MW01514775

A BOX OF
ROCKS
A PAIR OF
BOOTS

Larry Antone Ludwig 9-24-22

To Art & Barb

Thanks for stepping in

LARRY ANTONE LUDWIG

and rescuing me when my

Truck broke down.

Copyright © 2009 – 2021 Larry Antone Ludwig
All cover art copyright © 2021 Larry Antone Ludwig
All Rights Reserved

Interior Design by www.formatting4U.com

This is a work of fiction. Names, places, characters and incidents are either the product of the author's imagination or are used fictitiously and any resemblance to any actual persons living or dead, businesses organizations, events or locales is entirely coincidental.

No part of this book may be reproduced or transmitted in any form by any means electronic or mechanical. Including photocopying, recording or by any information storage and retrieval system without permission in writing from the author.

DEDICATION

To the many men and women who served in the Armed Forces during the Korean Conflict and to those who remained at home supporting their efforts. This Nation owes each of you a debt of gratitude. May you lift your heads high and be proud of what you have done. This war is not a forgotten war. It lives within the hearts of those who gave their best to this country, we so proudly call America.

IN APPRECIATION

To my loving wife Shirley Earnestine Ludwig, who lost her fight with cancer. She had the heart to tell me when my story was running adrift and not ringing true. Without her editing and continual words of encouragement, this story may not have found a happy ending. She had managed to endure and nurture my passion, while aiding in the construction of this story, as much as I attempted to create it. Thanks love, for the beautiful memories and the countless times you read aloud the entire story so that I may hear the bumps.

AUTHOR'S COMMENT

It is my fondest hope that this book although a piece of fiction, may reflect favorably upon the men and women who served in Korea. Not to be forgotten are the families that remained behind holding down the home front, while a part of their hearts served in a conflict during a turbulent time.

You're about to read a story, written in two parts. Eddie Day managed to survive the Korean War, a POW Camp and an extended stay in a North Korean Prison. Years later he would return to Montana where he would rebuild his life on a horse ranch in Gallatin County. He received the love from his wife, family, a grateful community and State. Because he was much more than their hero.

KOREAN SERVICE MEDAL

CHAPTER 1

A Community Celebrates Veteran's Day Week – 1995

They say every coin has two sides. Such is the case with the state of Montana. On one end is the beauty of the Rocky Mountains and Glacier National Park. On the other side is the prairie flat land, rich soil for farming cash crops like alfalfa, sugar beets, wheat, corn for silage and some land left over for range cattle. Some random parts of the land are spotted with alkali flats. In the land beneath the soil are deposits of history, prehistoric dinosaur bones that have been preserved by nature. In each community there is a reason for community pride and you don't have to dig deep to find the reason.

~ ~ ~ ~

The flat horizon of the eastern Montana landscape dominated by farming operations began to show some color as it shook the darkness of the night. Distant yard lights no longer could be seen as dots in the night marking each farm. The blanket of darkness was slowly beginning to surrender to the soft pastel colors of yellow and pink that began to fill the eastern sky. The subtle change became more brilliant in color, lighting up the outer space. The heavens some distant behind the local landscape developed into a backdrop of brilliant orange moments before the sun began to mark its point of entry into a new day.

It was November 2nd, Saturday morning a week before the Veterans Day Parade was celebrated by the scouts as a yearly tradition. Moments after sunup the local Boy Scout Troop in uniform began fulfilling one of their yearly community duties. They started at one end of Main Street and planned to make it to the other end of town as quickly as they could. The

1

two-and-a-half-ton truck Mr. Art Forsyth the Boy Scout Master had borrowed from the MFA grain elevator was used to haul the many American flags rolled up on their staffs. No longer was the dust, dirt and grain chaffing evident on the truck. It had been washed and wiped down. Art eased the truck forward after finding the granny gear and left it there. A team of scouts in the truck bed removed the canvas protective covering from around each American flag. They handed them down lower end of the staff first. Two teams of scouts approached the truck from each side. As a scout received a flag he would dash off towards the sidewalk. He unrolled the flag and placing it in a designated hole in the sidewalk in front of each business. There were slight gusts of chilling wind that swept in from the north and across the community. A glance back down the street showed a wonderful display. The flags moved freely in the light breeze. Each business owner would be responsible to bring the flag into their business at sunset and have it displayed each day by 8:00 A.M.. The Boy Scout Troop would pick up the flags at sunset on Veterans Day.

When the flag detail was completed, Art drove the grain truck to the high school and parked it inside the Agricultural building. In the days to come it would be decorated for the parade scheduled to begin at 10:00 A.M. the next Saturday. Art hopped down from the cab and said, "OK boys, let's get it ready for the parade. You have a week." The traditional swagging red, white and blue bunting would drape the sides of the Scout's project. The troop members not in the color guard would ride during the parade with their Veterans Day project rising high above their heads in the middle of the truck bed. Three of the older boys would not be in their scout uniforms that day because they were in the high school band.

~ ~ ~ ~

The night before the parade, some of the floats had arrived and were placed in their order for the parade. Bessie Margrave the parade coordinator was busy in the staging area lining up floats. She allowed space for others that had yet to arrive. The scout master had made arrangements to keep their project in the Ag building protecting it from any bad weather and would join the lineup an hour before the parade was scheduled to begin.

Shortly after 8:00 A.M. on the 9th of November, the Veterans Day parade entries were finally lined up. They waited for the Grand Marshal and dignitaries to arrive before the parade began. Between nine and ten, the streets of the community were filled with spectators of all ages. The younger children were excited and ready to scamper into the street when the parade passed by. There was always a small amount of wrapped candy that would be tossed to the crowd. After the parade the community would gather at the football field for the awards and dismantling of the floats.

On Sunday morning the churches were filled with worshipers proud of their involvement in the church of their choice. The support they gave helped the local school and community honor their many veterans. After worship services a planned ceremony was scheduled at the high school shortly after the noon hour.

When the community gathered at the high school for an unveiling the crowd grew quiet as the first of several speakers stepped forward and picked up the microphone. There was a series of short comments praising Eddie Day for what he meant to the community and our nation. He and his wife Jody sat in the front row of chairs next to his parents. They were awed by the reflective statements so many of the town folks gave concerning Eddie's impact on the community due to his military service.

When Eddie's oldest daughter Mari spoke so eloquently the crowd was moved to near tears as she pointed out, "My sister and I only knew my father from a hand full of photographs. We were told he was killed in action during the Korean conflict and his body was not recovered. I was nearly a teenager before we finally met."

When his youngest daughter Kari spoke, she mentioned her father's commitment to life. His word being his bond and the example he set for them before saying, "He came home to be a part of our lives and love us he did. He taught us by example how to live and have faith and how to forgive our enemies. It was hard to forgive those people because they had kept him from us for so long."

One of Eddie's adopted pair from Vietnam stepped forward. His son Hanh, spoke highly with feeling and reverence of the man he loved. He ended his reflection by declaring, "He was my second father the protector and mentor in my life. He took my sister and me out of a war-torn country so that we may experience family love in a peaceful time."

The softest and most gentle praise came from his adopted daughter Lien. She was the last to speak. After a brief comment she added, "I began each day wanting to stand in his shadow. He touched our hearts so softly each morning and in such a tender way as if to allow the birds in the meadow to sing with joy. As we honor him today let others learn of his importance."

At that moment the large bronze plaque with Eddie Day's image above a lengthy inscription was unveiled for all to see.

CHAPTER 2

A Winter Accident – A Local Hero – 1947

Snow had been falling off and on during the day. But it began in earnest after school had let out and during football practice. Their used leather helmets the school district had purchased last year showed age. But the sports equipment was in good shape and offered the latest protection. Their white-with-green-numbering practice jerseys that fit loosely over their shoulder pads showed an accumulation of snow as the team sat on the bench. The team regrouped after running a new play option, the coach insisting it be executed precisely and with lightning speed. Coach Ted Higgins had called the team to the sidelines to discuss the option and a defensive move. He demanded they commit the plays to memory before the following week's game. His favorite saying after explaining every play as if engraining his wisdom, "Don't drop the ball! You can't be successful if you do. So, protect the ball. Whatever you do don't drop the ball!" The talk was short because of the weather.

The coach reluctantly said, "Men, this weather is getting to look rough. I'm calling off practice. For those of you who drive home, I want you to get there before the roads get too bad. Commit the plays to memory and I'll see you all next week."

Eddie Day the team's quarterback raced to the locker room where he had his books and a change of clothing. His practice uniform was too wet to wear home. He hurriedly changed and would shower after he got home. He would leave the helmet, padded equipment and cleats in the locker room. Wasting little time, he quickly changed into his Levi pants, a western shirt and a lined Levi winter jacket with buckskin-lined gloves jammed in the pockets. He left the locker room and cut across the snow-covered school lawn towards his 1943 blue Ford pickup truck. He tossed his books and practice uniform across the seat. The windshield had an accumulation of snow. He reached across the windshield with his outstretched arms on the passenger side of the truck to wipe off most of the snow and did the same on the driver's side. Then he crawled into the cab. He would rely on the heater and wipers to do their best.

Upon approaching the highway, he could see the stop sign was partially obscured from the snow. He stopped before entering the highway took off his gloves and laid them on the dash to dry from the heater. He noticed the roads were beginning to accumulate some snow packing into ice. He was thankful for the traffic that preceded him. They had left a path upon the highway to follow. The snow was beginning to blow sideways and it was getting close to a white out. Without warning the pickup fishtailed. He let up on the gas and turned into the skid. The back tires hit some underlying grass at the shoulder of the road. The bump seemed to keep the truck in check and it slowly came under control. For a few moments his stomach was tied in knots feeling uneasy from losing control. He knew he would have to park his truck in the tractor shed when he got home. He could change tires over the weekend and put on the snow treads. Weather like this was no place for standard-tread tires. The curves of the highway had his truck sliding from the lack of traction a couple of times. But nothing as severe as the first skid. Eddie slowed down and kept his wipers going full speed. The snow was coming down so fast it was hard to see the tracks beyond the hood of the truck. The wind was constantly blowing sideways with no letup in sight. He had his radio on and was listening to some country music on his favorite western station. The sound coming from the speakers filled the cab of the truck but failed to register in his mind. Driving in this storm required his full concentration.

The music was interrupted by an advisory getting Eddie's attention, "We have just received word from the weather bureau that we are in blizzard conditions and white outs have occurred. Those of you who are at home please stay there and do not venture out on the roads. The highway patrol advises motorists to use extreme caution. The highway department has all available snowplows out on the streets and highways. Travelers who can hear my voice are advised to take extreme caution. Weather conditions are not favorable at this time." The country music returned as he gripped the steering wheel and tried to remain on the slippery road.

Rounding the corner of a large bluff there was a slight break in the weather because of the contour of the hillside. Eddie could see where a vehicle had left the road. It had to be recent, because the markings were so clear. He stopped his truck threw it out of gear and set the emergency brake. He kept the motor running and went to the edge of the road where could see a light green Studebaker. It had left the road and plowed through some thick willows. It had clipped some bark off a large cottonwood tree and was partially submerged in a creek. A thicket of willows had slowed the car down some before it came to rest. The back tires were on the embankment. The other half of the car was in the snow-covered slush that was beginning to freeze. The front of the car was slowly sinking.

Eddie scampered over the embankment and down a slippery slope keeping his feet out in front of him. Using his hands to keep his body in check he wondered why he left his gloves behind. He made his way down the wet slope over loose rock covered with fresh wet snow. When he arrived at the car, he could see that the driver was Mrs. Edna Shoemake. She was dazed and moaning with pain. She was clad in a house dress and a jacket without a hood. Her hair was held in place by a doubled triangular silk scarf tied under her chin. As he looked past her, he could see her daughter Sarah. She was one of the high school cheerleaders. Her face was bloodied but there was movement. She was wearing a winter coat with a hood resting at the back of her neck and she had her skimpy cheerleading uniform on with nothing protecting her legs. Suddenly there was a shift from the car as the back wheels slid off the bank of the creek and the bumper seemed to grab at twisted willow saplings lodged under the car. The front end of the car had moved forward and began to sink under the cold water.

All he could think about was getting them out of the car and he needed to hurry. A small gravel bed below the mud bank allowed Eddie to step down into the frigid water without having it come over the top of his western boots. Now he could get some leverage but the driver's door was damaged and stubborn. "Come on, come on!" he hissed through his clinched teeth as he grunted while applying muscle. With his third brute force effort the door opened with a metal-against-metal scraping sound.

When it gave way, he asked, "Mrs. Shoemake, I need to get you out of the car. Where are you hurt?"

"My head. My chest and my right leg hurt. Is Sarah ok, she was with me?" Her teeth chattered from the icy chill and her voice wavered emotionally from losing control of the car. She sobbed from the pain. Her voice was as cold as the rocks in the creek bottom.

He removed her from behind the wheel and sat her on the ground near the base of the cottonwood tree she had just skinned. He raced to the far side of the partially submerged car. His heart hammering hard within his chest. He tugged at the door and it produced the same results as the other side. He gave a second jerk before the bent door gave way with a metal grinding sound. "Sarah, are you alright?"

"I think so. I hit the windshield and the dash pretty hard."

"Let me give you a hand." He reached over and offered his out-stretched hand. Guiding her from the car he took her to her mother's side.

"Sarah, we have to get out of here. I'll take you up the bank to my truck and then I'll come back here and get your mother."

While guiding Sarah up the steep slope Eddie held on to her arm tightly. Her feet slipped out from under her several times but they finally got to the top of the embankment. He opened the passenger door and reached inside to scoot his books to the floor and tossed his wet practice jersey and pants to the bed of the truck. "Here Sarah, hop in. The heater should help get you warm."

Moments later he was sliding down the embankment half on his backside. He braced his slide with his left hand until he got to the bottom. His palms felt numb from the cold and sharp jabs of pain ripped through his hands after hitting sharp rocks and roots on the way down the incline. Mrs. Shoemake didn't look good. He quickly cradled her up in his arms and carried her for a short distance thankful for his weight training. He paused for a moment before making his upward climb to the road that rested at the top of the slope.

Not until he arrived at the snow-covered blacktop did he see a highway patrol cruiser. The flasher and stop lights were flashing after he had pulled up behind Eddie's truck. The officer had hopped from his car and was approaching the cab of his truck when he happened to see Eddie carrying Mrs. Shoemake. He hurried to Eddie's side checking his balance on a slick snow-covered surface. When the trooper arrived, he said, "Let me give you a hand. We'll place her in the back seat of my car."

When Mrs. Shoemake was placed in the patrol car he said, "Get that young lady out of your truck and get her back here with her mother."

With all the excitement Eddie opened the passenger side of the truck and said, "Sarah, we need to get to the patrolman's car. Can you make it?"

"I think so."

As she stepped from the truck, Eddie retrieved his truck keys and closed the door. He said "Give me your hand Sarah, and I will assist you on this slick road until we get to the trooper's car."

State trooper Gene Glass said, "I have called for an ambulance to meet me at the crossroads."

Sarah cried out, "Mom, are you ok?" When there was no response, she turned and pleaded, "Eddie, tell me she is going to be alright, I need to know."

Deep within him he knew that Mrs. Shoemake's chances didn't look promising. He knew that once the trooper had turned them over to the ambulance crew they would be with strangers. Instead of returning to his truck, he slid in alongside of Sarah and cradled her in his arms and told the trooper, "I'm going where they're going. I'll come back for my truck later."

Within moments the patrol car was making its way to the nearest junction where an ambulance would be waiting for those injured. Trooper Glass said, "You need to get back to your truck as soon as possible because of the snowplows. They'll need to keep the roads open." The squelch and abbreviated talk included code numbers over the communication equipment. It filled the interior of the car.

Eddie said, "I'll have my parents go out and pick it up. They have an extra set of keys and the farm isn't that far away. Right now, I think I should be with the both of them."

He fought hard to control his emotions. Eddie knew what pressure was in the heat of a close football game, but this was something totally different. He had to keep his head and be ready to respond when needed. Right now, Sarah needed his comforting shoulder and he would be there for her later.

It didn't take long before the trooper was approaching the intersection. From a distance, the ambulance was a huge soft flashing glow. As the patrol car got closer, the three flashing lights became more distinguishable. The lights were the center of a glow reflecting off the frozen landscape and the loose snow that was being whipped across the land by a heavy wind. Patrolman Glass slowed his cruiser and pulled up alongside the ambulance that had its lights flashing and the crew waiting. With the blizzard conditions, the figures stepping from the ambulance appeared as if they were behind frosted glass, their moving shadows pressed upon a white backdrop.

When the doors were opened on both sides of the car, the ambulance crew was ready to take care of the injured. Eddie quickly removed himself from the car, allowing the men to do their work. The padded metal stretchers seemed to snap to attention alongside the patrol car. The Shoemakes were placed upon them and quickly ushered to the interior of the ambulance. One of the medical crew began making an evaluation of each patient. The trooper had already made arrangements for Eddie to ride to the hospital with the pair. He was not allowed in the back, but took over the shotgun seat up front. He glanced into the back and gave what information he could about the accident and those injured.

As the rear door of the ambulance was shut, the medic in the back began making his assessment, while talking on phone equipment and relaying some information to the driver. Eddie sat in the passenger's seat and was asked several more questions as the ambulance made its way through thick unplowed snow. The highways would be blocked before too long if the snow didn't let up. The road crews would surely have their hands full clearing the roads.

The crewman in the back determined that Sarah had a fractured arm and collarbone and a possible fractured ankle. His primary care was for Mrs. Shoemake who had internal and facial injuries as a result of hitting the steering wheel. He was having problems with her vital signs and spoke in medical terms with the driver, attempting to defend Sarah from understanding the distress her mother was in.

When they arrived at the hospital, the emergency crew was waiting for them and the women were ushered into an exam room. One of the staff called Eddie to the front desk for what information he could provide. Moments later he was asked to reenter the emergency room because Mrs. Shoemake wanted to speak to him personally.

When he entered the small exam room, a doctor was hovering over Mrs. Shoemake while making his evaluation. The staff was collecting blood for lab work and she had been wired up for an EKG before having to go to X-ray. The doctor and several nurses were working feverishly to put as much information together before they would send the Shoemakes to the surgical ward. When he arrived, Mrs. Shoemake held out her hand and said, "Eddie, we thank our lucky stars that you found us. They say I'm busted up a bit and will need surgery. I won't be able to be close to my daughter for a while. Can I ask a big favor from you?"

"Sure, what is it?"

"We don't have family, be with Sarah, at least while I'm going through surgery, would you? Just be there for her, so that she knows there is someone close by who cares."

"I promise," Eddie said. "They say I have to be in the waiting room for now, but I'll be here for her."

"Bless you and thanks ever so much."

The nurse began ushering Eddie out of the exam room, but allowed him to look in on Sarah for just a moment.

Eddie called out, "Hey, Sarah, are you okay?"

"I guess. They say I'm going to be a mess of plaster before too long. From what I gather, I'll have to stay the night for observation. They just told me that Mom is going to be in surgery and I'll get to see her after she recovers."

"Sarah, I'll be here for you until you get to see your mother. The nurse told me I would have to stay in the waiting room for now. But when they assign you your room, I can visit with you for a while. I'll call my folks and let them know where I am and that I left the pickup alongside the road."

"That will be nice. Catch you later?"

"Sure thing," Eddie added, before he was ushered out of the room and directed to the waiting room.

He used the telephone in the waiting room to call home. His father answered. "Dad, this is Eddie. Don't panic, but there was an accident on the way home and I'm here at the hospital. I'm not the one hurt, it's the Shoemakes. I rode in the highway patrol car and the ambulance to get here. You'll need the second set of keys for Old Blue. I've left my truck off the side of the road at the creek about a mile from our turnoff, can you get it? Tell Mom not to worry, because I'm not the one hurt. Can you make it here, so I can get a ride home?" They talked for a moment before they hung up.

The waiting room suddenly became filled with a news announcer and several journalists. They wanted to cover the accident and talk to the hero who had saved the women.

The nurse at the emergency desk spoke briefly with some of the press journalists before she directed them into the waiting room.

When the news crew entered the waiting room, one of the news reporters asked, "Which one of you is Mr. Eddie Day?"

Eddie stood up and said, "I am."

The journalist pointed the microphone in Eddie's direction.

~ ~ ~ ~

Edward Day lowered the receiver after talking with his son and turned to his wife Kathy, who was calling out as she listened to the radio, "Ed, they have a special report on the weather!"

"This is a Special News Bulletin," the station announcer said.

A female news reporter spoke, "We are gathered here at General Memorial where two very lucky women are now being tended to by the staff of this hospital. We have with us the young man who was instrumental in saving them from certain death. He had pulled them from their automobile that had left the roadway in the blinding snow and nearly submerged in the icy waters of a swollen creek. Highway patrolman Gene Glass confirmed moments ago, had it not been for the heroic actions of Eddie Day, Mrs. Edna Shoemake and her daughter Sarah might have gone unnoticed due to the blizzard conditions. Mrs. Shoemake apparently lost control of her car and careened off an embankment and into the icy waters. She is listed in serious condition, suffering from internal injuries and is at this time being evaluated prior to surgery. Her daughter Sarah has suffered a fractured arm and ankle, a broken collarbone, along with facial lacerations."

Mrs. Day gasped at what she had heard as her son's name was mentioned over the radio.

"He's ok, Kathy, that was him on the telephone."

The news reporter continued, "We are fortunate to have our young hero here at the hospital. Eddie, how does it feel knowing that because of your heroic action this evening you have saved the lives of two people?"

They could hear their son Eddie reply, "I don't call myself a hero. I just happened to see where a car had run off the road and I stopped to help."

"According to the highway patrol, you single handedly removed both women from a sinking car in the creek and carried them to the roadway to safety."

"Yes, but all I did is what had to be done."

The reporter added, "Eddie, that is what makes you a hero." As she spoke into the microphone adding, "We will have an in-depth interview with our hero on the nine P.M. edition of the news. This concludes our special report from Memorial General, now back to the station for a weather update."

Kathy turned to Edward and said, "How in the world did he get to the hospital?"

Ed said, "I'll tell you on the way. We need to get his truck off the highway and then we'll drive over to get him from the hospital. He'll need a ride home. You best get bundled up. We'll take the tractor in case the truck doesn't start. That snow is piling up some and we don't need to be out there any longer than need be."

Moments later Kathy could hear the chain clanging against the tractor. A short time later there was the distinctive sound of the Massey Ferguson kicking over. She threw a scarf around her neck before getting into her winter farm coat. She took another winter scarf anticipating her husband would need it. At the door she reached over on a shelf and grabbed two pairs of winter gloves: a pair for her and a pair for Edward, in case he had neglected grabbing his. She stepped from the house closing the unlocked door behind her. As the screen door snapped shut from a cold spring stretched out in the frigid winter air, she heard the tractor approaching. She would not feel comfortable until they had Eddie's truck back at the farm and had completed the round trip to the hospital. She wanted her son and husband home where it was warm, because the Montana snowstorms could sometimes go on for days.

CHAPTER 3

High School Days – Graduation – 1947

The life of a high school senior can be a whirlwind of events leading up to graduation. For Eddie Day, this was no exception, from all the notoriety he received from his actions on a cold winter night, to the final football game and the State Championship. He received honors as being named All State on the first team. Then came a successful year for the baseball team, where he played first base. He did well academically and was popular among his classmates.

Eddie supported Sarah Shoemake in making adjustments in her life after losing her mother. He felt compelled to ask her to the prom. The accident last winter allowed them to become closer as classmates and friends. Eddie began to see Sarah as a very close friend, instead of just one of the many girls he attended high school with. Maybe it would be too soon, but Eddie felt Sarah was his only true choice for that special night. He knew the death of her mother had hit her hard and left her without a caring guardian, until one of the teachers stepped in. He cared for Sarah, but felt uneasy in exposing her to all the notoriety he was getting, knowing she needed some private moments. He was unsure how to handle himself, other than being friendly at school and being ready to listen to her when she was ready to talk.

His heart felt understanding with Sarah, who had lost her mother two months following the automobile accident. Mrs. Shoemake had made a valiant effort and never lost her faith in Jesus during her attempt to recover. But her body was broken beyond what current medical knowledge had available to save her.

Sarah had remained in school, as a promise to her mother and through the generosity of the girl's home economics teacher. Mrs. York, a recent widow of a young articulate Baptist pastor, took Sarah into her home the church provided as a parsonage. She could remain there until she graduated and was able to get out on her own. Mrs. York would remain in the parsonage until the church settled on a new pastor on a full-time basis. Because of the death of her mother, Sarah's grades slipped and hindered her from getting a scholarship. Her fall into depression seemed to end when Eddie Day talked to her one after noon on her way home.

"Sarah," he called out.

She stopped for a moment to see Eddie trotting across the school lawn. When he approached, he said, "Sarah, I hope no one has asked you for the prom, because I would be honored if you would go with me. Can I get a yes now, or are you going to play hard to get and make me wait for your answer?"

Sarah smiled and looked up into his face. She had no choice as Eddie's muscular frame towered over her. When her lips moved, she uttered softly, "That is the sweetest thing I have heard today. I will be pleased to be with you and thank you for asking."

"Great, let me give you a lift home."

She smiled and said, "That really isn't necessary, it's walking distance, but it is a nice offer."

"I've got my truck parked within walking distance and it would be my pleasure."

They turned and walked to his truck trading small talk on an upcoming class project and speculating who would team up with who before the big dance. Eddie walked with big strides and Sarah suddenly seemed to have a bounce in her step. She felt the first jolt of her emotions, as they began to change directions. Eddie Day was considered a top catch for any of the girls, especially for the big dance.

As they approached the pickup, he opened the passenger door for her and waited for her to be seated before he gently closed the door. Within moments he was behind the wheel and driving the short distance to where Sarah now called home.

When they arrived at the old two-story Victorian-style house the First Baptist Church furnished as a parsonage, he turned off the motor and was out his door, on his way to the passenger side. Sarah didn't make an attempt to open the door herself, knowing that Eddie had intentions of being a gentleman. When she stepped out, she said, "Thank you, Eddie," as he closed the door behind her.

"Do you have a way to school in the morning?"

"Sure do, I ride in with Mrs. York."

Eddie smiled at her and said, "Then I'll catch you in class tomorrow."

"I'll see you then." She smiled as she saw her prom date slowly make his way to the other side of his truck. She walked halfway to the door and turned to wave at him as he drove out of the circular drive.

Eddie headed for the highway and drove straight home. He had chores to do and if there was any amount of sunlight left, he would lend a hand to his father before the sun made its way down behind the western horizon.

With calving in the early spring there was work to do on the open range adjacent to the family farm. The Day family had a few acres of land in a fertile valley next to the river where irrigation wasn't a problem for the farm. They also had a string of livestock that was turned loose on the public range. During the early months of each year, they would join with others who used the open range to ride and have a roundup. The government land offered nothing more than sage brush, cheatgrass, prairie grass and cactus. In the draws near the water, cottonwood trees overshadowed scrubby pines and competed with the cedar trees and smaller cedar brush. Large sandstone outcroppings and bluffs highlighted the upper portions of the hills. In the flatland, the prairie dogs would build their community and a rider would have to be careful not to ride too close to them. Close to the sandstone bluffs and near the cedar brush, it was possible to run across a rattlesnake now and then. The mule tail deer would avoid the stock, but they would come down from the hills near dusk for water located on the lower range.

The neighbors did their best not to have their stock too close to the others. But at times there was an occasion when the brands had to be determined on a range cow as to who was allowed the privilege of branding the calf. It was a casual affair with the neighbors cooperating with each other. During the weeklong roundup, the chores included branding, vaccinating, castration and dehorning. The wives would team up together and bring food out in a pickup truck rather than using a chuck wagon. After supper the men would remain behind as the wives headed for home. The men would sleep on the open range and rise early for a long day's work. After a hearty breakfast consisting of whatever the wives left behind, they would make do until the women returned in the evening.

On the third day of the roundup, a calf was roped and readied for branding, when its mama a rugged range cow decided, it wasn't going to happen. She put up a fuss, threatening with her extended horns; she was mad. One of the wranglers roped her and was in hopes of guiding her off to the side. This wasn't an easy task and Eddie rode up and felt he could settle things if he bulldogged her.

"Get 'er!" the wrangler yelled out.

Eddie leaned from the saddle and latched on to the horns protruding from her head. From the time his feet left the stirrups, he was in trouble. He lacked precious time for his feet to hit the ground, when suddenly the range cow managed to break the lariat rope and began shaking her head. Eddie didn't have a chance to set his heels and was whipped unceremoniously over sagebrush and rock. Eddie looked up through the clouds of dust, only to see the wrangler sitting in the saddle having a laugh. Eddie tried to weigh his options, either hang on or turn loose, not sure of either option. Ultimately the cow won and trotted off to the side after losing a young cowboy from around her neck, for the moment the calf was forgotten.

Eddie got to his feet half shook out of his boots and yelled, "Some help you were. I could have been hurt!"

The wrangler stopped laughing long enough to say, "From the looks of things, you need more practice. I think this be the first time I laid me tired ol' eyes on a butt sprung cowboy afoot."

All Eddie could do was stand momentarily in his dust covered-clothing with a naked face in front of his more experienced neighbor. He hobbled over to his horse that was trained to be ground hitched, mounted and rode off to help with the roping of other calves.

~ ~ ~ ~

With spring calving completed, the chores shifted to those around the farm, with preparation for early planting and the cleaning of irrigation ditches. School activities from student council, the prom dance with Sarah and preparation for graduation filled most of Eddie's days. From Prom night on, it was inevitable they were a match.

Every Saturday night, his dress boots left prints on the dusty sidewalk leading to the York doorstep. He would be asked to step in while Sarah did her last-minute preparation on her hair before they went on a date, most often a movie.

Mrs. York would speak up, "Mr. Day, at what reasonable hour do you plan to bring Sarah back to this household?"

Eddie would tell her of the time and location where he planned to take Sarah.

"That will be fine," Mrs. York would say, "so long as the both of you are in by that hour. If there is trouble, I know at least one of you should call and not keep me waiting with worry."

Eddie knew Sarah had to be in at a reasonable hour because Mrs. York attended Sunday school and church. Sarah was expected to be at her side.

~ ~ ~ ~

The night of graduation was a fun-filled evening. The senior class gathered in the study hall, before marching over to the gymnasium in alphabetical order. They were clad in cap and gown ready to receive their diplomas before all the town folks. Eddie could feel the excitement as the procession entered the gymnasium on their way to take their seats. They would listen to the principal and a guest speaker before being called on stage one at a time to receive their diplomas. The program didn't seem long and when it ended, family and friends gathered around the graduates to wish them well.

Sarah stood at Eddie's side while his family and friends gathered around. She was left shy of a family to share her accomplishments with, outside of her church family. When the crowd began to break up, Eddie excused himself and took Sarah to his truck. "I'm mighty proud of you tonight, Sarah. I know this last year hasn't been easy for you and I just think it's great you finished and got your diploma."

"Can I ask a favor of you?" she inquired.

"Sure thing, what will it be?"

"Could you drive me to the cemetery, just for a few minutes? There's something I'd like to do."

When they got to the truck, there was the customary courtesy of opening the passenger's door for Sarah, then he trotted off to the other side and got behind the wheel. He drove to the cemetery knowing she was going to visit her mother's grave.

When they arrived, Eddie pulled to the side of the entrance and shut off the motor. He opened the door for her and she stepped out only to

19

look into his face and softly said, "Eddie, I need to say a few words at my mother's grave. You can come along if you wish."

Eddie knew that he was invited or she would have excused herself. "Let's go together," he replied.

When they approached the grave, Sarah said, "Mama, I did it. I got my diploma as I promised. I miss you something fierce. I don't know where I'm heading from here, but you will always be a part of my daily thoughts. Mama, I'm here with Eddie, he's been a great help to me. Without him, I might have quit going to school, because I felt so bad. He's been my spirit picker-upper and I owe him for saving us at the accident and being there for me through some pretty tough times. I love you, Mama."

She stood there for a long time as if in deep thought. Eddie was compelled to remain silent and be there for her, when she was ready. When she turned from the grave, she had tears in her eyes and began sniffing trying to control the hurt that she held within.

Eddie held out both hands and cupped her face and stroked at the tears that were running down her face. "You ready?" he asked.

Not saying a word, she nodded her head in agreement.

They turned and went to the truck. Eddie asked, "Where to from here?"

"Home, I guess. I'd like to spend the remainder of the day alone; I hope you understand."

"Sarah, no need to apologize. I know of your hurt."

When they returned to the parsonage, Sarah went inside and before the door was closed Eddie said, "Mrs. York, could I ask something in confidence?"

Mrs. York stepped out on the porch and said, "Yes you may, Eddie."

"Where does Sarah go from here?"

She replied, "The church is still seeking a full-time pastor. I understand it may be in the fall before they expect to have the position filled. I will remain here with the blessings of the church until that time. As for Sarah, she is most welcome to stay with me until then. After that I guess we'll have to see what the good Lord has in store for the both of us. Is there a reason why you ask?"

"Well, we have been dating, as you know. But I don't think we've been dating long enough to get serious enough for me to ask and have her respond. I think the world of her and I guess we need a bit more time together to sort things out."

"Eddie Day, you add cheer to my heart and I know that when the time comes, you will also add cheer to Sarah's. You both have time and when the time is right for the both of you, you'll both know. As for dropping by to visit with her, you have my blessings."

Eddie looked into Mrs. York's face to find a reassuring smile. "Thanks," he uttered, as he turned and walked off the porch.

During the following months, there was work on the farm and some on the open range, checking on the stock. As for Sarah, she found a job at the drugstore as a cashier during the day and didn't have to work past six in the evenings. There were the usual telephone calls during the evening hours, where they compared daily events and expressed how they felt for each other. On Saturday nights, Eddie's familiar knock was answered and he found his boots making prints in the plush rug inside the parsonage door. He always seemed to have to wait momentarily for Sarah to complete her hair. They would take in a movie and later enjoyed a treat at the Empty Cup café.

When there was a movie not to their liking, they drove to the farm where Sarah enjoyed visiting with Kathy and Edward Day. Ed as he liked to be called, thought the world of Sarah and always greeted her with a loud rip snorting, "Howdy, Sarah, you're a sight for dry dusty eyes."

Kathy on the other hand smiled and with a twinkle in her eye would motion for Sarah to come into the kitchen for a chat. Before the night was over, there was generally some sort of pastry made, leaving Eddie and his father wondering which one of them had made it.

~ ~ ~ ~

It was the first of August after being paid, when Eddie tapped on the parsonage door. Mrs. York opened the door and without an exchange of words called out, "Sarah, you have a visitor." Turning to Eddie she said, "Come in, you two have the living room to yourselves. I have a sink full of dishes to take care of."

Eddie remained standing until Sarah entered the room. They both sat next to each other on the sofa. He turned to have his broad shoulders facing her and said, "Sarah, there is no use foolin' around trying to find the best time to say it, so I'm saying it now. I think the world of you, I love you and would you consider being my wife?"

The high squeal alerted Mrs. York in the kitchen who responded

21

quickly, only to hear Sarah proclaim, "Yes. Yes, Eddie Day, I'll marry you!"

Mrs. York stopped at the doorway to hear Eddie say, "I thought I would ask first and if I got a yes, we could go to the jewelry store together to pick the ring you'd like to wear."

They both looked up to see Mrs. York standing in the doorway half in half out of the living room with a smile on her face. "When is the blessed event going to happen?" she asked.

Sarah turned to look at Eddie to hear him say, "Soon?" Her eyes were tearing from happiness, as she nodded to the affirmative.

Mrs. York said, "Not so fast you two. There are family and friends on both sides to consider. Get the ring and set the date, but allow both sides to prepare for the wedding. Congratulations to the both of you. You both have my blessings and I think I best get back into the kitchen."

~ ~ ~ ~

The ring was purchased and she wore it out of the jewelry store. They had decided on an October first wedding date and began making plans for the future. He would remain on the farm and help out on the range. One of the houses for the hired help was set aside for the soon-to-be couple. The wedding plans seemed to take on community involvement. This was going to be bigger than a simple wedding.

CHAPTER 4

Family Fears - The Draft -1949

The large wedding that included nearly all of the community in one form or another was a distant memory, being replaced by the anticipation of their first child. Sarah smiled as she made her way across the large farmyard, happy with life and the enjoyment of collecting the eggs from the motherly hens. When she arrived at the chicken yard, she lifted the lid off a barrel containing scratch. After reaching into the barrel and filling a big scoop, she scattered the scratch outside the hen yard. The Days had several varieties of chickens which were allowed to run loose. She took another scoop of feed with her into an enclosed chicken yard and scattered the scratch before going into the chicken coop. There were several laying hens on their nests. Her mother-in-law was pleased they had several good layers. Between the eggs and the cream, they sold at the Farmers Market, it helped offset the cost of groceries. Sarah had agreed to take care of the chickens, because it was one of the few chores on the farm, she could handle during her later stages of expecting a child.

She carefully filled the watering jars and placed them on the floor of the coop. In an empty milk bucket, she placed a soft hand towel, allowing a soft bottom for several eggs she would gather. She went from nest to nest running her hand beneath each hen to collect the eggs. She spoke to each hen, as if they could understand, "Goodness it looks as if you've been busy today."

Sarah had collected the eggs and was ready to leave the layers when she was suddenly stricken with a pain that started the labor process. She quickly took the bucket and left the coop, closing it for the night and carefully putting the latch in place. She crossed the small hen yard, passed through the chicken wire gate, secured the latch and managed to get to the back porch of Edward and Kathy's house. It was there she was forced to stop. The pain just seemed to take center stage and anything else was secondary. Sarah called out and Kathy heard her plea for help. Nothing gets things done on a farm faster than an expectant grandmother, especially for the first grandchild.

Half out of breath, Kathy made her appearance and asked, "What's the problem, Sarah?"

"I'm cramping something fierce. I nearly dumped the bucket of eggs before I got here."

"Land's sakes, Sarah, sit down on the divan. How far apart are the pains?"

Sarah looked up into the concerned face of her sweet mother-in-law and said, "They come and go, but they're getting closer together and like to have doubled me over with the last few."

It didn't take Kathy long to time the contractions and when she figured out the intervals, she looked Sarah in the eyes and said, "It won't be long now. You just sit there and try to relax, while I get the men."

Kathy opened the screen door to the back porch that faced the large red barn and yelled out with considerable volume, "Edward! Edward Day, poke your head out of that hay loft!"

Edward and Eddie had been working in the loft shifting bales of alfalfa hay and stacking them so that they could be used more readily. Sometimes the Montana snow storms at their worst could cause delays during the chores of feeding stock. The smell of baled hay and the dust it creates is a pleasant odor to a working farmer. But it is a far cry from the smell of hay that is freshly mown. They could tell by the smell in the loft that it was good hay. It would make excellent feed for the stock when the snow was on the ground. Between the grunts and groans produced from their handling of the heavy bales, Edward thought he heard Kathy call his name and went to the loft door to see if he was hearing her voice.

The white loft door in need of painting rolled to one side with a squeak and Edward yelled back, "What is it, Kathy?"

"Get Eddie and the both of you get here in a hurry. That grandbaby wants to come into this world!"

There was no answer from the barn, but the loft door rolled shut in a hurry and within moments the two men were running for the house.

~ ~ ~ ~

Eddie had to run to his house and get the suitcase for Sarah's stay in the maternity ward. He drove fast enough to catch up and managed to ride the back bumper of his father's car, for his solo journey to the hospital in his pickup truck.

During the trip to the hospital, Edward's wife Kathy was seated in the back seat of their car. She was giving Ed a handful of concerns and instructions, after seeing their son driving so close behind, while she cared for Sarah. With no time to read signs, Edward Day made a quick turn and drove his station wagon into the emergency entrance drive of the hospital.

Several nurses in their light blue smock uniforms came out of the emergency door after witnessing the car and pickup coming to an abrupt stop in the emergency lane clearly marked for ambulance use only. Edward hopped out and bellowed, "She's about to make me a grandpa! I got her here as fast as I could."

One of the nurses turned to retrieve a wheelchair, while the others attended to Sarah, once Kathy had gotten out of the car.

Eddie had stopped so close to the back bumper of his father's car, he had to backtrack around his truck, before he could come up alongside his wife. "Sarah, are you ok?"

She replied, "Yes," followed by a muffled sound of discomfort.

One of the nurses took the suitcase, as the others managed to get Sarah into the wheelchair before heading to the labor room. Edward and Eddie were told to get their vehicles out of the emergency lane and park in the lot. Eddie was asked to stop by the admission desk when he returned, while Edward and Kathy were told where the waiting room would be for expecting grandparents.

Edward had returned from the parking lot and was with Kathy when a nurse came to the waiting room and called out, "Mrs. Day?"

Kathy spoke up, "Yes?"

"Sarah has asked that you be allowed to come back to the labor room. The nurses are prepping her now and the doctor should be down to see her in a few minutes." The nurse looked at Edward and said, "When the father is through with admitting, he can come back too, but you stay put."

Kathy jumped to her feet and the nurse took her back to where Sarah

25

was being prepared to give birth to her first child. Eddie had yet to return from the admitting desk.

When Eddie returned to the waiting room his father looked at him and smiled, "She all checked in?"

"That she is. I'm glad we went through the pre-admitting last week; it sure made things simple."

The doctor came to the door wearing his scrubs and said, "The both of you can go back to see her for just a moment. You'll have to leave when they take Sarah to the delivery room."

Eddie and his father quickly followed the doctor to Sarah's bedside. No sooner had they arrived, when Sarah let out a scream signaling that the baby would soon fill the room with its first cry. The nurse urgently called out, "Doctor!"

The doctor moved quickly to get in position and the nurse ushered the family back against the wall. The birth of Mari Day was taking place right before their eyes.

A nurse gathered Eddie's attention and asked him to wash his hands right quick. When he turned around the doctor looked up and said, "Ok, Eddie, you can cut the cord right here."

Eddie stood uneasy in his skin, but did as he was instructed. His parents looked on, proud to be present for such a blessed event. Moments later, Eddie and his parents were ushered into the waiting room for a few moments, while the staff did their job. Mari would be taken to the nursery and Sarah to her room.

After a short visit with Sarah, Edward spoke up and said, "Eddie, bring your mother home when they kick the two of you out. As for me, I'll have to get back to the farm to make sure the hired hands have milked the cows, the milk run through the separator and the cream cans set out for the truck to pick up in the morning."

~ ~ ~ ~

After a three-day stay in the hospital, Sarah and Mari were free to go home. Eddie had showed up in the truck and had the front of the cab cleaned out for the first time in months. The seat was cleaned, the dash washed down and the windows cleaned, but not a thing was done to the bed; after all it was a working truck. Just before entering the hospital, he looked down and saw a small rock about the size of his fist in the landscape shrubbery. Eddie quickly picked it up and stuck it in his back pocket.

Eddie was in high spirits as he entered the room to see Sarah and Mari all set to leave the hospital. He asked, "You two good-looking girls ready to go home with me?"

Sarah looked up and said, "We sure are. Honey, would you get the suitcase and those bags? I'll carry Mari."

"Not so fast!" the nurse's voice rang out. "We'll wheelchair you and that precious bundle to the car, our pleasure and hospital policy."

Sarah laughed, "There's no car, it's his old truck we'll be riding in." Eddie gave the nurse a provoking grin, as if to say his old truck was better than any car.

When they got outside, Eddie hurried to the side of the truck. He put the loose articles in the cab and the suitcase in the bed of the truck close to the cab, covering it with the business end of a pitchfork to keep it in place, and quickly opened the passenger door.

With the wheelchair close to the truck, the nurse held the baby while Sarah slowly lifted her body into the cab. After handing the baby to her mother and before leaving, the nurse said, "Best wishes to the both of you."

It was a cheerful departure. Eddie closed the passenger door, before he ran to the driver's side and hopped in. They were heading home not as a couple, but as a family. "We have one stop before we get home."

Sarah asked, "And where might that be?"

"Mom and Dad gave instructions that we had best stop in as soon as we got there. Dinner will be warming and ready for the table."

The days and months on the farm would pass from winter operations to the spring planting and the calving chores on the open range. Eddie seemed to have his hands full, rising early to begin his chores and working until the setting sun curtailed his work. When the day was done, he would rush home, always to be greeted with a hug and kiss from Sarah and precious time to be with his family.

~ ~ ~ ~

It was nearly a year later when the doctor informed the family that Sarah was expecting again. The joy of having another child seemed to be overshadowed by the trouble in the Far East. The news on the radio focused on the conflict in Korea, when the North invaded the South on the 25th of June 1950. On the Sunday evening news, there was talk of the Selective Service calling up a large number of men for the draft to bolster the ranks of the military. America would enter into the conflict under the United Nations into a police action rather than a war. Eddie was concerned about a possible deferment and was unsure if he remained eligible for the call-up.

~ ~ ~ ~

When he visited the Selective Service Office, the clerk was cordial but informed him, "You have an older brother still living, although he served in WWII, so you are not a sole surviving son. You do not qualify for a farm deferment, because your father owns the land. You aren't in college, so that leaves out a student deferment. And you haven't had a physical that would show you are unfit for military service. Although you have a family, a dependency deferment would have to be granted by the board, you'll need to apply for that consideration. As it stands, you are currently classified as 1-A."

Eddie said, "I would like to apply for the deferment. If it is denied, when do you think they'd be calling me up?"

The clerk looked up into his face and said, "I don't have anything to do with that. The Selective Service Board meets once a month. From that meeting, they send me a list and I send out the notices for those men to report for their physical."

Eddie completed the paperwork to file for his deferment. He left the Selective Service building, ready to finish the other chores he had in town.

When he arrived at the feed mill, he was surprised to hear a car horn honk as the car approached the loading dock. He turned around to see his high school football running back. "What's up, Eric?"

Eric got out of the car and both of them leaned against the front fender while talking. Unconsciously, as if out of old habit, one or both would adjust their hat or spit in the dirt. They would take one of their boots from time to time and make a smooth long swipe in the soft dry soil. Then they would pat the dust down with their foot, as if it was ceremonial, before smoothing it over again and repeating the same movements. Both looked down while listening to the other's comments.

28

At times, they would turn their head to the side rendering a cocked eye, to see if the other was looking back.

"I had a couple of days off from classes and came home to be with the family," Eric explained. "Grandma Elders has taken a turn for the worse. The folks thought it would be nice if I returned home for a few days and visited with her because she had been asking about me a lot."

"Sorry to hear the bad news."

Eric said, "It was to be expected, her health has been slipping here of late. But why the long face; you look tired?"

Eddie looked at his friend and said, "Same amount of work, sunup to sundown. Sarah and I have Mari and any day now the second one is due to arrive."

"Congratulations! What are the chances of us getting together? We can talk over old times and let me catch up on the news."

"Call me anytime at the farm after it gets dark," Eddie said, "I'll be around the place doing odd chores or with the family. I'd sure enjoy visiting with you. I'd like to hear about your college and how you're getting along."

"Mostly classes and loads of lab work. I'll be getting a degree in Chemical Engineering, hopefully in a couple of years."

"Enjoy it while you can. As for me, I found out today I might face the draft."

Eric said, "From what I hear, there are going to be a bunch called up. Talk on campus is either keep up the grades or they stand to lose their deferments."

"If I get drafted," Eddie said, "I at least have my folks who can look after the family. They are not in the best of health, but I'm sure they can make do. We'll kick the subject around later when we get together. I need to get this feed back to the farm. Be sure to give my regards to your family."

"Sure will. Give my regards to Sarah and I hope you two have a boy."

"Call and we'll get together." Eddie finished loading the feed sacks that had been deposited on the loading dock and headed out to the farm.

Eric's grandmother lost her fight with ill health the day after his return home. Eddie attended the funeral with his family and allowed Eric and his family time to grieve.

Eddie still had two additional days to visit with Eric Elders before

29

he had to go back to college. During their visits, Eddie and Eric developed a bond and commitment between them. There were things men talk about if this or that happens, mulling over what the other would do. The talk was of serious things and of course there was the fun of looking back on their school days, while making light jokes of life only a few years in the past. Eric was invited for dinner one evening and enjoyed Sarah's cooking and seeing Mari before he had to leave and return to college.

~ ~ ~ ~

The month of preparation and the second dash to the hospital was less hectic following the days he had visited with Eric Elders. Kari Day came into this world kicking and crying louder than her sister had. Unlike her sister, she waited until her mother was in the delivery room before she entered the world. Eddie had to experience the emptiness of spending some free time in the waiting room. There was excitement around the second child. Eddie was so proud and when he made the call to the farm, he told his parents they could tell Kari's big sister she had arrived. Kari was red cheeked and had a head of hair that put the rest of the newborn babies in a distant second place.

On his way to the truck after visiting hours at the hospital, Eddie picked up a rock and slid it into his back pocket. Some three days later they returned to the farm. Eddie returned to his routine of taking care of the crops and the livestock. He would put in a full day and could hardly wait until he could see his family at the end of the day.

It was on the 9th of August 1950, after putting in a long day fixing fence when he walked into the house for supper. Sarah held out the letter he had received from the Selective Service Board. When Eddie opened the letter, he discovered his request for a deferment had been denied and was ordered to report for his physical on the 15th of August and he would be inducted into the military on that date.

He lowered the letter and saw Sarah brace herself, as if she knew the contents. "It's not good news, Sarah. I'm being inducted on the 15th. I'm not even sure which branch of the military they will put me in."

Sarah said, "We'll make it! Honey, it isn't the end of the world. We're here and your folks are within walking distance, it'll be ok." She was doing her best to put a positive spin on things, although the thought of having him leave so soon jolted her being.

He said, "After supper, we'll take the kids and go see the folks and let them know the latest."

When Eddie, Sarah and the kids arrived at his folk's house, Edward had some of the hired hands gathered around the milk separator on the porch. He was giving them assignments for the following day, a detailed list of things he expected them to do before the day was done.

Eddie and his family eased through the screen door and made their way into the living room. They found Kathy nearly finished with the dishes in the kitchen. She tossed the towel on the counter and immediately came into the living room to coddle and extend her loving ways over the children. Sarah made her way into the kitchen to finish the dishes, knowing when Kathy heard the news she would be devastated and wouldn't feel like completing the chore. Eddie dropped his weight into a stuffed leather chair and seemed to wilt, as if the air had been knocked out of his sails, after a long day's work.

When Edward returned to the interior of the house, he likewise found a comfortable chair after greeting Sarah and making a quick fuss over Mari and Kari. "Nice of you two to drop over with the girls," Edward uttered. He groaned while lowering himself into the chair, before asking his son, "How was your day along the ditch line?"

"We set the water gates for the top of the alfalfa field for tomorrow. It looks as if we'll get another cut before fall. Dad and Mom, there is something Sarah and I need to share with you. I'm being drafted!"

Kathy inhaled sharply, as a mother would, and Edward moved forward on his chair and asked, "When do you have to report?"

Eddie said, "I have the letter here. They say I need to catch the train on the 14th and go to Butte for the physical and be ready to be shipped out to one of the basic training stations. They gave me some paperwork, so I don't have to pay for the transportation."

Kathy cried out, "Neil had his time in the military. Why do I have to go through this with my youngest son?"

Edward rocked back in his chair seeming to swallow hard and said, "Kathy, if the country needs him, this is their way of having him do his duties. Son, news of this nature doesn't come easy, but we'll manage here on the farm. As for taking care of Sarah and the girls, we'll manage."

Eddie said, "I know that you and Mom are not in the best of health.

31

While Eric Elders was back visiting home, we did some talking. He promised to check in on Sarah and the kids and on you two from time to time, if I was drafted."

Kathy uttered, "Son, it's the worry that will take its measure on the both of us, as well as Sarah. Some of the domestic things we'll just have to adjust to. It'll be nice to have Eric drop by, but he can't help us none with the worry."

Edward spoke up, "Sarah, the times don't get easy, but we'll manage, you can bank on that. Seems when they draft someone it is almost set in concrete. We'll be here for you when the time comes; that is what folks are for."

Kathy leaned over and threw her arms around Sarah's neck giving her some comfort, "We'll make do and we'll be here, for you and the girls."

The visit went well into the evening before Eddie and his family returned to their house.

~ ~ ~ ~

Time had passed and on the morning of the 14th of August, the Day families gathered together and drove into town for Eddie to catch the troop train at the Northern Pacific Railway depot. The telegrapher, a thin older man with a green visor that rested mid forehead above an old pair of glasses that straddled his long nose, was on duty. He looked at the material furnished by the local draft board. The railway agent made out the necessary pass for Eddie to give to the conductor, once he had boarded the train. The depot agent looked at the line-up furnished by the dispatcher earlier in the day, then stepped in front of the depot and adjusted one of the signals to indicate that the westbound train needed to stop. This action caused the signal arm about a mile or so down the track to adjust and move to the slow down or caution position. The train was on time and Eddie had to say his goodbyes out on the platform. As the large black steam-powered locomotive noisily made its way past them, the large wheels began breaking with the steam hissing out the side of the engine a few inches above the platform floor. A conductor stepped down from the train and dropped a small metal step down on the platform for passengers to use as they stepped up onto the train.

Within moments, the train began to move and Eddie looked out the window to see his family waving, left behind on the depot platform. His father held his mother around the waist, while each waved with their free arm. Sarah held the girls in close to her side, as she knelt between them and with her hands would take each of the girls by the hand in unison and lift them up slightly to wave their goodbyes. He couldn't see, but he knew there were tears falling from Sarah's eyes. With every revolution of the passenger train wheels, his family began to fade from his view.

CHAPTER 5

Valor In Combat – POW In North Korea -1950

At the induction center on August 15th, the military-style physical was given in the early morning. The men were lined up against the wall, told to strip, leave their clothing on top of their shoes and walk into the next room barefoot. Eddie could tell who had not experienced athletics in school. The mere idea of standing naked in front of so many others brought out visible shyness in some during the crudeness of the examination. When the physical was complete, a battery of tests was administered before the noon hour.

The group of draftees and a few who enlisted were told to report back to a large waiting room after lunch with the belongings they had brought with them. Most of the men had small gym bags, a few had small suitcases and two fellows had what little they brought along stuffed in large paper bags.

When they were seated, one of the doctors in a smock and three military men entered the room. The Army officer spoke. "Listen up! If your name is called, pick up your gear and step forward. The following men will be returning home today." Three names were called out and they stepped forward and were taken into another room by the doctor. After the exit of those men, the remaining men were randomly divided into three groups, as to who would go into the Army, Navy or Marine Corps. The largest group was for the Army, the Marine Corp took a smaller group and the Navy accepted only five. There was additional paperwork for each group before they entered a ceremonial room and were sworn into the Military.

The groups were taken to the train station or the airport for transportation to their basic training. Each group had one individual in charge of the personal paperwork and tickets. Eddie was assigned to a group heading for Army basic training at Fort Ord, California. A fellow named Danny Doyle who had prior service carried the paperwork.

Danny called the group together and told them, "We need to stick together when we get to Fort Ord for training. We might be able to stay in the same company."

Eddie took a liking to Danny and asked, "What is to be expected of us, when we get there?"

He said, "Don't volunteer for nothing, keep your eyes open and your mouth shut for a week or so and you'll catch on to the training. Those that don't will get chewed out something unimaginable. Expect your turn to be chewed on; know that when it happens, you knew it was coming and you're not going to take it to heart. They will do it just to test you and the fact that you didn't volunteer could be a reason or on the other hand maybe for no reason at all."

Eddie said, "How about you?"

"I've been in the military before," Danny replied, "I pretty well know what I can get away with. I may wind up having my parade rained on by one of the drill sergeants. They do that to test your leadership, or lack thereof, and take any chance to unnerve a person in one of his weaker moments. If it happens, in the back of my mind, I know it's their job to train and dig at my weakness, if they can find it."

~ ~ ~ ~

Upon their arrival at Monterey, California, they were bused to Fort Ord. The new arrivals received the traditional haircut - zip and it's gone - and a duffle bag and clothing, which included brown combat boots and leggings. The training company was formed at the reception area, before they were moved to the training area for six weeks of basic combat training.

Danny Doyle was given the duties as a company platoon guide and he picked Eddie to be the first squad's leader. This put Eddie responsible for fourteen other men.

Eddie asked, "Danny, you told me not to volunteer for anything, now you went and picked me for this position. Why?"

Danny looked at Eddie and the other three squad leaders and said, "I chose you four because I feel you have the leadership to lead your men and get them through this training without a lot of trouble. If there is anything you want to know or if there is a problem, ask me. You need to show some leadership and I feel the men will listen to you four. You may have to demonstrate first to show the others what is expected of them. If that's the case, then do it, but insist they follow your leadership."

Eddie figured it was almost like football. Danny was the coach; he was the quarterback and responsible for the team to move forward. He knew he had to be a quick learner to his initiation in the army. By being a squad leader and adjusting to a new way of life, the training might be easier on him and his men.

~ ~ ~ ~

On graduation day, before the ceremonies began, word came over the radio that the Marines had landed at Inchon, Korea and had cut the supply route from the North Koreans. The enemy previously had managed to fight their way to the southern portion of the peninsula. The North Koreans meeting stiff resistance had managed to fight their way back north and reports where they were above the 38th Parallel. The advancing marines had recaptured the capitol city of Seoul, South Korea. With such good news, most of those who were graduating felt that the war would soon be over and when they arrived in Korea, they may not see much fighting.

After the graduation ceremony, Eddie was allowed to go home on furlough for 15 days before having to report to Treasure Island in the San Francisco Bay. When he arrived at home on the troop train, he was met by the whole family. His mother and father had brought Sarah and the girls into town before supper, so they could meet the troop train.

When they arrived at the depot, Sarah asked Edward, "Why is he arriving on the troop train instead of the regular passenger train?"

He replied, "Mighty fine question. Guess you'll just have to ask Eddie when he gets here. The regular passenger train isn't due through here until about ten tonight."

It wasn't long before the large black steam-powered locomotive came whistling and rumbling down the tracks. About the time it got even with the platform on which the family had been standing, the brakes began to squeak and squeal on the rails. Several gushes of steam shot out from the locomotive above the platform floor about ankle high, getting everyone's attention. The air seemed to fill with the smell of coal and oil with a light shower of cinders added in, as the locomotive passed by. Sarah thought to herself, it certainly isn't like the sleek vista dome North Coast Limited the Northern Pacific Railroad had for a passenger train.

When the train came to a stop way down at the far end of the platform, a conductor stepped from the train and dropped the metal box below the steps leading up to one of the cars. Within moments they could see Eddie in uniform stepping down and handling his duffle bag. As the family walked down the platform towards Eddie, there were several military members in uniform leaning out the window and making light conversation as they passed by.

They were nearing the end of the platform when the conductor stepped back on the train and waved his lantern. The shrilling whistle from the train with its 'A woof-woof' blast preceded the sound of the couplings between each rail car banging into place, as the locomotive engine began to pull numerous passenger cars and picked up speed.

Eddie dropped his duffle bag and ran toward the family. Edward held on to Mari and Kathy held Kari in her arms allowing Sarah to run on ahead.

When Eddie and Sarah came together, he picked her up into his arms and swung her around in a complete circle. She held her feet inches off the ground, a split second before they kissed.

Within moments, the family was together for handshakes, hugs and kisses. When they were ready to leave the platform, Eddie ran to get his duffle bag from where he had left it and joined the family on their way back to the farm.

Edward asked, "Son, where do they have you going and when do you have to report back for duty?"

Eddie replied for all to hear, "I will need to catch the troop train in about nine days and head for California again. When I get to San Francisco, I'll go to the bay area and board the naval ship USS Barnstable APA 93. It's a troop transport for my passage to Korea. I was told I would be assigned to a unit after I arrived there."

The first stop was at Edward and Kathy's house, where supper was ready in the warmer above the majestic range. The visit lasted for a couple of hours before Sarah and Eddie made their journey to their house.

When the girls were tucked into bed, Eddie turned to Sarah and they embraced, as he whispered into her hair, "Sarah, I have missed you every single day I was gone."

She replied, "I want to hold you forever and not let go." They held each other close for a kissing marathon and then settled for a peck now and then, back and forth. They settled on the sofa for a brief time, catching up on the latest news around home and sharing his experiences during training, before they kissed each other deeply and went to bed.

When morning came, Eddie prepared himself for work on the farm and headed for his folk's house. The hired hands were just leaving when he heard his father say, "And just what in the world do you think you're going to be doing?"

Eddie replied, "I thought I'd give a hand."

"No, you're not, I won't hear of it!" Edward replied.

Kathy had entered the porch and upon hearing the comments, she added, "Son, you take those legs of yours and march your britches right back to your house and get your family! You came back to spoil that family first and visit with us once in a while. Tell Sarah I have a batch of cinnamon rolls just out of the oven. Her and the girls can come and get them while their hot. There just might be one or two left for you."

Edward laughed and said, "You know we can't win when she has made up her mind. Go get Sarah. I've got a cup of coffee still waiting for my attention."

Eddie returned home and got his family. On the way back to his folk's house he said, "Sarah, when I showed up a few minutes ago in my work cloths, it seemed to set a fire under the both of them."

Sarah laughed, "They sure have both been great to me and the girls. I love them both. But I love you more."

Eddie smiled, "I love you far more than words can say. You're my wife, my love, you gave me two wonderful girls to love and you fill my heart with more happiness than I can say. You put a glow in my life, you're my sunshine."

Sarah smiled and teasingly said, "I'll let you tell me more when we get back to the house."

~ ~ ~ ~

The furlough was short lived and the dreaded day came when the family gathered on the platform of the Northern Pacific Railroad near the depot. They were waiting for the westbound troop train to arrive. The telegrapher acting as the depot agent adjusted the signal outside the depot office indicating that the troop train needed to stop. By adjusting the signal for a stop, the signal a mile or so east of town would indicate for the engineer to slow the train.

There were long faces and guarded conversations not to allow the premature release of tears and crying. It was going to be a tough departure. The devotion to family not only ran from the grandparents down, but up as well. Kathy was fearful for his departure because her oldest son Neil had served during WWII and was wounded by the Japanese in the battle for the Philippines. Her fears were guarded, in hopes of not causing more pain and anguish for Sarah and the children.

Edward stood with his arm wrapped around Kathy's back knowing her deepest feelings. His broad shoulders were sagging, as if the weight of the world was upon them. "Don't go fretting about how things are here at home," he assured Eddie. "Do your best, don't get hurt and come back as soon as you can."

Eddie nodded his head and turned to Sarah and said, "I'll keep the photo of you and the girls right here in my shirt pocket, right over my heart. I'll be all right and I'll be home before you know it."

Sarah wasn't fooled. She knew the length of their separation would be a long time. She had heard that some of the men who entered the military would be committed for the duration of the fighting plus six months. She hadn't been a military wife all that long, but she knew the separation could be for nearly a year if the fighting on the Korean peninsula lasted. "Eddie, I love you and we'll manage. Mom and Dad have been so good to me and I have the girls to keep me busy. Be careful and come back soon."

"They only drafted me for two years," Eddie replied. "Don't reckon they will be keeping me longer than that. This whole fuss may be over in a few months. Then I'll be back stateside, where I can come home on furlough and visit again. Don't any of you spoil the girls too much. Leave some of that for me to do when I get back."

Edward said, "Son, your mother and I have our first priority of spoiling those two girls and we'll spoil Sarah as well. When you get back, you're going to have to accept them as they are, spoiled or not." A bit of laughter followed only to be interrupted by the whistle of the train some distance down the track to the east, as it blew its whistle for one of the crossings.

When the train slowly rolled into the station, the locomotive belched steam and cinders before it rolled to a stop. As one of the passenger cars slowly passed by before coming to a stop, one of the soldiers called out from the window, "There is plenty of seating in this car. What's your name?"

As he looked up to reply he said, "Eddie Day, I'll be right there." Turning to the family, he said his last few words before giving each a hug and a kiss. Sarah was last and the best was saved for her. They embraced with passion and kissed each other so forcefully that they nearly bruised each other's lips.

The embrace was interrupted by the conductor who bellowed out, "All aboard!"

Eddie grabbed his duffle bag and boarded the train. The family could see him making his way to a seat inside the passenger car. Before the train began to move, he was partially hanging from the window waving his arm and trying to say something that he had failed to mention. But the train began moving and the conversation was lost in the movement of the troop train.

~ ~ ~ ~

When the ship anchored within the Inchon harbor in South Korea, most of the men were taken ashore, where they were quickly processed and shipped out to their units. Eddie Day was assigned to the 8th US Army's 7th Infantry Division. It didn't take long for him to get a good taste of battle and in no time was considered a seasoned soldier.

In the East at the Battle of Chosin Reservoir in the later part of 1950, the Chinese assault came at them hard. Some of the units were pulling back in an attempt to regroup. Eddie was caught facing the Chinese, as they came pouring over the landscape. There were times when his unit came close to running out of ammunition before another unit arrived to give support. Some of the enemy that fell in the fighting were close enough for men in his unit to see their faces. The hard reality of combat began to set in on those who experienced such a close call. There would be many more days of smothering combat, now that the Chinese were involved in the fighting.

When the Chinese began their spring offensive on April 22nd, 1951, many units in Eddie's outfit fell and, in the process, he saw a lieutenant from another platoon fall from shots to his leg and back. He ran from his position to where the wounded officer had fallen.

With a stunned expression, the lieutenant looked up into Eddie's face and uttered, "Take one of my tags and this letter. If I don't make it, get the letter to my wife. She's a nurse at the Army hospital and also works at the VA hospital in Frisco."

Eddie looked at the tag briefly and said "Lieutenant, we can't stay here long, there are just too many of them."

Eddie took one of the tags and the letter, shoving them down inside the inner part of his boot. He rose up from his position to see they had an opening. He bent over the lieutenant's face and said, "We're getting out of here." Eddie managed to get the lieutenant on his shoulders and began making his way to the rear. He was in hopes of finding someone to give fire support until he could get the wounded lieutenant somewhere safe. There were bodies and disabled equipment scattered about. Some of the men that had retreated only a short distance turned to lay down a line of fire to help him.

The weight of his equipment, weapon and the lieutenant slowed him down and before long the zip, zip popping of rounds near his feet encouraged Eddie to seek cover in a small nearby ditch.

He rolled the lieutenant from his back and reached for his weapon, only to be stopped by a Chinese soldier who was now pointing the business end of his weapon in Eddie's face.

The lieutenant was reaching for his sidearm when another Chinese soldier shot him at point blank range. The lieutenant fell back and was dead. The Chinese soldier holding Eddie at gun point motioned for him to get to his feet.

When Eddie stood up and stepped from the ditch he tried to use for cover, he could see most of those who had laid down a line of fire for him had been killed or overtaken and were now prisoners. He was ushered in the opposite direction of any friendly troops. A small handful of American and allied troops were hastily gathered up and marched from the battle area.

The rapid removal from the field of battle kept each soldier at a disadvantage. Several groups of recently captured men trudged across the battle torn land from varied pockets of fighting to a central location.

They were held in an area and segregated by the Chinese and North Koreans. Three Chinese manned the machine guns, as if they only needed a small excuse to open fire on the entire group of prisoners.

It was nearly nightfall when several North Korean trucks arrived and began loading up the prisoners. As the trucks became full, they would

42

drive from the make-shift compound and head north. It was well into the night when the trucks came to a stop and the prisoners were ordered out of the truck two at a time. The Americans were briefly searched once more and ushered into a building with mats on the floor. The buildings had no windows and only one door from which they entered. Undoubtedly there would be a guard on the outside. Few men fell asleep, fearing what was going to happen next.

Eddie looked at the tag; the lieutenant's name was Donald Sutton and the letter on a half piece of paper was to his wife Jody - VA Hospital San Francisco. Eddie took the boot string tab and began making a pocket inside his left leather boot. The metal dog tag helped separate the thick layer of leather for the small pocket. It took over an hour before two openings were large enough to hold the tag and letter. Eddie felt he had the tag and letter concealed with one in each boot in a way not to be rubbing his foot.

The night was short lived, when a guard opened the door and yelled out to the prisoners. They were ushered into a formation outside the small boarded up hut. Eddie could see several huts with the same formations in front of each. Each formation had an unfriendly North Korean manning a machine gun.

Eddie spoke out of the side of his mouth, "My name's Eddie. Wonder what they have in store for us today?"

A prisoner to his right said, "Um Teddy, just wish I not be here right now."

"I'm from Montana, where you from?" Eddie managed to say.

"Sidney," came the reply.

Inquisitive Eddie asked, "Montana or Australia?"

His answer was cut short when a dingy looking North Korean came up to the group and in a pidgin English said, "This line, then next you follow to kitchen," as he turned and walked off.

The morning breakfast was a spoon of rice and a liquid mixture of something stirred in a large pot, its vapors swirling in the cold mountain air. Three prisoners complained and threw their food to the ground. They were taken a short distance away and shot.

When breakfast was over, the men were ushered into their formations. They were marched to a road site, where they were put to work under the watchful eyes of those manning the machine guns. A small prisoner detail remained behind and was given the responsibility of digging

43

graves and burying the men who had been shot. The remaining prisoners were put to work gathering up stones and placing them in the roadway. Some of the men were assigned with sledgehammers breaking up big ones into little ones. They were luckier than the other prisoners who had to squat and use a hammer and chisel. Most of the prisoners carried rocks of various sizes to the roadway and placed them in a certain order. The stoop labor and the meager rations was more than some could stand.

When the day was done, the evening formation before the huts allowed a short North Korean to take several prisoners one at a time for interrogation. The cries from the rooms fell on the others' ears, knowing there was torture involved. When it came Eddie's turn, he knew the visit inside the interrogation hut wasn't going to be pleasant. The interrogation and Eddie's reply according to the code of conduct brought on a savage beating. The door opened and Eddie was tossed onto the frozen ground and forced to crawl to a group of prisoners for comfort.

His body ached as he crawled, but Eddie returned to the prisoner formation. An hour after the interrogation was over, he heard another North Korean say to the formation, "If you work with explosives to break rock, you get double rations." He stood there waiting, as if there would be a bunch to volunteer.

Eddie thought about the situation. He was hungry and he knew that in order to make it through the rough winter ahead, he would need more food in his body. Within moments, the formation was marched to the kitchen for their ration of rice and very little meat.

During the night, Eddie told Teddy Olsen, one of his fellow prisoners, "I'm going to volunteer for the explosive detail. I'm not going to work like this and starve before I have a chance to get out of here. The first chance I get, I'll use the explosives to blast my way out of this place."

Olsen said, "That's nuts! It makes some sense to me, but it's crazy. I'll go with you if you volunteer." They made plans and shared a note of each other's name and information about their folks back home in case the other didn't make it.

The morning came with a new layer of snow on the ground. The morning formation brought out the offer once more. The guard said, "Added rations for those who work with explosives."

That is when Eddie, Teddy and five others volunteered. That evening, they were placed at the head of the line and given extra rations and made to stand aside so that the other prisoners could see the added rations against their meager rice helping. That evening after supper, Teddy and Eddie were ordered into another formation with other explosive volunteers. They were marched a short distance from the remaining prisoners to a housing unit within the same camp.

The following morning, they were given orders on how to handle the explosives and directed to a rocky ridge and put to work. A single guard supervised two prisoners. Some of the explosive material was unpredictable. It would either explode beforehand or not at all after the plunger was pushed. The unexploded material was checked out shortly after the blast and some of the volunteers lost their lives when the delayed charge exploded with a roar.

~ ~ ~ ~

Several weeks had passed and the prisoners receiving single rations within the huts began to succumb to the lack of rations and from the cold. Early in the mornings, some of the bodies upon the mats no longer responded. When the work detail was sent to the rocky roadbed, a few remained in the camp to dispose of the bodies in a crude cemetery behind the camp. Several of the men on single rations on the work detail fell to the ground from malnourishment and exposure to the cold while working. They died next to their weakened fellow prisoners causing them anguish and yet another gruesome burial detail.

It was late January in 1952 when Teddy and Eddie along with a few others were transferred to another labor camp. The camp was located in the northern-most part of North Korea near the Russian border. Some of the guards were North Korean and supervised by Chinese and Russian officers. There was a large area that needed flattening for a roadway and an airfield was to be built in the rugged terrain. After the first week, Teddy and Eddie were separated and placed on different details. This separation hampered their ability to make plans to use the explosives in aiding their escape.

~ ~ ~ ~

Winter was gone and the summer months allowed blasting and the leveling of the mountainside to be suitable as an airfield and roads leading into the unknown. Eddie wondered what was at the end of the road if he decided to make a run for it, but the control of the guards never allowed such an attempt. There were no rumors of anyone dying or being blasted to bits, but Eddie had lost contact with Teddy Olsen and wondered how he was. Day and night, MiG-17 fighters that were flying south were now using the airstrip. For those prisoners on the work site, it created a sadness that engulfed them knowing the flights were going against American and allied forces.

Eddie Day was shuffled from one working project to another over the years, working with explosives to blast away at the mountainous terrain in preparation for yet another airstrip or storage area. He began to understand the predictability of the explosives and made sure the charges were properly handled. It was during this time that he fell under the increased scrutiny of the guards and their mistrust.

Unknown to the prisoners, in June 1953, talk of an armistice was being made and the war effort was slowing down while negotiations were offered. The project of building an airstrip and road in a remote portion of North Korea was falling behind schedule. The use of explosives was increased, but that did little to advance the delay. The terrain would need to be flattened before the project could be completed. The North Koreans wanted the airstrip and storage facility completed before any such peace agreements were made. Eddie was assigned to a project and who but Teddy Olsen was ordered to assist.

Eddie said, "Teddy, you're a sight for sore eyes. I thought I would never get to see you again."

"They have a way of splitting up any friendships, don't they? But they couldn't keep two Montanans from seeing each other now, could they?" Teddy responded.

Eddie uttered softly, "I've got to get out of here. I'd like to get to friendly lines if I could, but they watch me like a hawk on how I use the charges."

"They've watched me so close, I'm ready to skedaddle first chance I get. I'm with you if we get a chance to do it. I'll be right on your heels, so don't trip on our way out," Teddy answered back.

The face of a mountain had to be blasted away and it seemed that the enemy knew they would have to rely on the two best explosive-handling prisoners to get the job done. Eddie and Teddy slowly drilled holes, placed charges, ran wire and were finally in the process of placing the last charge. One of the guards approached them and ordered the setting of additional charges. The pressure to speed up the blasting in this area was unsafe for anyone working with the unpredictable explosive.

Eddie protested and tried to explain what would happen.

The guard leveled his rifle at Eddie and said, "I order you to set the charge."

Teddy spoke up and said, "Come on, Eddie. I'll work with you. We can do it if we're mighty careful. This might be our lucky day."

When Eddie turned to do what he was told, the guard swung his rifle and struck Eddie across the back and knocked him to the ground some eight feet from where he was standing.

Eddie was in pain when Teddy pulled him from the ground. He said, "Eddie, we'll get the job done and if the face of the hill careens down on a bunch of them, so be it. Are you fit to split if we get the chance?"

Unspoken words were shared as both smiled at each other knowing this may be the day.

The added charges and wiring were in place and the two of them were halfway back to where the plunger was situated when one of the charges prematurely detonated, causing the other charges to blast away as if a delayed timer was rigged to each explosive device.

Eddie had managed to dive into a shallow area only to see Teddy get knocked around with some of the flying debris. Eddie was unhurt from the blast, but Teddy had the wind knocked out of him for a moment and his back and legs were lacerated from several pieces of the flying chards of rock and timber. When the dust settled, several pieces of expensive equipment were buried under the debris, three advisors were killed and a good number of North Koreans were injured.

Eddie would face an inquiry as to why he had set the charges as he did and rebelling against the wishes of his guard. The parting of two explosive-handling friends from Montana was sad. Teddy would be sent south to a hospital and possibly on to another blasting area because of his skills or repatriated when the Armistice was signed. Eddie, on the other hand, would face some pretty serious charges and possibly death.

The parting of friends was short. Eddie said, "I may not make it. If they release you, get in touch with my wife and let her know what we did and that I love her and the girls."

Teddy Olsen was sent south to a hospital to remove some debris from his body and for observation. Some of the wounds were so deep, the enemy aid man was unable to remove some of the pieces.

47

The following morning, Eddie Day had to explain why he set so many of the charges in such a dangerous way, causing the death of three and injury to so many others as well as the destruction of so much equipment. His punishment was yet to come.

CHAPTER 6

Status: POW – KIA Body Not Recovered – 1953

The ceasefire may have been signed in July and the repatriation of POWs scheduled to start in September, but for Eddie Day, his situation would remain the same: detained and imprisoned. He was to be punished for negligence with explosives. He could have been executed, but politics within the North Korean government and the military gave cause for a lenient sentence. He could very well be used as a bargaining chip later, if need be, or easily disposed of. For now, his name would remain off the POW list that they were required to give to the officials in Panmunjom.

Months of confinement followed the sham hearing. They claimed they were looking into what went wrong at the air strip. They knew many of the explosives detonated prematurely or was the detonation intentional? The guard that knocked Eddie to the ground was wounded and later died from his wounds, but not before marking Eddie as a troublemaker. Eddie had been led from the hearing room and placed into a cell of near total darkness in a nearby prison. There were a few days of hard labor on details outside in the daylight. Then he was left alone within the cell he was assigned. The dingy musty hall outside his cell had a dim light bulb. As Eddie sat and pondered if it was daylight or dark, he began to lose all concepts of time. He was fed once a day and figured it was the evening meal. But as time passed, his meager rations were placed outside the slot of his cell door and the rations were cold when he discovered them.

For a time early on, there was a rhythmic beating on the pipes from someone else down the row of cells. Eddie would tap back while mentally scolding himself for not knowing Morse Code. In the darkness of his cell, he couldn't even scratch down the dits and dahs, even if the sender was patient with him. Then again, he didn't know if it was a friendly or the enemy doing the tapping. Over time there was nothing, only the silence and darkness.

Standing in the darkness to stretch his legs, he would sing the National Anthem and God Bless America out loud before crouching as does a quarterback, "Hike, Hike". A few steps back and he would go through the motions to pass. In his mind's eye, he would look left then right, but wind up throwing down the middle. Sometimes he would call out a play, only to pivot to hand the ball off, remembering Coach Higgins's repeated cry, "Don't drop the ball". After playing the game, he would mentally find himself in the chicken coop down on the farm, "Don't drop the eggs, place them in the bucket, but don't drop the eggs." Over time, he lifted more bales of alfalfa to a flatbed than what his father's farm had produced all summer. He had to keep moving. Then there were the visits with his wife and the bouncing of Mari on his knee and holding Kari. He would go through the motions of fly fishing with his father and carry on an imaginary conversation. From time to time, he would think back on the time he was in his mother's kitchen, eating a freshly baked bun with butter or an iced cinnamon roll. He couldn't waste away by sitting down and giving up. He had to stay active and mentally tough.

~ ~ ~ ~

It was Friday October 2nd, 1953 when the Army-brown four door sedan pulled off the highway and drove down the long dirt road to the Edward Day farm. A young enlisted man was driving with his commanding officer and the unit chaplain in the back seat. He knew their duties would be to inform the family of a tragedy or death to another family member.

Edward saw the sedan coming as he went into the house and said, "Sarah and Kathy, go to the living room and have a seat. I'll go to the gate to see what those fellows want."

Kathy questioned, "What do you mean?"

"We got company. I'll tend to it and be back in once I find out."

Sarah went to the window to see the sedan pull up in front of the house. Her heart sank as she let out a gasping sound, "No, it can't be, no!"

50

Kathy ran to Sarah's side and looked outside. She saw her husband open the gate to the yard and approach the sedan as two army officers got out.

The officer asked, "Is there a Mrs. Eddie Day nearby?"

"I'm Edward Day. Eddie is my son and his wife Sarah is inside with my wife."

The chaplain spoke up, "Mr. Day, we are here to share some unpleasant news."

Edward swallowed hard. His throat felt as if the moisture had raced from it, "I didn't figure your trip to the farm was something good. Let's go into the house, where we can hear it all at the same time."

After a short introduction, the officers were made comfortable before the commanding officer spoke. He said "I have the sad duty to inform you that Eddie Day has been listed as missing in action and assumed to be a prisoner of war. The North Korean government has furnished a list of prisoners that are to be repatriated. The army has gone over the list of POWs held by the North Koreans and has no choice but to change his status to killed in action."

Kathy grabbed at the upper part of her chest and gasped as she cried out, "Eddie, my dear Eddie!"

Sarah couldn't contain herself as she wheezed to catch her breath. The words of pain refused to reach her lips.

The chaplain rose and stood before the women. He stretched out his hands and laid them on the shoulders of the two women. Not a word was uttered from the chaplain for a short period of time.

Edward looked at the commanding officer and said, "Is there any chance at all that there has been a mistake?"

The officer said, "The North Korean government doesn't admit to even having held Eddie as a prisoner. They furnished the list and that is all the army has to go on. I'm terribly sorry. I am not only the notification officer, but the benefit officer as well." He handed over a card with several numbers the family could call for assistance. He briefly told Edward what benefits were available to the family.

The chaplain offered up a pray with the family before they excused themselves and made their way back to the waiting sedan.

~ ~ ~ ~

51

Unsure of the time during the week, two guards would come by and open the cell door. They would motion for Eddie to grab his slop jar and carry it to a slit in a concrete floor where he was instructed by motion to empty it. When he heard them coming, he would hide the two rocks he had smuggled into the cell with him. He would pull his prison garb pants up and roll the waist around the rocks so they wouldn't drop. He imagined his cell was searched whenever he left. When the messy chore was completed, he was escorted back to his cell. Eddie could tell that someone had been in his cell, as the mat he laid upon on the floor usually had been moved and a meager amount of sanitary paper was left behind. The guards apparently spoke no English, as none was shared with him while he was being escorted. Upon returning to the cell, the door was closed and the snap seemed to echo a seeming finality in the hollowness of his darkened world.

Eddie knew he had to hold up and be mentally tough. In the beginning he would pray out loud. His voice was stronger then, now it was but a mere whisper as his body began to weaken. He would ask for strength and guidance, mentally crawling into himself to reach his spiritual being. There were times he would talk out loud, as if his wife could hear him, "Sarah, today is a day where the darkness has blotted out the color of my world, as once I knew it. You and the girls are on my mind and I hope all is well in Montana. Tell Mom and Dad, I am alive and doing fine. I'll see all of you one of these days." The prayers and conversations would exercise his mental process, in hopes of not going mad with the solitude and silence. When lying upon the mat trying to find sleep, he hoped that the dreams he would have been of a gentler time and not the horrors of war and captivity. The good dreams were a way to escape reality. He would be able to share them with his family when he talked with them after he woke up. Early in the mornings, he would softly sing the National Anthem and at times during the day he would try the exercise of remembering the song backwards. He didn't do too well. Somewhere in the middle, he would lose and would give up for another day.

At times, Eddie would feel a need to measure his cell to be sure in his own mind how big his world was. He knew his tattered government-issue boots were about twelve inches as he laid his boots down end to end, one in front of the other. Long ago, the laces had been removed from his boots to discourage any escape attempt. When his exercise was done, he came up with a total of eight feet wide and nine feet long. Sometimes he would use the width of the back of his palm and measure hand over fist, coming up with a total of twenty-four hands wide and twenty-seven hands long. When his knees were not hurting, he would bend over and rest his weight on his forearms, as he took his index fingers and place them one over the other. Sometimes he would miscount and have to return to the corner and begin counting again. He had to keep his mind occupied and not be satisfied with guessing.

When the tedious exercise was done, he concluded that the cell was 120 index fingers wide and 135 index fingers long. Some days he would come up with one or two more index fingers in length or width. He wasn't sure if he had miscounted, or if he was losing weight and his fingers were not as wide as they once were. He knew that the opening to the cell door was a three foot by five-foot door. Not paying attention had caused him to bump his head several times. Sometimes it would give him reason to measure the room again to make sure of his figures. He knew that near the door, the floor was dry and at the rear of his cell, there was a bit of moisture that gathered at times. When he felt the dampness, sometimes he could feel a bug or two that were sharing his cell. When he was through counting in this fashion, he would rub his knees before standing and stretching. He would prepare mentally to go into the river and stand almost hip deep in the water and cast out line from his fly rod several times, in hopes of catching that elusive brown trout. One thing for sure, he would never let the enemy know he was exercising. When he heard their footsteps in the darkened hallway, he would stop what he was doing and be sitting on the mat when they opened the cell door.

When he emptied his slop jar and returned to the cell, he would measure the mat again to see if it was the old mat or if they had replaced it. He would slowly count from the top to the bottom and from one end to the other. He found the length of flat fibers counted 115 and at each end, the fibers were folded under to give a small ridge. The width of the mat was 43 flat fibers folded under at the ends, the same way to keep the mat together. There was no pillow provided and he would use his clothing rolled up to improvise. The slop jar with little paper, a pair of Korean paper-thin slippers, his boots, clothing and a thin blanket were all that remained in the cell with him.

~ ~ ~ ~

53

Eric Elders had kept in close contact with Edward and Kathy Day when he visited the farm. He would always ask about Sarah and the girls. Eric made it a point that his meetings with Sarah had been at Edward's and Kathy's home. Following his graduation from college, he had been given a route to travel checking on different refinery operations and meter stations throughout the state. When he came to the turnoff to the Day farm, it made no difference, going west or east. He would always turn down the lane and at least give a short visit.

The Days informed him that the army had changed Eddie's status from missing in action to killed in action, body not recovered and the presumptive finding of death. The Army claimed his name had not appeared on a prisoner of war list furnished by the Communist North Korean Authorities for the repatriation of prisoners. Eric began taking on a protective role as far as Sarah and the girls were concerned. The promise to Eddie would remain solid: he would look after Sarah and the girls should something happen to him. Eric had not been seeing anyone seriously and felt a strong pull towards Sarah. Over the years following the notification, Eric had called on Sarah and had remained understanding, knowing the laws of Montana would dictate the length of time she could not be his. It took time for their relationship to get serious; undo delays were limited by the rules of law.

~ ~ ~ ~

Several months after the standard seven years of waiting for someone to be declared legally dead in Montana, the Day family and Eric Elders went to the county seat where they had to appear before a judge. For Edward and Kathy Day, the court documents would reflect on the assets they owned and the change to the family will. For Eric and Sarah, the proceedings included Eddie's death certificate, court docket information, so that a marriage license could be applied for. They declined being married before the same magistrate. The following week in a private ceremony, they were married by the local Methodist minister in the church the family had always attended.

Edward and Kathy Day insisted that Eric and Sarah stay at the house on the farm that Sarah had enjoyed for so long. They wanted the grandchildren, Mari and Kari, available so that they could have the joy of seeing them grow up. They would be nearby when Eric was gone on his long road trips across the state for the refineries, in case Sarah needed anything.

~ ~ ~ ~

For Eddie, the winter snows had come and gone tenfold, as well as the rainy monsoon seasons in this prison compound. But the passage of time for someone held in darkness and captivity, the marking of seasons went on without meaning. Early on when he first arrived, they placed him with prisoners doing hard labor on the prison labor gangs. Later on, came the total isolation, which became a customary punishment handed out by the guards for little or no reason. To work, you could see sunlight and lose your strength from withheld nourishment because you failed to meet a required amount of work. Isolation was in the depth of the prison where in near total darkness it weakened the mind over the passage of time. Recently Eddie found it hard to stand anymore and would remain sitting on his mat during the time he was awake. All his bones ached from the lack of activity, but his hands hurt the most, as the fingers grew stiff. Between his shoulders, there was a constant ache and the spinal column seemed to bend him forward over time, not allowing him to stand as tall as he once did so proudly. At times, there was a period of despair, when he nearly lost all hope. But deep within himself he found a grain of faith that seemed to rekindle the fighting spirit within his body. He realized that the strength he once held within his body had left. Folding his arms across his chest, he could feel his ribcage; there wasn't much there. No longer did he stand to play his imaginary football game, or stand to sing aloud. His voice had all but left him. No longer did he move his body as if he was doing the farm chores, or the physical feat of loading hay with the up sweep of his arms or the fluid motions required of casting while fishing with a fly rod. The weight of his arms was more than what little strength he had within them. He was unable to go through such strenuous exercises trying to match the movements of his body with those that played out in his mind. The images of those he left behind so long ago were like photos flashing through his mind at an uncontrollable speed. The corners of his lips gave way to an uncontrollable twitch, his face was shallow and his shoulders sagged, giving way to the weight of his arms. They dangled allowing his hands to fold into his lap when he was able to sit up. His legs were thin from his hips to his ankles. A small bowl of rice began to feel like an overwhelming amount of food to eat. Despite trying to hang in there and not let his captivity get the best of him, he knew he was behind in the score.

~ ~ ~ ~

For some unknown reason in 1963 the isolation came to an end. Two guards unlocked the cell door and motioned for him to get his belongings and come with them. Eddie crawled to the back of the cell to pick up his worn old combat boots. He concealed his actions from the guards, as he quickly palmed the two rocks. He wrapped part of his old shirt haphazardly around them, holding them tightly to his body, as he tried to stand. Both of the guards entered the cell and, with their help, Eddie's frail legs wobbled like those of a newborn colt before they gained the strength to hold up his body. Each step was with considerable pain and effort, but for some unknown reason, the guards checked his balance.

Eddie thought, 'Maybe today is the day he would stand before a machine gun like so many of the other POW's had in the past and meet the same kind of fate. Maybe they would be merciful and provide a chair for him to sit in while viewing the machine gun and listen to the enemy laugh at his weakened state of being.' Eddie finally snapped out of his dismal thoughts and nearly spoke out loud through his parched thin lips, 'I'll do my best to stand on my feet and grit my teeth into a smile, I won't let them have the satisfaction and knowledge they have broken my spirits.' The gauntness in his face showed the lack of muscle control and his eyes were shallow and deep into his face. He held his wadded shirt tightly, as if he was in pain. He walked along in his combat boots minus the laces.

Eddie was ushered into an office where a North Korean officer and a Korean government official sat at a table. The officer spoke in deprived English, "Eddie Day, we have decided to end your punishment. The fighting with the Americans has ended. When you see doctor and you eat, we take you to Panmunjom."

He was given back his wallet empty of any currency and handed his dog tags along with the photo of Sarah and the girls, Mari and Kari. Time hadn't treated the photograph very well, the edges were tattered, but he could still cast his eyes upon his family.

As he left the prison, with pain racking his body, Eddie leaned over and picked up a small rock. The escort paid little attention to him, as he was ushered to a truck for transportation from the prison.

Eddie looked back over a compound much different from the days when he first arrived. Now the neglected buildings showed poor mortar and cinderblocks with rusted iron doors. Around the grounds, several wilted plants tried to grow among the encroaching weeds that were taking over. Buildings that once had a painted surface were in disrepair. Eddie thought the prison was as forgotten as he was. The jostling in the truck over the rough roads brought out the sharpness of the aches within his weakened body.

Moments before arriving at Panmunjom, Eddie thought back on the quick physical or lack of and the skimpy meal set down before him, had he finally worn out his welcome? When the truck rolled to a stop, he was supported by his escorts and taken inside a small building with several guards posted directly outside. Eddie remained under the constant control of the two North Korean Guards, as they stood on each side of the chair, he was sitting in. He was allowed to cling to the ragged end of his shirt, concealing the small stones he held to one side, as if he was in pain.

A handful of American army people and nearly twice as many of the enemy were seated at a table. One of the American officers spoke up and said, "What is your name, son?"

When Eddie tried to talk, his voice barely registered a wheeze of a whisper and he was unable to communicate. His lips twitched instead of saying something audible, trying to identify who he really was. Mentally he was concerned and afraid he would lose his ability to reach out for help.

The officer continued, "How long have you been held captive?"

Eddie didn't know the answer and instead of shrugging the weight of his thin arms kept his shoulders sagging.

The string of questions seemed to be endless and Eddie was beginning to wonder why they were asking so many questions. One of the guards reached down and took Eddie's dog tags off and handed them over to those seated at the conference table. Slowly the dog tags found themselves in front of the senior officer, where they remained on the table. Eddie sat unaware that his identity had to be confirmed, that he was part of a prisoner exchange and the negotiations had a certain type of protocol on each side.

There were a few moments of negotiating before one of the doors opened and a North Korean was escorted into the room guarded by a military policeman from the South Korean army. The North Koreans talked with the prisoner and finally settled on his identification.

There was more negotiating before both parties signed something in a large ledger. With that completed the North Korean was given over to the North Korean delegation and Eddie was given over to the delegation of American army officers.

When they left the building, Eddie paused and struggled through the pain long enough to pick up a rock directly outside the building. He was ushered away in an American army sedan and driven to an area inside friendly lines, where he was flown to Seoul, Korea in a helicopter. At Eighth Army Headquarters, Eddie was interviewed, then taken directly to the hospital and fed before he underwent a complete physical.

After a few days of observation by numerous army personnel, they informed Eddie he would be stateside within the week. Those who interviewed him shook their heads in disbelief, when the answers they sought were answered with mumbled words, confusion and incoherent sentences. The doctors and nurses were challenged at trying to render medication and food into such a gaunt figure. When his vitals were stable and it appeared that he was responding well to nourishment by a slight weight gain, he was ready to make the journey home. Eddie was issued a complete set of military clothing before he was air lifted from Korea. He was surprised that the shoes and new boots were black. He was assigned to a hospital in Japan for a week before his flight back to American soil.

CHAPTER 7

Korea - Japan - USA - A Flight into Rehabilitation - 1963

W hen Eddie left the hospital in Japan, he was ushered to an aircraft that was scheduled to puddle jump back to the States. Next to him in the aircraft was a nurse in dress khaki, assigned to see he received the best medical care on his way home. The DC-7 had ample seating, where he could stretch out his legs and not have to feel cramped during the long flight. Between the seating and the cockpit, a stack of mail bags was heaped in the passageway. He held his old tattered brown combat boots in his lap, where he could feel them and know they were near.

The first stop was on the island of Guam for added passengers and refueling. The plane pulled up to a terminal that looked partially abandoned. A brown army tanker truck pulled up near the right wing where two men rushed about connecting hoses, before going about refueling. A jeep with the dusty windshield resting on the hood drove up near the tanker truck. Several pieces of luggage were placed in a compartment in the belly of the plane.

Lieutenant Shirley Swanson, an army nurse asked, "Private Day, are you comfortable?"

Eddie responded only with a slight nod of the head.

She smiled and said, "I'm Lieutenant Swanson, I'll be your nurse on the way back to the States." The line of her jaw got closer, as if she had to see his face up close in order to tell him. "I'll need to check your vitals while we're on the ground. That way if you feel like sleeping while in flight, I won't have to bother you." She did her duties and entered the information in his medical chart. "You might want to stand up for a short spell and stretch your legs. Sometimes sitting in one position buckled in can get uncomfortable over time."

He did as he was told and unbuckled his seat belt before standing up in front of his seat. He didn't have much headroom and the nurse moved out of his way, allowing him to stand between the rows of seats. When he felt he had stood long enough he reclaimed his seat and buckled the seatbelt. He continued to look out the window with interest at what was happening below the wing. The nurse claimed her seat next to Eddie and began reading a Saturday Evening Post magazine that was available for the passengers.

Two army officers, one in dress uniform the other in khaki, came onboard the plane. One took a seat in the rear of the plane, while the other held out two in-flight meals to the nurse in his passing. He went to the cock pit and handed the pilot a small briefcase and a meal box before he turned and left the plane. Lieutenant Swanson handed one of the meals to Eddie and said, "A bit of nourishment would help." Eddie took the package and could only return a gaze with expressionless eyes.

The cabin door was closed and Eddie could see the men refueling had done their duties and were winding the hose on the truck before they drove off. Within moments, the propellers began turning slowly and the engines began to smoke before the propellers picked up speed. The plane began to move on the tarmac and immediately sped down the runway for lift off. Eddie looked out the window to see the land fade before he saw the outline of the island bordering the Pacific Ocean. Hazy and puffy clouds began to interrupt his view, as the DC-7 gained altitude and headed for another stop closer to getting home.

~ ~ ~ ~

Eddie had been sleeping for some time and Lieutenant Swanson had some trouble rousing him from his deep sleep. She was scheduled to check his vitals. "Eddie, can you hear me? Eddie, wake up for me, can you?" He wasn't responding as she would like and his readings were beginning to show a drop in pressure. He came to for a brief moment, with unclear vision to see the nurse hovering over him and patting his face. Her brows made perfect arches behind the hair that had come loose from the hairpins and several strands of her long hair bounced, as it framed her face.

When the aircraft began to lose altitude, Eddie's eyes flew open. He didn't know what startled him from his slumber, the sensation of the plane dropping or the nurse. Lieutenant Swanson rested her hand upon his arm and said, "We'll be landing in Wake Island in a few minutes, how are you feeling?"

Eddie did not answer. He looked at her without focus, then turned away to look out the window, where he could see the whitecaps in the ocean. His eyes became teary and he got the shakes from a chill that ran deep to his bones.

The stay on Wake Island was short and the fuel was topped off. The nurse stood up, recovered a couple of blankets from the overhead rack and wrapped them around his body, "Keep this one arm uncovered, so that I can check your blood pressure. Let me know if the blankets make you feel warmer."

Eddie smiled and with a struggling whisper said, "I hope so, I feel so cold."

Lieutenant Swanson opened up the in-flight boxes that still had packets of salt in them. She opened his mouth with her hands and poured the contents into his mouth, "Eat that, it's salt and it should help bring up your readings. The altitude is causing your blood pressure to drop."

The cock pit door was open and Lieutenant Swanson got the pilot's attention when he glanced back in her direction. He came back to her side and asked, "What is the problem?

She said, "His blood pressure seems to keep dropping, is there any medical help at our next stop?" She went about putting her hair back in place as she talked.

The pilot said, "Not much to speak of. We have some rough weather ahead that will cause some flight delay. I need to make a quick stop at Midway and then we'll head directly for Pearl." He returned to his seat and could be seen talking with someone over his communication equipment. The flight was beginning to feel rough as the plane was jostled around in the turbulent air currents.

The pilot was apparently skirting a typhoon in his flight pattern as the sky was filled with dark gray menacing clouds and the ocean seemed to have large groundswells that would certainly cause problems for local shipping and naval operations. They kept getting closer and closer to the whitecaps causing Eddie to feel uneasy, as the plane dipped down a bit and the wings shuttered up and down. The uplifting tips of the angry ocean waters were replaced with a sandy beach that quickly disappeared beneath the wings, before the airstrip began racing beneath the belly of the plane. Relief came upon hearing and feeling the screeching and bumping of the tires as they made contact with the airstrip followed by the whining thrust of the engines. They had landed. The landing on Midway Island was much the same as landing on the other islands. The plane had to come in low to get every bit of runway under its wheels, turn at the end of the runway and return midfield, to the area where the aviation fuel was available.

During the landing, Lieutenant Swanson removed the blankets from Eddie, placing them in the overhead rack and asked, "Can you get to your feet for a spell? I think you need to get some of that blood circulating and stretch that thin frame of yours."

Eddie had no sooner got to his feet when the cabin door opened and one of the maintenance men handed up a thermos of coffee and a couple of cups. Eddie sat in his seat cradling the cup in the palms of his hands, soaking up the warmth of the cup. After his second cup the thermos and cups were passed back to one of the maintenance men.

With the fueling completed, the plane began to head down the uneven strip of runway becoming airborne just before the sandy beach at the water's edge. In a flash, the island of Midway vanished behind the plane's view. Eddie looked out the window seeing the dark clouds off in the distance. He was beginning to feel warmer and the nurse smiled after checking his blood pressure and said, "Now that is much better. How do you feel now?" Eddie returned a shallow stare, as if her words didn't fully register in his mind.

It was a short flight and out the window, Eddie could see the Hawaiian Islands standing out in the still clear blue ocean water of the Pacific. As the Islands came closer, it was evident which one of the Islands the plane was headed for. In time, the natural feature of Diamond Head could be seen, as the plane changed direction to enter into an approach pattern. The ocean below the plane was calm and the colors began to reflect the depth from a dark blue green to a blue and yet a lighter color of blue, as the coral beneath forced the reflective shallowness. The plane came in over Barbers Point and the destruction of Battleship row could be seen, as the plane lowered its landing gears in preparation for landing at Hickham Field. The touchdown was smooth and within minutes the plane had pulled up close to the terminal and shut off its engines. A navy ambulance pulled up close to the plane, before a doctor and a medic boarded the plane to assist Lieutenant Swanson in caring for Eddie.

After a three-hour delay from their scheduled takeoff due to a faulty oil indicator light, the DC-7 was airborne once more. Lieutenant Swanson smiled as Eddie fell asleep. The delay had allowed the navy doctor and medic additional time to help care for Eddie. This gave her time to exercise her legs in the terminal and take care of her personal needs before returning to the plane. When she returned to Eddie's side his, vital readings and pulse were stable and he had good color. She would be happy to arrive in California where she would be relieved of her responsibility of Private Eddie Day and be on her way home on a much-needed furlough. She knew that her duties of caring for him would hold a special part in her heart. He was a young man caught up in the clutches of war and imprisonment and somehow had found the strength to come out alive. She could see how traumatized he was from his experience. She felt his recovery in the hospital at the Presidio in San Francisco would mend his tattered body, at least she hoped so. She would always wonder about the tattered combat boots and the importance they held in his life.

~ ~ ~ ~

The news of Eddie's release from the North Korean prison was good news for the Day family. Edward and Kathy would make plans for their trip to San Francisco, California and be there shortly after he arrived at the military hospital on the Presidio. Eric Elders had some vacation time coming and had promised to look after the farm while they were gone. If Eric wasn't around the house at the time the school bus arrived, Sarah would see that the girls got off to school. Edward and Kathy had instructions from the Elder family to go and see Eddie and convey their best wishes as well.

Upon their arrival at the Letterman General Hospital at the Presidio of San Francisco, they were ushered into a conference room where several doctors greeted them. The family was informed of Eddie's current condition and not to expect a lot out of their son on the first visit. The doctors reported that he was extremely malnourished from his captivity. His vocal cords only allow small sounds from lack of use and the trauma associated with being held captive had left him psychologically scarred. The briefing painted a bleak picture of how life had dealt their son a terrible blow and that the army would allow a limited number of visits from the family, but discouraged unlimited timely visits. Kathy looked at the briefing doctor and said, "I'm his mother. His father and I have come a long way and we wish to see our son! The army told us at one time he was dead. Well, he isn't! And we plan to see him as much as we can. I trust that the army will not hinder the length of our visits with him before we decide to go back to Montana."

The doctor said, "We are concerned not only for your son's health, but the impact on him mentally-"

"I thank you for being concerned," Kathy said, "but the army wasn't so concerned on the impact to his family when they came and told us he was dead. When the army officer and Chaplin left the farm, they probably felt that was the end of their concern. His widow at the time had little assistance to get what was due her and the girls. How many other families across this country felt the same military concern when they were notified? Well, we're here and we plan to see our son for as long we as feel he is comfortable having us around."

Edward held on to Kathy's arm and reinforced her statement, "That's my boy you're tending to and I wouldn't argue with my wife, 'cause she laid it right on the line, just like I would. If we feel it is too much for him, we'll make arrangements to visit less and allow him to rest."

The medical doctors didn't want to be confrontational and chose to be sympathetic and cordial. They allowed the comments to stand as stated. Their main concern was for the health of Eddie Day and should his medical needs be necessary to override the parents' wishes, they would deal with the problems at that time.

The Days were ushered into the intensive care ward and down a shiny waxed corridor. The wax reflected the pictures that hung on the walls, doorways as they passed and the overhead lights, much like the mountains of Montana being reflected in the stillness of Glacier Lake, on their way towards Eddie's room. One of the staff nurses stepped into the hallway after preparing him for company. In her passing, the squeak of her medical shoes against the surface of the floor diminished as she continued down the corridor. The delegation of doctors and staff walked some in front of and some behind the Day family. When they arrived at the room, the door was held open. Edward and Kathy were allowed to enter the room. An attending nurse was tending to an IV in Eddie's arm.

Edward and Kathy were taken aback by the extremely thin figure of their son beneath the single sheet upon the bed. His face was gaunt and his complexion was pale. He looked at them from behind a variety of monitoring devices attached to his body. The nurse stepped back but remained in the room and allowed them to approach the bed. "Hello, Eddie," Kathy managed to squeeze out of her throat as she reached out and held his hand, "I'm so glad to see you."

Eddie strained his eyes, while trying to see through tears, to eke out one scratchy word, "Mama."

Edward reached over and placed his hand atop Kathy's, "Son we're here to let you know we love and have missed you."

"Dad, I'm…" The vocal cords strained, but failed to resonate adequately in volume, as the uttered comment drifted off to an inaudible whisper, erased from its ability to be heard.

The nurse spoke up, "His voice is so weak from not being used for so long the vocal cords need to be stretched. He will be going through some extensive speech therapy. It will be like teaching him how to talk all over. But in time he'll bounce back."

Edward said, "Son, we'll sit close to the bed for a while and tell you some of what is going on in this world. Then we'll let you get some rest and we'll come back later. We made the trip from the farm to come out here to check on your hide and give you some support."

"I'm… so… thirsty," he managed to say.

Kathy went to get a glass of water for him, when the nurse said, "Mrs. Day, he can't have a lot of water to drink because he had a treatment spray in his throat. We are using the sponge applicators to moisten his lips and tongue, but too much water would dilute the medicine."

"Please, call me Kathy and this is my husband, Edward. We'll try not to go against the treatment; I guess its best we ask before doing too much of anything."

The nurse smiled and said, "I'm here if there are any questions on his treatment or progress. There isn't much on progress, he just recently arrived. The staff is evaluating him and making diagnoses as quickly as they can, so he can get the best of care."

Edward turned to look at the nurse and said, "That's good to hear."

Kathy was bedside, dampening the sponge swab, leaning over the cold metal bed railings and wetting her son's lips. She allowed some of the moisture to be sucked from the sponge. "Eddie, your girls are fine.

Mari is now thirteen years old and Kari is almost twelve. They may look like their mother, but they sure have your eyes. Mari likes to have her hair freefalling, while Kari likes having her hair done up in a French braid. They are partial towards a dress for school and church, but around the farm they wear britches. They sure enjoy school. Both have made the honor roll together this last period. One is good in math the other excels in science."

"Is… Sarah… ok?" Eddie uttered.

The one topic that hit the hardest had been brought to the forefront. They had tried to talk about the topic on the way to California and were wondering, when would be a good time to tell their son the whole truth. Kathy swallowed hard, not wanting to be deceitful. She managed to say, "Sarah is doing fine, making sure those girls get their homework done and trying to keep up with all the demands of supporting the girls' class projects."

"Tell her, keep up…," he coughed several times before finishing, "the good work." The comment was nearly inaudible, as if there was a lack of lung power to throw the words past his vocal cords.

Edward chimed in from time to time, talking of the chores on the farm and the stock that was released on the government range. The awkward visit lasted about forty-five minutes. When they saw Eddie growing tired and his eyes were nearly shut, Kathy stood and placed a kiss on his forehead. Edward patted his shoulder and said, "We'll let you sleep and we'll be back tomorrow. Now get your rest."

The bravest of mothers turned and left the room. When Edward met her in the hallway, she threw her arms around him for support and cried with big emotional sobs. Nurses came running and encouraged her to have a seat up near the nurse's station until she felt better. "He's so sick and thin, my goodness what in the world have they done to our son?" The questions were not to be answered but uttered from the lips of a caring mother who could no longer hold back the words or thoughts within. A few minutes later, they were informed of Eddie's treatment schedule. They were also apprised of when it would be a good time to return. They left the hospital for the first time and headed toward their guest lodging on the post.

~ ~ ~ ~

The three weeks in California were drawing to an end. The last visit with their son was at hand, as they entered his room. Eddie had been taken off of some of the medical equipment. It was placed alongside the wall in the room to be used only as needed. Instead of an IV stuck in his arm, he was placed on a soft food diet that was packed with loads of nutrients for strength and weight gain. He was beginning to speak somewhat better and tried to add to the conversation. The Days had no sooner entered his room, when a nurse brought in his supper tray. Kathy helped with the bread and butter and tried to lend a hand in his feeding.

Eddie smiled and said, "I can do… that, Mom." He managed to tell the family of his progress in the speech and physical therapy treatments they were putting him through.

Edward and Kathy spoke of the preparations they were making in getting ready for their return to Montana. Eddie smiled when Kathy said, "I'll bet that Sarah will be happy to see us come home. She has been taking care of the cooking for the hired hands as well."

Edward had alerted the nurse of the impending bad news he would tell his son. The ward nurse called for the senior nurse to be present in the room. When she arrived, she introduced herself to the family, "Hello, I'm Major Jody Sutton. I'm in charge of the nursing staff here at Letterman. We're here to see that your son gets the best medical care this hospital can provide."

Kathy and Edward nodded in unison and Kathy said, "So nice to meet you."

Edward said, "I'm Ed and that is my wife, Kathy." He quietly informed the major of his intentions. He turned to his son and said, "Eddie, I have some hard news to tell you, so please let me finish before you say anything. I want you to know we all love you at home. But when that Armistice was signed in Korea and the list of POWs was given, your name was not on the list. The army visited the house and told us that you were probably killed in action and your body wasn't recovered. It tore the family up pretty bad. Well, Eric Elders, your high school buddy had been checking in on us, Sarah and the girls. When this news came, he tried to help, but stayed back not knowing what to do. Well son, in Montana you have to be missing seven years before the State declares you dead. That time had come and when the judge issued a death certificate, Eric and Sarah began seeing each other and they eventually got married. He is looking out for the family, wishes you well and wants you to hurry up and have a speedy recovery, so that you can come home."

The saying 'you could have heard a pin drop' would have been an understatement, as the nurses prepared themselves for what might come next. Kathy held on to his forearm patting it ever so softly. Eddie stared at his father, as if what he heard was almost too much to swallow. His intense stare lasted a long time.

Eddie thought back on the time he had asked Eric to look in after the family. He considered himself immortal and that he would be returning, not ever considering he may be captured or killed. Nothing was mentioned of Sarah possibly being available after a period of time, should he never return. "How long have I been gone?"

Kathy spoke up and softly said, "Son, it's going on fourteen years since you entered the army in August of 1950. It is now 1964."

There was a long pause. They could tell Eddie was thinking, trying to recollect events from his past, before he spoke, "That is a long time, isn't it?" Eddie replied.

His father said, "Eddie, Eric and Sarah waited quite a spell, and Eric has taken care of the family without asking anything in return for all those years, before you were legally dead by Montana statutes. Only then did I see him make himself available for Sarah. He has done well for her and the girls."

Kathy said, "Mari and Kari come by the house to look at your old photographs and ask about you. Eric has encouraged them to be proud of you and the sacrifice you made. They had accepted your death and are so excited that the army has made a mistake. They wanted to quit school long enough to come out here to see you, but we discouraged that. If you can't make it home this summer, they may want to make the trip during their summer vacation. You'll be so proud of them."

He listened and pondered what he had heard before saying, "Tell Eric and Sarah, I'll try to understand and I'll...," his voice choked silent for a moment, "see them when I get back home. If I can't make it home this summer, maybe I'll be home shortly after that. It depends on what they have in store for me around here. I would prefer the girls don't see me in the hospital, not like this. I would rather see them have fun and enjoy a visit instead of feeling sorry for me. I hope you understand, but please ask them to write. I'd like that a lot."

You could almost hear a sigh of relief from the nurse standing next to Jody before Kathy spoke, "Eddie, we love you and would never intend to hurt you. I don't believe Eric or Sarah intended to hurt you either. Their main concern was seeing that the girls had a stable home for them to come home to when they got out of school."

The last visit before heading to Montana was nearing an end and Edward said, "I plan to take your mother across the Golden Gate Bridge if that old station wagon will hold out and then we plan to visit Fisherman's Warf and do some shopping before we leave. On our way home, we plan to see the Grand Canyon before we cut a trail north to Jackson Hole, Wyoming. We plan to visit Yellowstone Park and see Old Faithful, before leaving the park at Silver Gate and dropping into Red Lodge on our way home."

Eddie's eyes twinkled, as he motioned for his father to lean down to where he could whisper in his ear, "Get something special for the both of you and a gift for the girls. Let me know how much it costs and I'll pay for it. Have a safe trip home, let me know when you get there and ask the girls to write me. Tell Sarah and Eric they can write if they want. I'll try to write back, but I'm not sure what I could say." Tears welled up in his eyes, but he made no effort to stop them.

"You going to be ok, Eddie?" his mother asked.

"I'll be fine. I have a lot of mending to do physically, mentally and I guess spiritually and a whole lot of catching up."

The family expressed their love once more before Kathy gave her son a good-bye kiss and hug. Edward gave him a handshake and a man's hug that conveyed much more meaning. They turned, nodded at the staff and left the room glancing back inside the door to give a slight wave. Their son waved in return.

Major Jody Sutton was reviewing the progress and medical chart when Eddie asked, "Major, can I talk to you?"

She sat near the bed and replied, "You most certainly can, how may I help you?"

The talk covered a large range of topics, the first one being, "They claim there were two more stars added to the flag since I was captured."

"That is true, Eddie," Jody said softly, "We have Alaska as our 49th State and then Hawaii was admitted into the union later that same year making it the 50th State."

Eddie thought for a moment, as if absorbing what he was told then said, "They issued me a new pair of black combat boots, shortly after

I was set free. They tell me that there is no longer a 'Brown Shoe Army'."

"This is another truth. From the beginning of the Korean Conflict to now, the military uniforms have changed to include the shoes and boots. Eddie, there have been many changes in the military and in our country since you became a prisoner of war. Now that you are released, it will take time to understand and accept most of the changes. That is why I am here. I want to help you adjust right along with seeing that your medical needs are carried out."

The talk continued with several more questions being asked or comments on how he felt. Major Sutton either answered or would have to get back to him. Several questions were about his spiritual needs, his hurts, anger and how to best handle the news he had just received. She said, "Eddie, some of what you're seeking cannot come from me, but the Chaplain in the Protestant faith is available."

Eddie said, "If you know the Chaplain, would you ask him to drop by my room later today? I'd like to talk to him."

Major Sutton said, "I sure will. I am almost off duty, so I'll stop by his office on my way to the Veteran's Hospital and I'll see you tomorrow."

"Thanks, I appreciate that." Eddie uttered.

~ ~ ~ ~

After months of examinations and vigorous speech and physical therapy behind him, Eddie was allowed some quiet time in the day room of the hospital. He stood at the window looking out at the green grass, the tall palm trees, blue skies and the new-looking automobiles that were parked or going up and down the street. Had things changed that much while he was gone? He wondered how many things had changed back home in Montana.

Major Jody Sutton had been an army nurse for a number of years, and was struck by the Eddie Day's introverted behavior. He had come out of his shell to a small degree recently, but was uncomfortable with the news media and public relations officers. He had withdrawn so deeply; it was almost painful to see him over the past few months in his solitude. As she approached him, she said, "Eddie, is there something I can get you?"

He stood at the window staring outside into another world. He shook his head in a negative fashion and didn't turn around.

She had a seat near where he was standing and noticed that he still clutched those tattered combat boots. "I'll sit here for a few moments, Eddie. You can join me if you like, when you get tired of standing."

There was no response for a few minutes and then Eddie turned to see the familiar major. She patted the chair near her, as if indicating she would like Eddie to sit in that particular chair. After a period of loose idle talk, she asked, "Eddie, those boots can get mighty heavy if you carry them with you all the time. Is there something important about them that make them so special?"

Eddie looked at the boots then up into her face as his eyes began to tear up. "I don't know who to give them to."

She inquired in a soft voice, "Is there something about those boots? I'll listen if you would care to tell me about them."

There was a long silence between the two of them, as if Eddie was trying to determine in his own mind if he should trust her. He softly said, "I'm thirsty."

She smiled and said, "I am, too. What would you like to drink?"

"Coffee, if it's fresh and black."

Without hesitation, she got up and crossed the lobby of the lounge to the concession stand and returned with two cups of coffee. She smiled as she handed Eddie his coffee, explaining, "I need a bit of cream and sugar in mine."

She sat back in an overstuffed chair, a soft smile radiated from her face and her eyes took in all of his actions. She knew he was traumatized and would only let things out if he felt he could trust her.

Eddie drank his coffee, and when the cup was empty, he set the cup gingerly on the floor next to the chair. He sat back in the chair staring at her. His eyes had cleared for a time, but the thought of telling her what was on his mind caused them to fill up with tears. He moistened his lips and uttered softly, as if almost talking to himself, "I don't know who to give my boots to. I just don't know who to give them to."

In a soft whisper, Jody asked, "Why do you have to give your boots to anyone?"

"I made a promise a long time ago." His answer was clear, but it also reflected hurt and inner turmoil.

Jody thought for a spell, feeling that there was a deep-rooted part of his past that was beginning to surface and she wasn't sure what direction it was going to go. She looked at Eddie over the cup of remaining cold coffee in her hand and asked, "Who did you make the promise to?"

"I don't remember his name. I see his face in my mind a lot, but I just don't remember his name." Tears welled up in his eyes and fell uncontrollably down his gaunt face. His body shook, as if he was experiencing a cold chill that wouldn't leave his body. Eddie held the boots closer to his body, as if hugging onto them gave him comfort. He wept with pain from a memory that was held within.

Jody was about to call for assistance in trying to give comfort to Eddie when the crying slowed and he began to relax. She said, "Eddie, I am here to listen to you if you would like to share with me the promise you made and what the boots have to do with that promise. You can tell me when you feel ready, and if you don't want to share that information with me, that is okay, too."

Eddie sat for a few moments trying to gather his thoughts, while wanting to step away from his crying spell. "I have four rocks!" he announced with some conviction.

She thought the change of subject was odd, but listened and went along with what he was saying. "That is nice, where are they now?"

"They're wedged into the toes of my boots."

Feeling that this may be a stretch of his imagination, or a crude joke he was about to pull on her, she asked, "May I see them?"

Eddie looked deeply into her face and replied, "Only if you promise not to take them from me."

"I promise, I won't touch them and if they're inside the boots you can put them back in their place, after you let me see them." Major Sutton was beginning to feel that an imaginary situation was about to come to a head. She was uncertain of his behavior and in what direction it was headed. Eddie was calm and didn't show any signs of becoming out of control.

Eddie loosened the grip on his boots and stuck his right hand into one of them and true to his word there were two rocks. He took the other boot and placed his hand down inside and pulled out two more. He explained, "This one I picked up after I was turned over to the American army, just before I left North Korea. This one is from the prison yard, where they kept me in a dark cell for so long. This one is from the first prison camp I was assigned to." He paused for a short spell before he continued. "There were a lot of American and allied soldiers that got gunned down for hardly anything at all. Sometimes they didn't seem to have any reason. They just took a handful, shot them and had the rest of the prisoners bury them."

Jody sat in silence, allowing him to say what he had to get out of his system. He was silent for quite a while when she asked, "What is the last one for?"

Eddie thought for a while, as if going backwards into a deep trance searching his memory before he said, "It was in April of fifty-one. There were so many Chinese coming over the hills at us, I picked up this rock figuring if I made it out of there, I'd have a bit of the land where we had fought so hard." He suddenly burst into tears and grabbed the rocks stuffing them back into his combat boots and held them close to his chest. His face grimaced and the muscles about his face became taut and twisted.

Jody cleared her throat and said, "Eddie, I thank you for telling me and for showing me those rocks. I promise you that you will be able to keep your rocks. You will have to excuse me. I will be going off duty and I need to drive a short distance to the west of here in order to do some work at the Veteran's Hospital. I will be back tomorrow and if you like, I'll meet you here right after lunch. You can sleep on the possibility of telling me about the importance of those combat boots, okay?"

Eddie smiled and said, "I'd like that. I'll be waiting over by the big window again, like I was today."

~ ~ ~ ~

Eddie was standing by the window looking out over the large lawn bordered with palms, watching the new automobiles drive up and down the street, when he heard footsteps come up and stop next to him. He held on to the tattered combat boots as he turned to the major and said, "I knew it was you before you came close."

She smiled and said, "How did you know it was me?"

"When you're in prison and the only sound you hear is a person's footsteps, you remember who they belong to. When you walked away yesterday, I wanted to remember your footsteps."

She said, "Eddie, that was really sweet of you."

He smiled and said, "Sometimes you have to listen hard to hear little things."

Major Sutton said, "The lounge is rather crowded today, would you feel more comfortable talking to me in my office?"

"Do you have good coffee in there?"

"I will see that we have a good cup of coffee for each of us. You will have it hot and black and mine will be with cream and sugar."

"I guess it will be okay, but I left the rocks locked up in my locker today."

They walked across the lounge where Major Sutton ordered the coffee from the concession and carried the nearly brim-full paper cups to her office. She was pleased to see Eddie following at her side.

She had nearly dropped the cups when the heat of the coffee penetrated the thick paper cups and heated her soft tender fingers. She placed the cups on her desk, closed the door before sitting behind her desk and motioned for Eddie to sit in a chair across from her. She reached over and took the receiver off the phone and said, "We don't want to be disturbed. Eddie, I will be happy to listen, when you're ready to tell me about the importance of your boots."

"I'll tell you about the boots, but you will have to promise you will help me and tell me who I have to give them to."

"Eddie, I will help you in any way that I can."

For a long moment he looked at her. Then he scooted forward in the chair and said, "I thought about this a lot last night. I have to trust someone and I trust you." He placed the combat boots on the front part of her desk. The soles were nearly worn through. He was careful not to disturb or touch any papers or the back part of the photograph she had in a small frame. Major Jody Sutton listened as Eddie began his story. "These are the boots I had on when the Chinese Army came running over the hills and smothered us. There was just too many of them, they just kept coming. It didn't make any difference with all the shooting, they just still kept coming."

Tears formed in his eyes, as Eddie recalled what had gone on. His face grimaced and it appeared his body was beginning to shake as if cold, before he continued. "There was this lieutenant, I don't remember his name. We were all trying to back up and regroup, as we laid down a line of fire for some of the others. This lieutenant got hit bad; I saw him go down. I raced to get to him and had him on my shoulders for a time running scared. When the shots got really close to my feet, we ducked into a hole." Eddie shook his head in a negative fashion and seemed to get choked up.

Major Sutton said, "Eddie, your coffee may help. It might taste better if you drank it while it is still hot."

Her voice seemed to bring Eddie to a state of less shaking. He looked at the coffee, but failed to drink and said, "Before they got close, the lieutenant gave me one of his tags and a short note for his wife. I jammed them in my combat boots and tried to save him. I grabbed for my rifle, but there was a foot on it and three Chinese were right on top of us, a muzzle pointed right at my face. The lieutenant moved and they shot him! They stood right over us and shot him. That is when they took me prisoner. When I looked around there were bodies all over the place. I don't think there was a half dozen of us left and we were now prisoners. All that shooting and when they took us prisoners, it was funny, there was no more shooting or shelling, it was quiet."

Jody said, "What happened to the lieutenant's dog tag and the note?"

"They're in my boots! When they took us to the prison camp that night, I separated the leather of the boot and pushed the tags and the note inside the pockets I made. That's where I kept them all this time."

The major said, "And now you want me to help you find out who the note and dog tag go to?"

"I made the lieutenant a promise. I'd sure like to keep it, after all the trouble I went through trying to keep it a secret this long." He released his grip, took the boots and held them loosely in his lap. Placing his hand inside each one he retrieved the items and laid them on her desk, leaving the boots in his lap.

She reached across the desk and took the items in her hand, saying, "Let's see who the tags are from and who the note goes…" She choked up and gasped, tears filled her eyes and she suddenly felt sick.

Eddie said, "I didn't mean to make you upset; I just need your help."

She cried out, "Eddie, tell me more. This is the dog tag belonging to my late husband. Oh, my goodness, you'll have to tell me more about him after I read his note."

Eddie sat still watching her unfold the small note and slowly refold it before holding it to her breast. She closed her eyes, but the tears still filled her eyes and rolled down her face. Eddie asked, "I hope you got good news, beings it was his last letter."

She said, "I'll treasure them both for as long as I live. Eddie, you have given me the best gift a person could ever hope for. She reached across the desk and took the photograph in its small wooden frame and handed it to Eddie asking, "Is he the person you helped?"

"I didn't mean to make you cry. Yes, it is. It's the lieutenant for sure. He was the platoon leader in one of the platoons in my unit." He handed the photograph back to the major. "That is a picture of him, in my mind, I can only see his face and all the…" He choked up and didn't continue.

Major Jody Sutton stood up walked around the desk and placed a kiss upon Eddie's head and said, "Thank you, Eddie, thank you so much. Now let's go get another cup of coffee." Jody placed the photograph back on her desk and continued, "I bet you need another cup of coffee, just like I do."

As they walked down the hall, Jody said, "Eddie, never in my fondest dreams, would I have ever imagined getting such a beautiful gift, as you have given me today. I was notified of my husband Donald's death in late April 1951 and we had his funereal early in May of that year.

They walked to the concession stand in the lounge and got themselves a cup of coffee, before sitting at a deserted table, where they could talk without interruption. Eddie told her as much as he could about seeing her husband in Korea. He was glad that his body was recovered. She told Eddie about Donald and the happiness he had brought into her life. She said, "All the fun ran out of my life when they told me he was killed in action. The funeral was hard and when they played taps and the rifle salute, I just lost it and cried. It took me several months to finally pull myself together. Then today you gave me one of the most precious gifts. I am pleased beyond words, how you have cared for those mementos over the years and your commitment to see that they were delivered. I have his dog tag and last letter, thanks to you. I will always remember you for your sacrifice. You're just awesome. And if you ever get tired of carrying those boots, they can find a home with me."

The time together was cut short when Major Sutton had to get ready to go off duty and make the short journey across the tip of the peninsula to the VA Medical Center, where she was filling in for a shortage in staffing at the VA. Before she left, she said, "Eddie, tomorrow we will be appearing with some of the staff and talking about some of the things that are important in your rehabilitation. We will talk about some of the news that has taken place while you were held prisoner. Can we meet here in the lounge about 9:00 A.M.? That way the meeting can be adjourned before lunch?"

With a smile on his face he replied, "That will be fine with me. I'll be right over there by the big window, again."

~ ~ ~ ~

Eddie was standing by the large window looking out upon a damp lawn. He was having trouble seeing the palm trees that bordered the street, because of the dense fog that had rolled into the Bay Area overnight. The headlights on the cars were like dimly-lit glows being driven up and down a street that was now illusive in the field of white. The moisture dripped from the supporting frames of varied shapes of glass higher up in the large window. The rivulets ran down several panes, streaking the glass. There was a squeaking of rubber-soled shoes walking across the freshly waxed lounge and Eddie knew Major Sutton had arrived. Without turning around to face her, he said, "You're a bit early, it isn't 9 o'clock yet."

Jody came to a stop next to him and said, "That is typical weather here at the Presidio."

Eddie turned to look at her and stated, "I've been standing here for a long time and didn't see you coming up the sidewalk."

She smiled and said, "I have a parking spot on the opposite side of the hospital and I came in the back door." As she stood there, she couldn't help but notice he was standing with his hands folded in front of him. From the time he had left Korea throughout his trip home, all the time throughout various therapy sessions and evaluations in the hospital, he had always held on to his boots. "I see you don't have your boots with you today."

"They done lived out their purpose. I thought it best to leave them in my room. They're in the locker with the rocks."

Major Sutton asked, "Why are you always standing by this large window?"

Eddie replied, "While I was in prison, there were no windows. I want to look out on my world through the biggest window I can find. Maybe someday I will have one whole room with no walls, if that is possible." He smiled not only with his lips, but the sparkle in his eyes gave way to the inner joy he felt, "I think I'm going to make it out of here before long, thanks to your help and all the coffee."

"The meeting is at the far end of the corridor. Shall we head that way?"

"I feel good today. I got rid of a lot of worry yesterday and now I'm ready to face the staff and listen to what they have to say."

The meeting was a lengthy process with army officers, medical officers and a few staff members from the physical therapy and psychiatric departments. Eddie was told of his wife remarrying and all the data that had been compiled about his captivity. Major Jody Sutton sat next to Eddie and from time to time made eye contact with him, as he seemed to search the room for answers. He was informed that he would be eligible for a convalescent furlough. If he wished, he would be able to return to Montana for a short visit, but his trip would be made with the aid of a nurse, yet to be assigned. When he returned from his convalescent furlough, he would be discharged from the army and his medical treatment would be through the Veterans' Administration hospital in San Francisco for a period of time. He would be released from their care once his health was stable and the flashbacks of his experiences had subsided.

When Eddie and Jody left the conference room, she said, "I know where there is a good cup of coffee. Do you want to walk the length of the corridor to get to it, or should we duck into the staff lounge around the corner and grab a quick cup?"

"I think I need a long walk and a long talk, if you would like to listen to what I have to say. And I hope you can answer some of my burning questions."

"I owe you more than that, Eddie. Let's get that coffee and we'll have a talk in the lounge or in my office, wherever you would like."

"I like the lounge," Eddie replied, "it is more open and we can talk there if there aren't a lot of other patients close by."

She explained that she had to return to her office to do a little bit of paperwork, but she would see him in the lounge shortly. They departed company each going their separate ways as Eddie called out, "I won't be too hard to find."

~ ~ ~ ~

When she arrived in the lounge, she spotted Eddie at the concession stand and sadly enough, holding on to those boots again. As she approached, she asked, "Are you ordering coffee for two?"

The volunteer had caught her comment and when she set the coffee down, there were two cups. She smiled and stepped away to allow both of them some privacy.

Eddie said, "The Chaplain visited me for a long time. I guess I have hit him with some pretty tough questions from time to time. He said he would have to visit me more often, as he found me a challenge."

Jody laughed, "That you are. I'm so glad you came into my life; you make things right interesting. You're a quiet young man with complex problems I'd like to help."

"Good! I have a problem and I want you to fix it, if you can."

"What could it possibly be?"

"They said I could go home, but I would have to have a nurse come with me. I would like to ask you to be that nurse, if I'm not asking too much?"

Stunned that it would be her that he chose was one thing; she was honored that he would make such a statement. "Eddie, I'm not sure I'm the one to make that decision. This is normally done by the hospital administrator."

He became quiet, but sincere, "I trust you and if I have anything to say about it, I'd like to have you escort me back to Montana."

"Eddie, that is so sweet of you, but don't get your hopes up. The hospital has its rules and procedures. Even if they did say yes, I have to make arrangements at the VA Medical Center so that they will not be shorthanded."

"You are my only choice; just tell them it's important," he smiled as if he had made himself happy for the first time in a long time. "There is something else."

Jody looked on as if to wonder what he was about to say. "What is it, Eddie?"

He softly said, "These old boots of mine, I have no need for them any longer. If you were serious about having a home for them and still want them, they're yours." With a wrinkled brow and a soft smile that marked his face, he glanced at the boots, as if to bid them farewell before looking up.

When Eddie raised his head, he saw the tears overflowing from Major Sutton's eyes and falling down her face and heard her say, "Oh, Eddie, I'll cherish them! I'm touched deeply and you certainly have a way of making me happy." She knew he was beginning to heal, because the gift was from his heart.

Eddie added, "Even when I make you cry?"

"Yes, even then." Jody turned her head slightly, while trying to stifle the tears. She was an officer and it was frowned upon to fraternize with the enlisted. She was also a nurse and to become attached to a patient under her care was also frowned upon. But Eddie Day was bigger than all that. He touched the strings of her heart that seemed to make such wonderful music within her soul. She tried to control her emotions before she reached out and accepted the boots that he extended to her.

They finished their coffee and Jody said, "I must go now, I have the drive across town for my shift with the VA."

Eddie smiled and said, "I'll do my packing tonight and I'll be over by the big window again, about the time you come in."

When she got to her feet, she cradled the boots much the same way Eddie had carried them for so long. She said, "I'll ask the administrator to consider your request. I certainly hope the answer will be yes."

Eddie stood up and displayed the biggest smile he could produce. He was happy and silently watched as Major Sutton walked away from him across the lounge.

CHAPTER 8

Adjusting To Change - Medical Furlough -1964

It was afternoon in late November when the train slowed down for his hometown. Eddie and Jody reached for the overhead rack and pulled down their luggage before the train rolled to a stop. He was returning home, for the first time in a long, long time. Jody was his escort and in charge of his medical needs while he was on convalescent furlough. When the train slowed, it rolled forward moments before jerking and coming to a complete stop. Eddie looked out through the train's windows onto the platform and saw a delegation of family and friends. They had turned out in masse for his homecoming. He thought for a moment of when the football team returned home to the accolades of the community. Now it was just him returning to a life that had been denied him for so very long.

He turned to Jody and said, "I hope we're ready for this, because it looks like a lot of fanfare."

When they left the passenger car and stepped down onto the platform, the chilling Montana air greeted them. The high school band began playing the school fight song. It brought back a whole lot of memories for Eddie and he braced himself for the hugs, kisses and well wishes from the family.

His mother was the first into his arms. She cried out, "Oh my son, I'm so glad that your home. It has been such a long, long time."

"It sure has been. It's good to hug you. The last time you saw me, I was a bit on the puny side." Eddie replied before he gave her a kiss.

Edward was right behind her and held out his hand for a handshake that turned into a hug, as they continued to grip each other's hand. "Welcome home, Son."

"It's great to be home. Mom and Dad, I'd like you to meet Major Sutton. She was the head nurse you met briefly at the Presidio when you both were in California. She's in charge of my medical needs, if I have any."

The Days refrained from embracing Jody with their customary family hugs by choosing to express their happiness as they spoke. Kathy said, "Welcome to Montana, I hope you had a wonderful trip."

Jody smiled and said, "It was colorful. The scenery up this way is breath taking. I love the mountains and when we went through some of the tunnels, a bit of the smoke came through an open window somewhere to add to the magic of the trip."

"Makes no difference," Edward said, "if it had been overcast today, the two of you certainly bring sunshine. It sure beats being in a fog."

"Thank you very much, that sounds pretty poetic," Jody replied, knowing the jab about the fog was directed at San Francisco.

Mari and Kari stood off to the side witnessing the hugs and comments and wondering what they should do. They were there to welcome their father, but he was a man they didn't really know. Even the photographs their mother had shown of him didn't prepare them for this. Their father looked thin and rather sick, in contrast to the football player pictures they had at home.

Within moments, he was standing directly in front of them. "You have to be Mari and this has to be Kari. You have both grown up on me. Mari, you were just a toddler and Kari, you were just a newborn when I was inducted."

The girls softly chimed, "Hi, Daddy."

Eddie reached out and gave them a light embrace and the girls returned a light hug as well. "I saw you both briefly, before they sent me to Korea. It seems like yesterday, but we all know that that was a long, long time ago. I'm looking forward to knowing you both better."

The girls rendered a slight smile that barely registered on their faces, not really knowing what to say.

Mari asked, "Are you coming to the farm with us?"

"Yes, I am," Eddied replied, "and this is Major Sutton. She is my nurse and she will be coming with me."

Edward said, "Eric and Sarah are back at the farm getting supper ready. We'll head that way as soon as the community turns you loose. They sure have turned out, haven't they?"

Eddie waved to those in the crowd and was motioned to a microphone. The Mayor, Mr. Tom Craven; high school superintendent, Mr. Alfred Hayslip and the Methodist church was being represented by Pastor Ronald D. Waters. They were joined with others on a small, raised platform. There was a prayer said, a proclamation read and several welcoming home comments from those on the raised platform.

When the dignitaries had their say, Eddie was pulled before the microphone for a few comments. "I thank you so very much for coming down to the depot to welcome me home. Right now, I need to get reacquainted with the family. I'll see most of you in church Sunday. If there is a ball game before I leave, I'd like to attend. Seems I've been missing a game or two here or there. Thanks again for showing me your support. I'm in hopes of seeing some of you around town before I leave. Thanks again." When he stepped down from the platform, the crowd was cheering.

They had additional luggage to claim and Eddie looked beyond the crowd to the depot with its two-tone lighter brown over a deep chocolate paint, typical for the pattern on structures belonging to the Northern Pacific Railway. The depot had its ticket office jutting out onto the platform from the rest of the building, so that the agent could operate the two signals high above the building, one for eastbound and the other signal was for westbound trains. The majority of the depot was the baggage room. Inside the baggage room was two large metal trailers with iron-rimmed wheels, both stacked with boxes and mail sacks. The smell resonating from the room was a mixture of axle grease and the crushed cinders that made up part of the platform. For some unknown reason, some had been carried into the building on the metal rims. The ticket agent was jockeying one of the trailers after receiving several parcels from the passenger train. The thin old depot agent dressed in black pants, dark vest over a white shirt and a green visor to shade his eyes when he was outside, looked up and said, "Can I help you?"

Eddie said, "I have two boxes, I think I see them right up there. I have 'Day' written in big letters on them. Here are the stubs."

The agent took a quick look and retrieved the boxes. Moments later, Eddie carried them out of the baggage room, past some of the remaining crowd on his way to the family car. He was happy and all smiles. He passed several well-wishers anxious to pass on their greetings, without receiving a reply to all their comments.

When they left the crowded depot, the dusty station wagon driven by his father headed straight for the family farm. Edward drove while Eddie rode shotgun, Kathy and Jody sat in the seat behind them and the girls were sitting in a seat that faced the back window. The girls twisted around so that they could hear and visit with their grandmother and listen to what the major had to say.

The girls looked at each other with raised eyebrows and a shrug of their shoulders, as if to communicate their unsure feelings on how they should act around their father's return. Feeling awkward, they felt that being silent might be best for now, because they thought it was unusual for someone to be escorted by a nurse.

Edward barely stopped at the stop sign, before goosing the accelerator. The tires spun out on some loose gravel as the car lurched forward causing a chirp once the recaps hit the asphalt. Eddie smiled at the familiar sound and glanced at the driver. He saw a broad smile on his father's face, staring over the top of his hands resting on the top of the steering wheel. They were headed home. A few miles down the road, Edward would turn off the highway and head down the long dusty lane. He would need to check on his farmhands while Kathy helped remove the dinner from the warmer above the stove. Supper would be on the table shortly after they arrived.

When the station wagon pulled to a stop, the billowing dust caught up with the car and seemed to engulf it for a few moments. They left the car and made their way to the house. They found the farmhands standing outside the screened-in porch, relaxing after having the evening chores completed. They rendered a quick welcome to Eddie before turning their attention to the boss. Edward gave them instructions for the following day and prepared to go inside.

The family was welcomed by Eric and Sarah on their return. Eric held the screen door open and Sarah stood by his side. The girls followed Kathy and Jody inside and Edward followed.

Eddie somberly looked at Sarah and Eric with hurt in his eyes and asked, "Can we talk before we go inside?"

Eric sensed the uneasiness of their first meeting and had a hard time swallowing comfortably. He closed the screen door and said, "Sure, Eddie, let's talk over by the gate."

With tears in her eyes, Sarah felt she was in a terribly awkward position. She was facing the one who saved her and her mother, later married and had two children by him. Now she stood before him after remarrying one of his best friends from school. It didn't make any difference if the army had declared him killed in action. He was alive and standing before them. She loved both of them, and now it tugged painfully at her emotions. She walked with them to the fence near the gate and stood by Eric.

Eddie turned to the two of them and said, "I loved you, Sarah, and that love carried me through some miserable times in prison. I held out hopes of returning to you and starting over again. Eric, the whole time I was in prison, in my mind I thought you were looking after Sarah and the girls, until I got back. I want the both of you to know it hurt me when I was told the news. I didn't realize I had been gone for so long."

"Eddie, just a minute we . . ." Eric went to say.

"No, what I have to say needs said." Eddie interrupted. "I lost my wife, my children and a big part of my identity. It took a lot of counseling and treatments before I finally came to grips with how life is."

Eric said, "Eddie, Sarah and the girls had a rough time too. They waited all that time and then to have their hopes dashed when the army came and told her you were killed. It wasn't easy for her either."

"Eddie," Sarah spoke up, "we even waited the seven years that Montana requires for a person to be declared legally dead before we even considered dating. I have always loved you and I still do, but now it is in a different way, after I remarried. You will always be special in my heart, after all you are the father of our children."

Eddie looked at both of them and said, "We have all lived through a bad time. Sarah, I will always love you and I have come to accept what has happened. Eric, I did ask you to watch out for her and the girls, for that I am grateful and I thank you. As for marrying Sarah, I will admit that was tough to accept. But I wish the both of you well. I hope we can still remain good friends, so please take good care of her and my girls."

Sarah was wiping the tears from her face that continually overflowed her eyes, as she said, "He has and he has treated the girls well."

"I only hope that you will allow me to have the girls in my life," Eddie softly asked.

Eric answered, "That is something we can definitely all agree on."

"Great," Eddie remarked, "Now let us remain friends and I don't want either of you to feel uncomfortable around me while I'm here. I'll have to admit, the news was tough to accept for a long while. I didn't think we'd ever get to see eye to eye on anything. They made me realize that I was gone for so long and life goes on, makes no difference if it is fair or not. But I had to tell you how I felt instead of beating around the bush."

Eric said, "Thanks, Eddie. The girls would love to have you in their lives and I wouldn't for an instant try to keep them from seeing you, or you them."

Sarah said, "Eddie, we have always taught the girls to face some adversities in life, as our situation has become. I have told you, in my heart I will always love you, but time has been rather cruel on the both of us. I hope you understand why I remarried. Eric has been good to the girls, encouraging them to remember you, if only through the few photographs we have. They have always known you went off to war. They don't remember you being here, only knowing their father was a soldier caught up in a war. I know I speak for all of us when I say, we welcome you back into our lives and hope we can help you adjust to what life has to offer, from this day on."

Eddie turned to Eric and Sarah saying, "Life has treated us rather rough over the years and it certainly has tested our relationship. I hope we can accept what has been forced upon us. Let us set aside the hurt and remain close friends. I'm glad that the girls had the two of you to help them grow. What do you both say we go inside, where I can taste some good home cooking and visit with the whole bunch of you?"

Kathy had been looking outside with a nervousness that was getting the better of her before she said, "I'm going to go see if I can help!"

Edward reached out to stop her and softly uttered, "Please don't. Let them work it out. That way they can come to us and talk openly if they feel we're neutral and can use us as their sounding board."

Mari and Kari stood back and remained quiet. Neither said a word, because they were unsure what was going on outside and right now their grandparents weren't giving them any sense of direction.

Edward and Kathy had been looking at each other suddenly, they looked up to see the three of them coming through the screen door smiling and sharing loose talk. They were glad that the three of them had said what was needed to make Eddie's visit a good one.

Jody stood back to witness the transition Eddie had to make, if he was ever going to recover and start anew.

Kathy proclaimed, "Wash up for supper, it'll be on the table before you can get there."

Eddie said, "I have presents."

From the kitchen, Kathy said, "They can wait. Sarah and Eric put the meal together and we'll eat it while it's hot. When we are through eating, you can give me mine first, because I'm your mama." Laughter filled the room in response to her statement.

As the gifts were handed out, they remained wrapped when Eddie said, "You can't look until everyone has theirs."

Jody sat back and watched as the presents were handed out to everyone in the family. When they were opened, there were gasps of excitement at scarves, sets of coffee cups, bracelets, square pillows with a San Francisco theme printed on them, stationary boxes, toiletries and other gifts. There was an abundance of wrapping paper atop the table before the second box of gifts was opened. Jody enjoyed looking on and seeing the family have such a good time. The second box was opened and the excitement began anew. Eddie was down to the last few gifts when he handed Jody a small package wrapped in bright red paper with a gold-colored cord. The eyes of all those gathered around the table seemed to fall upon her. She should have refused the gift because of protocol, but compelled by the moment, she graciously accepted the package. When she pulled on the cord, the tiny bow untied and she placed her fingers between the folds of wrapping paper, opening it up with great care. Inside, she found an angel pin of pewter about three inches tall and a note attached expressing Eddie's feelings, 'Thanks for being my nurse, signed Eddie Day'. There was an unexpected silence in the room, when she looked at Eddie and said, "It is lovely, thank you."

As the evening hours passed, the family was asking several questions and making comments. Mari got everyone's attention by her actions and facial expression and asked, "Kari and I were wondering, now that Daddy's back home, who do we have to live with?"

For the first time, the girls had asked a question that reflected the emotional problems the younger pair were facing. Both girls sat at the table nearly in tears, not knowing what the answer would be.

Eddie said, "Come over here, girls." He waited until they were seated on each side of him before he spoke. "I am your father, Sarah is your mother, Eric is your stepfather and we all love you very much. I had to go into the army a long time ago and fight some rather unfriendly people. They kept me in a prison for a long time. The army told everyone here I was dead. Now your mother still had to take care of you and my very best friend from high school days had promised he would look after your mother and the two of you, while I was gone. When everyone thought I was dead, your mother and Eric fell in love and they married. He didn't marry your mother to change the fact I am your father. He did so to love and care for all three of you. I am still sick and need some medical attention in order to get well. But just a few minutes ago, Eric told me that you girls will still remain in my life, as much as he and your mother can help with. And when I get well, I plan to move back to Montana, where I can see my girls grow up. But for now, it is best that you both stay right where you are. I know that I have all the support I need from the family right here. I'll be going back to San Francisco in a few days and I plan to get feeling better."

Kari squirmed and said, "How long is that going to take?"

Eddie said, "Now that the post office knows where to deliver my mail, we can start by writing letters and I can keep you up to date on how things are going."

The girls seemed to get all the inquisitive questions out of the way and were satisfied with the answers. When most of the uncomfortable conversation was pushed aside, they touched on the lighter side of life and began laughing about some of the funny things that had been happening.

When the hour grew late, Sarah and Eric took the girls to their home, while Edward and Kathy made a temporary exit to the kitchen. Jody said, "Eddie, I am so honored to be here with you and your family. They are such fun-loving people I know they'll be here to give you support when you need it."

"They haven't changed, even after I have been gone for so long."

"I'll have to give your mother a hand in the kitchen. I wouldn't feel right after such a good supper without lending a hand in cleaning up."

Jody went to the kitchen to help Kathy, while Edward inched his way into the living room and sat in his favorite chair to chat with his son alone. Jody shared her experiences with Kathy, about Eddie's attempt to save her late husband and the episode with the boots, the dog tags and the letter. "I am so beholden to him for his commitment to fulfill a promise he made years ago in Korea. I'll be his nurse at the veteran's hospital when he is released from the army. I'll get to see him every day then and I'll see that he gets the best of care."

"We'll appreciate that," Kathy said. She finished up by drying the roaster pans. "It literally broke our hearts when the army came here and said his status had been changed, from missing in action to killed in action and his body not recovered. I could never accept the fact that my son was dead and the army couldn't bring his body back for a proper burial. It left me hurt and bitter for a long time. But I'm so glad he pulled through that awful mess. Do you think he'll ever regain some of the weight he's lost?"

Jody said, "He'll bounce back. I remember, back in July of 1953 when Letterman General Hospital received six hundred and forty-four POWs. They were all suffering from maltreatment and lack of nourishment. It took them a long time to recover. Eddie's care is one of the most severe I've ever seen. But along with all the good treatments we have, he'll make it. Letterman can draw on its experience in handling cases of this nature; he'll be fine. It'll take some time, but this visit home is probably some of the best medicine he'll get. I see nothing but good coming from this visit. You're such a loving family and the support he needs is here. I think within the small frame of your son, Eddie knows it, too."

Kathy smiled and said, "I'm sure that your presence in his life has been a big factor, too. I can see the way he looks at you, as if you're a bit more than the medical support he needs."

Jody blushed and said, "He has certainly touched my life," she didn't comment further. Her heart had been touched in such a wonderful way and she wasn't sure how to deal with it, yet.

Sunday arrived with the Methodist church being filled to capacity knowing that Eddie Day would be visiting. His presence placed added meaning to thankfulness in the Thanksgiving Sunday service. The Pastor had called the house and talked with Eddie, asking if he would be receptive if called upon to say a few words. Eddie had agreed to a few moments at the pulpit to express his gratitude for the tremendous outpouring of support.

Sunday school classes were held in the hour preceding the traditional service. Major Jody Sutton joined Eddie, Sarah and Eric in the young adult class. The instructions were from a handbook that the class had ordered 'Understanding Faith That Moves Mountains'. Eddie enjoyed the instructions, as if thirsty for some of the teachings.

When Sunday services began, the Elders and the Days joined them along with Mari and Kari, nearly monopolizing one complete pew. When the time came to call on Eddie, the pastor had already embellished on his service and sacrifice while in captivity.

Eddie stood beside the pulpit, a small microphone in his hand and cleared his throat before speaking. The sanctuary became so silent, the unwrapping of a cough drop or a piece of candy interrupted neighboring worshipers. He said, "I am blessed with friends and family, but most of all I am blessed because I believe and know He lives. You may want to know what captivity is like. The answer is unpleasant, the work and the confinement. What does one do while in captivity, you may ask? The answer is, pray. I did a lot of that and I will not elaborate on what goes on in the mind when you're held captive. There are a few places in the Bible that encourage you to pray unceasingly. It may seem impossible to do, but I did a lot of it while in captivity. Fear will get you, but prayer will give you comfort. I admit this much: you do strange things that become habit, such as attempting to say the Lord's Prayer backwards. If you would like to read along, please go to Matthew 6:13 and you will follow along backwards until we get to 6:9. I do not want to sound blasphemous, but this was one of my mental exercises of a prayer and this is what I would say aloud. Amen forever glory the and power the and kingdom the is thine for Evil from us deliver but temptation into not us lead and debtors our forgive we as debts our us forgive and bread daily our day this us give heaven in is it as earth on done be will thy come kingdom thy name thy be hallowed heaven in art who Father Our. You see in prison; you challenge your mind. But when it came to the National Anthem, that challenge was much harder. The words I know, but I never mastered singing it backwards. You would hope that you don't go mad in some of your exercises, but you must keep a certain amount of mental toughness as well. In the darkness of a small cell, I played football. At one time I was a quarterback and I made several passes. I remembered the coach's words 'Don't drop the ball!' I went through the motions of fly-fishing countless times, trying to catch that elusive trout. At times I would mentally visualize the tying techniques required for a good fly. But when you hear the footsteps of the guards, you sit upon a small mat and wait to see if the door to your cell will be opened. I kept busy. The experience was unpleasant, but I had to believe and believe harder than anything else, He lives and I am alive today because of Him, Amen. While I was in prison, I understand that President Eisenhower signed a bill on Flag Day in 1955 allowing the words 'Under God' into the Pledge of Allegiance. I like it and it is so fitting." With that said, Eddie left the pulpit area to have a seat next to Jody. His journey to the pew was made in silence and he saw many with tears in their eyes. There was a closing hymn and the benediction with refreshments following the morning service in the fellowship hall.

Eddie was swallowed up by those who wanted to visit or just come and touch him if only to say, "Welcome back."

Jody was nearly in shock at what she had heard this morning. Not once during the time of his treatment in physical therapy or in the psychiatric sessions had Eddie opened up as he did today. She was overwhelmed by what she had heard during church. In the midst of the crowd in the fellowship room Eddie, found an abundance of support from within his church.

~ ~ ~ ~

When the Day family sat around the extended table for their Thanksgiving dinner at the farm, there was a brief period of silence that seemed to touch the souls of everyone. They bowed their heads to hear Edward clear his throat before he gave the blessings. His voice was jerky at first, as he offered up a prayer of Thanksgiving. The emotional impact was clear, his power of speech wavered as he gave thanks for all those present. The impact of the prayer had touched all those gathered. With an Amen, Edward, through moisture-filled eyes and a chest full of heavy emotion, looked at his son Eddie and said, "Welcome home, Son." Turning to Jody, he added, "And we're so pleased to have you here with us today."

Jody nodded, acknowledging his comment, her lips moved and made a silent thank you.

Kathy said, "Dig in before the food gets a chill and loses its flavor." There was laughter following her comment, while most began talking as the food was passed around the table.

When the meal began to slow, the offering of dessert was extended to the family. They began to chat and nibble, not wanting to be the first to leave the table. From the oldest to the youngest, their voices were heard with a comment or laughter that followed. They were a close-knit family and Jody felt a part of that closeness, as they opened their hearts to include her.

The day after Thanksgiving, the school had their home-opener basketball game. Prior to the tip-off, the announcer at the scoring table made mention that Eddie Day was in the crowd. There was a lengthy applause before he was called center court, where the basketball coach and officials were gathered. When Eddie arrived and stood at center court to be recognized, the band played the National Anthem.

He was honored to stand center court while the community showed respect for the flag and our nation. He waved at all those in attendance and then applauded the fans as well. The varsity coach, Mr. Hugh Holiday, presented Eddie a basketball with the inscription 'Welcome Home', and signed by the entire team and cheerleaders. Eddie went to the scorer's table where he took the microphone and briefly said, "Thanks for this warm welcome." Turning to the visiting team, he waved briefly before turning toward the home team saying, "Let's play ball." The applause ended when Eddie went into the bleachers to sit near Jody.

~ ~ ~ ~

With the passage of time, the convalescent furlough came to an end. On the 28th, the entire family was once again on the platform at the Northern Pacific Railroad train depot. The richness of the visit had brought out support for Eddie, not only from his family, but from the church and community as a whole. When the passenger train rolled into the station, the last-minute hugs and kisses were made. There were promises of writing letters and wishes for a speedy recovery when he got back to San Francisco.

Edward hugged Jody and said, "You're just as much a part of the family and we would be pleased to have you visit us again. Kathy hugged her and said, "Take care of my son. We have truly enjoyed meeting you and do keep in touch. You hold a special place in our hearts."

The conductor called out, "All aboard!" The loud command sent chills throughout the Day and Elders family knowing the visit was fast coming to an end. The last moments of saying good-bye, what needed to be said and who had to have a kiss or hug seemed to blend into quick touches or pats on the head, before Eddie and Jody stepped onboard the train. The family on the platform could see the pair making their way to a seat as the train began to pull out of the station.

Like so many times before with the turning of the passenger train's wheels, the image of family became reduced in the distance. Eddie and Jody sat next to each other momentarily without words, knowing in their hearts they would want to return to Montana.

Dinner in the dining car was at a small stationary table with chairs on each side. The table was adorned with a white linen tablecloth and a weighted centerpiece that stayed in place. The dinner was served by a black porter. The menu was limited to a beef plate or fried chicken, but the drinks varied from water, tea, coffee or a person's favorite mixed drink. Eddie and Jody had settled in on a fried chicken entree with cake for dessert. When the porter set the main dish down and returned to the kitchen area of the dining car, Eddie said, "It sure doesn't look like my mama's chicken, but it is chicken just the same."

With a smile, Jody replied, "Your mother spoiled me with her cooking. I love the way she seasons all her cooking. It makes your taste buds want to stand up and dance."

"She has always cooked that way. When I'm away from home, I miss Mom and Dad very much, but as far as food, well that is what I missed the most."

Jody thought Edward's strengths were numerous and a lot of his traits were evident within Eddie. As for his mother, her cooking loved Eddie from the inside, as much as Kathy loved him from the outside. She was a mother who had a lot of loving to give to her entire family. Jody's visit to their farm was one of duty. Now she was leaving Montana, returning to her assignment at Letterman General Hospital at the Presidio of San Francisco. Eddie had touched her life and his family had left their mark as well. They are really wonderful people.

The train sped down the tracks with a rhythmic sound of the rails filling the quiet times with the clickity clack and the rocking motion from side to side. They ate their dinner while looking out the dining car window to see the majestic mountains in the distance, the pasture lands and small houses closer to the tracks and the blur of the telephone poles that were near the track's right of way. When the train passed through a small town that had a railroad crossing light, the ding, ding, ding, ding sound of the warning light could be heard as the train approached and faded after the train passed the signal. Jody commented, "The porters sure have a sense of balance. They walk as if the train's motion doesn't bother them."

"It bothers me," Eddie replied, "I have to either brace an arm on the wall of the passageways or check my balance with the seating. Here in the dining room, I had to check myself on the edge of the tables."

After dinner, they made their way to their passenger car and went to their seats and made themselves comfortable. Eddie insisted that Jody sit near the window, where she could take in most of the scenery. The passenger train didn't have any Pullman cars and the passengers sat in upright seats with the seat in front of them adjusted so that the seat faced backwards facing them, for added room and comfort. Beneath each seat was a leg rest, which could be pulled up on both of the seats they were sitting on and the one's facing them, allowing each passenger to stretch out their legs and sleep in comfort once the seat was adjusted, as far back as it would go.

The conductor or brakeman would pass by from time to time. When they left the passenger car going to the next rail car, a blast of cool air filled the passageway before the door closed. When the train picked up passengers, sometimes in passing, they would bang their suitcases haphazardly against the seats or the exposed legs of other passengers while they made their way to their seats.

When a porter passed through the car, Eddie stopped him and asked, "Are there a couple of blankets available? There's a bit of a chill."

Within moments, the porter returned with two blankets that had been warmed. Eddie said, "Thank you," and gave him a tip. The porter smiled and continued through the car to his next assignment. Eddie took the blankets and spread them out on the both of them. They began to settle in for the night. The scenery slowly dimmed and darkened before it faded from sight. It was replaced by the reflection of activities within the passenger car.

Although the trip had been with proper protocol going to Montana, during the night Jody awoke, finding her head resting on Eddie's shoulder. She lifted her head and looked at him His eyes were wide awake and looking back at her, accompanied with a large smile on his face. "How long have I been sleeping like that?"

He wrinkled his forehead causing furrows before replying, "About twenty minutes or so. You were asleep and I didn't want to disturb you. It's alright. I enjoyed it and your hair smells so nice."

Jody adjusted herself in the seat, "Thank you for the compliment. That was sweet of you." She smiled in a way that didn't convey any embarrassment in what had happened, although military rule was strictly against an officer fraternizing with an enlisted. She was also a nurse and wasn't supposed to get involved with her patient. She would have to do her best not to encourage a relationship beyond the mere accidental touching, regardless how beholden she was for Eddie's actions. Her heart was in conflict with the military rules.

Eddie was aware of something troubling the major over the incident and knew she was restricted from showing her affection to a patient. He would have to consider her feelings first, then cope with how he felt about her. Now was not the time to say anything confrontational on the subjects. He hoped maybe things would find a way of working out.

~ ~ ~ ~

When Eddie returned to Letterman General Hospital, there was news he would appear before two groups of doctors. The Medical Evaluation Board and Physical Evaluation Board both were recommended by the staff while Eddie was in Montana on medical furlough. He would undergo extensive therapy and appear before two medical boards. His first appearance was before a Medical Evaluation Board where they discussed his health, impaired posture and weakened body from years of captivity. The mounds of medical papers before each doctor were copies from their reviews. Two days later, Eddie was before another group of doctors and several psychologists. He was questioned about his flashbacks, his deep-thinking periods and the behavior he had exhibited after his release and during treatment. Both boards took the better part of a full day each for Eddie's appearance. He knew the doctors had a lot of reading to do before they would make their decision.

Two weeks later, Eddie was informed of his scheduled discharge date on the last day of January 1965. Arrangements were being made for him to be assigned to the VA Medical Center for a period of approximately three months. If at that time he had adjusted well to the physical and psychological therapy, he would be released and allowed to move to a location of his choice. He was encouraged to apply for disability through the Veterans Administration in his home state when he had finished his move.

~ ~ ~ ~

When morning came, Eddie was scheduled for several rounds of physical therapy, before lunchtime and went without seeing Major Jody Sutton. In the afternoon, he was informed the Army approved the recommendations of the Medical and Psychological Evaluation Boards for his pending retirement, rather than a separation from active duty. There was an abundance of additional paperwork to be approved in preparation for his medical retirement from active duty as a sergeant. His promotion would be dated back to September 4th, 1953, the repatriation date in Korea. All back pay and allowances for three dependents were included from the army finance center from his captivity to the date when Sarah had remarried.

It was midday when Eddie finished with most of the paperwork. He returned to his room to deposit some of the forms in his locker before going to the lounge to enjoy a cup of coffee. He enjoyed the view from the large window across the large room from the concession stand. It was beautiful outside and the green lawn was greener than anything he had seen in Montana. Whoever they had doing the lawn sure knew what he was doing. He watched as traffic sped down the street in one direction, while others were going the other way. From time to time, a car would turn off the street onto the circular driveway that came up to the hospital entrance. Military, as well as civilians, including the nurses walked on the clean sidewalk leading to and from the hospital.

Eddie was wondering about Major Sutton when he heard the familiar footsteps approaching. He smiled and in turning, saw her sidestepping a chair that hadn't been placed under the table.

"Hello Eddie, I might have known I would find you here, looking out of this big window."

"Major, they are fixing to release me from the hospital at the end of January. They say I will be assigned to the VA Medical Center here in San Francisco on the first of February."

Jody smiled and said, "That is where I work, when I'm not working here. I'll be able to see you over there."

"I received most of the news earlier this morning. They will be medically retiring me with the rank of sergeant, dated way back when the war in Korea ended."

Major Sutton said, "Congratulations on the promotion. You get yours and I was told I will be a Lieutenant Colonel in March."

"If anyone deserves it, you do," Eddie announced.

"But along with the promotion is an assignment to Vietnam."

Eddie was shocked, "I'm sorry. When do you leave?"

"I will be having a port call of early June, I imagine. Nothing firm yet. I'm still waiting for the orders to be cut. So that gives me some time to see that you meet your therapy treatments here and at the VA as scheduled," she was smiling. "If you're ready for a cup of coffee and a short visit from me, we better hop to it before I leave. I have to be at the VA early today."

The visit seemed short over the first and only cup of coffee he had to share with her today. There was so much he wanted to share with her. Now was not the time and the army had put a time limit on a lot of things. Beyond his discharge, the recuperation at the VA would be for three months and in that time, he could only see and visit with Jody Sutton when she had completed her duties here at the Presidio.

~ ~ ~ ~

Time moves at a rapid pace when your life is full of activities. Jody Sutton had been promoted to Lieutenant Colonel in March. Eddie had been living at the VA Medical Center for nearly a month, where Jody worked half a shift five days a week. He would finish his therapy sessions and return to his room and wait for his daily visitor. There was no large window for him to look out of and it seemed as though he was retreating instead of going forward.

He felt sad because his need for space and light from the outside was reduced. The large window that allowed sunshine into his world was at the Presidio. He saw Colonel Sutton as his window of happiness and she would soon be taken from him and sent to Vietnam. The pleasurable things he enjoyed seemed slowly being taken away.

When Jody arrived one evening, she said, "It is such a beautiful day outside, would you like to go on a short walk around the Medical Center's grounds?"

"I sure would," he quipped with enthusiasm. "This room is a bit confining."

"Eddie, I have nearly an hour before I must leave." She teased, "You best put your walking shoes on."

The walk was casual and slow. They talked over a multitude of things that were related to his treatment. The time passed with guarded conversation, until they started back towards the main door of the hospital. Eddie stopped and turned to face her and they looked deep into each other's eyes. "Jody, I hope you're not offended that I call you by your first name. But I'm not in the military anymore and I have something I'd like to say before the day is out. I will be leaving from here before too long and you will be going to Vietnam. I will be going back to Montana to pick up the pieces of my life, as best as I can. By being the head nurse, you know me probably better than a lot of folks in the medical field. You know my parents, my children and my friends. I want you to take good care of yourself while you're gone and remember that I care so much for you it is hard to put into words. But if you feel like I do, I hope we can pick up the pieces when you get back."

Jody's eyes filled with tears and she said, "Eddie, of all the men I have ever met since my husband's death, you have certainly taken my heart for a ride. I care for you deeply, but I have a year in a combat zone facing me and I'll have another six months or so after I get back to keep the rating of lieutenant colonel for my retirement. At my stage in life, I may not be able to give you a son, if that is something you're hoping for. We are looking at a long time of not being together. Our feelings toward each other would certainly be tested."

"I plan to go back to Montana and make a go of it. I need to get to know my girls and catch up on a lot of things. I plan to make things ready for your return. We can keep in touch while you are gone and I can let you know how things are going in Montana. I know you have a military commitment and I realize that there may not be time in our lives to have a child. I'm comfortable with that, but when you get back, I would like to have us make a commitment. Is there a chance?"

"Eddie, the answer within my heart right now is yes. Let's just take it slow to see what happens during the time we're apart. When I get back to the states, we can pick up the pieces if we still feel the same towards each other."

"I love you, Jody."

"And I have loved you from the day you gave me Donald's dog tag and the letter you carried for so long."

"I made a promise and I kept it."

"Eddie, your words are a contract of commitment and you have proven you live by your words. You have gone through some very tough circumstances. You have touched my heart and my life in a way that has put life and meaning back into me. After Donald's death I buried myself in my nursing career on active duty and at the VA Medical Center. I have seen many young men come and go through the hospitals here and at the Presidio. I even had a long assignment at the school of nursing at Fort Sam Houston in Texas before returning as head nurse at the Presidio. If there ever was a reason to turn loose of a career, it is with a man that honors a commitment. I love you, Eddie Day." With all precaution thrown out the window, they kissed ever so slightly in broad daylight and in full view of several patients and nurses upon the Medical Center's grounds. The kiss that followed was longer and more powerful.

The remaining time they had together at the VA was short and painful. While visiting one day, Jody said, "I guess you're ready to go back to Montana at the end of the month?"

"I'll soon be on my way. Mom and Dad called last night and we had a pretty long talk. They claim to have spotted a large established ranch that might be for sale. As soon as I get home, I'll need to take a look at it. They figure I might be interested in the ranch because it is up near Bozeman, Montana. I have completed all the therapy they have for me and they say the VA hospital at Fort Harrison in Helena, Montana is available on an outpatient basis if I need them."

"Eddie, you'll do fine. I dropped by to see if you would like to have me tag along to Montana for about a week before I have to report to Travis Air Force Base? The orders will be cut this week and I have an early June port call for transportation to Vietnam."

"I'd like that very much. That makes me very happy. I'll call the folks tonight and let them know you're coming back to Montana with me."

Eddie pulled Jody in close and they kissed deeply once more.

CHAPTER 9

Discharged - The Return Home - 1965

Eddie and Jody stepped down from the Northern Pacific passenger train into a crisp May breeze that was blowing across the Montana landscape. It was a good twenty degrees colder from what they had left in San Francisco. Edward and Kathy came to the train station to greet them along with Eddie's daughters, Mari and Kari.

Edward gave both a hug as well as a kiss on Jody's cheek and a handshake to his son. Kathy also hugged both along with a soft kiss on each of their cheeks and said, "Goodness, its sure is good to see the both of you." A bit reserved, Mari and Kari gave their father a kiss and hug. To be polite, they smiled and offered a light hug to Jody.

Edward said, "Son, it's great to see you back home. Jody, by golly it's a joy to see you too. You're a sight for a set of tired eyes."

Eddie smiled as he hugged his daughters. He heard Jody tell his parents, "I enjoyed the last visit so much, I had to come for another because you both treated me so well."

"I was hoping you'd come back," Kathy replied. "You're so interesting to be around. I enjoyed the talks we shared on your last visit. How long do you get to stay this time?"

Jody said, "I'll have to leave for my next assignment before the week is out."

Kathy replied, "Eddie wrote and told us that you will be going to Vietnam."

"I'll be there for at least a year working with the medical staff and nurses, taking care of those who are doing the fighting."

Edward tried to squeeze into the conversation and added, "I hear there isn't a spot over there that is safe. You best keep that pretty head of yours down and protected." He received a smile in return for his concern.

While everyone was trying to say something at the same time, they didn't realize the train was pulling out of the station, leaving them at the far end of the platform talking. "I got the station wagon ready for the trip to the farm," Edward remarked, "What do you say we get this luggage and head that a way?"

Sarah had remained behind at the farm to see that supper was ready for their return. When they arrived, the food was ready for the table. Most of the fixings rested above the majestic range's surface in both of the warmers. The sweet smell of fresh bread, apple pies and beef roast competed with the aroma of freshly brewed coffee. The table setting had already been put in place. The milk and water would be served up when everyone got to the table. When dessert was served, an ample amount of homemade ice cream was available to go with the pie.

When the dishes were cleared and returned to the kitchen, Sarah said, "Mom, you stay in here and visit, I'll take care of things in the kitchen." While remaining in the kitchen to do the dishes and put away the leftovers, Sarah was standing at the sink when she felt a hand on her shoulders. She turned to see Jody facing her with a smile, "Sarah, can I help with the dishes?"

"The dish towels are over there, I'll wash," she said before her voice reflected shakiness, "I feel somewhat awkward."

"Please don't," Jody pleaded, "that's your family in there. Eddie understands and I believe he has come to grips with you remarrying. I would like to know you and the girls better before I have to leave. I've heard some great things about you."

Sarah looked at Jody through eyes that had nearly filled with tears, "Thanks, you seem so understanding."

The rest of the family was gathered around the supper table with cups partially filled with coffee, with exception of the girls whose milk glasses were empty. Edward said, "The letter your mother sent you on that piece of property up near Bozeman sounds good and might be available, if you're interested."

Eddie asked, "How in the world did you find out about it way up there?"

"Your brother Neil went to listen to a speaker. This veteran was a POW in a German Prison Camp during World War II by the name of

Gunther Weismann. He spoke at the American Legion in Billings a while back. They got to gabbing about the war and you being held for so long by the North Koreans and whatever the veterans talk about. Gun invited Neil out to his place anytime he was in the Bozeman area. Your brother was up that way a while back and stopped in for a visit. Mr. Weismann wasn't there, but his foreman, a full-blooded Shoshone named Johnny Tracks-a-Wolf, told him that his boss had a terrible accident. He had a horse fall on him and busted his back up really bad. The foreman told your brother that his boss was in and out of hospitals for treatments. He was more than likely facing having to go to one of them nursing homes. Neil visited with him in the hospital in Bozeman, where he told Neil he was headed out of state for some kind of treatment. Your brother claims that old Gun is concerned about holding on to his folk's old homestead and may have to put it up for sale one of these days. Neil wasn't sure you'd be interested in ranching, but took down all the information just the same. He let us know about it, so we could pass the information on to you. Your mother and I drove up that way to get a bird's eye view of the place. We think it might be a good buy if that fellow is fixing to sell."

Eddie asked, "What does it look like?"

"As for the old ranch house, it's in need of some repair, but the land is ideal. There are several thousand acres available and according to Neil, you don't have to buy all of it. There is a river that fronts the property and it's butted up against a mountain range. Gun might even offer some of the mountainside for property speculation. We just drove by the land to get a good look and drove up to the ranch house to take a peek. Like I said, it's a fixer upper, but the land, well you're just going to have to see it to appreciate it."

Kathy said, "The outside needs a good paint job, but looking through the windows, it appears to be in pretty good shape. It most likely needs a woman's touch on the inside."

Eddie said, "I have talked with Jody about the possibilities. She came back with me to see more of Montana. I'm sure she'd like to see it before she heads overseas."

"Take the car and make the trip. That way you can get your facts first and look at what's being offered. Then check the hospital to see if that rascal is still there. Or he might be in a nursing home. Get to know him and find out first hand."

When Sarah and Jody rejoined the family, Eddie asked, "Jody, would you like to make that trip to Bozeman, where we can look at that property in Gallatin County?"

She smiled while saying, "That would be nice." She turned to Mari and Kari who were mostly left out of the conversation and asked, "And would the both of you like to come along, if we get permission from your mother?" She turned to Sarah with a pleading expression for the girls, "They are most welcome and they won't be any trouble, will they, Eddie?"

"Sarah, it would give us a chance to be with my girls for a short time." He waited in anticipation for her answer.

"Okay," she turned to her daughters and added, "but you two had best mind your manners."

Mari and Kari giggled and promised in unison, "We will."

The visiting continued after the sun went down. Sarah suddenly jumped to her feet, causing the others to take notice, stopping them from what they were saying. She gasped, "I'll be right back!"

She left the house and moments later returned with a cardboard box of old letters, halting the conversations a second time. She sat in her chair with the box on the floor and lifted a hand full of letters that were loosely bound with a string. Placing them on the table, she looked through them and found what she was looking for. She took the letter and handed it to Eddie saying, "I remember getting this letter about a month after the fighting had stopped. It is from someone who knew you in Korea and was letting us know you were held as a POW. I didn't answer it, because the army visited a day or so later and told us that you were dead."

Eddie took the letter and recognized the name. He read the letter, folded it and placed it back in the envelope before he said, "That old rascal! We were together in a prison camp. We were on a work detail together, when there was an accident. Teddy got hurt and was taken to a hospital. It was near the end of the war. I asked him to contact the family and to tell them where I was, if he got out of there alive. The North Koreans thought I had purposely caused the accident, so they placed me in solitary confinement in one of their prisons after that. Goodness, that has been a long time back. He has his phone number in there. Could I keep it for a day or so?"

"The letter is yours, now." Sarah replied.

Jody sat stunned at seeing what was happening. Eddie had brought her the dog tags and a letter from Donald. Today Sarah is handing Eddie a letter that was written by one of his POW buddies in Korea, postmarked some ten years ago.

Eddie excused himself for a moment and went to the telephone. He called the hospital in Bozeman, but the information desk said Mr. Weismann had been discharged months ago and had gone to Minneapolis for treatment. She was unsure where he could be contacted. Then he placed a call to Powderhorn, Colorado. The voice on the other end of the telephone was that of an older gentleman. Eddie asked, "Is Teddy Olsen there by chance?" There was a pause before Eddie continued. "When he gets in would you have him call Eddie Day?" he left the number for Teddy to call. Moments later Eddie returned to the table and said, "That was his father. Teddy had gone to town for supplies and may not get back until tomorrow."

The rest of the evening was small talk topped off with a piece of warmed up apple pie and homemade ice cream before they called it a day. Sarah took the girls home and Kathy made sure the rooms were made ready for the visitors.

~ ~ ~ ~

Teddy Olsen had called the house and talked with Eddie. During the lengthy phone call, they laughed over some of the old times. As Jody watched, she could see that there were tears forming in Eddie's eyes before he wiped them away. The phone call was nice as Eddie could talk to someone who had been there with him. But resurrecting the memories of what had taken place there, and for those who would never be returning, it brought back some painful memories. Eddie had promised to return the call when he had returned from the Bozeman area. With the time in between, they would both try to figure out when and where they might be able to get together.

~ ~ ~ ~

Eddie and Jody prepared to make the trip to Bozeman. They had the map Neil had scratched out for his folks. The piece of property was north of town near Dry Creek on the East Gallatin River. Dry Creek empties into the East Gallatin River, a short distance from the property. The two bodies of water would eventually empty into the headwaters of the Missouri River near Logan and the Three Forks area, some ten to fifteen miles northwest and downstream. They left the farm with Mari and Kari choosing the middle set of seats. In the back seat was a water cooler containing twelve Nehi soda bottles of various flavors and a paper sack of assorted snacks that rested nearby.

When they arrived in Bozeman, they followed the directions to the property. Leaving town and heading north, they could see the swooping panoramic view to the west, with its various colors reflecting from the distant landscape. They blended together for nearly a hundred miles to the smaller Tobacco Mountains on the eastern side of the Continental Divide of the Rocky Mountains. Little did either of them realize the homestead would be cradled in the folds of one of the most beautiful pieces of soil Montana has to display. Enormous, rugged granite slabs jutted skyward through the layers of soil marking the entrance into the valley.

To the north beyond the fertile valley were the Big Belt Mountains and the beauty of Sacagawea Peak. To the east, the majestic granite ridgeline of the Bridger Mountains, across the ridgeline to the north northeast, was the Crazy Mountains. An enormous up-cropping on the Bridger Range reached to the heavens. It stood between the valley floor and any morning sunrise before its elevation dropped down to the southeast forming the Bozeman Pass. During the winter months, the pass was treacherous. Its elevation and snow accumulation generally caused problems for travelers. Between south southeast and due south some distance away is the Absoraka, or often called the Absorakee Range, the Bear Tooth Mountains, Mount Blackmore and the community of Bozeman.

Beyond the community to the south southwest, the Madison Range appears flattened out before the base of Blaze Mountain, which stretches out across the landscape and juts up toward the heavens. They were outdone by the gigantic Rocky Mountains in the background marking the land northward through the State of Montana with its ridgeline called the Continental Divide. On the Pacific side, snowmelt flows across the western counties of Montana on its way into Idaho and points west. On the eastern side of the divide, the water will flow north and east. A point west to north northwest of the ranch property is the community of Three Forks.

Beyond the town are the Lewis and Clark Caverns with the lower slopes of the Rampart Mountains. They extend to the southeast from the

Rockies. The head waters of the Missouri River form near Three Forks, where the tributaries of the Gallatin, Madison and Jefferson Rivers twist and turn their way across the landscape. They flow across the land like a pattern of discarded lengthy shoestrings tossed upon the face of the earth. The small streams are formed from the watersheds in higher elevations and grow in width and depth. They join together cutting a path through the rugged terrain on their way to form the Missouri River outside of Three Forks. The Missouri flows north to Great Falls, where there are five falls. Then the river meanders across the top of the State of Montana into North Dakota and points south and east. In the center of all this beauty is the homestead located in a land called Gallatin County.

They could only peer through the window near the door and other windows along the wraparound porch, when they arrived. The interior of the old ranch house would remain a mystery beyond what they could see. When they were through peering through the windows they walked to the varied outbuildings on the ranch.

They were met near the barn by a working Indian who was tall and lean. He was wearing dust covered Levi britches and a long-sleeved western shirt that was partially covered by a dingy looking vest. A felt hat that had seen better days rested on top of his head, as his dark braids that showed some graying dangled down over his shoulders. He had a hard-looking leathery face with piercing eyes that seemed to rest above a soiled bandanna. He said, "I'm Johnny the foreman. What are you folks doing out here?"

Eddie said, "Looking at the property and trying to get in touch with the owner."

"He is gone for medical treatment, out of state. Maybe he'll be back later this month."

"I realize the ranch hasn't been listed for sale," Eddie replied, "but I understand he may be considering it. I'd like permission to look at the place and maybe make him an offer, when he gets back this way."

The Indian nodded his head, "He tell me to let people look if they come, but not inside his house or bunkhouse, not yet."

"We'll just look around at the outbuildings and then drive over a portion of his land. We'll close any gates we go through before we leave if that is permissible?"

The foreman smiled and said, "You can do so, or I will show you." The Shoshone said, "The owner's parents homesteaded this piece of property, which was passed down for Mr. Weismann to live on. He has spent a long time trying to get his back fixed."

Jody spoke up and asked, "How bad is the owner's back?"

"Maybe I shouldn't be telling you this," the foreman said. As he continued, he softly added, "He suffered from back injuries after being thrown from one of his horses. Signs on the ground say maybe the horse rolled on him. No one saw the accident happen, we just found him in bad shape. He's had several operations out of state and returns to the ranch looking better. But he is in pain most of the time."

When the abbreviated tour was complete, they walked down on the riverbank of the East Gallatin to get a view of the river that borders the property. When Eddie bent over and picked up a rock he bragged, "Girls, look at this, a Montana agate rock."

Jody looked upon it with interest. However, the stone failed to gather anything but a mere glance from the girls.

Eddie turned to the girls and said, "Well, Mari and Kari, what do you think of the place?"

Mari said, "It's a big place. Are you going to have cows and horses here?"

Kari chimed in, "It's got a pretty view. But it seems colder here than back at the farm. If you buy it, can we have a pony? You know one for me and one for Mari, maybe?"

"I won't make a promise I can't keep. We're just having a curious look today. We'll have to see if Mr. Weismann is willing to sell and if I can afford it." He turned to Jody and asked, "Any comments?"

Jody smiled and said, "The view is breathtaking up here. There's about any type of terrain you want to look at. I also see a lot of potential. The ranch house will need a tremendous amount of work and I have to agree with your mother, the inside does need a woman's touch."

They rode back up to the ranch house to let Johnny know they would check out the rest of the property on their way out. Eddie said, "Thanks for the information," only to see the foreman walk off without saying a word, only raising his hand briefly in response.

Eddie drove over the remaining open property and the adjoining piece of land before they made their way back into Bozeman. They would stop at the Four B's restaurant for a nice sit-down meal before heading down the highway for home. When they left the restaurant, Eddie walked ahead. The girls deliberately sandwiched Jody by having their arms around her waist. Jody responded by placing her hands on their outside shoulders, as giggles filled the air.

No sooner had they left the parking lot when Jody said, "Turn in here. I want to take the girls shopping." Eddie pulled the station wagon to a stop in front of the department store and they all went inside. Jody looked at Eddie and asked, "Can we girls have a bit of time together to shop for girl things?"

Eddie replied, "I get the message. I'll be in the sporting goods section when you get through."

When they left the department store, each one of the girls had a large shopping bag stuffed with items Jody had chosen to pay for. Eddie had a small box in a sack that was small enough to slip in his shirt pocket. Jody had asked one of the clerks where the hospital was located and received directions. When they left the store, the girls were side by side stepping in unison as Eddie ventured ahead to unlock the car. Inside the car, Jody gave directions to Eddie and within moments they pulled up in front of the hospital.

Eddie gave Jody a funny look only to hear her answer, "No emergency, I want to have a word with the administrator, if he or she is in."

Eddie and the girls waited in the waiting room. They saw Jody being ushered into the administrator's office. Eddie took the numbers for the nursing homes in the area and started making calls and leaving messages. Eddie hit pay dirt when one of the nursing homes said that they anticipated Mr. Weismann in about two weeks. They would have Mr. Weismann contact him. A short time later, they were all leaving the hospital and the car was headed down the highway on their way to the farm.

~ ~ ~ ~

The visit to Montana was quickly over for Jody. The fun times had come to an end. It was time for her to leave those she had enjoyed being around for such a short period of time. She had to return to active duty with the military and report for her assignment overseas.

Before they piled into the cars at the farm, Eddie caught Jody alone and in full uniform. They had a rare private moment together. He said, "Jody, this is for you." as he held out a small box.

109

Jody took the small box and opened it to find a heart shaped agate stone on a silver necklace chain. "My goodness, it's beautiful Please put it around my neck."

Eddie opened the delicate clasp and lifted the chain over her head. She stepped into it before he hooked the clasp. She held the stone in one hand and turned towards Eddie and kissed him in a way that had more meaning than an appreciation of the gift. "I will always have it around my neck, close to my heart and remember you every day."

Eddie looked into a compassionate face with eyes on the verge of tears and softly uttered a commitment to her, "I don't care if it takes a year of waiting." He cupped her face with his hands, and with open eyes and an open heart gently whispered, "I love you and you know my intentions." Then he kissed her softly and felt her respond as well. "You're in my heart and I will always love you. I will patiently wait out the year, in hopes nothing will interfere with our plans."

"Eddie, I'm so glad we agreed to control our emotions, as unfair it may seem to you. I have denied myself the temptation over the years not wanting to fall into a pattern of behavior I would live to regret. If our hearts are truly meant for the other, this absence will certainly prove that point."

Their private time was interrupted when the telephone rang. It was the nursing home in Bozeman calling to pass along a message from Mr. Weismann for Eddie to drop by and see him when he was in the area. He would be at the nursing home for approximately six months. Eddie shared the news with Jody before they headed outside to the cars waiting in the drive. Within moments they were headed down the highway for Great Falls and Malmstrom Air Force Base. When they drove through Lewiston and headed west, Jody took note of the difference in the landscape and told Eddie, "The land is so different up here on the high plains you can see for miles and only see a butte popping up every so often."

"Montana has a variety of features. Charlie Russell painted a lot of this kind of landscape in his art. We'll go to his museum before you leave, but we'll take a look at the falls on the Missouri first."

When they arrived in Great Falls, the first stop was at the falls on the Missouri River that the community was named after. When they stopped the cars at the third falls, Jody said, "Look down there. It's a rainbow across the Missouri and the land seems to go on forever."

"Not too far from here is the Canadian border, nothing but flat prairie land between here and there. There are two other falls on the river, but we won't see them today because of our time limit." Eddie said.

When they returned to their cars, they drove into Great Falls to the Russell Museum. They would see the cabin he lived in while he did his paintings. In the museum, there was a multitude of paintings framed and hanging on the walls. There were catalogs you could page through and to find a piece of Charlie Russell's works and get a number for a reproduction. Jody loved the paintings and ordered two reproductions for Eddie. One was a cowboy riding a bucking horse with a jack rabbit running out from under the horse. The other was a cowboy who was raising a rifle while in the saddle. The horse he was riding and a pack horse cowered against the rocks as a grizzly bear confronted them.

When she presented Eddie with the paintings she said, "You're my kind of cowboy." When he looked at the second, she said, "And don't mess with the bear," before she laughed.

He smiled and said, "Thanks, I'll have them framed and think of you often."

The sightseeing was limited and it was time to face the inevitable. Jody was to catch the medical flight out of Scott Air Force Base that would be making its weekly flight across the northern tier states. This flight began outside of Belleview, Illinois to Fargo, North Dakota, on to Great Falls, Montana, then Spokane and Seattle in Washington, with a turning around point at Travis Air Force Base near Fairfield a short distance northeast of San Francisco, California. From Travis A.F.B.. Lieutenant Colonel Jody Sutton would fly overseas ending up in the Republic of Vietnam for her scheduled tour of duty.

The two-car caravan left the museum and headed for the Malstrom front gate. They stopped at the Air Policeman's gate, where Jody had a lot of talking to do in order to have the two vehicles and the nonmilitary guests accompany her to the terminal. She was lucky, as the Strategic Air Command Base had just recently ended their alert status. One of the Air Police cars escorted them to the terminal. After they had their vehicles checked and the insurance and registration noted, each visiting driver and passengers were properly identified before being allowed on the Base.

It was a small operations terminal of two stories attached to the seven-story flight operations tower, where the Air Force air traffic controllers performed their duties. The building indicated an elevation of 3526 feet, the 40th Air Division and home of the firsts, 301st Air

111

Refueling Wing, Heavy, a unit that provides support by in-flight refueling operations for the Strategic and Tactical Air Commands large bombers and the 341st Strategic Missile Wing, units of the minute man missile that were placed across Montana. The visitors watched as Jody approached the terminal desk on the main floor and made arrangements to catch the military flight. After showing them a copy of her orders, they placed her name on the flight manifest. With the necessary paperwork completed, Jody returned to the side of her friends.

Kari said, "You sure look different with your uniform on, but you're still pretty."

"Thank you, Kari, what a nice thing to say. I'll remember you every day that I'm gone." Jody gave her a hug.

"Mari, you're so sweet, look after your sister while I'm gone and I'll miss you deeply." She gave Mari a hug as well.

Eric and Sarah stood to the side only to have Jody turn to them and say, "I have truly enjoyed my visit. Eric, you have married a beautiful lady. Sarah, I'll always remember our short talks. I'll miss you and will always look forward to visiting with you again."

Eric nodded and Sarah got teary eyed and gave her a hug. She spoke into Jody's ear, "I love your open heart and your honesty. You're like a sister I never had. Take care of yourself and I hope you and Eddie wind up being a match."

Jody went to Kathy and Edward to say, "You two have made me so welcome in your home. There isn't enough time to say how I feel, but thank you both very much and I'll miss being spoiled."

Kathy received her hug and the two kissed each other on the cheeks. Edward received his hug and he planted a kiss on Jody's forehead. "Keep the noggin down if the shelling gets heavy and come back safely."

Turning to Eddie, she grabbed at the lower part of her throat indicating the place where the heart shaped agate was, beneath her uniform. Tears for the first time since they had been together entered her eyes. She stepped forward to kiss and hug the one who had made such an impact in her life. As they embraced, she whispered, "I love you, Eddie Day. It is going to be a long separation."

Eddie whispered back, "I know, I love you too. But don't let them keep you over there as long as they did me. I'll keep in touch." As they separated, there was a smile on their faces. She had heard his humor and he had heard her say how she felt.

Without warning, through the glass of the terminal, the flight from Scott A.F.B. taxied up in front of the fueling pump and the boarding gate. The call for the flight and the last-minute pandemonium of a sendoff filled the terminal area, as Lieutenant Colonel Jody Sutton turned to board her flight. At the door leading outside, she turned once more to wave good-bye. She turned and was last seen climbing the ramp to board the airplane.

The terminal manager notified the Air policeman nearby that the guests were ready to leave the base and they were escorted to the gate. As they passed through the gate and started to head down the highway, they could see the large plane leave the runway and fly a short distance above them, before it was quickly out of sight.

CHAPTER 10

A Horse Operation - 1965

Nothing gets a man around any better than his old pickup truck. When Eddie was drafted, his truck was placed in the corner of the old tool shed and placed on blocks with the fluids drained. The old tarp that covered the hood and cab had seen better days. It was spotted with feathers and droppings from the chickens that liked to roost on the rafters above the Ford pickup.

Eddie thought if he was going to have transportation, he had best get old blue tuned up and ready for the road. With the help of his father, they pulled the tarp from the truck, mounted a new set of tires and jacked up both ends one after the other, to knock the blocks out from under the frame. Edward installed a new battery, while Eddie tended to the spare tire. With the oil, transmission fluid and a shot of gas, Eddie hopped into the cab and pumped the gas as he turned the ignition key. It took a couple of tries before the motor seemed to hiccup and gave a sluggish groan before it turned over. Edward hollered, "Did you put water in the radiator?"

Eddie quickly shut off the motor and sheepishly said, "I thought you had."

Time for laughing had found no better place, "I did, but I didn't figure you saw me. You'd better check the carbonator points and condenser, fuel and air filters. While you're at it, check the brake fluid level and consider bleeding the lines before you drive it too far, plus that old master cylinder might need to be replaced."

"Do you think we need to do that before I kick her over?" Eddie inquired, as if there was going to be a sequence of things that needed to be done and in what order.

His father planned to help, but saw an opening and let his son have it, "We? I've got a farm to run. It's your truck and the way I see it you have all day." The jab and the laugh that followed brought back memories for both of them. One would say something and then hang the other out to dry, but they worked well together.

It took the better part of the morning tuning up the truck after mounting the tires. Mari and Kari showed up at the tool shed to watch what was going on. They found two badly-worn brooms and were in the bed of the truck making more dust than cleaning. Eddie removed the heavy logging chain and some long-forgotten fencing tools from the bed before driving it from the old shed. Kari sat near her father, while Mari sat by the passenger door. Eddie drove the truck up to the highway and back to the yard of the farm. His father proudly watched and waited by the gate leading into the house. Eddie jumped out of the cab and said, "It looks as if I'm about ready to make the trip to Colorado."

Edward said, "I don't think so, not before you go to town and get that relic registered and some insurance placed on her."

Eddie said, "I'll tend to that right after lunch."

No sooner had they sat down at the table for lunch when the telephone rang. It was for Eddie.

"Hello," Eddie spoke into the phone.

The voice was coming in loud and could be heard clear over to the table, "Eddie, this is Teddy are you coming down this way?"

"It may be a bit before I can get the old Ford checked out for such a long trip. Dad and I just got her running."

The booming voice said, "No problem, I called to cancel your trip, at least part of it."

"What do you mean?" Eddie inquired.

In the midst of static on the line, Teddy said, "Dad wants me to head up to St. Ignatius to check out four or five broodmares. I'll be driving his truck with a stock trailer. I can head your way, pick you up and drive up to Missoula before I cut north to look at the horses. If I buy them, I'll be going into Dillon and cutting south through Idaho Falls and into Utah, before I cut back east to the ranch. That way I don't have to contend with driving the mountain roads so much. Can you be ready to go, say in about a week? I'll bring you down here to the ranch and take you back home in a month or so."

"Sure, I can be ready by then. I was wondering if the old truck could make the trip."

"No need to break down along the way. Keep that old relic in Montana, there's enough junk cars around here."

"I'll be ready, just give me a call before you get here."

The rest of the afternoon was spent with his daughters. They washed down the faded blue pickup truck and dried it off to where it wouldn't streak. The girls got wet and Eddie got his truck looking pretty good. Now it was ready to be registered and licensed the following day.

~ ~ ~ ~

Days later, Eddie had received a call from Teddy who had gassed up his truck about ten miles down the road. While looking for his friend to show, he watched a farmhand assemble and operate the milk separator. A cup of coffee was hooked in Eddie's right index finger. It supported a measured amount of java he was nursing, as he glanced up the lane.

Off the highway came a red pickup truck pulling a long stock trailer. The dust in the lane boiled high following the trailer's passing. It gradually pulled to a stop in front of the house. The emblem on the truck was the silhouette of a horse's head with a powder horn under the neck. The faded printing read 'Powderhorn Horse Ranch Ted and Teddy Olsen Owners Est. 1953.

The figure behind the wheel bumped the door open and jumped to the ground, as agile as a teenager, and dashed around the front of the truck. They spotted each other and ran to embrace and hug, as only men with their past POW experiences could understand. Teddy's soiled cream colored felt western hat fell from his head. There was a love between the two of them that ran deep and the conflict in Korea had forged that bond. Teddy retrieved his hat, slapped it against his leg to knock the dust off and proceeded to try and reshape it.

They went into the house and Teddy with his hat in hand was introduced to Eddie's parents, where a short visit took place. Running short on time, Teddy said, "We best be heading down the road. I'd like to at least get to St. Ignatius by nightfall."

"I'll be right with you," Eddie quipped. He rushed to his bedroom to grab the luggage he planned to take with him.

Kathy asked, "How long are you planning to keep my son in Colorado?"

"I think he plans on a month or so," Edward assured her.

Teddy said, "He'll be alright down at the ranch. I had one heck of a time adjusting after the war and I was only held for two years. I imagine Eddie will have a lot more issues to deal with before he can finally put his captivity behind him and get on with life. He'll need a lot of support. Here is a ranch business card with the ranch house number on it," as he handed her a card. "I plan to show him the operation Dad and I got started, after I got back from the fighting. Dad has a good head on his shoulders. He dealt with me and the problems I brought back home. Maybe the horse ranch helped me adjust, too. He knows how to handle horses and maybe he used good horse sense on me from time to time. He's good at handling the books and making those high-priced sales. He's been around horses all his life and finally managed to put our ranching business in the black."

Edward asked, "Where's your market for all those horses?"

"You name it and you'll probably be right on target," replied Teddy. Last year we ran a few Arabians on the market. A pair was sold to some fellow overseas and a few went to an outfit in Southern California. That is where the market is for registered stock. Some of the breeders that hang around the tracks at Santa Anita and Del Mar call Dad from time to time."

Eddie came from the bedroom dragging two suitcases, gave his parents a kiss then a hug and said, "I'll be back in about a month, so take care of each other."

When they left the house, Mari and Kari were out by the truck and trailer admiring the long rig. Eddie called out to them and said, "Come here young ladies, there is someone I want you to meet." When they arrived, he said, "This is Teddy Olsen. We were captured and worked in the same POW camp in Korea. Teddy, these are my girls, Mari and Kari."

"Hello, young ladies," Teddy smiled and tipped his remolded hat as he spoke.

"Nice to meet you," they chimed in unison.

Eddie gave them each a hug and a kiss on their foreheads and said, "I'll be gone for about a month, and you two behave yourselves while I'm gone."

"We will," Mari answered, while her sister nodded in the affirmative. Eddie hopped into the truck and within moments, the rig had turned in the large yard and was headed for the highway.

They talked little of their war experiences and preferred to discuss where they were, during the current time. Eddie talked of his looking for something to put his efforts into and make a showing. He needed to keep busy while waiting for Jody's return from Vietnam. Teddy talked of the horse ranch and the large operation his father had built up. Between the two of them, they had done well.

Teddy stopped to top off the gas tank in Livingston. He pulled the truck and trailer out onto the highway after leaving town, as they headed west. Eddie had told his friend all about the property near Bozeman and the old German that had fallen on some hard luck. Teddy said, "We're making good time, we can stop in and see Mr. Weismann if you like. If we can't make it to St. Ignatius by dark, we may have to bunk down in one of those roadside motels."

"If it isn't too much trouble, my asking you to jockey this rig around the city streets. I would like to meet him face to face, instead of discussing business over the phone with someone I haven't met."

When they arrived in Bozeman, Teddy pulled into the nearest gas station to get directions to the nursing home. They were in luck as the outer road next to the gas station went right by the nursing home. When Teddy jumped back into the cab he said, "This must be our lucky day."

Moments later, the rig was parked in the nursing home parking lot so that there was a straight shot to the exit. When they went inside, a nurse directed them to a day room. She knew Mr. Weismann was in a wheelchair visiting with other residents.

When they arrived in the day room, Eddie approached the man in the wheelchair and asked, "Are you Mr. Weismann?"

The healthy-looking gentleman looked up from his chair and said, "Just depends on who you might be," as he showed a spark of tenacity.

"Eddie Day and this is my friend Teddy Olsen."

"You don't say. I had you pictured in my mind's eye as being a bit bigger than what you are. The nurses gave me the impression you were a self-confident young man from the inflection of your voice. That's what threw me off a bit. Guess that's what I get for thinking. I'm Gunther Weismann. Most who know me just call me "Gun". I'm a bit under the weather right now. The nurse just gave me some medicine to nip at the pain I have in my back."

Eddie said, "I thought, I would drop by and chat a spell with you, beings my brother Neil told me all about you. He sent me to look at your ranch and I had the chance to meet your foreman. The nursing home called and left word for me to drop by, according to your wishes."

Gun grabbed the wheels of his chair and spun around and said,

119

"Let's go over here, where you two can have a chair and we can get eye level. I don't plan on adding a neck ache by constantly looking up at the both of you, on top of how I already feel."

When they were situated, Eddie asked, "Neil said you might consider selling all or part of your land?"

"Let me see, is he the fella who had a brother held by the North Koreans?"

"That's him. He's my older brother and was wounded in WW II."

"I remember him well. It was in Billings when we met. He's one heck of a talker and hard to shut up. Now I get to see if you're as windy as he was," Gun chuckled.

Eddie said, "I was captured and sent to a POW camp in North Korea where I met Teddy. We worked with explosives on a work detail on a meager amount of rice, until the accident. Teddy was injured when the blast went off ahead of time. He was repatriated and I was blamed for the whole mess and sent to a North Korean prison."

"You don't say," Gun interjected, "the both of you?"

The talk was not going to be short lived and lasted where Gun talked of his captivity. He covered his time in a German Prison camp, while Eddie and Teddy shared some comments about their experiences.

Gun talked about the family homesteading, "My folks came to Montana with Dad's two brothers. They ventured this way because of the encouragement of Mr. Hill of the Northern Pacific Railroad. He provided free transportation to this area. They each paid out a $10.00 filing fee to the government and insisted their 640 acres joined the others. Mom and Dad were married and my two uncles were single. The five-year period to live on the property and improve it was one problem. But they failed to find a woman that would stick it out with them. That hurt them more than this harsh land."

Eddie asked, "Why did most of the homesteads fail?"

"While some of the homesteaders east of here faced a drought, others were plagued with those blasted grasshoppers," Gun continued. "If you couldn't plow it or get water on the fields, Mother Nature would send the harsh winds in to ruin what you hoped for. That is why this homestead managed to survive. All three pieces bordered the Dry Creek or the East Gallatin River. It nearly took all the money my folks had to buy my uncles out. They had it rough for a few years right after that. What hurt most was when the businesses that followed the homesteaders to Montana left with all the others, taking their machinery, money and dry goods."

"That had to be pretty hard to handle," Teddy replied.

"Dad was as hardheaded as any German could get, and my mother stood by his convictions. They made it, thanks to the help of some of the Shoshone Indians that live near Three Forks. When they proved up, they still had problems, but the land was theirs. That is why I love the homestead. It's a part of my family history and as important as the blood that runs through my veins." Gun reflected.

"I can certainly see the importance the land holds to you and the strength of your family," Eddie remarked.

"In their passing," Gun added, "they left the homestead to me, as I am their only child. Every year, I worked hard to improve and make a profit, Mother Nature has been good. But I had a riding accident and don't remember how it happened. My ranch foreman and his hands came looking for me. They found me in an area where there were tracks of wild animals but couldn't figure what caused my horse to lose footing and roll over me. My doctors seem to think the saddle and the weight of the horse messed up my back in several places. I have seen a lot of doctors, even those out of state. The pain is there and will remain and is only relieved by some powerful pain killer."

Teddy talked of his experience with his father in Colorado and building the horse ranch and wanting to help Eddie get into ranching and setting up a string of horses. He looked at Gun and said, "We may not have the same blood in our veins, but we're like brothers just the same. We share some pretty hefty mean memories."

Gun nodded his head to the affirmative and uttered, almost out of ear shot, "As do I."

Their conversation touched on several subjects, with Gun not coming right out and agreeing to sell any part of his homestead. He said, "I love that place out there, I'd sure hate to lose it. I'll give it some serious thought and I'll call you at your father's place."

"I'm going to Colorado to see Teddy's horse ranch and how the operation is run," Eddie said, "I won't be home for about a month or so."

"That will give me some time to think things over. What say you call me when you get back and we'll toss the subject around then?"

~ ~ ~ ~

121

Eddie and Teddy finished their trip to St. Ignatius and the long journey to the Olsen Ranch in Powderhorn, Colorado. Eddie enjoyed Ted Olsen, and among the three of them, a bonding of business and friendship developed. There was a desire from the Olsen's to share their experiences so that Eddie could get a running start with his ranch, if things worked out. He was exposed to a horse ranch and its operation that most people would never get to see. Ted sat down with him one afternoon and went through all the books, covering any item pertaining to the operation, from handling registration forms to the contacts he had managed to compile over the years and the veterinarian medical forms.

During his stay in Colorado, there were several letters from Jody forwarded to him from the farm. In the evenings Eddie would read them and send a reply to Vietnam, to let Jody know how things were progressing. The first part and the very last of every letter shared their feelings for each other. It was clear they were a match biding time to be paired up with a commitment and they were in love. One of the letters included photos of the unit and some of the nurses that Jody worked with. Near the end of the month there was a letter that contained the photographs of two orphaned Vietnamese children. They had lost their parents, who were the Phan family that supported the U.S. units; before their village was hit hard by a Viet Cong artillery bombardment. Jody wrote that the boy was an energetic gopher and was the only support for his sister. He was talkative and did a variety of errands and duties. His name was Hanh and was around ten years old. The meaning of his name was 'has good conduct'. His sister, a year or so younger, was Lien and the meaning of her name was like a 'Lotus flower'. She was quieter than her brother and did small errands for the nurses outside the hospital setting. She would help make up the bunk beds of the nurses. Her brother was good at carrying the dirty laundry to where it could be cleaned. They were a pair and the hospital unit seemed to adopt them and care for them to some extent. Jody thought they were a joy to see. Her letters always began the same and the ending was always sweet. She referred to the middle of the letters as the pain of reality.

~ ~ ~ ~

When Eddie returned to the farm, he had several letters waiting for him to answer. His friend Teddy was off running down registered stock to take back to Colorado. When Eddie told his parents of the talk he had with Gunther Weismann in Bozeman, they listened with interest. Edward asked, "Is there a chance for a sale, or do you think he'll consider a long-term lease?"

Kathy said, "When you talk with Mr. Weismann, see if he'll consider hiring a nurse and returning to the ranch. It would certainly be less costly for him and he'll be back where he wants to live."

Eddie said, "I'll give him a call tomorrow. If things work out, I'll ask him about the prospects."

The topic was discussed at length throughout the afternoon. Nearing supper time, Kathy said, "I've invited Sarah and the girls for supper beings Eric is on the road."

"How have the girls been doing?" Eddie asked.

Edward laughed, "Shoot, they're a bundle of energy. They help out a lot around the house here. If they have that much energy at home, Sarah won't have much housework to do. Those two are a pair of sweeties. They don't fuss between themselves and seem to be willing to help others."

"I'll be glad to see them tonight. I was wondering why they haven't come to the house yet."

Kathy said, "They knew you were coming, so they headed to town with Sarah to get some shopping done."

When Sarah returned from town, she dropped the girls off at Kathy's with the special parcels they needed to take into the kitchen. She would join them later, after she had taken her items from the car into her house.

Mari and Kari chimed in unison, as they darted for the kitchen, "Hi, Daddy!" They were on a mission and didn't want anyone to know their secret until they were ready.

A short time later, supper was served and the girls squirmed throughout the meal until it was time for dessert. Then they went to the kitchen together. When they returned, they were carrying a blueberry cobbler they had baked for dessert and placed it down before their father, knowing that was his favorite." Kari said, "Daddy, you get first helping. Mari said it was your very best, favorite, kind of dessert."

"Girls, you have won my heart. Now let me see, do I start at this corner or these others?"

The girls laughed and Mari said, "In the middle is the best, unless you want a lot of crust."

There was laughter and a pleasant evening talking about what had happened while he was gone. The girls had rushed from the supper table to pick up the dishes and take them to the sink in the kitchen. The dishes were washed, dried and put away before they returned to the living room to visit with the family. They sat on either side of Eddie, who hugged them and pulled them in close, as he said, "You both do me so proud."

The visit went deep into the night. When Eddie had pulled out the photographs from Vietnam, the entire family was interested in seeing the hospital and the nurses. The girls were particularly interested in the two children. Eddie didn't read the letters, but did share the information that was written on the back of the photographs.

Mari said, "They sure look smaller than we are and they dress funny."

Eddie said, "In the orient, there is a different culture."

Kari looked inquisitive and asked, "What is culture?"

Eddie said, "Girls, in different parts of the world, people live differently. They dress differently and some of their food is different."

"How come?" Kari asked.

"We enjoy eating meat and potatoes." Eddie went on to explain, "In their country, they eat a lot of rice and fish."

The questions and answers flowed for a time, until Sarah told the girls, "I think it is time we went home and let these folks get some rest. Within moments the farmhouse fell into silence, as each went their own way to grab some much-needed sleep.

Eddie went to his room. He had more recent letters to read and to answer before he called it a day. He chose not to answer several letters in one reply, but to take the time to answer each, so that when it was mail call in Vietnam, Jody would get more news and the assurance that his heart was focused on their love and he was waiting for her return.

When morning came, there was the smell of coffee and bacon coming from the kitchen. If he wasn't mistaken, he also smelled a hint of cinnamon rolls. It didn't take much of a guess. Kathy had breakfast on the table and was on her way to wake him, when he stepped through the bedroom door. "Your father's filling his plate and if you don't want to be left out, I'd suggest you wash up at the sink and join us."

After breakfast, Eddie called the nursing home in Bozeman to talk with Mr. Weismann. The talk was rather brief and when Eddie hung up the phone he said, "Gun wants me or us to come up and see him, if I'm still interested. He wouldn't say much on selling or leasing, just that he wanted to talk to me. I told him I'd be up there day after tomorrow."

~ ~ ~ ~

The trip to Bozeman was one of excitement and the talk was of the ranch, but with guarded optimism. When they arrived at the nursing home, they found Mr. Weismann in the recreation room. He had asked for a private room and was wheeled into one of the staff offices.

No one sat at the desk, but upon a sofa and chairs while Mr. Weismann remained in his wheelchair after the door was shut. He asked, "Eddie, with whom do I have the pleasure of meeting for the first time?"

"Gun, these are my parents, Edward and Kathy Day."

Mr. Weismann smiled at Kathy and looked into Edward's eyes for a moment before he said, "It is not only nice, but an honor to meet the parents of a man who has been taught respect and value while serving in the military of our country. He has done well and it shows from the upbringing you two have provided."

Kathy was caught a bit off guard but enjoyed the compliment. Edward smiled and said, "I'm mighty proud of him, he's been through a lot."

Mr. Weismann nodded and said, "Eddie, I have given it a lot of thought about your willingness to buy. I'll be right up front with you; I don't want to sell one acre of the place unless I downright have to. I may consider leasing the place, but you'll have to convince me that you have what it takes to get the ranch up and running. And I'll tell you something else: Johnny and his hands will remain on the property as long as I'm alive. He came to the ranch when I was a teenager and worked for my folks during some pretty tough times. He could have left several times, but he stayed and put in a hard day's work, not worrying about a payday."

Eddie said, "Who is Johnny?"

"He's my foreman. He and the boys are Shoshone and they are downright good around horses. They take care of the horses to see that they are saddle broke or for pack. I've seen them work wonders with stock. They are good and I'm indebted to them. I'd dearly love to return to the ranch, but this blasted back problem hampers that. I don't have the medical care out there that I need."

Kathy spoke up and said, "Mr. Weismann, have you ever considered hiring a nurse that has the skills you need her to have? Seems to me it would be more reasonable to do that instead of being here in a nursing home. You're paying for something that you're not really enjoying and at least you would be back on your ranch."

"I hadn't thought of that. Now that is something for me to mull over in my mind. I'll do that, while your son is trying to convince me he knows what he'll be doing on the ranch."

"It's just a thought," Kathy added, "you'll be able to see the daily operation and know what is going on."

Edward smiled as he looked at Mr. Weismann and said, "She can come up with some good ones once in a while. She's got a good head on her shoulders. She has given me a lot of good advice over the years, on farming and running stock on the open range."

The meeting was rather lengthy, talking of one thing and another. As the meeting drew to a close, Gun turned to Eddie saying, "I sure hope you've got what I think you have. Get things together as best you can and give me a call, let's say in about thirty days. We'll have a serious talk at that time to see if you can convince me you're not a flash without a bang." He smiled and rolled his wheelchair to the door and opened it for them to step through. Eddie recognized it as a gesture to show them he wasn't completely disabled, that he had not lost everything.

When they left the nursing home, Edward said, "Well, Son, it looks as if you have a lot of things to get together in a short period of time. We'll help if you need us."

Kathy said, "What a visit, he is truly interesting."

Eddie added, "I could surely learn a lot by being around him. I hope I can convince him I'm serious and have a good handle on a large horse ranch operation."

Kathy said, "Eddie, I'll bet he's lonely; he needs someone who cares. I imagine a day nurse or a close friend. He needs something more than what a nursing home can provide. He needs that and a pan of my cinnamon rolls should help."

Edward looked at Eddie and said, "I think it would be nice if you took the both of us out to eat, pick up the tab and offer to do the driving back home."

CHAPTER 11

POW's From Different Conflicts Meet – 1966

When morning came, most everyone on the Edward Day farm was up and getting ready for a full day. Before Eddie reached the breakfast table, he could smell the sweet aroma of his mother's cooking. It whetted his appetite, along with the smell of morning coffee freshly brewed. The last platter of food had been prepared in the kitchen before being placed in the center of the table. Following Grace, they all dug into the ham and eggs, with a helping of French toast and hot maple syrup over home-churned butter.

Kathy said, "I wonder how they're treating Mr. Weismann in Bozeman?"

"He was a little long-winded yesterday," Eddie said. "Goodness that man can talk. I guess he enjoys having someone listen to him." He rested his fork for a moment, swallowed and said, "I'll need to make a call to Colorado today. I'm in hopes of getting some help from the Olsen's in putting my proposal together before I make the trip back to see Gun."

"You want some good fatherly advice?" Eddie lowered the cup of coffee he had just managed to grab a swig from and nodded. "The way I see it, you should scratch out what you plan to present. Take and do some research first. Then fill in with what information you can get from the local veterinarian, livestock brokers and those raising horses as well as cattle. Then have Teddy and his father furnish you with some facts, to round out what you really plan to do."

"That's what I planned on doing," Eddie replied, "I just wasn't sure in what order I had to start. I knew I could count on you for some input." There was a short pause before he added with a smile, "As usual."

Edward reared back in his chair, winked at Kathy and said, "I got a whole lot of advice. It's free and I'm only about three and a half feet away from you, if you'd ask," then he laughed. "I have to line out some work with the hands today. There's nothing pressing, so why don't you take the day off and concentrate on getting things together?"

Breakfast was coming to an end, when suddenly the screen door opened and banged shut. They could hear the girls coming into the house. Eddie and his father tried to garner some of the attention, but the girls knew Kathy was always baking up some goodies, or had a treat close by. They raced to her side, giving her a big hug first.

Kathy smiled and said, "Come with me. I have some special cookies and a bit of fudge I brought back from Bozeman. I just know you'll like them. They're in the kitchen."

When they returned to the dining table, Mari and Kari each held a large cookie in each hand. The fudge was already in their mouths. Edward reprimanded in a kidding way, "Here, here! These girls might not have had their breakfast yet!"

"Yes, we have," chimed Kari, as she looked at Kathy stating, "and the fudge sure was good."

The girls stood on either side of Eddie and waited patiently for his attention. They had waited a couple of days at home and now they were ready to talk a spell. Eddie scooted his chair back and grabbed the girls around the waist and said, "Come over here to the sofa and tell me what has been going on around the farm while I was gone."

Their visit was short, as Sarah had planned to take them to town when she did her grocery shopping. Before they left their father's side, he knew what was going on and what was important in their young lives.

When the girls left the farmhouse, Eddie went to his bedroom and sat at a small desk in the corner. He had several letters he needed to write to Jody. He began the first one and wrote of his love and devotion to her, while expressing how much he missed her. Then he mentioned the meeting with Mr. Weismann and the presentation he had to put together. He expressed his hopes of convincing Gun that he was serious about a horse ranch operation. He had to show in writing his knowledge of such an undertaking, the pros and cons and how he planned to address those issues when they arose. He had to lay out a progressive plan of action and show his expertise in black and white within the thirty-day timeframe. At the close of the letter, he would reflect back on their happiness and add a sweet comment or so before he signed the letter. There were several letters to answer and he would put the news of what was happening in the middle of the letter, along with answering her questions. He always wanted her to know how he felt as soon as she began to read and the last to remember him by with his sweet comments.

With the letter writing completed, Eddie drew a sketch of what he would like to have in an open and honest detailed presentation. He smiled, thinking back on his high school English teacher's requirements and chapter outlines. It didn't take long for the outline to take shape and it gave Eddie a guide on what needed to be filled in.

There was a light tap on the door and his mother stepped into the bedroom, "I thought you could go for a hot cup of coffee about now."

"Thanks, Mom. You didn't have to, but I appreciate it."

Kathy smiled, set the cup down and said, "I know," and rubbed the top of his head. "It's the mother in me that made me do it." She turned and quietly left the room.

Eddie took his outline and gave each part a priority. There were suspense dates on when he had to have the information, in order to complete the presentation.

~ ~ ~ ~

He called the Olsen's in Powderhorn, Colorado to discuss what he needed and was reassured by Teddy that the information would be in the mail within the next couple of days.

With his outline and note pad in hand, he headed for the kitchen with his empty cup. "Mom, I'm heading into town to talk with the veterinarian and find out what I can from some of the farmers and ranchers down at the MFA. I'll grab a bite to eat in town, but I'll be home for supper." He left his empty cup in the sink.

Kathy said, "Stop by the store and get me some cinnamon and I'll need a sack of sugar if you plan on eating rolls tomorrow."

"I'll get them," Eddie replied over his shoulder. He headed out onto the porch; the screen door snapped shut behind him.

~ ~ ~ ~

With the folder nearing completion, Eddie had placed tabs on the individual pages that were mentioned in the index. He placed the presentation in a three-ring, soft leather binder embossed with black lettering. There was only one thing left to do. He approached his father and asked, "Dad, I would like you to look over my work on the presentation and give me any last-minute advice."

Edward smiled at his newfound importance and replied, "Bring it to the table and let's look at it together."

Within moments Eddie had returned from his room with the binder and placed it in front of his father. He smiled while pulling up a chair next to his mentor. He knew his father would point out any small detail missing because of the importance of the presentation.

Edward grunted slightly as he viewed the cover of the binder. He read the cover letter detailing Eddie's desire to operate a horse ranch and the reason for the enclosed information. Looking at the index, he took his thumb and forefinger and lifted each tab to view the contents. He was slow and deliberate, knowing his son was patiently waiting on a remark along the way. At the end of the presentation, the summation expressed his conviction. He was prepared to meet all obligations concerning the horse ranch operation on Mr. Weismann's old homestead. He asked the owner to respond within a reasonable timeframe. Edward closed the binder, looked at Eddie and said, "I am surprised and pleased with your presentation. There's a wealth of information, neatly compiled and easy to read. I hope he considers it. I know you have put your heart into it, not only for yourself, but for Jody as well. I wouldn't change a thing; it shows you're a straight shooter and knows what needs to be done."

That evening, Eddie called Mr. Weismann in Bozeman at the nursing home. Gun asked him to come up the following week on a Thursday, where he could look at the presentation and he would appreciate it if Eddie could stick around throughout the weekend, to answer any questions that may come up.

~ ~ ~ ~

When Eddie arrived in Bozeman, he went directly to the nursing home to look up Mr. Weismann. When he pulled his truck to a stop into the parking lot, hot steam escaped the hood, like that of Old Faithful in Yellowstone Park. He hopped out of the cab, went to the front of the truck and lifted the hood. While being careful not to get burned from the steam, the smell of hot water, anti-freeze, damaged rubber and oil under the hood assaulted his nasal passages. Not only did it have its own distinctive odor, but it also poked at his frustration. The fluid seeped from under the truck and encircled the pavement at his feet. When things settled down, he could see that it was a busted radiator hose, not the worst thing in the world. Was this an indication of how his day was going to go, he thought for a fraction of time? If so, he might just as well turn tail and head back down the road. Then the calamity of the situation caused his lips to turn upward into a smile. At least he made it this far. It could have happened back down the road and left him stranded and looking for a ride into town.

When he entered the nursing home, he asked one of the nurses at the desk, "I just busted my radiator hose, how far is it to a parts store?"

He was in luck, the nurse replied, "There is one three blocks down the road."

Eddie said, "Thanks," and asked, "Is Mr. Weismann in the activity room today?"

The nurse replied, "He's been there since right after breakfast. He doesn't spend too much time in his room. He claims it's too confining."

Eddie walked to the activity room and was greeted by Gun, with a wave of his hand and directions to go over to a table at the far side of the room. Gun said, "You have a mighty long face for this early in the day. Anything bothering you?"

"I busted the radiator hose in my truck out in the parking lot. I'll tend to it after our visit," Eddie replied.

Gun laughed, "I haven't done that in a spell. Just chalk it off to one of those happenings that are meant to get a good man flustered."

Eddie smiled and said, "I brought my proposal. We can skim over the highlights and when you read it at your leisure, you'll understand why I made the entries as I did."

Mr. Weismann took the folder and viewed the cover with interest before turning the cover back and glancing through the contents. The index drew his interest where the content of the proposal would be briefly outlined. When he finished reading the index, he chose, and turned to, a couple of pages and began a quick read.

Eddie sat in total silence, as if sitting on needles and pins, while having his stomach twisted into knots. He was hoping all the work in the proposal would render a positive response from his pain-stricken acquaintance. His mouth became dry and he was wondering if he would be able to speak clearly if asked a question.

Gun smiled as he closed the proposal and looked up, "I took your mother's advice, after you all left last month. I love that homestead and I'd certainly hate to give her up, just because I'm stoved up with a batch of pain. I hired a Shoshone nurse that's related to my foreman. She'll be tending to my medical needs out at the homestead."

The look of dejection must have been readable on his face as Eddie spoke, "I take it the proposal may not be needed?"

Gun smiled and replied, "I won't be able to work the place as I would like to, but at least I'd be living back home. As for your proposal, I'm going to go over it with a fine-toothed comb when I take it to my room. Like I told you over the phone, I'd like you to stay in Bozeman over the weekend and if your proposal is convincing, we can get together and make some of the necessary arrangements."

Eddie forced himself to relax and commented, "I need to get the truck fixed and find a place to stay for a couple of days. After driving straight through, I'm rather bushed."

Gun said, "Get a good night's rest and I'd like to see you about nine in the morning, if that isn't too early for you. I should have my decision made by then, and we can go from there." He closed the proposal and let it rest in his lap, as he turned the wheelchair from the table. Setting business aside for the time being, he said, "Eddie, it looks as if we're going to have a thunderstorm move in later today. I rolled this contraption out on the patio a few minutes ago and I can smell it in the air."

"I don't think they're forecasting rain or a thunderstorm," Eddie replied.

"Your bones don't talk to you as much as mine do," Gun said with a grimace on his face. He adjusted his sitting position in the wheelchair. "Seems since the accident I can tell when a storm is approaching without having to listen to the weatherman. I get an ache deep in my back and it stays there until after the storm passes."

The visit lasted for the better part of the hour before Eddie excused himself and said, "I'll fix my truck today and see you in the morning. Get feeling better."

"I'll do just that," Gun returned, as he watched Eddie walk from the dayroom.

~ ~ ~ ~

When morning came, Eddie found himself in the recreation room of the nursing home at 8:45 A.M. sitting comfortably in one of the lounge chairs. Gun wheeled his chair in right at 9 A.M. and was surprised to see Eddie relaxing. It was a calm morning and the recreation room was void of other residents. Eddie said, "Good morning," as Mr. Weismann rolled his chair up next to him.

"Bright day outside, isn't it?" Gun commented. "I looked over the presentation and have a handful of questions. I'd like you to clarify a few things."

"I'll answer them as best I know how. What is it you would like to know?" Eddie asked. He felt his plan had fallen short of what Gun might be expecting.

"Right here," Gun pointed to a page in the presentation. "You plan to run several head of livestock along with the horses. I thought you wanted to run a horse ranch operation."

Eddie thought for sure his future plans were being dashed before they had a chance to develop. "Yes, I did make the provisions for livestock. I'm not sure if we could come to an agreement on horses only or if there would be ample grasslands for livestock. I thought of the possibility of running livestock to diversify the operation. The horse operation may take longer to make the financial turnover I wanted. The livestock is a wise approach instead of gambling on a market that hasn't been tested by someone just starting out."

Gun seemed to pull at his chin with his right hand and said, "How many head of livestock are you planning to start out with?"

"That depends on how many acres are available to pasture the horses and how many are available to run the livestock."

"Who do you expect to furnish veterinarian care should you need it?" Gun asked.

"I have a choice of two here in the Bozeman area," Eddie replied. "I have already talked with them and they both will work with me should the other be busy."

"You seem to have all the answers," Gun commented, "I certainly hope you have the operational know-how to keep an operation this size in the black. It may take time. The material for the livestock stables, show arena area and clinic space is not cheap."

Eddie smiled and said, "I may not know all the answers, but I'm not shy of asking for a comment or help here and there. I hope I could ask you and then there is my father and my friends in Colorado."

Gun smiled and said, "Eddie, I'll have my attorney draw up an agreement, but we'll have to wait until he gets in his office on Monday. What I would like to do is have you follow me and my nurse out to the homestead today. We can cover some of the property and I'll show you the operation I have and how yours might fit in."

Their wait was short lived when the tall figure of a middle-aged Shoshone woman walked into the activity room and smiled at her boss. "I have talked with the Nursing Home Doctor and the Director of Nursing and have signed off on all the medications you will need out at the ranch. I brought along my two children; they will ride in the back of the station wagon. Your seat up front has been padded with cushions to make the ride more comfortable. Johnny has the rest of my belongings in his truck. He is in your room gathering up what belongs to you and then you can check out."

Eddie had listened to her approach. There was a distinctive sound to the way she walked, as if almost sliding her feet on the ball of her foot before the heel touched the floor. She wore store-bought moccasins with a thick sole, possibly the reason for the sound. If it had been soft skinned moccasins, the sound would have been almost inaudible and hard to pick up. He would remember her walk, like so many others that had entered his life.

Gun looked at her and said, "Susie, this is Eddie Day. We will be working together on the homestead, if we can come to an agreement."

Susie looked at Eddie to hear him say, "Mighty nice to meet you, I'm sure glad Mr. Weismann has you to take care of him."

"Eddie, if we're going to be working together let's can the formality and just call me Gun."

Johnny, the ranch foreman, came through the door and walked across the tile floor, his walk was marked by the toes of his boots spread outward, most likely from bronc busting and dug hard into his walk, as if the heels of his boots were worn down. His right leg looked as if it had been badly broken at one time. "Gun, I have your belongings ready for the truck. I'll fetch what you have in the room if you're planning to check out of this place."

Gun wheeled his chair around and said, "Eddie, I need to check out. It might be best if you follow Susie's station wagon out to the homestead."

When Eddie left the nursing home, he headed for his truck. He could see the station wagon with two children playing in the back seat. The wagon was pulled up to the curb, leaving him to believe that would be Gun's ride. When Susie came out of the nursing home, she was pushing Gun in his new wheelchair. He adjusted himself upon the thick foam cushion on the front seat of the station wagon. She looked at Eddie and said, "I'll try not to lose you in the dust."

Eddie smiled and replied, "I'll be right behind you in my truck," as he pointed in the direction of the blue relic parked a short distance away. Johnny the foreman walked bow-legged, hampered by one boot heel that was worn and twisted. He was carrying out the last of Gun's possessions and placing them in the cab of the tired old truck he was driving. The back was loaded down with boxes and other items most likely belonging to Susie for her trip to the homestead.

The parade of vehicles left the parking lot and headed out of Bozeman. Johnny was in the lead and paid no attention to his speed as he shot ahead of the others. Susie drove her car slower at times, pulling to one side of the road or the other in an attempt to miss potholes, ruts and slowed before crossing the cattle guards that crossed the road at fence lines. Eddie followed at a short distance behind the station wagon, amused at her driving. He realized the ride might be a rough experience for his friend. When they hit the dry dirt section of the road, the dust from Susie's car sailed into the air like a rooster's tail and filtered into the cab of Eddie's truck. He was forced to slow down and not follow so close.

When they all entered the ranch house, Gun looked at Eddie and said, "The room at the top of the stairs is available for you to use until you get married. It's too small for a newly-married couple. I imagine you'll be looking for other suitable housing by then. Feel free to go take a look. Susie will be my nurse and do the cooking for the both of us, but you'll be responsible for the cleaning of your room."

Eddie expressed his gratitude and declined to go up at that moment to check out the room. Gun had one of the bedrooms on the main floor and the adjoining two bedrooms were for Susie and her children. Johnny and the children were busy unloading the car and the belongings from the ranch truck before bringing them into the house. Gun said, "Let me get that foam padding. I'll put it in your truck for my comfort while we make a quick trip around the homestead. Maybe Susie will have us a bite to eat when we get back."

The trip covered three family homestead pieces of land that were adjoining. Gun said, "I have an agreement with the neighbors north of the homestead land to run horses on their open pastures." Some of the trip was over well-traveled roadbed and a few jaunts off the well-beaten path were over seldom traveled ground. There was no choice of roadbed to get from one side of the homestead to the other. Before they headed back to the ranch house, Gun had Eddie drive down to a set of corrals where Johnny and his men routinely saddle broke some of the horses. On their way back, Gun had Eddie drive to an area that was rather remote. When they arrived, Gun said, "This is where I had my accident. I guess the horse rolled over me and I laid out here for quite a while before they found me. The doctors seem to think the saddle did most of the damage to my back."

"Is there any hope you can walk and ride again?" Eddie asked.

"It looks as if I'll have to accept the inevitable. The main thing I'm trying to do now is get treatment and adjustments on my back so the pain isn't so overpowering. I'd like to get off most of that pain medicine."

"Is there anything I can do for you?" Eddie inquired.

"No, I'll not force my pain on another man. I have a crew here on the ranch and our operation goes on. I'll handle all that I can and Johnny takes care of the rest. I'll give you full rein on your operation and allow Johnny and the men to help when they're not tied up with my end of the ranch. Their wages will need to be agreed upon ahead of time."

"That sounds mighty fair," Eddie replied. "When would you like to sit down and discuss all the particulars?"

"I wanted you to see what I have first, that way you can make a rational decision on your part," Gun pointed out. "We can get together after we eat, if you like."

~ ~ ~ ~

It was after supper when the two of them entered the library in the ranch house and business was discussed to its finest detail. When the meeting was over, Gun excused himself, saying he was rather tired and would see him in the morning.

Eddie climbed the stairs and for the first time looked into the room he would stay in over the weekend. Eddie had chosen to return to the family farm and await the papers from the attorney. Gun was rather reasonable in terms of the agreement much to Eddie's surprise. Maybe it was because they both shared the scars of captivity while being in the military. But Eddie knew he had found a very dear friend with an understanding heart. One major part of the agreement reflected back to the homesteading requirements of having to prove up. The agreement would be for a period of five years and in that time, he would have to prove up by showing he had an operation that was successful. Anything short of the basic requirement would allow Gun to recommend Eddie take up another line of work and not consider an extension of the agreement. To show a successful operation and a good profit margin, the agreement tended to favor Eddie. The terms reflected a chance for an extension of five years with an option for another five. He could hardly wait to tell his folks. That evening he remained in his room and wrote one of the lengthiest letters he had ever written to Jody. She had to know of his love and his happiness concerning the ranch.

The stay at the ranch over the weekend was filled with talk of ranching and a bit of other experiences on both sides. It became a fun-filled time and both men seemed to enjoy the frankness, honesty and humor of the other. It was nearly noon on Monday when Eddie gave his farewell and left the ranch. When he arrived in Bozeman, he drove directly to the post office, where he mailed Jody's letter. Then he hit the highway and headed for home, wanting to get there before dark. He was happy when he got home, knowing they could all stick their heads into the cab of his truck and sniff at the sweet smell of the dust lingering from the Gallatin area.

When Eddie drove into the yard at the farm, the whole family came out to meet him. His girls, their mother and his parents were all eager to hear what had happened in the Bozeman area. Dinner that night had to be at the elder Day's family table. The talk went deep into the night. When Sarah and the girls went home, Eddie excused himself and went to his room.

When he entered his bedroom, he sat at the desk in the far corner of the room to read the letters he had received. He wrote another long letter to Jody. It was a happy letter with all the news of the day and his plans for the many tomorrows. He was in hopes the letter from Gun's lawyer would come soon, where he could keep Jody up to date on all that was going on. There were the many planned trips here and there to buy stock and supplies. The effort to make things fall into place would need to take on a sense of urgency. His mind was swirling and his letter showed his lack of current organization, bouncing from one subject to the next and back again at times. He was happy and it showed in his writing. With drooping eyes, he closed the letter and made plans to get a good night's rest. He was tired from the long trip home.

~ ~ ~ ~

The following week a letter arrived from Mr. Weismann's attorney. The documents enclosed needed to be signed, witnessed and returned within thirty days. He would notify Eddie when the papers had been properly recorded. Eddie was surprised to read that all of Gun's verbal agreements were to the letter, nothing added and nothing left out. Eddie thought to himself how fortunate he was to be dealing with someone who was straightforward and honest. As the contract was passed to his father and then to his mother and back again, they sat with smiles of happiness knowing something good was about to happen.

"Now that is a contract a man can live with." Edward said.

Not to be outdone Kathy added, "Eddie, he sure has taken a liking to you. You both have a lot in common. I hope the two of you can work together and become the best of friends. He sure seems like he needs a special friend in his life. I hope you will be that friend in all your dealings with each other."

Scooting his chair back, Eddie got up, went to the desk and picked up a pen and returned to the table. As he looked at his parents, he could see the depth of the unguarded happiness in their eyes. "Would the two of you do me the honor and be witnesses?"

When they nodded, Eddie took the pen and signed his name and slid the contract across the table for his parents to sign. When the contract came back in his direction, he had already positioned the stamped envelope to receive the contents and with a swipe of his tongue over the glue, it was sealed, "We'll get this in the mail tomorrow."

~ ~ ~ ~

Eddie was allowed to get settled in at his ranch before Eric and Sarah Elders brought Mari and Kari to the homestead. They would drop off the girls for the better part of the day and go into Bozeman to do some shopping, while Eddie and the girls had some time together.

When their car left the ranch in a trail of dust, Eddie and the girls were walking to the river, each with a pole in hand.

Eddie said, "I have a surprise for the both of you when we get back to the ranch."

Mari asked, "What is it, Daddy?"

"Yeah," Kari chimed in, "tell us now, so we won't be worrying all day what the surprise is."

"The surprise will wait. I have a dilemma on who gets to choose their surprise first."

"I'm the littlest, so I get to choose first," Kari cried out.

"Not so," Mari countered, "I'm the first born, so I should be first."

Eddie said, "I'll tell you how we can settle this."

Mari asked, "How are you going to do that?"

"We're going fishing first. Let's say we fish for two hours from the time we get to the river. When the two hours is up, the one with the most fish gets to choose first."

The girls were excited. When they began fishing, the thrill of landing a trout was magnified by taking the lead over her sister. It kept Eddie busy baiting the hooks and the girls wasted little time in landing a few fish. When the time limit was up, Kari had the most fish.

Back at the ranch, they stopped by the barn where two saddle broke colts were in a corral. When they approached the corral, Eddie said, "This is your surprise. Kari you may choose first. Which one of the colts would you like to have as your horse to ride each time you come to visit?"

Within the confines of the corral, the colts were prancing around first one direction then the other. The colts were kicking up a bit of dust into the air for the girls to breath. Both were two-year old's; one was an appaloosa, the other a palomino. Kari said, "I like the one with the blond tail."

Mari added her assessment, "She is pretty, but I love the appaloosa. She reminds me of my favorite breakfast fruit. I'm going to call her Raspberry."

Not to be outdone by her sister, Kari declared, "I'm going to name mine Golden Girl."

Mari asked, "Can we ride them, now?"

Eddie turned to the girls and said, "Let's go to the house and give these fish to Susie. Maybe her children are about. If they are, maybe all four of you can go horseback riding in the neighboring pastureland."

When they arrived at the house Susie, was chasing Shad and Kim out of the house after they had their glass of milk. Eddie said, "Susie, the girls have caught a mess of fish. Is there a chance they can have fried fish before they go home? Oh, and can Kim and Shad get saddled up and go with my girls for a short ride in the west pasture?"

"Mr. Day, are you asking me to fry the fish for the girls or for the rest of us to enjoy?"

"There is more fish than the girls can eat," Eddie noted, "I'm asking so that all of us might have a taste."

"Fish it will be," Susie stated with a smile on her face, "and

yes, the kids can go riding for a while. At least they will be out from under foot and I'll know where they'll be." She took the fish from the stringer that Eddie offered before he turned and walked to the barn with four young riders anticipating a carefree ride. Susie stood on the porch watching the group make their way to the barn. His girls walked ladylike, while her two kicked up dust, as they kicked at rocks lying in their path. No wonder she had to replace their shoes quite often. She turned and took the fish into the kitchen.

In the barn, the saddles were removed from the tack room along with the bridles. Eddie checked the cinch on each one of the saddles and helped each rider into position. They rode their horses from the barn, led by Eddie on foot as he opened the gate to the west pasture. The four riders rode away talking and laughing amongst themselves.

~ ~ ~ ~

When the time came, Eddie whistled and called out so that his voice could be heard across the pasture, for the kids to return to the barn. There was no race in the return trip, but they did have their horses at a trot. They would have to take care of their mounts first and then prepare for supper. After supper, Mari and Kari waited for their ride home. They spent the last few minutes of their visit with their father on the porch. They watched the long road for the tell-tale rooster tail of dust.

When the day came to a close, Eric and Sarah had arrived and were promptly escorted to the barn to look into the corral at the girl's horses. They hugged their father, each giving their thanks before they hopped into the car. Eddie said, "I hope we can get the girls up this way more often."

Eric said, "There will be no trouble getting them here. Just let us know when you're at the ranch."

"Call the house any time, Eddie," Sarah added, "I know the girls would love talking to you."

Within moments, the car was headed down the dusty road toward Bozeman and Eddie was making his way back onto the porch.

The months seemed to blend together with work at the homestead, trips to buy stock and the days his daughters came to visit. At the end of each day, he would pause and reflect upon his blessings and write a letter to his Jody.

~ ~ ~ ~

1967

Eddie had been gone from his parent's farm for nearly two weeks travelling around the state making purchases of horses and stock and delivering them to their new home, when the phone rang. Kathy picked up the phone and said, "Hello."

Jody's voice filled the receiver, so clear it sounded as if she were calling from a neighbor's phone. "Hello Kathy, Jody on this end. I just landed in Travis Air Force Base in California."

"Oh, my goodness," Kathy gasped. "I'll bet you want to talk with Eddie."

"I sure would. I have thirty days leave coming before I have to report to my next assignment in Texas."

"Jody," Kathy said with excitement in her voice. "Eddie isn't here at the farm, but he's supposed to be here for supper tonight. He's been out purchasing stock for his place. I sure hope you're planning to visit up this way. You've just got to because you're sure welcome."

"If you're sure you don't mind."

"I won't be off this phone five minutes and the whole neighborhood will be buzzing over the excitement of you visiting. We're all looking forward to seeing you. Goodness it is pure pleasure to hear your voice."

"I have been looking forward to visiting with you again," Jody said as she spoke into the public telephone. "I truly enjoyed my last visit up your way."

"I'll be looking forward to seeing you when you get here and Edward will be excited as well. And I know Eddie will be popping buttons when he hears that you're on your way. You can tell us all of your experiences once you get here."

"I'll need to make my flight reservations and I'll let Eddie know later tonight when I call back. He'll need to know what time the flight will arrive in Billings. There are several others wanting to use the phone, so I'll make it short."

"So nice talking to you," Kathy said, as she hung up the phone.

Kathy had gently placed the receiver down before she went into the kitchen. She began making supper for her husband and an added amount for her son. She knew they would be hungry when they came to the table.

When she heard the screen door open and snap shut on the porch, she knew it was a hungry man coming in from work. She talked loud enough for her voice to be heard without turning around, "Wash up, supper will be ready in a few minutes."

"You best set another plate; our Eddie just pulled off the highway. He should be coming in, in a little bit." She had no sooner heard Edward's words when he entered the kitchen and planted a kiss on the back of her neck. The day-old bristles from an unshaven face bit into her skin, but she loved the way he always showed his affection.

Edward had finished washing his hands and face at the porch sink, when Eddie bounded out of the cab of his truck. He was like a yearling turned loose for the day to romp in the open meadows and entered the porch. "You best wash up. Your mother chased me out here to clean up. She claims supper will be on the table shortly."

Eddie looked at the wash pan and saw that his father was not making an effort to toss his water, so he did it for him. Then he added a couple of dippers of fresh before he cleaned up.

"Your trailer sounded empty. Thought you was going to have a load of stock."

Eddie had splashed water on his face and looked up to answer before he dried his face. "I hit the asphalt early and managed to get a trailer load to Bozeman before lunch. I left the ranch kicking up a tail of dust and when I pulled out on the interstate, manure flew out the back of the trailer to leave a slick spot as I headed for home. I didn't plan on missing Mom's cookin'."

The table was set when they arrived and following grace, Kathy said, "I received an interesting phone call about two hours ago."

In the middle of one scooping mashed potatoes from a bowl to his plate and the other taking a helping of meat and sliding it to his clean plate, Kathy had gotten their attention. They both looked up as if to say, ok, tell us who it was from.

She continued, "Jody just arrived in California and has some leave time. I insisted that she come see us. Eddie, she wanted to talk to you. I told her you'd be in later. She'll be calling back and I guess she plans to fly up this way. She told me she had to report to some place in Texas later on."

Edward sat with a big smile on his face and they heard Eddie say, "She's back. Goodness I'm happy about that. Did she say when she would be calling?" For the first time in his life, his Mama's cooking was taking second place to satisfying his curiosity.

"She didn't say, just said she will be giving you a call later on. After she figures you had enough time to get in off the road. I told her you should be home around supper time."

"When she does call," Edward said, "you tell her your mom and I are looking forward to seeing her."

Eddie found it hard to concentrate on eating and was looking forward to hearing the phone ring. It didn't through the mealtime, or on past the dessert and quite a while after Kathy had cleared the table. But when it did ring, it was a sound that resonated throughout the house and seemed to jerk everyone's nerves to attention.

When Eddie answered the phone, it was Jody on the other end of the line. Kathy and Edward quietly went into the kitchen to give Eddie some privacy while talking to her.

On the way into the kitchen, they heard him say, "I'll pick you up in Billings and we will come back to the farm. Then you can join me on one of my runs and see what we have waiting for us in Bozeman."

~ ~ ~ ~

The stock trailer was left at the farm and Eddie drove the truck to Billings. He had business in Hardin and looked at a pair of broodmares before he took I-90 north and would catch I-94 heading west. As he drove over a rise in the road near Lockwood, he looked the sun in the face as it was setting. He adjusted his visor and could see the refineries to the southeast of the community. He would be facing the congested streets as

143

he drove up 27th through the heart of Billings. He would drive past the Deaconess Medical Center and Hospital and the campus of Eastern Montana College of Education at the base of the rims. After driving to the top of the rims on the Airport Road, he glanced out over the sprawling community that filled the valley from the base of the rims to the bluff above the southern bank of the Yellowstone River to the south. He pulled his truck into the parking lot at Logan International airport and glanced at his watch. He was cutting it close as Jody's flight would be arriving before long.

When Eddie stepped into the airport terminal, he could see where some construction was being done for an expansion on one end of the terminal, the crowd was located at the far side. When he arrived at the waiting area one flight of stairs up, there were families gathered with tickets in hand waiting for their flight to be called. Departing passengers were eager to finally be on their way. He walked over to the window where he could look down onto the concourse to see the workers going about their duties. As he lifted his gaze, he could see a flight touching down on the runway and making its way to the far end of the airstrip. He watched as the small vehicles drove about, one went out near the edge of the tarmac and directed the flight in towards the terminal. An airport worker had wands in his hand and lined up the plane before the crowd inside the terminal could hear the engines shut down.

Eddie was oblivious to the information the airline's representative was saying to the general public. He was searching the line of passengers as they stepped to the doorway of the plane and walked down the aluminum ramp. It was dusk and the fluorescent lights within the terminal waiting room were competing with the lighting outside the terminal.

Suddenly there she was, not in uniform, but in a stunning dress, its pattern indistinguishable at this distance. She stood in the doorway of the plane, as if to take in the beauty of the distant sunset and breathe in some of the fresh Montana air. The oval shape of the doorway framed her and made the blood within Eddie surge to capacity with excitement. As she stepped forward onto the ramp, Eddie seemed to count the steps she was making, until her feet touched the asphalt.

His unguarded walk to the stairs was unhindered by the crowd as he raced down them to stand close to the door. He wanted to be close enough where he could call out her name if she didn't see him first.

Words to draw attention were not needed when they saw each other in the same light. They were drawn quickly together, as if there was a magnetic pull. There was nearly a collision when they came together for an embrace and a welcoming kiss.

"You look stunning and I see that you have the agate heart around your neck," before Eddie managed to say. "Here let me carry that," as he reached for the small suite case. "How was your flight?"

Jody smiled, handed over the suitcase and said, "Thanks for the compliment. The flight was smooth until Denver. It was turbulent going in and coming out, but seemed to settle down over Wyoming. I have two other bags in check in."

Eddie smiled and said, "If we follow the crowd, I reckon we'll find it."

On their way to the baggage carrousel Jody said, "I sent most of my clothing to Texas and only brought along what I thought I would use."

When they arrived at the baggage claim area, Eddie placed the luggage on the floor of the terminal once Jody was satisfied that all her baggage was accounted for. He made no effort to pick up any of the suitcases, instead he turned to her, looked deep into her eyes and said, "Jody, it has been a long wait. I love you and I'm asking you; will you give me your hand in marriage?"

Jody smiled and slowly placed the articles she had been carrying in her hands atop one of the suitcases and turned to gaze upon an inquisitive face. "Eddie, I was yours the first time you asked. Yes, you may have my hand. I will marry you as soon as we can set the date."

They came together for a kiss that caused the others in the terminal to turn and look upon the happy couple. When they separated, Eddie was smiling and said, "Goodness, it took you a long time to give me a positive answer."

Jody was radiant and replied, "I hesitated to give you my answer because I wasn't sure if my tour of duty in Vietnam would have caused you to change your mind. It was a long wait for the both of us. I love you Eddie Day, and you have made me the happiest woman in all of… wow, what a homecoming."

He winked at her and said, "Let's get these out to the truck."

She agreed, and when they left the terminal, other folks cast smiles at them as they walked into the night.

When they left the terminal and headed across the parking lot to the truck, Eddie said, "Mom and Dad will be waiting up for us. They are both looking forward to seeing you. They're so excited, for a time I thought they would make this trip with me."

Jody laughed and said, "Your mother doesn't take no for an answer. When I called, she insisted I get on a plane and head up this way that instant."

"Sounds like Mom when she has her mind made up," Eddie commented.

"Do your folks know of our plans?" Jody asked.

"Not yet," Eddie replied as he hoisted the suitcases into the back of the pickup bed. He opened her door and took a box from the glove compartment, turned and said, "This is for you with all my love."

Jody opened the box to see her engagement ring. She said, "Eddie it is simply beautiful." She leaned towards him and gave him a kiss that punctuated the moment.

Eddie took the ring and placed it on the ring finger of her hand that was nervously extended in excitement. When the ring slid onto her finger so easily, she said, "How in the world did you know my ring size?"

The headlights of a car turning into the parking lot illuminated Eddie's face, as he explained. "It was at the Presidio a long time back, shortly after I shared your husband's dog tag and the note from my boots. You had removed your rings while working in some hand lotion. When you turned to get a tissue to remove the excess, I quickly grabbed your ring and slid it on my little finger and then replaced it before you turned around. I never forgot how far down on the finger it went. So, when I visited the jewelry store the other day, I told the manager it was a ring that reached down to here." He held out his hand to point out where the ring had once rested. He held back the truck door and Jody entered the cab of the truck as she took her index finger and gingerly tapped him on the nose in her passing.

It wasn't long before they were leaving the parking lot and driving down off the rims on Airport Road to 27th into Billings, caught I-94 and headed east for the farm. When they arrive at the farm, they expected there to be a period of greetings and talk deeper into the night. Farm folks like to greet, and if you haven't been around in a spell, there's a bit of catching up to do before going to bed is even considered.

A short distance from Billings, Eddie asked, "Are you as hungry as I am?"

"The last I ate was in Denver," Jody replied. "The flight didn't have any snacks and I have eaten what little I took onboard the plane."

"The truck is thirsty," Eddie explained, "We'll top off the tank and what do you say about a burger and a cup of coffee for starters?"

Jody smiled and said, "A burger sounds great and I certainly hope their coffee is good. That stuff they served at the Denver airport wasn't fit to drink."

He turned off the interstate at Huntley to top off his truck before they decided to grab a cup of coffee and a burger in the local café. When they walked in, all the eyes of the locals seemed to focus on Jody and Eddie felt like one happy fellow. Here he was wearing western attire, smell on his boots and a dusty excuse for a Stetson that had seen better days on the back of his head and escorting his love. She was dressed as if she had stepped off the front cover of a California fashion magazine. They took a booth, the locals continued doing what they were doing before they entered and the waitress took their order. They enjoyed small talk over the meal and Jody admired the engagement ring, looking at it and then at Eddie. Before long they were on their way down the highway.

The excitement and loose chatter kept them both awake, laughing and alert for the long trip. Late in the night, the truck's cab picked up the dust from the lane when they turned off the asphalt and headed for the farmhouse.

CHAPTER 12

A Wedding – A Cabin In Gallatin County -1967

The yard light illuminated the area in front of the farmhouse and all the way to the barn. When Eddie pulled his truck to a stop in front of the gate leading to the house, his father and mother were pushing the screen door open. They came out into the yard that was bordered by a white picket fence. Eddie exited the truck and was hastily making his way to the passenger's side to open the door. His father opened the yard gate and bellowed out, "Glad your home, Son, and Jody you're a welcome sight for tired eyes."

When Jody's feet hit the ground, she was met with Edward's extended arms who softly said, "Goodness its sure good to see you."

Edward had no sooner stepped back, as to not crowd their newly - arrived guest, when Kathy threw her arms around Jody and gave her a welcoming hug. "I'm sure glad you came. Come inside where you can relax and get comfortable."

They entered the old farmhouse and went directly to the kitchen table. Eddie was bringing up the rear with Jody's luggage. The coffee was fresh and Kathy had baked a fresh batch of cinnamon rolls. They gathered around the kitchen table to enjoy a bit of family talking. Kathy was the first to speak and said, "Well what is happening in your life since I last talked with you on the phone?"

Jody was all smiles and replied, "I believe Eddie has something to tell the both of you."

When three pairs of eyes fell on Eddie, he smiled, took in a small breath and proclaimed, "I asked Jody to marry me, right after she got off the plane and she accepted."

Kathy squealed with excitement and looked at Jody saying, "I'm so happy for you, for the both of you." As Jody pulled her hand from beneath the concealment of the table to show off her ring, Kathy gasped with excitement again, "Oh Edward, would you look at her ring!"

"It looks mighty pretty on your hand and the news is a pleasant surprise worth waiting up for," Edward replied. "Jody, welcome to the family. Kathy and I couldn't be more pleased. And just why did you two keep it a secret until now?"

Eddie seemed lost for words, but was saved by Jody when she said, "He asked for my hand nearly a year and a half ago. I told him I had the tour in Vietnam facing me. I thought it would be best to wait and see if we felt the same when I returned. It was all I could think about during the long flight home. I was relieved when he popped the question the second time."

Kathy laughed and remarked, "I've never known him to be at a loss for words."

Edward butted in and added, "As a little tike, he waited the longest time to talk. But when he did, he hasn't found a way to stop. He can shut up at times and apparently did while keeping this secret from all of us."

Eddie blushed a bit before he spoke up in defense of his actions. "I didn't know if she would say yes or no, so there was no need to talk of something that hadn't happened yet."

"Have you two set a date?" Kathy asked.

Jody smiled and looked at Eddie. He stared back with a hopeful look and said, "The sooner the better." She nodded with approval, her smile was wide and her eyes seemed to dance with excitement.

"How about a cup of that coffee and another one of these rolls?" Edward asked. No need to get all worked up over a wedding date, as long as we know by tomorrow." Laughter filled the room and the pause for humor after some serious talk was welcomed by the young couple.

Jody said, "If we get married while I'm on leave, the name change on all the retirement papers will reflect our married name."

Eddie said, "We'll have a lot to do if we plan on getting the knot tied before you have to report in. We'll have to file for the license keeping in mind the waiting period, as well as make arrangements with the church and preacher. On top of that, I have a commitment to look at some broodmares later next week. I passed on a pair in Hardin yesterday."

The talk lasted late into the night with laughter breaking out numerous times before the pot was empty and the plate of cinnamon rolls was no more. They would retire for the day and get up early in the morning with work and more visiting to do. As they departed for their respective bedrooms, Eddie said, "See, I told you the welcome would go deep into the night."

Jody smiled and said, "It was wonderful, I'll see you in the morning."

They kissed lightly and Jody turned to join Kathy who was waiting in the hall to show her to a guest room. Kathy said, "We plan on attending church in the morning, would you care to join us or would you rather rest in after such a long trip?"

With a big smile on her face, Jody hugged Kathy goodnight and said, "I would be happy to attend."

~ ~ ~ ~

After returning from church services and talking with Pastor Waters, the rest of the afternoon was spent relaxing and discussing plans for the limited time to get so much accomplished. When they started talking of a house to live in, Eddie said, "I would like to have a log cabin built, a nice big one with a room without any walls, if that is possible."

Edward laughed and said, "You always had a stretch of an imagination."

Eddie got a piece of paper and began to draw out his design as Jody leaned her head over, resting it on his shoulder the entire time. "You smell good," she said.

"It has to be Dad's shaving lotion," Eddie whispered. "I took a good scrubbing this morning and shaved using his supplies before church."

When Eddie had sketched out his floor plan drawing of what he would like in a cabin, he showed Jody first. She nodded with approval before he handed the tablet over to his father.

"About as close to the shape of a cross, if you look from the top," Edward said.

"The hallways going north to south and east to west form the rooms on the bottom floor and in the middle, I have my room without any walls." As Eddie turned to look at Jody and his father, he explained, "The upstairs over the center of the house will be our bedroom."

Kathy chimed in, "I think it's sweet. If that is what you both want, I think it is lovely."

Jody asked, "Mom and Dad, could I use your phone?"

151

There was an urgent plea in Jody's voice when she had placed the call to her friend, who served with her in Vietnam. The house was quiet and her voice could be heard in the other room. "Hi Deb, this is Jody. Remember when we left Nam, you said I could call on you if there was anything you could do. There was a pause before she continued, "I'm getting married and I'd like to have you as my Maid of Honor. There was another pause before she spoke again, "I know it is short notice, but we're saying our vows a week from today at noon. Can you make it?"

Edward spoke up and said, "It sounds as if your young lady is getting serious."

Eddie replied, "I'm glad she is. I believe she's the most wonderful woman I have run into in years. Sarah was my first love, but the war took care of that. On the other hand, that same war gave me Jody. She has put my life back together in more ways than one."

Kathy said, "I'm glad you two are coming together. I think she will be good for you and she's so special. She has a good head on her shoulders, a heart of gold and I enjoy visiting with her."

Moments later, Jody rejoined the family saying, "Deb owed me big time and I thought I'd collect. She'll be here for the wedding. We'll just have to get the rest of the details lined up." Laughter filled the house.

Moments later, Eddie called his friend in Colorado asking him to be the Best Man. The phone call was lengthy and the issue was finally settled: Teddy and his wife Autumn Song would be coming in from Colorado for the wedding.

From the drawing of the log cabin, to the wedding and other subjects, laughter weaved in and out of their conversation. The talk was smooth, as if it were freely flowing through the eyelets of a new pair of shoes. Their chatter and laughter crossed back and forth like shoestrings above the tongue of a comfortable pair of shoes. It was a casual afternoon and when it came time to prepare supper, Jody was in the kitchen insisting she help. The women had their time to talk while preparing the food and at the same time the men discussed other subjects.

Over the dinner table and deep into the night, the visiting continued. Not one subject was discussed in depth, only a comfortable flow of ideas and subjects that marked the night. When the coffee pot had been lifted and the last of its contents poured out, the last of the crumbs from the cake plate were lifted to Edward's lips. The casual mention of turning in became the topic. Tomorrow would be a big day with Eddie and Jody traveling across the state to check out stock and the travel to the homestead while there was plenty of work to do on the farm.

The following day was filled with activity, including several long-distance phone calls. Shortly after breakfast, Eddie in his western attire waited for Jody to join him. It was her first-time wearing Wrangler jeans, a short sleeve western blouse and a new pair of western boots. The leather was tight-fitting and itching to collect their first scuff mark or smell to the bottom of the boots. They rode in Eddie's pickup truck with an empty stock trailer dragging behind to the county courthouse to get their marriage license.

When they arrived, they received a lot of chatter from a pudgy female clerk, "You can file and pay for the license, but with the waiting period, it won't be available to pick it up until Thursday." Then with a smile, she looked at Jody and added, "It gives us girls a day or so to change our mind, if we want."

When they left the courthouse, they were hand in hand, each filled with the excitement of their pending wedding. When they got to the pickup truck, Jody was escorted to her side with proper protocol before he opened the cab door. Eddie went to his side passing behind the truck to double check the hitch before they headed down the highway.

Upon entering the highway Jody asked, "Where are we headed, to check on those horses?"

"There's a ranch out of Big Timber that has a pair of broodmares at a reasonable price," Eddie replied. "I made an appointment to drop by and have a look. If they look promising, we'll load them up and take them to Bozeman."

~ ~ ~ ~

When the pickup truck and trailer entered the highway, after a visit to the ranch at Big Timber, they headed west for Bozeman.

Jody asked, "Why buy just the one mare, why not both?"

"The other mare was older and showed signs of breaking down," Eddie replied. "That sweet one in the back will be good for several years. She appears to be in pretty good health and won't need a lot of attention from a veterinarian."

"So that's what they mean by saying you have horse sense," Jody kidded.

With a big smile on his face and a wink of the eye, he cast a quick look her way saying, "There is a lot to learn and I'm learning more every day. I just hope in my judgment, I don't make a big mistake along the way."

She reached over and placed her hand atop his right hand that was resting on the seat and said, "I can see that you're pretty much on top of things, least ways I trust you." Her smile lit up the cab of the truck like a bright dome light on the darkest night and here it was broad daylight.

~ ~ ~ ~

The dust in the air was beginning to settle when Eddie opened the truck door to let Jody step down to the ground. "We'll go up to the house to see if Gun is around before we place the mare in the corral."

Just as they arrived at the door, Johnny the foreman stepped through, "I'm just leaving. Do you want me to take care of your horse while you're visiting the boss?"

Eddie said, "Thanks, keep her isolated for a week in one of the corrals with plenty of feed and water. Call the vet and have him take a good look at her before she is put to pasture. I won't be around for about two weeks, because I'm getting married."

Johnny pulled up short, looked Eddie in the eye and said, "You do okay judging good horse flesh, I hope you have the same luck with a wife." He left the porch without another word.

Jody looked at Eddie and said, "He's a bit outspoken, isn't he?"

"Must be the Shoshone showing up in his vocabulary," Eddie replied.

"That's not the answer I anticipated," Jody said, "but it's original."

Susie, Gun's nurse, was standing in the doorway and said, "Come in, and Miss Jody please excuse him, my brother sometimes has a sharp tongue. He likes to think of the old days, but he is a good man most of the time."

Jody smiled and said, "Eddie has told me a lot about you. I'm very pleased to meet you."

She said, "I must prepare supper. Please, the both of you go on in, Gun is in the library. He'll be happy to see you both."

The visit was like sitting down with family and the invitation to stay for supper was made very clear early. They visited deep into the night with Susie sitting in a wooden rocker a short distance from her boss.

It was near time to call it a day when Eddie asked, "Gun, I'm getting married Sunday and I'd like to have you in the wedding party as one of the groom's men. Do you think you can make it?"

Gun seemed to sit up straight, thought hard for a moment, while producing a smile that nearly reached both ears. "I'm totally honored, but I can't stand for very long."

"No need," Eddie replied, "your wheelchair is acceptable. We'll have the rehearsal Saturday evening and you and Susie are invited to stay at the farm."

Jody spoke up and said, "Susie, I would like to have you as one of the bridesmaids. Would you accept the invitation?"

Tears welled up in Susie's eyes as she looked at her boss. He said, "I'll need you nearby, but it is you that will have to make your decision."

The tears rolled down her cheeks as her dark eyes snapped with excitement. "Yes, I Susie Two-Clouds will be there and I too am so very much honored to be asked. But what should I wear?"

Jody calmly said, "What would be traditional for you?"

"You mean Shoshone?"

With a reassuring smile Jody said, "If you feel comfortable wearing something traditional that will be acceptable and I would be pleased, or you may choose a gown. Think of it overnight and we'll talk about it in the morning."

It was getting late Susie showed Jody her room and Eddie went to the top of the stairs to his. Susie returned to the library to see that Mr. Weismann had what he needed before he entered his bedroom for the night and then she would go to hers.

When morning came, Susie had her talk with Jody and Eddie had a short visit with Gun. Eddie and Jody went to the pickup truck and headed for the highway for the long trip back to the farm.

When they pulled onto the highway, Eddie asked, "Did you two settle what she would be wearing?"

"We sure did," Jody replied, "and it is going to be stunning. Did you and Gus figure out a tux or a suit?

Eddie said, "No time for everyone to go formal. I thought a dark navy suit for each would be about right. Most of us guys have one hanging in the closet. I hope you'll wear your uniform."

"I will if it is your request," Jody replied. I was beginning to wonder

155

where I would find a gown on short order and in what color, beings I was married at one time."

"Then it is settled," Eddie added, "I think it is very fitting and you're right, time is limited."

Jody said, "When we get back to the farm, I'll call Deb and tell her to wear her uniform. I'm so pleased. I'm beginning to see everything fall into place."

"I'm looking forward to seeing Teddy again. He was in the same POW outfit with me. He was telling me how happy he has been after he got married to Autumn Song shortly after he came back from the war. They had a Ute wedding and I believe Teddy had to cough up a few ponies to get her hand."

Jody laughed then asked, "Maybe his wife can be one of the bridesmaids? I'd like to call her to see if she would consider doing us the honor, beings Teddy is your best man. I'd like to see if she would also consider her traditional Ute dress and shawl because Susie is going to wear hers."

"We'll call and ask," Eddie remarked. "I know she will be with Teddy and I'm sure Teddy's folks, Ted and Margaret, will make the trip up from Powderhorn, Colorado, too. Before we left the farm, I talked with Eric and Sarah. They thought it best not to be in the wedding party, but we're pleased that we are having Mari and Kari as flower girls and ring bearer."

"I can understand how Sarah feels and it is very thoughtful of her," Jody responded. "But it's going to be sweet having the girls take part. I couldn't be happier and my father will be escorting me one more time. I'm so happy."

"Me too," Eddie whispered barely loud enough for her to hear over the roar of the truck motor. The oncoming traffic going in the opposite direction seemed louder than usual. "I look forward to meeting your father."

"His name is Walter Rauch, but he goes by Walt most of the time. He married my mother, Eva. She died nearly fifteen years ago in a storm in Missouri. She made it to the barn, but it was no protection for her when the twister cut a swath across the countryside."

Eddie softly said, "I'm sorry to hear that."

"Folks that live back in Missouri know the dangers and accept them as a part of Mother Nature. I'm sure you'll like Daddy. He took Mom's death hard and now claims he's as hard to deal with as Missouri sod. He'd never consider moving beings that mama is buried back there."

There was a pause for a time on past reflections. The miles went by, the sweet talk and wedding plans began to fill the cab of the truck again, keeping both in an excited mood. The trip back to the farm was a long one, but the distance would pass almost unnoticed.

Eddie glanced over at Jody after she was unusually quiet for several moments. She was suddenly quiet and deep in thought. He glanced at her and detected a shiver rippling through her body.

"Jody, what is it?" he asked.

She shivered once more and said, "For a moment, I was seeing one of the soldiers back in Vietnam. He was near death on the operating table, all shot up. His last few words were of his wedding plans when he returned home."

"Sweetheart, I've been there with my experiences. Those flashbacks will come and go for a long time. It's something we don't like to talk about."

She looked at Eddie and said, "But the image was so real. Does it get worse or diminish over time?"

Eddie smiled and recalled, "Remember when you and your staff were working with me at the Presidio?" He didn't wait for her response but continued. "I had a duffle bag full of flashbacks and the treatment I received helped me pull through a lot of it. When they happen, let me know and we'll work through them together. If they get to the point where they are bothersome, we'll get treatment for you. If they interfere with your work at Fort Sam Houston, get help there on post before you retire."

She reached out and touched his arm saying, "Eddie, you're so understanding."

Eddie kept his eyes on the road and replied, "I hope I can be. We've been exposed to things the folks around here don't understand. I experienced it in Korea and you have in Vietnam. When we're together, just open up and let me know what you're experiencing. We'll try to work through it together." He paused for a moment and then continued, "Some folks wonder why veterans don't talk of their wartime experiences. They're just bad memories for the most part and something we'd prefer to set aside in our minds. But I'll be here for you when the flash backs occur. Together we'll try to put some space between them."

She patted his arm and said, "Thanks, I love you for your understanding heart."

The trip back to the farm was a long one, but the distance would pass almost unnoticed, as they talked of one thing and another.

~ ~ ~ ~

When breakfast was finished Wednesday morning, Kathy and Jody were in the kitchen and Eddie and Edward were in the living room, when the telephone rang. It was for Eddie. "Hello," on the other end was Pastor Waters, the Methodist minister who informed him that the arrangements for the wedding had been made for the following Sunday, immediately following Sunday services. Church services would have to be in the high school gymnasium because the community was coming together for an all-denominations service. This year, the Methodist's would be officiating over the services. He asked Eddie if the wedding could be held at the high school following services or would he prefer they go to the church to conduct the wedding? Eddie replied, "Let me talk with Jody and I'll call you back."

When he talked with Jody about the services, she said, "The high school would be fine. I think it would be an inconvenience for those attending church to have to get up and leave the high school and go back to the church just for the wedding. I'm comfortable with that if you are."

Eddie nodded his head in agreement and called the minister back to let him know it would be ok to have the wedding at the school following the religious services. He asked if the wedding rehearsal would be at the school or at the church. He was informed it would be at the high school at 7 P.M. on Saturday.

Kathy spoke up and said, "I don't recall them having an all-denomination church service last year."

Edward looked at his wife, as if to silently shush her from causing any additional concern. He nodded his head and headed into the kitchen and she followed. When they were out of ear shot Edward said, "Don't let on, but the town pastors have something up their sleeves."

Kathy accepted the explanation to some degree, smiled, but added, "Why is it I am the last to know something about this little secret?"

Edward said, "There is no time to mail invitations and the pastors thought it would be nice for the town to see their hero get married. All the worshipers know is that there is going to be just the one joint service with a potluck reception to follow on Sunday. They don't realize it now, but the wedding is going to follow a very special sermon designed to put the teachings of the Bible into the center piece of everyone's marriage. All of the preachers thought the opportunity had come for such a sermon. They are using the wedding as a reason to use the gymnasium for both functions. Each church is going to split the fees to cover the school district's charge for the gymnasium and funds for the barbeque chicken and beef. There just isn't enough time to have others buy wedding presents and to my knowledge, I don't believe they're even going to collect a love offering for the kids. It's just a show of support."

Kathy gave him one of those looks, as if to say you better keep me informed and conceded, "The gesture of support is a nice thought."

Edward nodded his head to in the affirmative, "I got your message and I'll let you know when I know. Most of what will be happening hinged on how the kids reacted about having the wedding at the school. I guess each preacher will begin to put the rest in motion."

~ ~ ~ ~

The next three days were filled with a variety of activities. They shopped for floral arrangements, a wedding cake, greeting guests and making arrangements for lodging for those coming in. Fold out sofas, day beds and inflatable mattresses, anything to accommodate the guests overnight was scheduled for pick up. They also had to deal with the food and preparation to feed the guests. It was a whirlwind of events that led up to an evening of relaxing after the wedding rehearsal.

When morning came, the farmhouse was filled with several couples The women helped with breakfast in the kitchen and the men seemed to congregate on the long narrow porch until called to the table.

Jody remained in her room where her breakfast would be brought to her as she prepared for the wedding. The bedroom became filled with helpful guests who entered and left in a seemingly continuous stream. The room was also a changing place for the bridesmaids. The hair, makeup, perfume, corsages and last-minute touchups with eye liner and eyebrow pencil that always seem to accompany a wedding, led to laughter. The smell that permeated the room was much like entering a floral and perfume shop, only to have the total fragrance whisked under your nose. The last-minute nervous jitters seemed to be set aside, replaced by an abundance of laughter filling the small space that nearly cracked the windows. There was enough hair spray in the air to defoliate several acres, in their attempt to make each strand of hair stay in place. It was a room filled with love and laughter, with excitement turned loose.

After breakfast, Eddie and the groomsmen had entered his bedroom and went about changing into their suits. As each stepped from the bedroom, they were stopped by some of the women who checked to see that the boutonniere was attached properly.

Connie Summerfield, Eddie's sister and one of the bridesmaids, stepped into the hallway and called out, "Eddie and Neil, I need you both in the hallway."

When they appeared in the hallway, they heard Connie explain, "As your sister, it is my right to pin the boutonniere on both of you."

Both men stood still. She did her chosen duty and in response, Neil said, "Thanks Sis, I couldn't have done it without you."

"I'll take that as one of your smaller weaknesses big brother," Connie answered back.

Eddie gave her a slight kiss and said, "I love you, Connie, you're so thoughtful."

She replied, "Naturally, what are big sisters for?" Turning, she joined the others in the living room, allowing Eddie to join the other men.

Most of the other guests were on the porch and in the day-room, when Eric and Sarah Elders came to visit, with Mari and Kari all dolled up for the wedding. After introducing most of the guests, Eric joined the men and Sarah told Kathy, "The pillow for the rings and the flower petals are in the car. They would follow the others to the school."

Kathy said, "That would be fine." She turned her attention to the girls and said, "Goodness, Grandma is sure proud of you two. You both look so sweet."

Mari and Kari smiled and chimed, "Thanks, Grandma."

When it was time to leave the farmhouse and head into town for church services before the wedding, the men drove from the farm first. This kept Eddie from seeing the bride before the wedding. The parade of cars arrived at the high school and parked in a section already reserved.

Most of the wedding party was ushered to reserved seats up front near the center to the stage that had the curtain pulled closed. The bride and her bridesmaids were ushered to a balcony room overlooking the gymnasium floor. They could see and hear the sermon from there. When the services, began the stage curtain was pulled back, exposing the community choir on risers.

~ ~ ~ ~

Moments before the benediction, Pastor Waters motioned for the wedding party to exit and make their entry preparations. When the group had left the gymnasium, he addressed the combined congregation. "There will be a wedding in a couple of moments and the community is invited to witness this blessed event. The marriage will bring Mr. Eddie Day our Hometown Hero and his lovely bride Lieutenant Colonel Jody Sutton together as one. Within the wedding party today are three Prisoner of War veterans. One veteran experienced a German POW camp in WW II. Two experienced a POW camp in the Korean Conflict and a wounded veteran from fighting in the Philippines during WWII. They will stand with parents, a sister, wives and children, who have been exposed to the hardships our men and women in uniform have faced. We are also blessed to have two army nurses who have just returned from their tour of duty in Vietnam. One I am pleased to say is the bride. The two bridesmaids in tribal dress are Shoshone and Ute. They are an important part of this wedding. They share their lives with two of the men that were held as POWs in Korea and World War II. Closer to home, we cannot overlook the two youngest of the Day family, Mari and Kari. They are the daughters of our hero Eddie Day. He was kept from their lives for nearly 13 years, because of the Korean conflict and his imprisonment. Along with your pastors, let us join together, as a community, ready to witness such a blessed event and wish them well with our prayers and support."

The benediction began and the pastors filed from the gymnasium to later join the procession for the wedding. No sooner had the pastors exited the gymnasium then the curtains on the stage were opened. No longer were there risers on which the choir stood. They had been removed and in their place were three American flags, each symbolically representing WWII, the Korean and Vietnam conflicts, divided equally across the stage behind the altar that had been removed from the Methodist Church. Two sets of steps had been placed side by side on the gymnasium floor in front of the religious altar, allowing access to the center of the stage.

The ceremony would be conducted on the stage so that the entire community could see. When the organ and piano began playing, the groom and groomsmen filed on stage from the right side and took up their positions near the front and center. There was Eddie, Teddy, Gun, Johnny and Neil. From the left side of the stage, the Maid of Honor Deb, an army nurse captain in uniform, two bridesmaids, Susie and Autumn Song with ceremonial Indian shawls over their native attire and Connie in a gown, they took up their positions at the same time.

The ministers entered the gym from behind the congregation and walked down the center aisle arriving on stage to stand between the two groups and turned to face the combined congregations.

When the 'Wedding March' began to play, the congregation stood and looked to the back of the gymnasium for the entrance of the bride. Kari Day entered first, casting down rose petals from a flowery wedding basket that she carried down the center aisle and slowly strolled to the front. A few steps behind Kari, was the bride. She paused only momentarily to accept the arm of her escort, her ailing father Walter Rauch. Behind them was Mari Day, the ring bearer.

Pastor Waters stepped down from the stage and met Jody and her father as they approached the steps. "Who gives this bride into this marriage?"

Walter Rauch said, "I do." He placed his daughter's hands in Pastor Water's extended hand and turned to be seated.

Mari handed Reverend Waters the pillow with the rings attached and joined Kari sitting next to their parents, Eric and Sarah.

Pastor Waters escorted Jody up the stairs to the stage and began the wedding ceremony.

When the vows were completed, Pastor Waters said, "You may now kiss your bride." Following the kiss, he added, "Please turn and face the congregation." While they were turning the minister announced, "May I present to you, this community and the entire world, Mr. and Mrs. Eddie Day."

There was applause and when it diminished the Pastor added, "Please allow the wedding party to exit before you follow the directions of the ushers. There will be a brief reception in the school cafeteria, where you may meet the bride and groom and partake of their wedding cake and refreshments along with the barbecued chicken or beef that is included in the potluck dinner."

When they returned to the farm, the remainder of the day was filled with visiting family and close friends who had showed up to make the wedding a blessed event. Jody's father was due to return to Missouri early the next day. Each would go their separate ways and return to life as they knew it. For Eddie and Jody, they had a number of things they had planned to do before she left for San Antonio. She would be leaving Eddie behind to build his business. They would wait on their honeymoon, as they planned to enjoy it immediately following her retirement from active duty.

The remaining time left on Jody's leave was spent at the side of her beloved Eddie. He journeyed east and west checking on stock in hopes of building a business that would be productive. On their first trip to Bozeman as husband and wife, they were informed that Gun was considering setting aside a portion of land on his homestead for them to build their home when the time came.

With all the excitement came the day when Jody had to prepare to leave those she loved in Montana. Eddie watched her flight leave Logan Field in Billings, Montana for a layover and change of flight in Denver, Colorado, allowing her arrival in San Antonio, Texas, later that day. Once there she would grab a cab and make her way to Fort Sam Houston for her new assignment. She felt happiness and pride within her heart when she initiated the necessary papers for the name change on her military records and immediately forecasted her retirement nearly seven months away. She would also seek treatment and counseling for her numerous flashbacks.

Eddie remained behind in Montana, driving one direction and the other looking at stock. In the quiet time, he would do his work on the homestead seeing that what stock he had was taken care of. Letters were exchanged for a time but were replaced with phone calls on the weekends.

~ ~ ~ ~

Time had passed and months later, Eddie boarded a flight out of Billings with a change of planes in Denver for a flight to San Antonio. He was on his way to see Jody's retirement from active duty and then they were off to enjoy a three-week honeymoon. They would not return to Bozeman until the last Saturday morning of the month. This was fine for those left behind in Montana, because there were plans that had been put in motion months earlier.

~ ~ ~ ~

The day following Eddie heading to Texas was a day when the dusts raised to the heavens north of Bozeman leading to the homestead. Gun and Susie were on the front porch when the first of several trucks began to arrive. In the lead were Edward and Kathy Day, their trailer loaded with building material. When they approached the porch, Gun, remaining in his wheelchair said, "Edward, I'm so glad to see you. This is going to be wild; what a challenge."

Susie said, "Kathy, please come inside. Before the day is through, there are going to be some hungry workers."

Edward shook hands with Gun, as if they hadn't seen each other for a spell. He turned to see the parade of vehicles coming to the job site. "I had to drive like the dickens to get here before the rest."

Edward Day had done his research and found Danny Doyle, one of Eddie's old service buddies doing business in Missoula. Danny's parents were big in building log cabins in Michigan and their son was looking to get a franchise built in the Missoula area. From the crude drawings Eddie had sketched out one night when Jody was visiting the farm, his father had shared them with Danny. The drawings were later shared with Danny's parents and the final blueprint layouts were in turn sent back to their son. The cabin would be made from Montana timber, each log precisely measured and marked according to the blueprints.

Roaring into the yard was a pickup pulling a trailer that contained the office for Danny Doyle, the head contractor. When he came to a stop, Danny joined Edward and Gun on the front porch. He informed them, "I have the prints in the trailer. You're welcome to look at them at any time. For now, I believe I'll go into the yard and greet our help."

Behind Doyle's rig came the Moot family. Tavis was a good sub-contractor and had worked with Danny on several projects in plumbing, heating and ventilation along with anything electrical. He was a man of dark complexion with large eyebrows, large sideburns, large hands, a tall muscular frame and agile features. His wife Peninah joined him and kept watch over their son Tobias, often called Toby, and their daughter Ja'Nell. Peninah was tall and slender complimenting her beautiful

164

features and a skin color like honey poured over bronze. The children were considered very good-looking, sharing some of the features of both parents.

Contractors and vendors contributed their time and material. Where there was a gap in contributed items, funds collected in a financial account from one source or another seemed to cover what wasn't freely given. Three bulldozers and two graders had been trucked in along with several backhoes to do the major excavation of the grounds and two cranes to handle the enormous logs for the cabin. Truckers hauling processed logs previously cut, notched and measured to specifications and eighteen wheelers filled with building materials began looking for a spot to park. Several smaller vans had electrical supplies, while others carried pre-fabricated glass windows. Most of all, behind the heavy equipment were a multitude of volunteer workers from Eddie's hometown. His dream home was going to be built and waiting for them when they returned from their honeymoon.

From his wheelchair, Gun looked up and asked, "Hey Danny, would you mind bringing the prints up here for a moment? I'd like to look at them."

Danny said, "I'll get them for you. Tavis, could you give me a hand?"

Moments later Danny and Tavis placed the prints on a large table where Mr. Weismann and Edward were waiting.

Danny glanced at Gun over the top of the spread-out material and said, "This set covers the necessary excavation, supporting wall dimensions, plumbing and electrical channels needed within the cabin's foundation. The other covers the construction of the cabin. Is there something you would like to add?"

"I'd like to take a look at the prints before the work begins," Gun replied. "I've set aside five acres for Eddie and Jody. I'd like to have their cabin built on that knoll over there. The house can be with its north south, east west lined up perfectly and the rise will allow for the garage under the south hall, like so," as he held the prints. That way there will be less excavation needed, don't you think?"

Danny replied, "Excellent, that way we can tie in to the access road. If you'll excuse me, I'll get with the survey crew to get things measured and staked out so the work can begin."

Edward, Tavis and Danny excused themselves from those gathered on the porch and returned to the contractor's trailer with the blueprints. They greeted the community of volunteers as they arrived.

Danny turned to Edward and said, "I'd like to use you as a liaison with the volunteers. You know most of them by name and it would help, if they have questions, to have their concerns channeled through you. Tavis and I will handle the construction end of things. We need to have teams assigned and specific duties and have the work done in sequence. That way we're not running over each other. Each project needs to be completed before moving to the next. We can't allow the construction to get ahead of any particular phase."

As the group of volunteers gathered near the trailer, Danny explained that Edward would be one of his right-hand men if they had questions. He asked for those with experience in certain fields. Five teams were put together and the volunteers were introduced to their crew chief. They would be sent out to begin their work after Danny had a short meeting with his crew chiefs.

Danny Doyle had been Eddie's platoon guide in basic training years ago. Now he was filling the shoes of a general contractor. He was honored that he had been chosen to be the contractor in charge of building such a majestic cabin for a very deserving veteran. He talked with the crew chiefs in his office before work began on the cabin. "I will need you five to work independently with your crews. Each side of the house is exactly alike and they will join the center. The logs have been marked and the assembly will be rather easy if you follow the blueprints. Check with the truckers and they will get the required logs to your jobsite in the order you need them. The excavating and foundation will come first. The retaining walls will need to get my approval before the cement is poured. We should have most of the exterior and inner walls of the first floor of the cabin up before the week is out. We'll go up as fast as we can, but safety comes first. There are a lot of volunteers helping out and we don't need anyone hurt. The plumbing and electrical, Tavis Moot will handle. Various sub-contractors will begin with crews handling the large glass for the windows and cabinetry. Contractors will come through me to get their volunteers. They shouldn't take anyone from your crew without a reason directed from me. If there are no questions, let's get out there and build Eddie and Jody their cabin."

The logs to the cabin had been marked and numbered and the entire structure would be put together like a giant set of Lincoln Logs and a detailed paint by number set. The blueprints were in a large book binder that took up all the space on a picnic table in the contractor's office.

When the crew quit for lunch, the top of the knoll had been scraped away and the foundation of the cabin was ready for the concrete and rock crew. A crew of Shoshones from Three Forks came over and had a large barbeque going full blast. The smoke lightly filled the area around the construction site, dancing with the dust that was raised above the Gallatin County soil. The smell of barbeque seemed to rest on every light finger of smoke. The women who accompanied their husbands had joined Kathy and Susie in making some of the salads, desserts and coffee for those who drank it, as well as the chilling of ice water and sodas for those who preferred them. The smell of baked goods no longer was contained to the kitchen area and soon found its way out onto the wraparound porch of the house.

Kathy nudged Susie and commented, "According to my watch, it took nearly an hour and a half to feed the crew at noon." As she motioned out the window, she added, "And look at those men. They finished eating early and are gathered in the shade waiting for their crew chief before they go back to work."

Susie replied, "They sure ate. The work they did made them plenty hungry." Then she laughed before adding, "My Shoshone brothers can make the meat, corn and beans taste pretty good."

When supper time came a short time before sunset, the excavating had been completed. The ground was scattered with material for each of the five projects which had been going on at the same time. One of the crews was assigned work on the middle of the cabin, while the others worked on their portion of the cabin. The material had been systematically laid out for the next day's work.

With each day's work came new challenges and the volunteer work force began to develop a growing pride. The cabin began to take shape and rise above the Montana soil. It was not only going to be a cabin, but a magnificent structure that contained an architectural design unmatched by current home building. A beautiful home was about to be presented to Eddie and Jody. The cabin would show the pride and workmanship of those who cared for someone, who had made them proud.

It had been an exhausting time for most of the volunteers who hadn't worked this hard for some time. They knew it was a surprise for the young couple who deserved the support from his home community. It was their way of saying thanks and the giving of their gift of time as a wedding present would certainly be appreciated.

With the cabin nearing completion, most of the subcontractors left the job site, but the volunteers who had worked so hard remained behind waiting for the happy couple. They were joined by others who had worked earlier on the cabin, but had to return to their homes or farms out of necessity.

Sixteen days had elapsed from the first gouge mark made in the knoll to a finished cabin of grand design. The next two days was filled with putting the finishing touches on the interior such as rugs, furniture, dishes, appliances, bedroom suits and coordinated linens. The exterior work included planting shrubbery and cleaning up from the construction process. The construction of the cabin was completed two days before Eddie and Jody were scheduled to return from their honeymoon. The remaining touch-ups on the cabin's interior took them up to the day before.

CHAPTER 13

A Gift From Many – Faith And Summer Camp – 1968

With the many miles they had covered during their honeymoon behind them, it would soon come to an end. Eddie drove Jody's deep blue Chevy Malibu with creamy white vinyl interior displaying Texas license plates off the interstate in Bozeman and onto the road leading to the homestead. A few miles to the north, they took a left turn that led them down an improved gravel road to the Weismann main house. They were followed by Teddy and Bird Song Olsen in a truck pulling an enclosed Calico trailer with a pair of quarter horses. Close behind Ted and Margaret Olsen drove their truck with four brood mares in a Powderhorn Ranch stock trailer.

The banner above the main gate said it all: 'WELCOME HOME'. Each post was decorated with a small staff flying the American flag.

Jody said, "Now if that isn't something. Someone was very thoughtful."

Eddie smiled and said, "Wonder who went to all that trouble?"

"I think it's wonderful," Jody added. "The folks up this way are sure nice and they seem to extend themselves to make others welcome."

When the car topped a rise in the road, they looked down upon the homestead. Eddie said, "What in the world?" What they saw left Jody speechless as well.

It looked as if there wouldn't be a parking space for them when they got there. Tractor trailer rigs, flatbed trailers, construction equipment, campers, fifth wheels, tents and a variety of automobiles that took on the appearance of a large dealership's stockpile were filling the yard. A large group of people gathered near Mr. Weismann's house, as if a county fair was taking place.

When Eddie pulled the car to a stop, he recognized a lot of the crowd. Turning to Jody he said, "Most of these folks are from my hometown."

Eddie stepped out of the car and opened the passenger's side for Jody to exit. There were cheers from the crowd accompanied with applause, hooting and hollering a big Montana welcome.

Gun and Susie remained on the porch of his home, while Edward and Kathy made their way to the new arrivals. Edward bellowed, "Welcome home you two, it's sure good to see you." He hugged Jody briefly and patted his son on the shoulders.

Eddie said, "You all will have to excuse me for a couple of minutes, I need to help with the horses that Teddy and his father brought up this way." He headed for the corral at the far end of the yard where the trailer had been backed up to a gate, near a loading shoot. Edward could be seen grabbing at the belt loops on his hips to give his pants a quick hike, as he tried to keep stride for stride with his son.

Kathy grabbed Jody and hugged her saying, "I bet you're exhausted from that long trip?"

"It has been a whirlwind of events," Jody replied. "From the day I retired, we've been traveling one direction and then another. We had a beautiful honeymoon and to come back to this, goodness it looks as if most of the folks from Eddie's hometown are here."

"Who are those folks that came in behind you?" Kathy asked.

With excitement marking her face, Jody smiled and said, "We stopped off and saw Teddy and Autumn Song Olsen in Powderhorn, Colorado for a couple of days. When we went to leave, Teddy and his father hooked up the trailers to the back of their trucks and followed us with two beautiful saddle horses and some broodmares."

When Eddie, his father, Teddy and his family arrived at the porch, they were in a festive mood. Eddie looked at his father and asked once more, "Ok, now that we are back at the ranch, will you please tell me what is going on."

Gun reached up and began pulling a cord that was attached to a bell off to the side of the house. As the bell rang out, people from around the barbeque area, the trailers and tents made their way to the Weismann house.

When they had arrived, Edward stood on the edge of the porch and said to the crowd, "My son and his wife are wondering why we are here, should I tell them?"

The roar of "Yes," came from the crowd. Edward turned to Eddie and Jody and saying, "The town folks didn't have time to shop for your wedding present a while back. So, we all got together with Gun and we had your first house built. If the both of you will look right over yonder, there she is."

Gun added, "You both can get a bite of barbeque first, the Shoshone are responsible for all the fine food, then we can all head over to the cabin."

The latest arrivals were placed at the head of the line. The food was served up with a choice of drinks that had been cooling in a metal water trough loaded with ice. They ate and when it appeared that all were through, they gathered, ready to make the short walk to the cabin.

When they arrived at the cabin, Pastor Waters, the Methodist minister from Eddie's hometown stepped forward along with the Shoshone religious elder from the Three Forks area. Gun spoke from his wheelchair, "Eddie and Jody, it is my privilege to deed you both five acres of land that sits on the old homestead, as your wedding present." as he held out the deed for the land.

Edward spoke up before Eddie or Jody had a chance to say a word. "The fine folks from your hometown have gathered together with us to complete this place. While you two were out celebrating, through their work, contributions and knowledge, along with a whole lot of muscle, we raised this cabin from good old Montana soil, to what you see today. It's their way of giving you both a great wedding present for your time in the military and what you both have endured over time. Your friend Teddy and his family knew what was going on here in Montana, but they couldn't be here. You two had planned to visit them, so they have added the horses they brought up from Colorado."

Eddie and Jody stood stunned at what was to be their new home and from the love of the people in Montana. The design and style of architecture marked the valley with a stunning jewel of a home. Jody waved her hand to some of the folks and mouthed a thank you. Eddie raised his voice to express his feelings, "We are thankful for this awesome gift." The crowd began whooping and hollering best wishes.

When the noise began to fade, Edward held his hands up to quiet the crowd and said, "Son, there is someone who you haven't seen in a long time and he has something for the both of you."

171

The door to the cabin opened and out walked Danny Doyle. The two men embraced for a moment before Danny said, "I'd like to present to you both, a set of keys to the cabin. I may have been the general contractor, but it was put together with the love of all these folks gathered here today."

Edward pointed out, "The cabin is based on those crude drawings you sketched out a long time back."

The crowd erupted with a lot of cheers and happy comments before Eddie looked upon the crowd once more and said, "We will always know of the love it took to build this home. Jody and I are so blessed."

Following the comments, the house was blessed by Pastor Waters, who spoke with a booming voice so that he could be heard by those in the rear of the crowd, as he offered up his prayer. "Lord Jesus, we are gathered here today to honor Eddie and Jody Day for their time in the military and offer them this home as a wedding present. The tragedies within the Korean conflict tore two families apart and allowed another to begin anew. As a loving Christian community, every congregation has joined together over these past few days to erect this lovely home. Bless their marriage and bless this home, because it was built with love. Amen."

The religious elder from the Shoshone people near Three Forks stepped forward wearing traditional attire and in his native tongue began chanting. He went about the exterior of the cabin blessing it and the ground on which it was built. When he had finished, he stepped back and nodded slightly to Eddie and Jody. There was silence that began to grow over the homestead. The crowd was still and the soft wind began to carry choir voices so that they could be heard by those gathered, as if an ancestral hand quelled any interference. Their voices would be heard. The many Shoshone that were present had joined Susie, Shad and Kim Red Cloud as they sang 'The Heart's Friend (Shoshone Love Song)'. They sang in their native tongue before they sang in English.

There was a brief moment of silence before all those gathered applauded. Jody turned to Eddie softly saying, "How sweet. This is so wonderful."

Pastor Waters spoke up once more, "My friends, just a reminder we'll have church services tomorrow at 10:00 A.M. near the barbeque area. We'll let the newlyweds tour their home now. Those who wish to join us are cordially invited."

Most of those gathered returned to the barbeque area to visit, while others went to their tent or trailers before joining others. Several joined the tour of the cabin, to be near the newlyweds.

Eddie and Jody entered the cabin and were awesomely struck by the openness of the halls and ceiling. The window glass allowed the scenic beauty of the valley, hills and mountain range to be seen from the interior. When they reached the center of the cabin, Eddie stood in the center of the structure awed by what he was seeing. It made no difference what direction he was looking, at the end of each hall was the great outdoors. The height of the two-story deep walls of the cabin allowed all of Gallatin County to come in and surround him. Where the halls came together in the middle of the house, an abbreviated octagon made the central room. A large fireplace was at one end, the opposite, shelving for books and memorabilia. The other walls across from each other were stairs leading to the upstairs master bedroom. He held on to Jody, as they pivoted around in the center of the cabin. Directly overhead was a chandelier that marked the center of the house. Penetrating an opening from the room above, it was attached to the upper peak of the cabin nearly three stories up.

Edward said, "You mentioned a while back you wanted a room with no walls, if that was at all possible,"

Eddie said, "It pretty well comes as close to satisfying that dream as I could have ever hoped for."

Those touring the house were taken into the spacious kitchen-dining area. The three other equally spacious rooms on the ground floor were the utility room and two guest bedrooms. Each room had large glass windows that allowed the outside in. When they climbed the stairs, they found themselves in an enormous master bedroom with glass windows in four directions to allow a panoramic view of the outside world. Above their heads at the peak of the ceiling they could see where the large chandelier was attached. It hung down to penetrate a circular opening in the master bedroom and illuminated the main floor. A decorated wooden railing surrounded the six-foot circular opening. The four rooms upstairs that touched the master bedroom were equal in size with two windows in each room. The second floor was an open-aired master bedroom with a master bath located in one of the spaces. The other two open spaces were designed with ample closet space, one for Eddie and the other for Jody. The fireplace on the main floor continued up to the master bedroom, where an additional fireplace was located in a library setting. The master bedroom was simply huge and spacious with full bath and shower with twin sinks.

Jody said, "My goodness, they have even placed linens and quilts on the beds. Everything is furnished. This is beyond what I could have ever hoped or dreamed for."

Eddie said, "You're so right about that."

There was a long sigh, as Jody thought back on her time overseas, "It's sad that those two children I left behind in their war-torn country don't have a bed like this, let alone a decent home to go to every night."

Eddie cupped his palms around her shoulders and held her at arm's length looking into her face. "Sounds like you grew attached to them and miss having them around?"

"I miss them very much," she replied. "They were half starved when a patrol brought them in. The hospital basically took the responsibility of caring for them. It was determined that their parents had been executed by the Viet Cong because they had helped our troops out near their village. I cried the day I had to leave them behind. I guess I grew attached to them while they were on the compound and underfoot."

Eddie asked, "Is there anything you can do from here, like checking on them?"

"I guess I could write a letter to the hospital. I'll do that later. I was just momentarily touched by what has been given to us. I'll be okay."

Eddie smiled and said, "We'll talk about this later, when we have some time to talk in depth. Right now, let's join the others and try to thank each and every one personally. I feel so overwhelmed by such a gift. I find it a bit hard to put into words exactly how I feel and how to say thanks for such an awesome gesture. I'm sure you feel the same way."

The rest of the day was centered near the barbeque where several tables had been set up. An area was set aside for the band from Bozeman to set up their equipment. They would entertain into the later hours. The music would be country and there would be dancing on the grass or in the parking area where some of the loose gravel was swept back to the side.

When the sun began to fade in the west behind the rugged snowcapped Rocky Mountains, the yard light was turned on illuminating the yard. The sky above the homestead began to show the beauty of its Montana sunsets as the outline of the terrain changed in hue before slipping into the darkness of the valley. The sunset began to fade in brilliance before surrendering to the night when the heavens began to fill with stars.

The band began to play, Eddie and Jody were encouraged to be the first to begin the dance. It was an extended dance with the music playing on and on. The crowd entered the dance area as couples and they would tag the newly married couple. The wives would dance with Eddie and the men would dance with Jody, until the next tag. Each couple had a brief time with the happy newlyweds. As each couple was tagged, they would find their mate and dance along with the music, adding to the crowd dancing in the yard.

When the music for the second dance began, Eddie and Jody tried to coax Gun and Susie onto the dance area. Gun was in his wheelchair and Jody held his hand and swayed to the music, while Eddie and Susie danced briefly. A couple of moments later, they separated and Susie turned to dance with Gun. Eddie and Jody were off dancing to the rhythm of a two-step. Before the tune came to an end, they could see Susie wheeling a smiling Gun off to the side. The wheelchair was turned so that Gun could see those having a good time.

Deep into the night, the crowd began to dwindle, as so many had worked from early morning. As they prepared to step into the night on their way to their tent or trailer, they would call out, "good night", and wave their hands in the air.

When the dancing came to an end, Eddie and Jody invited Teddy with Autumn Song and Ted with Margaret Olsen to sleep in the cabin. Their guests would sleep downstairs, while they slept upstairs in their master bedroom.

~ ~ ~ ~

Morning came early and the initiation of the kitchen area began to take place. Laughter began to fill the kitchen area as mild teasing was given out in varied amounts. Sliding eyes accompanied remarks intended for one or both newlyweds. The brunt of the jovial comments went from one to the other. The men found their place around the large rectangular wooden table, reflecting its glossy finish over a beautiful grain pattern. Eddie began to find his voice in returning a quip here or there.

The lighthearted conversation was new to Jody, but she managed to unleash a volley of defensive comments, drawing laughter from the women at her side. No mean-spirited jabs, just great early morning conversation before they talked of weather and current trends. Within minutes, the women had prepared bacon and eggs with a side of biscuits and gravy served up hot.

A quiet moment fell upon the group moments before Eddie said grace. With a coffee pot that suddenly became empty, a second pot was put on to brew while they ate. Breakfast was at a leisurely pace, but not a moment was wasted. Pastor Waters was to conduct an abbreviated church service near the barbeque area, where most of the seating was available before the crowd prepared to make their journey back home.

When the morning church services came to an end, Eddie addressed those gathered and expressed their deep appreciation for the hard work and gift of the cabin, "Jody and I are so very grateful for your love and hard work. May God bless each and every one of you and protect you on your way home. Please keep in touch and if you're ever up around this way, feel free to drop by."

The morning services concluded, Eddie and Jody stood with Pastor Waters. Those who had gathered passed by for a handshake or a hug and a last-minute word of congratulations and encouragement. Kathy and Edward were near the end of the group, both with the intent of passing out last minute motherly or fatherly advice to each before they would return home.

When Sarah and Eric approached with Mari and Kari, Jody spoke up, "I certainly hope you both will keep in touch. I would enjoy getting to know the both of you better. And as for the girls, I hope we can see them often."

Eric smiled and nodded, while Sarah gathered tears from her eyes, as she smiled and said, "I'm so glad you feel that way, I wasn't sure how we were going to work through the odd situation."

Jody said, "Sarah, war is unkind to those who serve and especially to those who are left behind. Let's not let those circumstances shortchange the girls. There is room for us to be friends." There were hugs and handshakes and a sweet display of emotions from Mari and Kari, as they embraced their father. Then they turned and lavished Jody with nearly the same amount of affection.

The crowd that had filled the homestead was gone long enough for the dust that had been kicked up on the road in their departure to finally settle. Family and friends had gone home. The Shoshone who had worked so hard to feed those who came to work had neatly cleaned the area around the barbeque area and the homestead was beginning to return to normal.

With supper finished and the dishes behind them, Eddie and Jody sat in the center of their cabin with their guests from Colorado near them. The sun began to drop in the western skies, behind a thin layer of clouds. The beauty of this sunset would gradually take place. The silver rim on the overcast skies marked the demarcation of the outflow stratus. It cut across the heavens allowing clear skies below its lining. When the sun dropped from behind the stratus, the blue gradually turned to gray and then to lavender. There was a burst of vibrant reddish glow that marked the sky. When the sun began to drop behind the mountains, the silver lining marking the top of the clouds took on a new color. When the sun fell behind the distant horizon of the darkened Rocky Mountain silhouette, the glow turned into a pastel pink and the clouds beneath the stratus showed reflections of the sunset that lightly touched their peaks. The sky was filled with color, as if a giant paint brush stroked a light blue canvas by the Master's hand.

"Oh, Eddie," Jody uttered, "it's beautiful. Those windows allow us to see quite a sight."

Autumn Song added, "It is a perfect way to end the day, a soft and wonderful sight to hold in your heart."

Eddie said, "Every sunset we see together will be special, as only the Montana skies can display."

The serene moment was interrupted with laughter and opposition, defending and comparing the sunsets in Colorado. Events in the past brought them together; now that kindred friendship grew into a deeper bonding by their happiness.

~ ~ ~ ~

When breakfast was completed the following morning, the men had bragged on the abundance of tasty food. It would keep them fit until noon. They backed their chairs away from the table and symbolically wiped at their chops or patted their belly, moments before they stood. Jody, Margaret and Autumn Song looked on to see the three men pleasingly satisfied and ready for the day.

Ted and Teddy joined Eddie on their way to see Gun and discuss additional business. When they arrived, Gun was in the mood for some fresh air and asked that they discuss their proposal outside. The four men made their way to the corral and casually went about making themselves comfortable. Gun looked up from his wheelchair and said, "Ok gentlemen what's on your minds?"

Eddie replied, "Gun, Ted and Teddy have their horse operation in Powderhorn, Colorado and I'd like to see if you're in agreement to some changes here on the homestead that would allow my operation to be a reflection of theirs?"

Gun smiled and asked, "How so?"

Ted spoke up and said, "Gun, I started the operation I have some eighteen years ago. Along the way I had to make some changes in the shape and purpose of the corral. In other words, I made it multipurpose. The corral needs metal fence dividers. These sections can be adjusted to a need on any given day. The configuration would aid in the showing of livestock or horses. For the convenience of guests that will eventually come to the ranch, we will provide a covered seating section to protect them from the elements while looking at what is offered. What we're looking at is a proposal, with your approval, to set up the corral for visitors to come to this ranch instead of Eddie having to truck his stock elsewhere. I believe the move will be widely accepted by western ranchers in the state coming here to buy and sell. It will become a focal point for buyers and sellers and will greatly put Eddie and you in a position to gain monetarily. This would allow you both the opportunity to purchase top stock that will be brought here to be bought by you or sold to others." He presented his proposal and felt it was time to see what Gun had to say. He leaned back against the corral fence and hooked the right heel of his boot on the bottom rung of the fence and waited.

Gun smiled and said, "And just how much is this going to cost me?"

Eddie spoke up and answered as best he could, "They had me do some research with what has been offered in the western part of the state. I have talked with a large number of ranchers with high quality breeding stock and those with registered and top-quality horses. They say something like this is needed, above what any of the local stockyards can provide. They are interested in bringing in the high-dollar buyers to one central location instead of using the local stockyards. A top-quality operation will also cut down on the possibility of diseases and will expose the buyers to only the top line of stock."

Gun looked on with an inquisitive nature and asked again, "How much?"

Ted replied, "Eddie needs your permission to make the changes and for you to realize that in the future, there will be a lot of folks visit and a good number of ranchers bringing in stock for a two- or three-day event on your homestead. The cost is something me and my son will help Eddie with. Unless you see that this is a profitable venture and you want to help out, that is a horse of a different color and is something you and Eddie will need to deal with. If you have any reservations, I'd like to invite you and Eddie to the ranch in Colorado next month. You'll see our operation and what you and Eddie may have to deal with here in Montana."

Gun looked at Eddie and said, "I'd like that and if I like what I see, you'll have my total support."

The rest of the morning was spent on talking of one subject and then another. But before long, the subject of fishing came up and before the noon hour, all four men were on the bank of the Gallatin River casting a line in hopes of catching the first of many trout.

The women were each notified of the men's intentions and they were left behind, making a snack lunch to take to the men on the riverbank, when the time came. When Jody and her guests left the house, they passed by and asked Susie to join them. They went to feed the men, knowing a fisherman's luck depended on not having a hungry gut. There was laughter between them and with the men when they arrived.

~ ~ ~ ~

When the following morning came, Ted and Teddy went about hitching their empty stock trailers and bringing them close to the cabin before breakfast. After the great breakfast Jody had prepared, they left the Day cabin and headed down the road for Powderhorn.

It was mid-morning when Susie came by the cabin. Eddie had answered the door. Half out of breath, she explained, "I need to talk to Jody!"

Eddie had her come in and called out for Jody, who was in the kitchen. When Jody arrived Susie said, "We got a call from Minneapolis and Gun has an appointment in a couple of days. Can I ask you to check in on Gun this afternoon and make sure he takes his medications? I need to make arrangements for my children to be in Three Forks with their

179

grandparents while I'm gone. I'll take them with me. I should be home later tonight and we'll be leaving early in the morning."

Jody said, "I sure will. When should I check in on him?"

"He'll need his medicine about three and then there are a couple of pills just before supper."

Jody replied, "Susie, you go and do what you have to with your family. Eddie and I will visit Gun and have him here for supper. When you get back, come by and visit for a spell, before you take him home, ok?"

~ ~ ~ ~

Later that evening, the two Vietnamese children were discussed in great detail. Eddie learned for the first time the depth of Jody's involvement with the children, as she served as Director of Nurses while in Vietnam. When it appeared she had said all there was to say about the two, Eddie suggested, "Why not write to whoever is in charge of the hospital and check on them. My understanding is that President Eisenhower has made it possible for adopting Vietnamese children, if this is something we'd like to do."

Tears filled her eyes and she asked, "Would you like me to check in on that, too?"

Eddie reached out and pulled her to him. He wrapped his arms around her and kissed her on the forehead before whispering into her ear, "If they are as precious to you as I believe they are, I want to see you happy and I support you one hundred percent."

They talked at length of the pros and cons of adoption and if this would be the right move for their happiness, as well as the children's. When they had considered all aspects of such a move, Jody said, "I'll write a letter tonight and check on them. If they're still there and okay, I'll write our intentions and see what happens."

Eddie said, "You have my blessings. Just let me know what I can do, to help make this become a reality."

~ ~ ~ ~

The following morning as dawn was breaking, the valley was quiet. The dust that had risen into the air was beginning to settle a considerable distance behind the car that Susie was driving. She was taking Gun to the

180

airport for a flight out of town for his medical appointment. He would return home in time to visit the Olsen operation in Colorado next month.

The builders had long gone home and when they did, they had left the area as clean as when they had found it. Eddie and Jody had the beauty of the homestead and the entire Gallatin valley to enjoy for themselves. It was a lovely day, and for the first time since their honeymoon, they found themselves alone to enjoy life to its fullest.

Standing at the doorway of the eastern wing, they watched the entrance of a newborn sun, as the sky changed colors in the east. The mountains to the east were beginning to lose their dark shape replaced with snowcapped peaks and an array of color from the trees and vegetation that grew up to the timberline.

Jody sighed and said reflectively, "Back home in Missouri, my father would call that an Osage sunrise."

Eddie looked at her for a moment and replied, "It is beautiful, but I reckon the Montana Indians might call it something else. I've never read where the Osage made it this far west. If you think the sunrise is wonderful, wait until you get to see the many sunsets that paint the Montana skies."

She looked deep into his eyes and whispered, "If I can spend my time with you for every sunset, I'm sure they will all be wonderful."

They stood side by side with an arm wrapped around the other's waist. It was a time to soak up the beauty of the land and to appreciate and feel their love for each other. They were truly happy. They would have the rest of the day to celebrate their marriage and a new beginning for both of them. While the Korean conflict had taken away from both of them, it had also been instrumental in bringing the two of them together. From the east wing of the cabin, they would enjoy the sun rises. But the traditional view as Eddie had suggested would be sitting in the rockers in the center of their home and watching the many varied beautiful sunsets that would close out each day.

When the sun poked its rays above the mountain peaks, they had found their way to the kitchen.

Jody was in the process of whipping up a pancake mixture and asked, "Do you want eggs and bacon with your flapjacks?"

"That sure sounds good. I'll fix the coffee," Eddie replied.

Breakfast was a leisurely affair with nibbles of food and a sip of coffee with lighthearted conversation. They expressed their love for each other and made plans for the day. She had her ideas on changing some of the interior of the cabin. He had to make plans for leaving the homestead the next day to visit both veterinarians he would be working with in Bozeman.

~ ~ ~ ~

When mid-morning came, the telephone rang. Much to their surprise, it wasn't from the veterinarians, but from Montana State University in Bozeman calling for Jody.

When she hung up the telephone, she turned to face Eddie with a big smile on her face. "The university is offering me a position in the school of nursing as a lecturer in emergency triage. The course will be covering a wide range of injuries that may happen on anything from a trail ride, to hunting and accidents around the water. I'm so excited. They are also offering a certified emergency medical course for hunting lodge personnel, and for hunters who use pack animals. It will be ideal for me. My work will be on Monday, Wednesday and Friday."

Eddie smiled and joined her in her excitement, "That will give you two days during the week and your weekends off. It fits in quite well."

She said, "I'm so glad. We'll get it all moving in a good direction before long, I just know things will work out."

"I'll be on the road a lot for the next couple of weeks buying horses during the day, but I'll be home at night," Eddie said. "I'll try to be home by sunset. That way we can enjoy the heavenly display together."

~ ~ ~ ~

It was nearly three weeks after Jody had mailed her letter to the Commanding Officer of the hospital in Vietnam when the phone rang. She picked up the receiver and said, "Hello."

The voice on the other end was the military base phone operator of the MARS station at Malmstrom Air Force Base in Great Falls. After realizing it was Jody on the line, he said, "Mrs. Day, I have Vietnam on the other line. I will patch you through, but I'll have to listen to your conversation so I can switch things to satellite. When you are through talking each time, say 'OVER'. There will be a short pause and then you should be able to hear them." After confirming she knew the procedures, the operator went about getting the MARS call lined up with the land line from Vietnam to Malmstrom and on to Bozeman.

Eddie had entered the cabin in time to hear Jody saying 'OVER', for the first time and found the one-sided conversation interesting and a bit on the comical side.

When the phone call was completed, Jody turned to Eddie with joy. "The children are okay. The hospital staff has checked on the adoption procedures over there. They are doing some work on that end and we'll have some to do on this end. The C.O. is recommending approval and it looks like a done deal on their end. Eddie, I'm so happy."

Eddie grabbed Jody and kissed her before asking, "What's left for us to do now?'

She said, "We'll get a packet of papers in a week or so with instructions on what we need to do to qualify. I'm so happy! The C.O. said the children are aware of our attempt to adopt them and are happy that 'Nurse Colonel with soft eyes' wants to bring them to America."

~ ~ ~ ~

When Gun and Susie returned from his medical treatments in Minnesota, they made plans with Eddie and Jody to make a hasty trip to Powderhorn, Colorado. They wanted to see the horse operation the Olsen's had put together. Eddie was sure that Gun would be interested in the local expansion once he saw how efficient Ted and Teddy's operation had become. They would make the trip over the weekend, avoiding interference with Jody's schedule at the university. Classes were due to resume on January 5, 1970, after the semester break.

Jody informed Susie, "I know there are times when you need some personal time off. I'd be willing to look in on Mr. Weismann and handle the medications should the need arise. I only have Tuesday and Thursdays where I'm not committed, if that would help?" Susie got excited over the offer and Gun smiled at the gracious offer as well.

~ ~ ~ ~

When they returned from Colorado, Gun was excited and encouraged Eddie to expand his operation with his blessings and an agreement to help finance some of the changes. There was excitement on the homestead and word quickly spread from Bozeman and across the state of the newly formed enterprise. Ranchers and specialized breeders were looking forward to such an operation and the word soon spilled out across the border into neighboring states. Horse breeders and their associations began using the facilities on the homestead. Eddie's prior planning was beginning to show promise, as it brought ranchers, breeders and other groups together.

While on the homestead, Jody would spare Susie a day or two once a month looking after Gun. So that she could do the necessary things with her children. It was a hectic schedule, but everything seemed to work out. The two households were bonding together on the homestead. Gun claimed this was the happiest he had been in years. Susie cared for Gun and when she needed time off, Jody spared her. Gun enjoyed seeing Eddie build a wonderful business and they were as close as brothers.

Eddie and Jody became involved in church and before long, Gun and Susie joined in as well. From their interest with the youth and the youth ministries program at the church, the Little Britches Riding For Jesus was formed. The youth group was affiliated with the church but would meet at the corral and arena area on the homestead two Saturdays a month for fellowship and learning life skills.

Mari and Kari would visit and help out along with Susie's children, Shad and Kim Two-Clouds. Some Saturdays after a short horseback ride, the children would gather on the banks of the Gallatin River and spend some time fishing.

When the girls visited, they had their own bedrooms on the main floor of the cabin. They knew if the adoption came to be, the rooms would become someone else's. Jody encouraged Mari and Kari to modify the décor of their bedroom when they were visiting. Eddie enjoyed their visits, cherishing and treasuring every moment. Their marriage was accepted by the girls and most evident was their bonding as a family unit. They loved Jody and she fit in so well.

CHAPTER 14

The Adoption Of Two - Horse Operation Expands - 1969

Eddie and Jody waited patiently for the Western airlines flight to land mid-day in Billings. Onboard were their adopted children, Hanh and Lien. The two Vietnamese children were orphaned because their parents were executed some four years ago. The Days stood before the massive glass window that allowed those inside the terminal to look upon the runway and see the vast amount of open prairie land, as far as the eye could see. Hot summer temperatures had been unkind to the local vegetation, giving the sage brush a light gray cast in color. The cheat and prairie grasses were dry and yellow, parched but satisfied to be a backdrop to the asphalt runway. The first touch of winter had left light skiffs of snow surviving in the shadows of the sage brush. Winter was late this year and the depth of snow that was needed across the farming belt was taking its time getting there.

The announcement of the flight's arrival had no sooner been completed when the thunderous roar of the plane filled the terminal. It touched down on the runway only to be diminished in size and volume, as it used up the remaining portion of the tarmac. Within a few moments, the plane taxied close to the terminal and the ground crew went about maneuvering the aluminum passenger ramp into place.

Passengers that had visited relatives in the Billings area were now lining up to board their flight and go back to where they had ventured from over the Christmas holiday.

Eddie had been holding Jody's nervous hand and suddenly felt a squeeze before she said, "I can hardly wait to see them. The suspense is getting to me."

He smiled and answered in a reassuring manner, "It certainly won't be long now."

To their surprise, several people left the plane, and then there seemed to be no one. A few moments lapsed before a stewardess stepped into the doorway with hand luggage in one hand and in the other was the hand of little Lien. She was bundled up to protect her from the expected cold weather. Directly behind them was another stewardess assisting Hanh. He was in his winter jacket and appeared along with his carry-on. A stewardess led him down the ramp with a helping hand and the remaining carry-on luggage.

The two stewardesses with the pair in custody no sooner entered the terminal, when Lien and Hanh broke free of their charges and rushed into the waiting arms of Jody. The stewardesses were right behind them with their arms full of carry-on luggage, while attempting to keep the two escapees in sight.

Jody held out her arms and gathered both of them in together with a hug. She was trying to reassure Lien who was breaking down with tears of happiness and Hanh who was chattering about how happy he was to see her. "Everything is going to be ok. I'm so glad to see the two of you," and the comforting went on for a spell.

Eddie saw that the stewardesses had papers for him to sign off on as to the custody in flight to clear the airlines. He offered, "Is there something I need to sign, while the wife is busy with them?"

There were a couple of forms to complete giving his whole name, the date and time and his signature. When this was completed, one of the stewardesses said, "This is their luggage from the cabin of the plane. They have additional items you will need to claim in the baggage room. There are three claim stubs attached to the receipts."

"We thank you for watching over them on the way here," Eddie expressed his feelings, unsure what else to add.

The other stewardess said, "They are sure well mannered. You have a quiet one and one that is full of conversation. We have heard of your wife's duties while in Vietnam. We wish the both of you the very best. These are two very lucky children."

Eddie said, "Thank you and Happy New Year." The stewardesses smiled and were on their way back to their duties on the plane.

When Eddie turned around to see Jody and the children, he was met with a young man who was sticking out his hand for an introductory handshake. As they did so, Hanh asked, "I shine your boots, cowboy?"

"Not today but are we glad to see the both of you. Now you're Hanh and this little cutie must be none other than your sister Lien. My name is Eddie."

When Eddie was introduced to Lien he said, "I am so proud that you have made this journey and it is nice to meet you." They all went to the baggage room and picked up the rest of their luggage and ventured into the parking lot. The contents were placed into the trunk of the Chevrolet Malibu that now displayed Montana license plates. The items that didn't fit in the trunk had to be placed in the back seat between Jody and Lien along with one box that rested between Eddie and his son in the front seat.

On their way down off the rims in Billings, Eddie pulled the car into the first McDonalds he found, on 27th Street. They went to the drive-up window and ordered what they were hungry for. The transaction was watched closely by the children.

A few minutes later, they were headed down the highway in an easterly direction toward his parents' farm. Eddie wanted to get there before dark. Hanh was in the front riding shotgun, a new term that seemed to hold importance. He was smiling and had his arm resting on the armrest, as if that was the most natural place for it to be, while he looked out the windshield and over at Eddie quite often.

Jody directed the conversation and would keep each of the children responding to the many questions. Time had passed by so quickly and the miles seemed to have gone unnoticed. They were nearing the turnoff to the lane leading to the farm.

When they arrived at the farm, the yard light was attempting to illuminate the yard. The sun was slowly dropping behind the western horizon. Edward and Kathy were in the yard when the car pulled to a stop. Before anyone got their feet on the ground outside the car, Edward said, "It's about time you got here, your mother has been pacing the floor in anticipation."

"Don't you pay any attention to him, Jody," Kathy interjected. "He's the one who has been pacing the floor and causing me more concern than I should have to put up with."

When the family began entering the gate to the fenced yard, Kathy said, "And just who do we have as our guests tonight?"

Jody was all smiles as Edward came over and gave her a hug while his son explained, "This young man is Hanh, a whopping eleven, and this is his sister Lien and she is nine years old."

Edward turned loose of Jody and turned to Hanh and stuck out his hand. "I'm mighty pleased to meet you," grasping a young man's hand offered in return for a shake. Then he turned to Lien and patted her on the head and said, "I'm so glad to meet you, too." He looked into a smile that melted his heart.

Kathy gathered both of the children in with a sweeping motion of her extended arms. She pulled them together saying, "I'm so happy, what do you say we go inside for some milk and cookies?"

When Kathy stood, she wrapped her arms around Jody and whispered, "This farm isn't the same without you and now you have brought me two to spoil." When she turned to go into the house she asked, "Have you had supper yet?"

"We grabbed a burger, fries and a drink at McDonalds when we left Billings," Jody replied, "but I imagine the kids will be interested in the milk and cookies. Will the children be able to meet the girls while we're here?"

Kathy smiled and said, "They most certainly can. Mari is about to finish up her degree work and is due to graduate the end of the semester. She and Gordon Shum have something important to ask Eddie while he is here. Kari is visiting her mother and introducing her to David Hostetler and I think they're getting serious. The big news is Eric Elders has been given a position in Houston, Texas. He and Sarah will be moving in that direction before long. That is going to leave Edward and me here on the farm with just a handful of seasonal hired hands."

Eddie and Edward unloaded the car and brought the luggage into the porch, where the contents could be gone through to determine if the children had pajamas for the night. When the men got to the kitchen table, milk and cookies were already before the children.

Hanh and Lien appeared exhausted from the trip. The jet lag and the long car ride had tired them. They were tucked in early and soon found sleep for the first time in their new land. The visiting went deep into the night, before Edward moaned, "I best get some shut eye. I need to talk to the men early in the morning, before they go to work."

When morning came most everyone was around the breakfast table ready to eat. Edward could be heard moments before he came through the screen door of the porch. He had a habit of stomping his boots to rid them of any barnyard collections. When he entered the dining area, he spoke up, "Am I too late?"

Kathy said, "Wash up, we're waiting on you. When you get to the table, you can say grace."

For Hanh and Lien, saying grace was not a practice they had been introduced to in Vietnam. When they were in the mess tent at the hospital compound, they grabbed their tray and got in line. After collecting their food, they went directly to a table and began eating. Jody was sitting between the pair and softly said, "Before we eat, we say grace. Here on this farm, that privilege is for the man of the house. When we get to our home, that privilege is for your new father." The children waited with anticipation.

The Saturday breakfast was nearing an end when there was a knock at the screen door. It suddenly opened and in walked Mari, Kari and the men in their lives. They went to the living room, deposited four small packages and joined the others in the dining area. Gordon and David gathered up additional chairs and wedged them in where they could find adequate space. Mari and Kari had gone to the kitchen counter where the coffee pot was and poured several cups of coffee. They made sure to take a few cinnamon rolls from the back of the stove, placed them on a plate and brought them to the table.

When the girls joined the family, Eddie introduced them to Hanh and Lien. He told the children that the girls were their sisters.

Hanh spoke up and asked, "They are our American sisters?"

"That is for real," Eddie said.

Jody spoke softly and said, "When I left Vietnam, I left my heart there, because that is where you two were. When I came back to America, I married a wonderful man. Before we married, he already had two daughters. Now they become your sisters."

"Now I have a brother and a little sister," Kari proclaimed.

Then Jody spoke again, to reassure the children, "In Vietnam your mother and father were heroes for what they had done. The Viet Cong took them away from the two of you and the hospital group began to take care of you. You must always remember your parents were very special. They are to be remembered with honor as your Vietnamese mother and father. In Vietnam, they would say that your parents are Number One. Eddie and I talked about you two being without parents and we decided to adopt you both. We are your American mother and father and the girls will be your sisters."

Lien smiled and said, "I like them both. They have smiles on their faces." With that, there was laughter marking a pleasant time to get acquainted.

Kathy spoke up and said, "Jody, that was so sweet. Now I get to add something. Hanh and Lien, that makes me your American Grandma and he is your American Grandpa." as she pointed towards Edward.

When the laughter settled down, Mari was holding Gordon Shum's hand as he cleared his throat. While looking at Eddie he said, "Mr. Day, I would like very much to have Mari's hand in marriage." His words seemed to be choked off. Then again, he had said all that was necessary; now he would wait for an answer.

Eddie looked at Gordon for a long moment and then an extended glance at Mari. He looked at his wife and said, "Jody, I need to talk with you in the other room." The dining room seemed to take on a quiet tone, as the two of them got up and went into the kitchen.

No sooner had Eddie and Jody cleared the doorway into the kitchen when he turned to Jody and said, "Do we give them our immediate approval or wait a few moments longer?" His question was met with a smile and for the first time, a mischievous nod. They stalled for time.

Walking slow and methodical, Eddie and Jody returned to the dining room moments later. He waited until Jody was seated before he slowly sat down, looking at both of them before focusing in on Gordon, he softly said. "We're honored that you asked! The answer however is…" following a long pause, Eddie continued, "we agree, yes you can."

There were cheers before Jody asked, "When is the happy occasion?"

Mari said, "Mom and Eric gave their blessings and we'd like to get married next month in the Methodist church, the weekend before they will be leaving for Texas." For the moment, there was talk of the pending wedding and best wishes added in alongside a bit of kidding.

Kari introduced David Hostetler and hinted of their upcoming engagement. There was a quiet time and David remained mute, thinking it best to ask for her hand at a later date instead of taking away the special moment from Mari and Gordon.

When the family left the dining room table, they went into the living room where there were several packages wrapped in colorful Christmas wrapping. It was no surprise to the others, but Hanh and Lien were excited because the packages were meant for them. When the children unwrapped the presents, there were scarves, mufflers, mittens, clothing and a doll for Lien and a radio-operated car for Hanh. Each received a small battery-operated radio for their individual listening pleasure. The family felt the mere presence of the children was their present for this day, as they had celebrated Christmas earlier.

The rest of the morning was filled with visiting and getting to know one another, after Gordon and David had been introduced to the family. But it was Hanh and Lien that remained the main topic of interest. It was mid-morning when the men took Hanh out to check on the stock and the women went into the kitchen to prepare dinner. Kathy said, "Come on, Lien, you and Grandma need to roll out some cinnamon rolls. I'll show you how I make that special treat."

~ ~ ~ ~

The following morning was Sunday and the Day families made their way to the Methodist church in town. Eddie and Jody were recognized before Hanh and Lien were introduced to the congregation. At the end of the services Mari and Gordon could be seen talking with Pastor Waters about the upcoming wedding.

Instead of returning to the farm, they ate dinner at the small diner in town. The proprietors were excited for the trade and opened one of the adjoining rooms to accommodate the entire family. At the back of the room, a tree was still decorated with lights plugged in and blinking. The rest of the room was decorated for the holidays from a banquet that had been there a few days earlier. Eddie said, "This is nice. We can eat and when we get to the farm, we'll load up and try to get home before dark."

Kathy said, "Yes, this is nice. your mother doesn't have to fix dinner for a change. I think I'm going to enjoy the meal more than the rest of you and I'm not going to order turkey!" There was a round of laughter that followed her comments.

Jody smiled and said softly, "I hope we can get home soon enough to get organized and have a good night's sleep. I have my position at the university and Eddie, you have a couple of mares to keep tabs on as they're about ready to foal."

"When you finish at the university," Eddie reminded her, "I'll meet you in town and we'll drop by the school and try to get the children enrolled. There should be ample staff available after school following the Christmas break. I'll call them for an appointment."

The visit with the family over dinner covered a variety of subjects,

191

but the main topic centered on the upcoming wedding. Eddie and family said most of their good-byes at the diner and kept their comments short. After all, they had a long drive facing them.

When they arrived at the farm, the belongings were loaded into the car and the last few words said before the long trip. Edward spoke as if the buttons on his shirt were about ready to come undone, "Hanh and Lien, I expect the two of you back this way real soon. You both have made me one proud grandpa."

The children nodded only to hear Kathy say, "I'm going to miss seeing the two of you, so come back real soon, where I can spoil you both."

There was the last round of hugs, kisses and fussing before the car made its way down the lane, headed for the highway.

~ ~ ~ ~

It wasn't quite dark when Eddie pulled the car off the highway and headed for the homestead. When they pulled up in front of the cabin, the car was quickly unloaded and the contents taken inside. The children were taken to one of the bedrooms where Hanh's belongings were left. He was in awe at the size of the room and the enormity of the bed. He stood in the center of the room and kept making a circle looking at all that was there. It was made for a boy. Hanh stood near his sister, who was quiet and almost lost for comment before she said, "There is just one bed in this room."

Jody spoke up and said, "Lien, this will be your brothers' room. The next room we see is going to be yours."

As they walked across the hall, they walked into another room the same size, where Lien was excited to see that the room was decorated with a young girl in mind. She looked the room over and stopped in the middle before she said, "I remember my home in Vietnam. It was small and could almost fit in this room. This is so large and beautiful." She walked over and touched the material on the bed before she replied, "It is so soft and the bed is so large. Not like the army cot they had me sleep on at the hospital compound."

"I hope some of those memories will become less painful in time," Jody said, as she hugged her daughter.

When they turned around, Eddie and Hanh were bringing in the last

192

of her belongings. When they left the room, they went to the center of the cabin where they could see Mother Nature at her best. Eddie had already retrieved two chairs from the kitchen and the whole family sat down to see one of the most brilliant displays in the heavens, west of the homestead.

The top of the heavens was a light blue. Looking toward the horizon, the sky had a light-yellow pastel cast. The banks of a winter thunderhead loomed off to the west and northwest. The southern side was white, with the northern side of the clouds a light purple, their bottoms a darker shade. The sun had just fallen behind the southern tip of one of the dominant thunderheads, where a burst of bright fiery orange glowed, over the soft yellow background. The small stratus of clouds was a light blue. When the sun dropped from behind the thunderhead, the color in the lines of stratus changed to a dark purple. The outline of the mountainous landscape was a dark silhouette with the sky behind it a soft orange glow. When the sun fell behind the horizon, the outline of orange behind the pines and cedars seemed to burst into a fiery orange. It resembled a forest fire of gigantic magnitude, beyond the snow-capped mountain peaks.

The heavenly display took about fifteen minutes. It left a mark on the family, because it was the first sunset, they would enjoy together under Montana skies.

Eddie said, "I hope as a family we will always be able to enjoy such a sight as we have seen."

Jody looked at the children and said, "If you two will bring your chairs back into the kitchen, I'll see what we can put on the table to satisfy the hunger in our tummies."

~ ~ ~ ~

When morning came, you didn't need to look outside twice to know it was cold. There was a touch of winter snow that had accumulated during the night. The pine branches outside the cabin did their best to hold up under the weight of the fresh snow. Jody left the homestead early and headed for her job at the university.

When Eddie was ready to check on the mares, he had the children bundled up for the cold to include overshoes. They tagged along at his side on their walk to the stables. The snow was a new experience for the children and they found a joy of being outside in the element. Eddie

193

noticed the smoke from the chimney at Gun's house, as it rose only a short distance above the roof line before it seemed to bend over and head toward the ground. In these parts, it was a clear sign that additional cold weather was on the way.

When they passed Gun's house, Shad and Kim came running down the slope of the hill to meet them. They were dressed warmly to stand the cold while they waited for the school bus that would pass by later. When they arrived their introductions were quick, "Hi, I'm Shad and this is my sister Kim." You could see their breath dance in the chilly morning air.

Eddie spoke up, "This is Hanh and over here is Lien. They arrived over the weekend and we got home late last night. By the way, are you two going to go to school today?"

"We sure are," Shad announced. "Hanh, are you going to be going to the same school as us?"

Hanh wasn't sure and looked at his new father who said, "We will be enrolling them later today. I'm not sure what classes they will be assigned."

Kim looked at Lien and said, "Do you want to make a snow angel?" Without hesitation, she plopped down on her back in the snow and began moving her arms and legs.

Lien looked at Eddie and he smiled and nodded. Lien slowly sat on the snow, then leaned backwards and made her snow angel. She got up to see if hers looked anything like Kim's. She was tickled, as her snow angel was perfect, just a bit smaller than Kim's.

Shad and Hanh looked on, not wanting to make an image in the snow and possibly look silly in front of the others on their first day of introduction.

Bright eyed, Kim asked, "After school, can you come to my house and we will play inside?"

Lien smiled and was unsure if she should agree, "If it is okay, I will come."

From the front door of Gun's house, Susie had stepped onto the porch slightly, more like half in and half out, while calling out, "You two get back in here and get the rest of your school supplies and get out there where you can catch that school bus." She waved at Eddie and called out, "I see you have your hands full."

Eddie waved back and they continued their journey to the stables, where most of the broodmares were housed. One of the stable hands was cleaning out stalls before the foreman came around. There were four other buildings with stalls that offered the same capacity and they were nearly full.

When they arrived, Eddie grabbed the large door that was on rollers and pushed it open. Once inside, he closed the door. The long building had seven stalls on each side of the passageway. There was bailed hay before each stall, along with a bucket for grain, a water bucket and various ropes and leather. Behind each door and in each stall was a horse. Most of them were mares about ready to foal. But there were a couple of yearlings that were being watched over after taking medicine. One of the stalls was empty.

Eddie entered into one of the stalls while the children stayed outside and look in. There was an older roan mare that was down. She had been a victim of rough horse play and troublesome behavior by another in the pasture weeks earlier. Now she was being watched closely in hopes she could carry the pregnancy full term. As he approached, the mare raised her head and softly nickered. He reached down and rubbed his hand on her neck before checking her more closely. "It won't be long now, girl. I'll be sitting up with you and I bet it will be sometime tonight."

Eddie looked up to see Lien looking on with interest and Hanh loaded with several questions. Upon leaving the stall, Lien grabbed his hand and said, "If it is tonight, can I be here with you to see the birth?"

Eddie said, "That might be arranged, if it is okay with your mother."

Hanh spoke up, "How many horses do you have?"

Eddie said, "I have several horses, some are for riding, some for selling and some for breeding. When you look down from our cabin, you can see some of them in the pasture to the west. Most of the broodmares I have were brought up closer to the stalls. We keep an eye on them and house those who will be delivering their foals before the others. On the northeastern part of the homestead, I have several head of registered beef cattle and a handful of bulls for breeding. They keep some of the hands around here busy. I have a big operation and I plan to have it get bigger, as time goes on. In the north pasture, I have several head of cattle and in a day or so I'll show you most of them."

Eddie was kept busy answering all the questions fired at him after leaving each stall, on his way to check on other mares. When they were through in the stables, Eddie made his way back to the cabin. Hanh and Lien trotted alongside of their father, leaving their footprints in the loose snow in a random zigzag pattern.

~ ~ ~ ~

Eddie and the children met Jody at the university, during an arranged extended noon hour and they made a quick trip to the elementary school. They talked with the principal and counselors regarding the enrollment and placement testing. They were informed that the children would be taking testing most of the week to determine what grade they would be assigned and what additional assistance they may need from the teacher of E.S.O.L. English to Speakers of Other Languages. Hanh and Lien spoke some English, but it was unclear what they could read and comprehend. They would be able to ride the school bus in with Shad and Kim Red Cloud. The counselor would be with the children during the day for testing and getting them acquainted with the school. When school was dismissed, the counselor would make sure that the children were on the right school bus. They would arrive at home with a note regarding their progress or any problems.

When they left the school, the principal said, "We'll expect to see them on the bus tomorrow."

They concurred while leaving the principal's office. Jody returned to the university and Eddie drove home with the children.

Supper had no sooner been cleared from the table, when Susie came to the cabin. She asked, "Jody, I need to be with some of my family in Three Forks this weekend, could you see that Mr. Gun gets his medicine on time? Sometimes he doesn't want to take all of it."

Jody smiled and said, "Susie, I'd be more than happy to spell you, for a little bit. You just go ahead and make plans and I'll look in on him."

"I will leave these extra bottles with you and here is a note on what he needs to take," Susie replied. "You're so good to me."

"Susie, we won't be here in about three weeks. The family is going back to the farm and Eddie's oldest daughter is getting married."

Susie cried out, "You're kidding me. You mean to tell me that Mari is getting married!"

"Eddie and I were told a couple of days ago. She's going to marry a nice young man by the name of Gordon Shum. I think you met him when Eddie and I got married."

Susie said, "I may have, I don't forget a face, but names I sometimes forget." They laughed and within moments she was gone.

When Jody turned around, she could see that Hanh was at the table staring into the bottles of medicine with a curious expression on his face. "Can you tell me about this medicine? Why are some of the pills a solid white, others are blue and why are some of the capsules with different colors? What do they do and what are they made of?"

When Jody took a chair next to Hanh to explain, Eddie said, "I need to go to the stables and keep an eye on the mare. I may not be back for a spell because she looked fairly motherly earlier in the day. I'll take Lien with me if she wants."

Lien leaped to her feet, "Hanh, I be with American father at the stables with the mother horse." Her comment let her brother know she had reached a point in her life where she did not need to be next to him to feel protected. Jody and Eddie both seemed to realize there was a subtle change taking place as they smiled at each other.

When Eddie and Lien left the cabin, Jody reached for a pharmaceutical book that showed the different kind of medicines and what they were named. In most cases, the chemical compound of ingredients was listed. There were many questions and she felt it was a time for them to grow closer.

~ ~ ~ ~

At the stables, Eddie did not allow Lien to enter the stall with the mare. He realized it was not safe enough to do so. He moved a bale of hay close to the bars in an adjoining stall and placed a saddle blanket over it, where Lien could sit and see the mare in safety. She sat on the bale of hay and would either place her feet on one of the bottom rungs or lean forward and place her arms comfortably on the bars and rest her head. She was excited and her eyes didn't miss much of the action in the stall. Lien asked, "Is she going to have her baby tonight?"

"I hope so. She had some trouble with another mare out in the pasture and was hurt. She is having a harder time because of her injuries," Eddie replied. "But I'm sure she will have it before morning." He entered the stall, walked over and patted the mare on the neck.

It was a long wait and at one time Eddie had to check the mare. When he had finished, he turned around only to see that his daughter had fallen asleep, her head resting on top of her arms that were placed on the bars between the stalls. He got up and went directly to her and made her comfortable with the aid of another bale of hay. He picked up another

197

saddle blanket and covered her to keep the night chill off. While watching the mare, he would also be close enough to arouse his daughter, when the time came. For now, he would let her sleep.

It was nearly an hour later when Lien felt her father nudging her awake. "Lien, wake up. The mare is about to have her colt." The contractions came and the thrashing began and the noise brought Lien out of her sleepiness.

Her eyes flew awake and she was all set to witness what she had waited so long to see. She was also happy that her father had taken a moment to awake her, knowing the importance of her feelings. She knew he was a good man and she wanted to learn more about him. Her American father was so kind, not only to her and her brother, but to the mare as well.

She had no sooner focused her eyes, when the mare raised her head and thrashed for a moment in the process of giving birth. Lien stood silent when she saw the front legs begin to show, then the head and within moments the rest of the colt was there. Upon delivery, the mare thrashed a bit in her attempt to get to her feet. Lien looked upon the colt that lay still for a moment, until Eddie helped it struggle to stand on all fours. He checked to see if the colt had any broken ribs or other injuries, which may result in him having to call a veterinarian.

When the colt maintained its footing, Eddie stroked the back of the mare. She stood still, as if resting quietly after the ordeal. Then he went about introducing the colt to where there was some nourishment.

Lien began to giggle. The wobbly colt stretched its head and neck forward seeking milk, not realizing that its unsteady legs needed to take a step or so to get into position.

When Eddie left the stall, he joined Lien for a few precious moments, looking on to see that mother and her offspring were happy together. The mare was relaxed and occasionally suffered a nudge from the colt's head against her lower abdomen when it lost contact from the milk supply.

Eddie and daughter walked happily back to the cabin. The moon was out and with the landscape fresh with snow. It glowed, as if the valley near the Gallatin River was happy and celebrating the new birth.

When they arrived at the cabin, they discovered Hanh had been tucked in for the night and Jody was waiting with a cup of coffee for Eddie and a glass of milk for Lien.

Jody asked, "Lien, did you learn something tonight?"

Lien was full of talk, and from the expression on her face, it was one of excitement. When she talked of Eddie, she would turn to face him for a moment and it showed he had become her idol.

Eddie told of her falling asleep and wasn't awake for the long haul. Jody spoke up, "Lien, you need to freshen up and go to bed, because you will be going to school in the morning."

When Jody returned to the kitchen after tucking Lien into her bed, she said, "That girl will be dreaming of horses, if I don't miss my guess."

Eddie wrapped his arms around her and said, "What a rewarding evening, and now I have the pleasure of being alone with you."

"Your coffee is going to get cold," she teased, as she surrendered to his affection.

~ ~ ~ ~

It was Sunday morning on the 11th of January when the Days entered the Methodist church in Bozeman with their extended family. Two boys from Hanh's class at school and Shad Red Cloud approached him and escorted him to their Sunday school class. A young lady from Lien's class at school and Kim Red Cloud came up to her and asked if she wanted to be their guest in class also. The children were accepted and they began to fit into the social fabric of the church community.

The children sat next to their parents after Sunday school class and listened to the minister deliver a sermon on the birth of the Christ child. When the services were over, there was a time for fellowship before everyone prepared to go home. The children were exposed to more love and friendship on this day than they may have ever experienced in Vietnam, following the death of their parents.

Both of the children found it hard to realize that there was clothing for school, for play and for church. In Vietnam they were lucky to have a change of clothing. Here in America, there was clothing for many things. When they attended school, they would see other children with clothing of many different colors and styles. They were about to be introduced to clothing for another purpose.

Hanh and Lien would be a part of their American Sister's wedding. After church, the family had an appointment at 'The Bride and Groom's Shop', where Hanh was fitted for a tux to include cummerbund, bow tie and patent leather shoes. Lien was fitted with formal wear that included a modest amount of lace and shiny new shoes that could barely be seen, even when she walked. After the fitting, the items were carefully prepared for transport to the wedding on the upcoming weekend.

~ ~ ~ ~

When Eddie escorted his daughter Mari down the aisle to her waiting Gordon Shum and others at the altar, he felt a happiness within that caused his heart to swell. He was happy for his daughter, knowing she was about to marry the love of her life. In front of them was his adopted daughter Lien, making her way down the aisle delicately casting down the rose petals in such a way as not to bruise them, as they floated to the floor. Behind them was his adopted son Hanh, standing tall in his tux, carrying the pillow with the rings attached, knowing his job held great importance to his American sister.

Pastor Waters asked, "Who gives this bride in this marriage?"

Eddie's throat suddenly felt dry for the first time. He looked into his daughter's eyes that were smiling back at him before he turned to the Pastor and said, "Her mother and I do." Pastor Waters looked at Sarah, who nodded. Eddie then went to his beloved Jody's side to witness the wedding of his first born.

During the reception, Eddie and Jody had the privilege of talking face to face with the Shum's at length. Prior to the wedding, the talks had been on the telephone, with calls to Colorado Springs, Colorado while coordinating the wedding.

Pete and Peggy were both talkative. They operated a touring business out of Colorado Springs that made trips to the Royal Gorge, Garden of the Gods and to the top of Pike's Peak. They talked as if there was an excitement in the air and they couldn't be happier knowing that their son was marrying Mari.

Peggy said, "Gordon brought Mari home for a visit last year. The first couple of minutes I was around her, it was apparent that she was meant for Gordon. I knew it was going to be church bells before long."

Jody laughed, "It was just a few weeks ago when Gordon asked for Mari's hand. They wanted to tie the knot before Sarah and Eric left for his assignment in Texas."

"It isn't every day," Pete replied, "that you run across a girl that your son has chosen to settle down with and instantly like her. We certainly can see why Gordon was so struck by her. We're glad to meet the two of you and we had a chance to talk with her mother and Eric earlier today. We're right proud to have Mari in the family."

"Mari went through a rough period when I was in the service," Eddie replied, "Jody and I are very pleased to have Gordon in the family. He has been to the ranch a couple of times. He's a joy to have around and we're happy he has chosen our Mari."

"When you're down around Colorado Springs," Pete offered, "give us a call. We'd love to show you around."

Eddie replied, "The same goes for you and your wife when you're up around the Bozeman area. You'll find a room and a plate waiting at our cabin. We have horseback riding and some mighty good fishing for trout."

Mari called out, "Moms and Dads over this way, we need to have another picture taken."

The rest of the evening was filled with chatter between dear friends and new acquaintances. When it was discovered the bride and groom had quietly snuck out, everyone seemed to go their separate ways.

~ ~ ~ ~

In the weeks that followed his sister's wedding, Hanh seemed to find comfort in being around Jody. He was full of questions regarding medicines and herbs. His science class project fit into his interests in herbs and he had to make a display chart on several different plants. Lien on the other hand, was practically tied to Eddie's back pocket. Wherever he went, she was either at his side, or never more than a pace or so behind him.

When they were at school, there was the immersion of English. There was a rush to learn the spelling and meaning of each word in order to stay in the class that they were assigned. The counselors at school worked with them and they usually had an abundance of homework when they returned home each day. Eddie and Jody would enjoy the Montana sunsets in the evenings before they sat down as a family at the kitchen table helping their children to understand their homework assignments.

Jody had purchased a small puzzle of some 500 pieces. The children thought it was interesting to try and get the pieces to fit and have a picture emerge. Then she said, "English is much like this puzzle. When the words fit, you will get to see the total picture in words."

Hanh asked, "How is it that you can say something and it might have other meanings."

"That depends," Jody answered. "It may depend on the inflection of how you say the words. Be patient and some of the questions you may have will be answered. But never, ever be afraid to ask, because that is how we learn." She smiled and patted him on the head. The study sessions at home were conducted as a close-knit family. They discussed each problem until it was no longer a problem. When Jody was up getting refreshments, Eddie would find a way to relate to the children and make the assignments easier. It was a fun time and when they were through for the night, there was a sense of accomplishment.

When the children were tucked away in their beds, Jody and Eddie enjoyed the fruits of being involved parents with an abundance of love to go around. They would pause at the end of the day and feel genuinely blessed.

~ ~ ~ ~

When the spring thaw came, there was the problem of tracking mud into the cabin. Some of the Montana soil has a habit of clinging to a pair of shoes or boots and the tracks of the most careful would sometimes mar the floors. But with spring comes the beauty of the spring flowers that randomly spring up to decorate the landscape. The foliage on the trees brings out the budding process and the pasture grasses begin to flourish. If the weather was cooperating during the early part of spring, both the mare and the colt would be turned out to pasture. During April and May, the weaning process takes place and the colts are watched over carefully with their feed and their habits monitored closely. The mares are kept away from their colts in another pasture for about sixty days to allow them to stop producing milk. One month there are mares with their colts dotting the greening pastures and the next, the separation of mothers from their offspring. Beyond the pastures are the trees that line the Gallatin River and the buds beginning to turn into leaves, allowing the fullness of the trees to flourish. Above the valley, the mountain peaks grudgingly gave up their snow to produce run off. When that happened, the granite rock formations began to peek from under their blankets of white. At higher elevations, the snow remained above the tree line year-round, nearly scratching the heavens.

When there was time for horseback riding or going fishing, the children had their fun with Shad and Kim Red Cloud. They were a perfect match from a social standpoint. The Red Clouds would talk of their Indian heritage and in turn Hanh and Lien would talk of their life in Vietnam. Shad and Kim were too young to remember the fighting that took place between the government and their ancestors. Hanh and Lien, however, would relate to the war that devastated their family. Now all four children were enjoying spring and summer in a more peaceful time.

It was quiet where they rode by horseback or where they fished. But there was always laughter that filled the air from these happy children. Shad and Kim knew how to saddle up and where to ride, while Hanh and Lien learned quickly. Shad was the fisherman and quickly taught the others the skills of how to fish and where the holes were in the river. Shad would point out the perfect gathering places for some of the biggest trout in the Gallatin River.

Sometimes Hanh would grow weary of fishing and would wander off on foot seeking various herbs. He would pluck them from their stock and take them home. He would slice into them with a sharp knife to see the inner makings of each plant. He had a scrapbook that he would draw in from what he saw, a habit he developed from his science class.

Jody and Eddie enjoyed the times when the children helped them in planting additional flowers and landscaping. Jody loved flowers and Eddie saw to it that there was plenty of the kind she enjoyed. It would not be uncommon for him to return from town where he had stopped off to buy a different Perkins rose for her rose garden. Their quiet times working together began to put the finishing touches around their home.

~ ~ ~ ~

The marriage of Kari Day to David Hostetler took place in Miles City in a large Methodist church. Eddie, Jody and the kids arrived shortly before the rehearsal. Lester and Cora Belle Hostetler had made arrangements for them to stay overnight at their house and were gracious hosts. The evening hours were reflective on the lives of the two getting married and the support both sides planned to make. Both sides enjoyed getting to know the other. The Hostetler's were paleontologists that enjoyed digging up dinosaur bones, in contrast to Jody and Eddie with their military experiences and the horse ranch.

When morning came, Eddie looked into Kari's eyes moments before he was to escort her down the aisle to wed David, saying, "I wish you much happiness. May the both of you enjoy life and love to its fullest."

The music played and when the time came to enter the sanctuary, Lien fulfilled her duties for her other American sister by being the flower girl. Hanh was more relaxed now after having experience being a ring bearer and followed a few steps behind the bride.

When the Pastor asked, "Who gives this bride in this marriage?"

Eddie turned to look into Kari's eyes before he winked, only to hear her whisper, "I love you, Daddy."

He turned and without hesitation said, "Her mother and I do," before he turned to have a seat next to Jody. The minister glanced over at Sarah who nodded her approval. Within moments, they were witnessing the ceremony. Eddie and Jody held hands, each giving the other a soft squeeze.

Kari and David had a free moment between being swallowed up by well wishes while Eddie and Jody wished them the best. Eddie added, "Don't be strangers, come by when you can or write. We'll be leaving in a few moments, after we chat with Lester and Cora Belle."

After the reception, Eddie approached the Hostetler's and said, "Thanks so much for your hospitality. You're invited to stop by the ranch, whenever you're up around Bozeman. If you'll excuse us, we'll head back down the road, as there is work to do."

Lester replied, "I'll take you up on that. I'd like to see the homestead and the horse operation. From your visit, my curiosity is up, I'll have to satisfy the itch sometime soon."

Jody hugged Cora Belle and softly said, "Keep in touch and do visit when you can."

Cora Belle responded, "Come back if you will, we enjoyed our lengthy chat last night. Maybe next time, I'll have better coffee," she chuckled, "do have a safe trip home."

~ ~ ~ ~

The years passed. Eddie and Jody celebrated becoming grand-parents. After Eddie's daughter Kari married David Hostetler, within a month his daughter Mari gave birth to her first born, and with Gordon's blessings, they named him Chet Shum. The following year, Kari and David Hostetler had their first child and named him Max. The excitement of having a family member get married, to the birth of grandchildren, filled the spaces around raising Hanh and Lien. With work at the university and the requirements around the homestead, they kept busy.

Just when they thought they had everything under control, Mari and Gordon had their second child and named him Chad. Kari and David had their second and they named him Tyler. The commitments Eddie and Jody had kept them hopping. There were more things happening daily that seemed to demand their time. They were proud parents of four and proud grandparents of four. In between, they filled in the gaps with a commitment to ethical work and growing in their faith within the teaching of the Bible.

~ ~ ~ ~

A year later Eddie was doing some work on a fence near Gun's house. Gun had rolled his wheelchair out on the porch and asked, "Eddie, when you get through with what you're doing, could you come to the house, I'd like to talk to you."

"I'll be right up," Eddie called back.

When Eddie entered the study, he noted that the large leather chairs showed use over the years. The room was clear of clutter with the exception of the top of Gun's desk. It resembled organized chaos; only Gun would know where things were or belonged. He found his friend behind his business desk shuffling papers. "What's on your mind?" Eddie asked. He had a seat in one of the overstuffed leather chairs and waited for a reply.

Gun looked up and said, "Do you realize we have an anniversary to celebrate?

Caught a bit flat footed, Eddie thought for a spell, then asked, "Who's?"

"Well," Gun continued, "if you look at the calendar, it is now midyear of 1978. It was five years ago today I gave you five years to prove up." He looked up from the papers and smiled at Eddie and teased. "Are you ready for another five years or are you about to give up."

"I believe I took root. I'd like another five and can we forget about having to prove up" Eddie jabbed back.

"It's okay by me. Oh, by the way, I have heard some talk from the folks that visit the homestead. The accommodations and trip in from Bozeman get to be a hassle at times. I thought I'd run something by you and see if we can work together on a project."

Eddie smiled and said, "Sure, tell me about it and we'll kick it around."

"I was thinking," Gun continued. "Instead of cluttering up our back yard, I'd like to expand the portion of the homestead above the access road. I'll bet we could build a lodge up close to the mountain, with several large guest rooms, a conference room, a small grocery for weekend essentials and fishing gear. We'd have the buyers right at home, here on the homestead. While they are here, they can be looking over the stock and enjoying some relaxation."

"It sure beats running back and forth into Bozeman for those interested in buying and enjoying some free time." Eddie replied.

"I thought," Gun added, "we could have the Shoshone run the store and offer some of their crafts for sale and work in cleaning up the rooms. I believe it would employ a handful of jobs around her."

"It sounds good to me. When would be a good time to get the project underway?"

Gun thought for a moment and then said, "Who was the contractor that did the cabin? I thought he did a great job and maybe we can add a touch of flair to the lodge. That would give the buyers something to appreciate while they're here and word should spread from there."

"Danny Doyle," Eddie said, "he'd be the one to put it all together, and Tavis Moot was his right-hand man as a sub-contractor. If we start by showing him a sketch, I'm sure he could come up with the blueprints. Then we could have him build it."

"Let me get with my attorney," Gun said "to get some legal advice from him. I'll check with the real estate people to see how the property value around the mountain is coming along. I think a joint venture on a lodge would be a wise investment. Should I decide later on to sell the upper part of the homestead, I imagine it would be a close fit for the skiing industry. Contact Danny and we'll see if we can come to terms where everyone is pleased with the project."

Twenty minutes later, Eddie was on his way to the tool shed, returning what he had been using. From there he was heading to the cabin for supper and prepare for the night. He had a sunset to share with his family and there was the study session working with Hanh. He had turned seventeen and was preparing to take the SAT for college next year. They also helped Lien get ready for State Scholastic Achievement Competitions.

Hanh was thinking of entering college and later going into medicine or pharmaceuticals. Lien would try to use her personality to win people over. If that didn't work, she would turn on her charm to show she was as sharp as a pup, intellectually and socially. She had an interest in business and didn't seem to find a person she couldn't be friends with. But her love for horses grew from the first time she sat up late with her father. That was the very first night when one of the mares was having such a difficult time delivering her colt.

~ ~ ~ ~

The following summer, the 'Homesteader's Lodge' with all the amenities had been built for the horse buyers' comforts while visiting the homestead. The Shoshone from Three Forks had goods on consignment at the store and several from the tribe had found employment there. Gun had remained at the homestead long enough to see the grand opening. He and Susie made another one of his medical trips out of state. Eddie was left to see that most of the homestead ran properly. A series of supervisors and Johnny Tracks-A-Wolf, the senior foreman, made Eddie's jobs easier. The aging Shoshone foreman knew horses and humans about as well as anyone in the state. He could tell a good one from a bad one.

~ ~ ~ ~

The Methodist summer retreat had fallen into disarray over the years and was in need of some massive renovations. Eddie and Jody approached the church about sponsoring the summer retreat at the homestead. She was a registered nurse and Eddie had the horses and equipment for someone interested in riding. The small group of riders from the Little Britches Riding For Jesus group could take on one novice and look out for them during any horseback rides. The fishing on the Gallatin River could be supervised by some of the counselors and the folks at the homestead. During the retreat they would have to bring their own tent. The fees for food and a few essentials would be paid for by the church member attending the retreat, with the church funding the rest.

207

Counselors from the church would be responsible for the religious lessons that were taught. While some worked at and enjoyed the retreat, others within the church could be at the old retreat working and preparing the facilities for the following summer. The proposal was approved and the church looked forward to the summer rebuilding project and the retreat at the homestead.

~ ~ ~ ~

When the pasture to the north of the housing area began to fill with tents and campers, it was evident there was going to be a good turnout for the summer retreat. Johnny Tracks-A-Wolf, the homestead foreman, and his men had marked off the pastureland and placed several small stakes for each camp site. When the sun fell beyond the mountainous horizon, the retreat grounds were filled with eager campers. In the center of the campgrounds was a large pit where wood had been brought in for a campfire. Counselors and youth would gather around the fire in the evening, enjoying fellowship and singing religious songs.

Morning came early and the first project was saddling up and getting ready for a trail ride following breakfast. To the surprise of many, there was a chuck wagon breakfast the very first day. As everyone lined up for the food, they held out their plates for a hefty helping. For the adults, there was coffee from a bucket over an open fire and milk for the younger generation. For some, the option of riding in a saddle was out of the question and they were loaded onto an open buckboard.

The morning ride took in most of the homestead and lasted over three hours. Some of the riders were comfortable handling the reins on their own, while others were learning to ride for the first time. When they returned to the campsite near noon, it was apparent who had ridden often. Those who had not been on a horse in a long time showed their riding history by the way they walked. The rest of the day would be spent with the counselors taking over and several small groups walked across the countryside. The evenings would be spent around the campfire singing.

The second day began much like the first with the exception of younger children being paired up with responsible adults and the fishing gear being loaded on the buckboard. It wasn't far to the Gallatin River and the fishing group walked on an established road to the riverbank.

Most of the poles had line hook and sinker, with a night crawler or a hellgrammite for bait. Squeals could be heard up and down the riverbank when the boys chased some of the girls with worms. Several were squeamish and screamed, hesitant to bait their own hook with the lures provided. For those who were avid fishermen, they could try the fly rods. The fishing group would finish up before noon and head back to the campsite for lunch.

Prior to the evening event, Jody received a telephone call from Susie letting her know that they would be back on the homestead on the weekend. She turned to Eddie and suggested, "Can we make a welcome home for Gun and Susie? We could get Shad and Kim and they could stay over with Hanh and Lien and we could do something nice for Gun and Susie for a change."

Eddie smiled and said, "That would be perfect."

"I'll talk with their grandparents at the retreat's evening event and get permission for them to stay over," she said. "Then I'll have the girls help me make some Rocky Mountain cookies."

"Hanh and Shad can help me make up a sign," Eddie replied. "We'll try to come up with something clever."

For the week-long retreat, the alternate days of horseback riding and fishing became standard, ending on Friday night. The religious lessons were structured but remained interesting and fun.

~ ~ ~ ~

On the last day of the retreat, family members who had not attended came to be with their children. Those who worked on the Methodist retreat made it to the homestead for the last part of the entertainment. One of the counselors stood up and said, "The children have studied the origin of the song 'Jesus Loves the Little Children'. They know now the words were written by C. Herbert Woolston and the music was originally composed for the American Civil War "Tramp, Tramp, Tramp" by George F. Root. The alternate refrain was modified to the song we know today. They will circle up and show you, their version."

While some of the youth that had attended the retreat gathered in a circle, three counselors began playing guitars. The children would circle one direction and sing:

Jesus loves the little children,
All the children of the world,

Red and yellow, black and white
They are precious in His sight
Jesus loves the little children of the world.

As each verse of the seven verses was sung, when the color was mentioned, two children of that color would step into the circle. On the next verse when the color was mentioned they would rejoin the circle and prepare for the next verse. At the end of the song, they all came together in the center of the circle to raise their hands and shout with happiness.

There was an exhibition of horsemanship given by the ranch hands and the Little Britches Riding For Jesus group in the afternoon. That evening, the Shoshone people came over and gave a demonstration of song and dance along with displaying some of their traditional crafts and workmanship.

When the summer retreat had ended, the final report showed two children had injuries to their fingers from fishhooks while trying to get a trout off and putting them on their stringer. Antiseptic and a band aid took care of the injuries. Those who enjoyed the retreat left with regrets that it wasn't longer. Eddie and Jody had made them welcome and the campers left knowing their church was so much richer by having them within the congregation.

~ ~ ~ ~

The day following the retreat, Jody invited Lien and Kim into the kitchen, "We are going to make some Rocky Mountain cookies. Then we'll have to get some flowers for a welcome home treat."

When the girls gathered around the table where the ingredients were placed, they made themselves busy under a watchful eye. The girls were excited that they would be doing the mixing and the baking. They could hardly wait to see the final results.

Jody suggested, "It would be nice if you two would get some wildflowers and place them in a vase."

Kim said, "The Bitter Root flower is beautiful; my grandparents make it into a good, tasty porridge. I will take Lien and we will go looking for some wildflowers, I know where some are located."

From beneath the kitchen sink Lien retrieved a fruit jar and said, "We can put them in this and set it next to the cookies."

When the girls left the house, they went across a pasture and began looking for those precious flowers. When they returned, they had the following in their collection: arrowhead balsamroot, Indian paintbrush, two Rocky Mountain Iris, a single cattail, yarrow, pussy toes, mountain arnica, avalanche lilies, bear grass, columbines and alpine asters. The girls worked together to make a beautiful arrangement.

Eddie had the boys in Hanh's room, where Shad sketched out a Shoshone pattern and Hanh drew in the 'Welcome Home'. Both boys colored in the sign according to Shad's directions, for he knew the colors in the Indian design. The sign was a large oval bordered with a narrow band border. It had a Shoshone beadwork design going up the middle under the Montana State flower, the Bitterroot, and a mountain design somewhat resembling the Bozeman pass in the upper half, with four eagle feathers hanging down from beneath the flower. Arcing the design at the top were the words 'Welcome Home' and cradling the design were the words 'Gun and Susie'. Beneath all this, the names of Eddie, Jody and the children were written with an Asian flare that only Hanh could muster up. Eddie had the boys help him make a small wooden frame. It would be placed on the porch in front of Weismann's front door before Gun and Susie got home.

~ ~ ~ ~

Gun and Susie had returned late Saturday from his medical appointment out of state. The hopes were that there would be a day he could walk with the aid of a walker. His medicine and the rugged physical therapy would have to be endured over the coming months to determine if this would come to be.

The welcome sign, cookies and flowers were appreciated and both Gun and Susie praised the children for what they had done. Susie took the flowers and placed them in the middle of the table and the cookies were brought inside and placed next to the arrangement. The welcome home sign was brought into the house. Gus said, "This is such a masterpiece, it will be placed on the wall in my library."

Gun was informed of the success of the retreat and he said, "Eddie, I'm so proud of you and Jody, for the life and vibrancy you two have brought to this tired old homestead. I knew from the day I first read your proposal, you were a man of conviction and foresight and I'm right proud of you both."

Eddie looked on, smiled and for a time, at a loss for words, before saying, "I couldn't have done it without you. Jody and I feel the same; we love you, Gun! Take the therapy seriously and we hope to see you walking someday."

"Thank you both," Gun said with a broad smile on his face.

CHAPTER 15

Horseback Riding – Trout Fishing – 1987

Breakfast of scrambled eggs and bacon with toast was the main course. But for Chet Shum and Max Hostetler, the larger than average cups Grandma Jody had pulled from the cupboard got their attention. It was for their hot chocolate with marshmallows on top. That's what topped off their meal.

Grandpa Eddie had wasted no time sitting at the table. There were things to do and little time to squeeze them all into a day. He had already slipped into his jacket and was looking for a pair of gloves for the two boys to use. He found two pair of leather gloves he thought would do the trick before he called out, "You two going to sit and admire breakfast, or are you planning to go with me?"

The ultimatum got their attention. Chet looked up and grabbed his cup and gulped the last of the hot chocolate. He bit into the marshmallow and was in the process of quickly chewing before swallowing. Max, on the other hand, felt pushed for time, dipped his fingers into the cup and removed the marshmallow before drinking the remaining chocolate. Then he ate the marshmallow with two quick bites before licking his fingers, in the process of leaping from the chair.

Jody jokingly replied, "Max you best wash your hands. You don't want to be getting your fingers stuck in the gloves."

Max ran to the nearest water, which happened to be in the kitchen sink. He dipped the tips of his fingers in the dishwater and dried his hands on the dishtowel, before saying, "Thanks Grandma, that cocoa sure tasted yummy."

"You boys run along," she encouraged, "have a good time."

The door to the cabin had no sooner closed, when Jody looked out

213

the window, seeing her husband being flanked by two excited boys. She often wondered how he kept up with the four grandchildren and the requirements on the homestead. Now she had some quiet time for herself, where she could do some baking. She wanted to surprise the three of them when they returned.

As Grandpa and the boys walked away from the cabin and headed for the stables, Eddie asked, "You two fit for some horseback riding, then stretching your legs on a good mountain trail hike?"

Chet said, "I'm looking forward to the horseback riding and I bet the hiking will be interesting, too."

Max asked, "This is going to be great. Grandpa, where are we riding today?"

Eddie said, "We'll saddle up first and then head over towards Sacagawea Peak. We'll ride up a way tether the horses and hike the rest of the way, until we get to the ridgeline. We'll go up quite a climb until I give out, or if you boys can't keep up with a man my age." Then he laughed, knowing it was a challenge the boys would be happy to meet.

When they had saddled their horses, they rode across the homestead three abreast, like they do in western movies on television. When they came to the trail and headed for higher elevations, Chet fell in behind Eddie and Max brought up the rear. Eddie would turn in the saddle often to check on those following him and ask, "Everything okay back there?"

Chet would give his response and shift his weight in the saddle, as he sent his own challenging comment back to Max. They were enjoying the ride while the horses climbed the steep terrain. In amazement, they could look back and off to the side to see how far up they had ridden.

The trail was getting narrow and was heavily covered with pinecones and needles. It was laced in and around the pines and cedars with low hanging branches and large boulders or granite chunks in the path. The old animal trail followed the path of least resistance on the slope heading for higher ground. They were nearing the top of the timberline, when Eddie reined in his horse and swung down from the saddle.

Chet reined up his horse and dismounted as well. Then Max arrived on the scene, he looked down from the saddle and gave his assessment saying, "Grandpa, I don't think there have been very many horses up this far on the trail before."

Eddie answered, "Most likely not. It looks like the elk use this part of the timber. I've seen some of their hoof prints in the soft soil. We'll tether the horses here and climb the rest of the way."

Max dismounted and tied the reins on an extended cedar limb near Chet's horse. He told his cousin, "I like it when we get to come up here and visit with Grandpa and Grandma for a week. It seems that we always do something different and interesting."

Chet replied, "When I get home and tell them of all the fun I had, my brother doesn't believe me."

"Mine neither," Max added.

The air was crisp and cool, as the upswept flow from the valley floor raced toward the crest of the ridge, far above the cabin they had left earlier. They had reached the baseline trail a fair walking distance below Sacagawea Peak.

Eddie had hit his fifty-seventh birthday a while back, but was in reasonable shape from working on the ranch. As for his guests, Chet had turned fourteen and Max was thirteen. They were enjoying a week-long stay, part of a yearly tradition. Eddie thought he would add the mountain hike along with the boys' usual horseback riding. The view of the valley was breath-taking from the lower elevations all the way up to the peaks. He felt they needed to see more by viewing it from above and the challenge of the hike fit in nicely.

The sweet smell of pine and cedar gave way ever so slightly to the smell of newly-mown hay. The smell rode the air currents from the valley floor only to be lifted toward the heavens. This is where the serenity of life was to be enjoyed, on the western slope of a rugged Montana mountain ridge.

Higher up, the jagged granite and Sacagawea Peak were pushed skyward, as if to scratch every passing low cloud. In the valleys far below, numerous boulders of varying sizes began to mark the landscape of the Rocky Mountain terrain. This was a common feature for the area north and west of Bozeman, Montana.

Eddie had grabbed a dry limb that was rather straight and made a walking stick out of it. The boys looked on and laughed, while Max added, "Is that stick going to help you, Grandpa?"

"It helps a bit on the steep slopes and helps the legs. Why don't the two of you make your own walking stick?"

"We don't need one, Grandpa, that's for someone older. We have strong legs, don't we, Max?"

Cousins can say the wildest things at times and without meaning to, they lay down a challenge. This may have been one of them. Max was put into a situation, had he wanted to use a stick, but he wasn't going to look like a wimp in front of his cousin. It just wasn't going to happen, not on this day or any other. "I'm with you, Chet, I don't have rubber legs."

The boy's laughter was cut short when Eddie said, "I heard that remark and we'll see before we get to the top."

When the game trail faded out, Eddie began taking the side of the hill in larger strides towards the top. It wasn't long before they reached the crest of a ridge. He paused and let the boys catch up with him. They both stood bent over, using the stiffness of both arms resting on their knees as the climb and the altitude seemed to catch up with the younger set.

"Boys," Eddie began, "I want the both of you to look out that way and then over that direction" as he pointed.

The panoramic view to the west was breathtaking. To the east, the famed Crazy Peak marking the Crazy Mountains seemed closer than it really was. From where they stood and rested, if only momentarily, they could look back down the steep incline they had covered. Beneath the rugged granite-covered western slope, a densely-covered pine and cedar timber line marked their trail. This was where their horses were secured. They had climbed almost straight up to get to the ridgeline. Sacagawea Peak was still another lengthy climb, even if they stayed on the ridge line. To the south they could see the small outline of Bozeman and far beyond was the Bear Tooth Mountains to the southeast and the Rampart Mountains to the west.

Eddie said, "Come over here boys." When they moved near him, he pointed, "Look down and over there. I think I see a herd of elk on the eastern ridge, am I right?"

The boys looked for a while before Max said, "I don't see anything."

Chet replied, "I see them over there!"

A long moment passed before Max said, "I see them now." Then there was laughter among the three of them.

Eddie said, "We'll walk the ridgeline for a distance and then we'll cut back to where the horses are. We don't have enough time to reach the peak today. We need to get back to the horses and be home before dark. We'll have to save that for another time."

When the time came to head down the rocky and jagged slope,

Eddie had the boys stop and rest before they made their descent. "I wanted to walk this far before we go down, because I've seen eagles off in the distance up this way. I'd like to know if they happen to have a nesting area nearby."

"Do you really think we'll see some up this high?" Chet asked.

Eddie said, "I'm not sure, we'll just have to keep an eye out for them. But when we start walking down, be careful where you put your feet. You don't need to slip and cause a slide. Once the rocks start moving downhill, sometimes they go a long way before they stop and I don't need you boys hurt."

Before they started their walk down, Eddie picked up a small piece of granite from the rocky terrain and placed it in his shirt pocket; it was destined for his collection. He kept the trail simple for the boys. They could put their feet where he had just left his. Slowly but gently, they came down from the ridgeline and finally reached the timber line. When they did, they rested for a moment.

Suddenly Max grabbed at Eddie and Chet's arms and pointed, "Look over there, that's an eagle, isn't it?"

"It sure is," Eddie replied, "We'll watch for a few minutes and see if it heads for a nesting area. Maybe it is out looking for food."

Time got away from them as they watched the eagle. It neither showed the direction of a nest or his art of finding food. It was time to move on and Eddie said, "We can't stay here all day, the horses are still quite a distance away."

When they reached the horses, Eddie reached into his saddle bag and produced three sandwiches. They each enjoyed their sandwich, then Eddie led the way down the trail and Chet followed behind Max. The boys thoroughly enjoyed the learning experience they were having and kept looking out to the side, seeking out the all kinds of interesting things to talk about.

When they reached the boundaries of the homestead, they rode three abreast again, sandwiching Eddie between them. There were questions and laughter all the way back to the stables.

When they arrived, Eddie said, "We had our fun, now it's time to care for your horse. They need a rub down, feed and fresh water. Then we'll go to the cabin."

A short time later, they were walking into the cabin and smelling something good. Eddie called out, "Honey, we're home."

"I'm in the kitchen," Jody replied. "Clean up, I have a treat for you and the boys."

When they arrived in the kitchen, they could see that grandma had been busy most of the day baking. There was an apple pie, a wonder berry pie and a large pan of cinnamon rolls for dessert as well as fresh bread and hot rolls.

When the boys recounted the events of the day, Jody sat and listened in amazement. She enjoyed the excitement on their faces and the reflection in their voices. They were allowed a cinnamon roll and a cup of hot chocolate before supper. She didn't want to spoil their supper; the roast was nearly done.

Moments before the sun began to sink behind the Rockies, they sat in the middle of the cabin and shared another one of the Montana sunsets. They talked of the events of the day and made plans for the next few. The boys were excited, but they showed signs of being tired, after such a day of climbing. The boys were ushered into their rooms for a good night's sleep with thoughts of what tomorrow would bring.

The leisurely pace of having fun was ideal for the boys. They took time each day to saddle up and go for a short ride. It was two cousins having fun and enjoying their vacation with their grandparents. When the time came, they both gathered in Eddie and Jody, showing their appreciation with a big hug, a kiss for Jody and a handshake for Eddie.

After the boys had left to go home, Eddie and Jody found their rockers in the center of the cabin and watched the sunset quietly.

~ ~ ~ ~

Eddie spent most of the morning at the stables tending to a colt that had gotten himself messed up with two strands of barbed wire. He had been summoned to the stables by a ranch hand because of the colt's violent behavior. He had fresh deep cuts to his abdomen and legs. His ears laid back and he was rearing and pawing frantically.

Tavis Moot was working on some electrical wiring in the stables and came to investigate. When he saw, the colt wasn't going to allow any of the stable help into the stall, he stepped into the stall, latching it behind him. Tavis hit a high-pitched Cajon sound matching the colt's high squeal, before he blew through his lips like a horse does at the end of a nicker. The horse suddenly stood still. The colt's ears that once lay back on its head were now upright listening. Tavis walked directly up in front of the colt, placed his large hands over the upper part of the head near the ears and mane, slowly pulling them down across the eyes with his thumbs touching softly, until he was near the muzzle.

At that moment Eddie arrived and came into the stall. Between the two of them, they were able to keep the colt quiet. Eddie checked the cuts and applied medication. Moot repeated the actions with his hands while softly saying. "Stand still, I know it hurts."

When Eddie asked, "Tavis what did you do to cause the colt to settle down?"

Tavis replied, "That horse has fresh scars that hurt. With them ears laid back, I could tell he was angry. But they perked up to listen to me. That was when I laid my hands on him. I got no use for a Croker sack. I jus' remember the scars on my back, not caused from no whip, jus' fresh wire. It broke when I help fix fence. I got caught up in the loose strands that snapped back when I was young. My Mama raise' her voice to get my attention, then held my head in her hands. As her palms covered my eyes, she tol' me to stand still, then she stroked my cheeks and rubbed the bridge of my nose for comfort. My Papa got me loose and dabbed my back with salve. That horse needed salve, too. I just tried to give the colt some comfort."

As they stepped from the stall, Eddie said, "Thanks Tavis, your point is well taken and I appreciate your help."

Eddie had doctored the colt best he could and had left instructions at the stables for the men to keep a close eye on the wire jumper.

When he arrived at the cabin, Mari and Kari came bounding out the door to greet him. Life on the homestead had no sooner returned to normal when Chad Shum, who had turned twelve and his cousin Tyler Hostetler, who was eleven, were able to pay them a visit. These two seemed to be inseparable when they were together.

Both were fishermen, at least they had the fever. The boys were about the same height, but Chad was chunkier and Tyler seemed to be built as thin as a willow.

Moments before their arrival, Jody had pulled a sheet of brownies out of the oven. "Come into the kitchen, boys," she beckoned, "have a hot brownie and a cold glass of milk."

She found that nothing got her grandsons to the table faster than a hot brownie and a cold glass of milk. They took to the treat and the glass of milk, nearly as fast as they had arrived at the table. Mari and Kari made their visit brief and had to rustle up the boys to give them a hug and leave them with last minute instructions on their behavior. They left them in the care of their grandparents.

"Hi, Daddy," Mari said, "Sis and I just dropped off double trouble for the two of you. Chad has been looking forward to going fishing with you."

Eddie smiled and looked at Kari, as if to hear what she was about to say. "Mari and I are sure happy you and Jody wanted to have them at this time. It gives us two a little bit of time to do some serious shopping before the men come back with Chet and Max."

"Where did they take those two off to this time?"

Kari said, "There was a rodeo over by Red Lodge and the four of them wanted to take it in."

"That's nice," Eddie remarked, "glad to see the boys are getting to do something enjoyable. Well, leave my two fishermen with me and we'll see if they can catch a big one while they're here."

The girls were on their way into Bozeman. Eddie entered the cabin to find the two boys hugging up to the table reaching for another brownie. He said, "Best eat while the eating is good. I have the poles all lined up for us to catch some fish if you're interested."

"Thanks, Grandma," Chad and Tyler seemed to chime at the same time. Tyler added, "Them brownies sure were good."

"Go have your fun fishing," Jody told the boys and added for Eddie's ears, "Supper will be ready about six tonight, don't be late."

He caught her at the kitchen stove and gave her a kiss and said, "We'll be back by then."

Eddie had planned for this day for a long time. He picked up four poles and two nets along with the other accessories to make the outing memorable.

When they left the cabin and headed across the field, the boys had two poles each and Eddie carried the rest. The boys walked next to each other a step or so away from Eddie's hip pocket. They were telling the other of their fun and experiences in school, especially sports and during the early part of summer. Eddie listened and was amused at the attempt of one to outdo the other.

When they arrived at the Gallatin River, Chad asked, "What pole are you going to use, Grandpa?"

Tyler looked on with an inquisitive ear only to hear him say, "Today is your day to fish, you make up your mind. If you want to fly fish, I'll do my best to teach you. If you would rather use hook and sinker, I'll teach you how to thread a worm on a hook and show you the best way to use a hellgrammite. It's your choice!"

Chad spoke up, "I'll start with the hook and sinker, Tyler wants to fly fish, then maybe we can switch off?"

Tyler smiled so quickly; the flash of his white teeth was as shiny as spinner bait. He was excited about learning how to fly fish and to be taught by none other than the man he admired.

Eddie had Chad lined up with a good-sized Canadian night crawler and a light weight, no bobber and left a small net on the bank. He saw Chad cast out into a small pocket of water that was partially hidden under some leaning willows. "You sure you can bait your own hook for a while?"

Chad's jaw was set for fishing and answered with a tight grin, "I can do it, Grandpa, and I'll prove it."

Eddie excused himself and took Tyler out on a narrow gravel bar and had Tyler make his choice of fly. He chose the Royal Coachman and heard Eddie say, "Great, I'll place it on the end of the tippet like so. I want you to watch me for a couple of casts. Then I'll reel in the line and we'll see if you can get the hang of things."

While Tyler was standing to his left, Eddie pulled on the line and showed him how to control the loose line in order to make his cast. Eddie began bringing the long fly rod back and forth at about two o'clock and after a couple of whips, released the line and the fly danced through the air. The line fed out through the eyelets with a whistle. The line had no sooner hit the water when Eddie pulled more line from the reel and showed Tyler how to bring the line in for a second cast in order to release more line and get further upstream and out into the river. He showed the young fisherman the art of handling the free line in the event of a strike. He reeled in the line and handed the pole to his grandson. "Here, now it's your turn. Nothing like learning by doing, is there?"

Tyler settled in and began to follow instructions. For a young lad of twelve to suddenly become coordinated and experienced at fly fishing, the first try would have been great. It didn't happen and it didn't happen over the next few tries.

The encouragement from someone older will always keep things going. Eddie said, "Patience, patience, never give up. Learning how to cast is like music, seeing a metronome that goes back and forth. Fly fishing is like music. Then you can relax and be patient and before long, 'BANG!' it'll happen. Then you'll have to know how to land it, without losing the fish and the fly."

"How is that, Grandpa?" Tyler tried to speak and fish at the same time. Nervousness showed in the tone of his voice, as he sought a supporting comment from Grandpa.

"That line that you have in your hand, if you get a strike, let a little bit of line out so that there isn't such a jerk in the line. You reel in when you can. When the trout decides to run, you play him out a little bit of line. Remember to keep the tip of the pole high enough and you can lower it as you play out some line. It takes a fisherman's touch. Most grownups don't have the touch and they have to learn or keep replacing a dandy fly. You're doing fine."

Eddie was standing back watching Tyler slowly become confident in what he was doing, only to hear Chad scream out in panic, "Grandpa! I got a big one, help me. I can't get him in and he's got my line tangled."

"Keep up the good work," Eddie said in parting. He raced through some willows and up the bank to give Chad a hand. Sure enough, the line was wrapped around a limb and some rocks by the time he arrived. "Stay on the bank and I'll try to get the line free." Grabbing a small limb, he placed it under the line and tried to lift up. The line came free of the rocks, but it was twisted around a limb. Eddie stuck his foot into the cold water, reached over and snapped the limb, freeing the line. This allowed the trout to head for deeper water. By the time Eddie had removed his leg from the water, Chad was reeling in and the pole was bowed near the tip.

"Help me, Grandpa, get the net," Chad cried out.

Eddie said, "Just this once, but next time you keep it close by."

There was a surprised look on Chad's face, when Eddie handed him the net. "Play him out a bit and the fight will soon be gone, then you can use the net by being careful and dipping in behind it and swooping up. You can do it; I have confidence in you."

Nervous tension sets in on almost any angler when he has a big trout on the line. To a young fisherman, the tension is almost too big to handle by himself. But the encouraging words of a grandfather will sometimes calm the nerves of an excited boy. Before long, Chad took the net, swooped under his catch and brought it up to the bank.

"Great job," Eddie boasted and was tickled to see that Chad had taken several steps back from the river, just in case the trout had ideas of getting set free. Within moments, the trout was on Chad's stringer and he was in the process of baiting his hook.

Eddie excused himself and went to see how Tyler was making out. When he arrived, he found the young lad standing alone, his pole on the gravel bar and looking up into the nearby tree. One quick look and Eddie could see that the fly was caught on the tip of a pine bough. It was about ten feet above the gravel bar. "Got yourself a snag and some trouble, don't you, Tyler?"

"I didn't mean to get hooked up like that, it just happened somehow," Tyler went on to explain.

Eddie laughed and said, "I forgot to tell you that things of this nature happen when you whip out too much line. Lesson number one, remember the trees behind you." With a piece of driftwood, Eddie managed to pull the long branch down far enough where he could pull at the sprig of pine needles. Within moments, the Royal Coachman was set free and Tyler was picking up the pole and making preparations to get back to fishing.

There is an art to fly fishing that takes time and patience. Tyler heard his cousin yell several times, indicating he had another one on. He was about to give up on his fly fishing, when suddenly the line that was once slack in the eyelets of the rod suddenly grew tight. The young lad gasped and dropped a hand full of line. He heard his grandfather coaching, "Get the line Tyler, reel in the slack. There you go, nice and easy. Keep the pole high, come on a bit higher, give him some slack now, not too much. Reel it in, nice and easy."

About that time, the rainbow broke water and did a dance on his tail that added excitement to Tyler's nervous jitters. It took time and some coaching, but before long, more line was reeled in. Eddie handed the net to his grandson in time for him to reach down and lift a beauty from the cold waters of the Gallatin River. Eddie calmly reached down, picked up a small smooth rock and placed it in his pocket.

Tyler asked, "Did you find a lucky rock?"

"I may have at that," Eddie replied, "I think I'll keep this one and add it to my collection."

The importance of the rock was set aside. There is no excitement in this world any more powerful for a fisherman to experience than setting the hook on a fighting rainbow trout with a fly. To say the fish was hooked would have been a misstatement. Tyler was hooked on being a fly fisherman. The joy and excitement were as explosive as a shook up can of cola pop with all that fizz.

Eddie ran back and forth assisting one grandson and then the other. It was a day of joy for all three. When the time came to go to the cabin, there were a few fish to be cleaned before they made their journey across the fields.

Before the week was out Eddie had the boys fishing once more and he was teaching Chad how to cast a fly. Tyler used the hook and sinker line. He tried to catch up on the fish count. In between bouts of fishing, Eddie would sit on the bank and visit with the boys, talking of one thing then another. The boys kept asking more questions than he could possibly answer, before it was time to get back to fishing again.

Eddie said, "I can't spend the entire day with you fishing, I have work to do. I'll get you started and be back later in the day to check on you both. Do you think you can fish without me being here?"

The challenge was made and he heard their response almost in unison, "We can handle it Grandpa, you'll see."

On the days they had gone fishing, Jody had baked something special just for them. One of their favorites was the Rocky Mountain cookies she made. The evenings would be spent watching the sunset and visiting before bedtime.

Time flies especially when you're enjoying yourself and the boys hated to see their week evaporate so quickly. When the families came to pick them up, there were stories that unfolded and true to being fishermen, their stories were from the lips of those learning the craft.

~ ~ ~ ~

1987

The flight from the Bozeman Gallatin air strip to Seattle on the Horizon Alaskan Air was a smooth one for Eddie and Jody. They were on a trip to celebrate their twentieth wedding anniversary. At the airport, Eddie insisted, "You can sit by the window, I'd like you to see the beauty of this land."

Jody replied, "Thanks, but what if I would like to stretch my legs?"

He thought for a moment then replied, "I'll do the gentlemanly thing and allow you to step into the aisle for a moment or so." His facial features, soft and loving, were meant to get her attention.

"You're all heart," she whispered, only for his ears. She showed her appreciation by tilting her head slightly with a sweet smile on her lips. Her eyes were dancing with excitement.

Their connecting flight on Alaskan Airlines to Anchorage, Alaska was to be a three-and-a-half-hour flight. When they left the Seattle airport and began gaining altitude, Jody said, "Eddie, the whole city of Seattle is spread out down there, as clear as a picture puzzle and there is the space needle. Woops, it's gone. Below us now are the Olympic Mountains and off in the distance, I think I can make out the Cascades. Now it looks as if we're headed out over the ocean."

Eddie reached out and patted her hand that seemed to have a powerful grip on the armrest between them. She was glued to the window and taking in all the scenery. She gave a narration of what she was seeing.

When the airplane leveled out, there were refreshments served by the stewardesses. Eddie and Jody sat back and became engaged in a reflective conversation. The flight was as smooth as sitting in a lounge chair in your own living room. Their talk drifted into the past and relived moments that had brought them together. Those special times meant so much to both of them. They had so much to be thankful for and this vacation would add to their treasured memories.

When the wheels touched down on the tarmac of the Anchorage airport, there seemed to be a sigh in Jody's voice. "What a wonderful flight. Now I'm ready to see Alaska."

Their stay in a local hotel in downtown Anchorage near the train depot allowed them to get some rest and be prepared for their Alaska excursion. When they were signing in, Jody said, "Eddie, look at this, they have a wakeup call if there are any Northern lights during the night."

The clerk overheard her and said, "There aren't very many during the summer months, but if one shows up, I'll have your room listed for a wakeup."

There was no wakeup call during the night. With breakfast behind them, they found themselves at the Alaska Railroad Depot in Anchorage. They had reservation tickets for a southerly journey to the town of Seward via the Portage Glacier. Onboard the train were young students the railroad had hired as guides to point out the different features along the way. Portage Glacier was one of the main attractions on the way down. The glaciated ice had been wedged between the rugged uplifting landscapes. Over time, the force of its weight began to make a journey to lower elevations. It moved only by inches each year to melt before flowing into a glacial lake. The train slowed and seemed to take its time, allowing the passengers a good look at the natural beauty of the glacier.

When the train arrived at Seward, there was a short stay before it was scheduled to begin making its return trip to Anchorage and points north. While in Seward, the train picked up several passengers from two different cruise ships. Many of the passengers were from foreign countries and some from the lower Forty-Eight. Their transfer from the ship to the train was made during the short stay. That allowed those passengers returning to Anchorage time to step from the train and do some shopping. Many of the new arrivals were planning to spend their vacations in Denali Park.

On the return trip to Anchorage, Eddie and Jody got off the train and stayed a second night in the sprawling community at the foot of the Chugach Mountains located east of town. They rented a car and with information maps in hand, drove throughout the community. During their stay, they toured the areas where the 1964 Earthquake of 9.2 magnitude had done the most damage in Anchorage and the surrounding area out near the airport. Numerous buildings and schools were affected and sustained severe damage. The community was recovering, but there were areas that still showed the marks of devastation. There were plenty of postcards and magazines full of photos from that dreadful day and numerous items of memorabilia available for purchase.

The following morning, Eddie and Jody left the hotel and headed for the Alaska Train Depot once more. They would board the Denali Star for a scenic rail tour. When they left Anchorage, they were told that the railroad hires high school students every year to act as guides while the train travels the interior of the 49th state. The train, with several domed observation cars, headed north along the Knik Arm of the Cook Inlet and approached the Alaska Range, passing through the small communities of Wasilla and northward to Talkeetna, where they could get their first good look at Mt. McKinley. As they approached, Eddie asked, "How would you like to have that view in your backyard?"

A look of disbelief crossed Jody's face. "Eddie, I'd rather have the view we have at the homestead. This is beautiful, but it's so rugged. I don't think I would be comfortable living up here in the tundra, so far away from civilization, even with the beauty of Mt. McKinley in the background. I'm a comfort creature." Her comment and smile stole Eddie's attention from the mountain for a few moments.

Upon leaving Talkeetna, the train slowly passed over Hurricane Gulch crossing a bridge some three hundred feet above the Chuitna River on their way to Denali Park. Most of the passengers got off the train in Denali. Eddie and Jody stayed on board and continued on to Fairbanks for a two-night stay.

The train left Denali and made its way along the edge of a cliff above the Nenana River Canyon to the legendary gold rush community of Fairbanks. One full day was set aside for touring the community. They tasted the great food and met some of the locals. They used their camera to photograph for some of the hot spots, but bought several of the postcards that were available instead of using a lot of film.

When they left Fairbanks by rail, they stopped off in Denali Park. They had reservations at the intimate Skyline Lodge in the middle of Denali Park where they would remain for four days. Dining at this facility was family style. They would be eating next to a tourist and on the other side of the table would be one of the local pilots who would bend your ear with stories of the area. The decks outside the rustic lodge overlooked Moose Creek and the beautiful Kanishka Valley.

On their second day, they boarded a de Havilland turbine otter, a fixed-wing aircraft and flew completely around Denali to view magnificent peaks, glacier-filled valleys, rugged peaks and mountain ranges in the Alaska Range. It also included a flight around Mount McKinley, Mount Foraker and Hunter to the south. They flew past the Great Gorge and landed on top of Ruth Glacier. There the passengers were allowed to get off the plane and take pictures. Eddie said, "The view from here is wonderful and the flight was almost breath taking."

Jody pulled in a deep breath of air and said, "Now I can understand why some people would like to climb or venture to the top of the world. It is simply stunning up here."

The landing back at Denali brought a welcome feeling. Travelers that left the plane were reflecting on the day's events and the beauty they experienced. Tours around the park were packed with information about the vegetation, such as the beautiful Fireweed and the abundance of sweet Alaska Blueberries. There was talk about everything from the small and

227

colorful Willow Ptarmigan, to the majestic bald eagle, black bear, wolves, moose and Dall sheep.

There were groups of adventurers leaving to go kayaking and others to enjoy fly fishing. Eddie and Jody had decided not to sign up for these outings before they made their trip. Instead, they would tag along to see those returning with tales of the day and the fishermen showing off their catch of large rainbow trout and Arctic Grayling.

On the third day, they took the Denali jeep Backcountry Safari. They would drive in a caravan throughout the wilderness to explore old gold-mining areas and things only seen off the beaten path. Eddie did the driving and was assigned to a lemon-yellow jeep with tattered brown seats. Jody sat across from him and in the backseat was a young college student turned park worker over the summer. She was from Tulsa, Oklahoma and her name was Maggie. She was hired for summer employment and was their guide on the Safari, telling them all there was to know, as if she had spent her life in Alaska. From the birds to the trees, the landscape and building features, she had a story to tell about it all.

When they returned to the lodge that evening, they ran into Jeff King, a four-time winner of the Iditarod race. While sitting at their table, he had tales of what it was like to be a musher and what it was like to homestead in Alaska. After the meal, the tourists in the dining area began migrating around their table to listen to Jeff talk of his sled dogs and some of the cold weather they have been through on the Iditarod.

At the end of their four-day stay at Denali, before leaving, Jody turned to Eddie and said, "I don't believe either of us will forget this trip."

"I won't, that is for sure," Eddie replied, as he took time to turn around and get one last view of the park. They rode the Alaskan Denali Star back to its main base of operation in Anchorage where they would spend the night.

The following day, they had a morning flight out of Anchorage. Jody sat by the window and gazed at the jagged peaks that marked the Alaskan landscape and marveled at the beauty this land holds. She turned to Eddie and said, "We couldn't have made a better choice for our anniversary trip. It has been one big, wonderful experience."

When the flight settled on altitude and direction, they shared bits of loving and tender conversation until they landed in Seattle. After a short layover, they caught a flight to the Bozeman Gallatin Field Airport and were soon home on the homestead with a host of memories about their anniversary trip.

When they arrived at home, the front entrance was blocked with an enormous package. Before opening the cabin, they looked at the tag attached to the lengthy ribbon that loosely surrounded the mysterious object. The note simply stated, 'Welcome Home, we love you, enjoy your sunsets,' signed Mari, Kari, Hanh and Lien.'

When they dismantled the wrapping, they discovered an oak loveseat rocker. Eddie opened the cabin door and the two of them carried the rocker into the center of the cabin. It would be used for their daily ritual and the other rockers were placed nearby for company, should the need arise.

~ ~ ~ ~

1988

Three years had passed since their trip to Alaska, when Jody was considering retirement from her position at the university. She had grown physically tired trying to keep up the rigorous schedule. She wanted to spend more time enjoying some of the finer things in life. Their life was filled with activities, and although enjoyable, there was little time to sit back and enjoy the fruits of their labor. Jody had retired from the military and with the upcoming retirement package from the university she would have time to be with the man she loved. She wanted to be near him and his involvement in the horse business.

They had a quiet supper and sat at the table for a time discussing quick vacation plans. The university was on a semester break and it would be a good time to notify them of her intentions to retire and make a visit to the family. When she returned from vacation, she would remain at work until the university filled her position. Eddie listened and softly commented, "It will be so nice to have you close by. You have always been my right-hand gal."

The comment playfully fell upon her ears and she replied, "OK, lefty!" The spontaneity of what one said, the other often took to the opposite. If one said white the other might say black. They both enjoyed the lighthearted play, before they settled down to more serious dis-cussions.

Eddie was the first to settle down and replied, "I've always enjoyed having you near me, here on the homestead. Sometimes I needed your advice. Sometimes, I want to let you know what I'd like to have for supper, but you were at the university. This will be a time when we can grow closer together and I'm looking forward to that."

Jody topped off his coffee cup before they went into the center of the cabin to enjoy the evening sunset. She softly responded, "You have a nice way with words and I like that, too."

The loveseat rocker had two overly stuffed pillows at each end and a Shoshone blanket draped over the back for comfort, should the need arise for warmth.

They had their coffee nearby, and as they sat next to each other, Jody leaned over and placed her head on Eddie's shoulder. This was their time to be together, enjoying the comforts of life in their home.

The sky to the west was beginning to show a change of color, as the sun began to drop behind the distant mountainous terrain. There were clouds to the north and some to the south when the sun gradually dipped from view behind the Rockies. The sky filled with a reddish orange glow sending the brilliant colors across the heavens in streaks of varied rays. The clouds to the north and south dotted the sky. A heavenly display of muted color brushed against the billowing stratus, as if a giant feather had borrowed some of the color in the west and whisked the bottoms of each cloud. Moments before the awesome display began to fade from view, two military jets far above the Gallatin landscape crossed the sky. They picked up a reflective glow against their fuselage and the contrails that marked the sky also picked up some of the color. It appeared the beauty of this sunset was being protected, for those who took time to notice.

When morning came, Jody called the University President and rendered her decision to retire. The call had apparently been warmly received and at times Jody was laughing into the phone, before she gave a cheerful, "Thanks," and hung up.

Eddie reached over and took the receiver and made a call home to his mother, letting her know they would be dropping by for a visit.

Kathy was excited about them returning to the farm and said, "Your father just left for a meeting in town at the MFA. He won't be home for a couple of hours. He'll be excited to know that the two of you are headed this way."

A short time after the phone calls with their suitcases packed, Eddie and Jody were in their car and heading east on I-90. They had several miles of blacktop ahead of them before they would turn onto the familiar lane.

When they arrived in Billings, Eddie took the Business Route 90 and headed to Montana Avenue and eventually found a parking spot. A short distance from the car, they made their way to the Stockman's Café, not far from the Billings stockyards. Jody was far from being impressed with the exterior of the building and asked, "May I ask, why is the Stockman the place to eat?"

Eddie held the door open for her to enter as he answered. "One of the buyers gave me a note several months back. I have it in my wallet. It grants me a meal for two because of the mares I sold him a year ago. I thought I'd collect. If the note is no good, no problem, but if it is good, I want him to know we had a meal on him." Eddie laughed before he continued. "Some of the people I deal with are talkers. We'll see if this note is legitimate."

When they ordered their meal, Eddie laid the note out and asked the waitress, "Will the Stockman honor such a thing?"

The waitress busted out laughing and added, "Order the highest priced meal on the menu if you want. Old Benjamin scratches these things out every once in a while. I haven't seen one in over a year. His notes are as good as cash. Just sign the back so he'll know who ate at his expense. There are very few men in this state who will live by their word, but Old Benjamin is one of them."

Eddie not only signed his name, but left his phone number and added a thank you remark. Their order was modest. They wanted to head down the road and be at the farm before the sun had a chance to leave the heavens. During lunch, the conversation centered on the note and the set of circumstances surrounding Eddie getting it.

When they entered I-90 again, they were ready to make a run for the farm. They had fair weather for such a long drive and the traffic on the interstate was mild. They made good time and before long, they turned from the interstate and wound up on the dusty lane leading to the farm.

~ ~ ~ ~

When they pulled up in front of the house, Edward and Kathy were standing in the yard. They were happy to be having company. Edward said, "I saw you coming down the lane and it gave my tired old body a lift. We don't get the company we once did and at times, being in the country is just that."

Jody got her customary hug and a peck on the cheek from Edward before she was warmly embraced by Kathy. They also fussed over Eddie a bit before they made their way into the house.

Kathy had been baking from a new recipe she had copied off a TV program last week. It was still in the oven and would be introduced to the family in about ten minutes. She said, "There's going to be some oatmeal cookies in a few minutes. The coffee is in the pot, just grab a cup and help yourself."

When they were all gathered around the table, Edward asked, "What brings you kids back this way, you both homesick?"

Jody spoke up and said, "I have decided to retire from my teaching position at the university. I have some time between the semesters, so we thought it would be an excellent time to visit. We plan to see both sides of the family before we get back to what needs to be done on the homestead."

Eddie said, "We plan to visit for a few days, then we're going to stop off in Billings and catch a flight to Springfield, Missouri. We'll drop in on her father after we get there. He isn't in the best of health and we thought it would be a good time to make the rounds."

Edward asked, "How long do we have the privilege of having you two in the house?"

Eddie replied, "We'll stay through Sunday and then we'll drive back to Billings."

Kathy responded, "It doesn't seem fair, putting a time limit on all the fun talk Jody and I are fixing to have." She got up from the table to check on the cookies and Jody followed.

It was a few minutes before the women returned to the table with a tray of hot oatmeal cookies and a fresh pot of coffee, both set in the middle of the table. Neither item lasted very long as the visiting lasted deep into the night.

Shortly after breakfast on Sunday morning, Jody was helping Kathy in the kitchen with the dishes before they went to church. They had been sharing small talk, when Kathy said, "Being on the farm, there's no such thing as being able to retire. But I don't think either of us would have it any other way. This is all we know."

The men entered the kitchen, each with an empty coffee cup dangling from his fingers on their way to the kitchen stove. They wanted another cup of java before they left the farm. Edward commanded, "Shake loose of those aprons and join us for a quick cup of coffee, then we'll head into town for church."

Kathy turned around and looked at Edward from top to bottom and finally uttered, "I hope you're not intending on wearing those farm-stained boots to church. You might want to change into your 'go to meeting boots' before you go telling me to shake loose of my apron." Laughter filled the kitchen before they sat down and enjoyed one last cup of coffee.

~ ~ ~ ~

The flight from Logan Field in Billings to Denver was on the bumpy side as the airplane was buffeted by some strong winds. The flight from Denver to Springfield, Missouri was as smooth as anyone could ask for. They rented a car, had their baggage loaded into the trunk and headed out of town. The beauty of the sunset was missed as they drove south through the western part of Springfield.

When they arrived at her father's home located on several acres outside the community of Clever, she could see that her father had already turned the yard light on. The two-bedroom wooden framed house was showing its age, but it was typical for the area.

When they drove into the yard, Jody's father was making his way back to the house from the barn. No longer did he have his large dairy herd and milking chores. He had cut back to two milk cows, leaving a handful of chickens to roam the yard during the day and roost in the barn at night. In the yard, a shepherd mix that was nearly blind sprawled out on the ground near the porch. A handful of cats showed up at the porch near the screen door and steps for their evening milk.

Walter was walking with his head down and didn't see or hear the car before Jody called out, "Daddy!"

He raised his head and began to pick up his pace. Jody met him halfway back to the house. In a Missouri drawl, Walter called out, "If you're not a sight for sore eyes. Come over here and let me hug the daylights out of you." He set the milk pail down and stepped away from it to embrace his daughter. He reached over, and instead of shaking

233

hands, wrapped his arms around Eddie's shoulders in a bear hug and said, "I'm glad to see the both of you. Come inside. I'll put the milk away and feed the cats, then we can get down to some serious visiting."

When they walked into the house over a tattered linoleum floor, they passed through the kitchen to get to the living room. In the corner of the living room, Walter had brought in the cream separator and stood it up in the corner. Here, he would run his milk through the machine and take some of the skim milk and feed his cats. Jody noticed the pots and pans on the stove. Nothing indicated he had his supper yet. "What would you like to eat for supper?"

Walter answered, "I'm set till morning."

"Dad, it doesn't look as if you have had your supper."

Eddie silently stood back, not saying a word and listened to Walter answer, "No need, I'm not hungry."

Jody could see a handful of medicine lined up on the table, with very little indication he had had much to eat since breakfast. "Well Eddie and I are starved. I'll fix a bite to eat and I think I'll have enough for you if you change your mind."

When supper was cleared from the table, three plates had been wiped clean with a last bit of bread before calling it quits. They sat in comfortable chairs in the living room and visited. When Walter's head began nodding to one side or the other, they decided to call it a night. The clock showed five minutes after nine.

When morning came, Jody looked out the kitchen window and called out, "Eddie, come over here and look at this."

When he stepped up next to her, she said, "Look at that. If that isn't one of the prettiest Osage sunrises I have seen in a while, I'll…" She neglected to finish what she was saying.

"That is beautiful," Eddie spoke with some conviction, "I'm sure glad God saw fit to put Mother Nature in charge of making sunrises and sunsets."

As they gazed out the window, the barbed wire fence across the road bordered a field of tall grain stalks. The silhouette of oak trees across the field lightly shrouded in the morning fog allowed the heavy dew to accumulate on the vegetation. As the sun began to make itself known, the sky was filled with a pink, lavender and soft pastel yellow haze. It seemed to protect the deer off in the distance and the squirrels in the nearby timber.

Jody made breakfast and watched her father. He seemed to ignore the medicine that was on the table. When her father got up from the table to do some chores outside, she said, "Eddie, Dad isn't taking care of himself very well."

Eddie said, "I've noticed. Do you think he'd give up this place and come live with us for a spell?"

"Oh, Eddie," Jody chimed, "You're so thoughtful. The thought had entered my mind, but I wasn't sure when I would ask. I'm sure we haven't seen all we need to see before asking Dad."

Eddie said, "It would make it much easier if he would. That way you wouldn't be worrying about him."

When they sat down to visit later in the day, Jody asked, "Daddy, how would you like to come live with us up in Montana?"

Walter looked at his daughter and then over at Eddie and said, "I can't. You know that your mother is buried down here and I don't want to leave the farm."

Jody replied, "I know Mama is buried down here, Daddy. If this is where you want to be laid to rest, when the time comes, we can make arrangements. You could be visiting us and I could see that you take your medicine as you should."

"The answer remains the same," he retorted, "I can't leave. When I get lonely, I go over and talk to her. I'd be just plumb miserable away from here."

Jody thought for a spell then countered, "If you won't consider visiting us, would you allow me to talk to some of the folks around here, so that they may drop by and visit every week That way they can see if you're doing fairly well?"

Walter bristled for a moment, "I don't need someone coming around here telling me what to do on my own place."

"No, Daddy, they would come to see that you are eating and that you're taking your medicine when you are supposed to. They'll visit, but not cause a problem."

The discussion went on into the evening hours before Walter agreed to have someone stop by and check on him. When her father went to bed, Jody and Eddie had a lengthy talk on what they could do in a limited period of time.

When morning came and breakfast was over, Eddie accompanied Walter when he went about doing his outside chores. Jody, on the other hand, was on the telephone calling the Office of the Aging and the county nurse.

When the men came in for lunch, Jody asked, "Daddy, we are going to drive over to Ozark in the morning to see some people over that way and arrange some care. Would you like to ride along?"

"Don't mind the lift," Walter replied, "thought I'd never get a ride in that direction. I need to stop by the grain store over there and pick up some seed, if you two don't mind."

~ ~ ~ ~

When morning came, they stopped by a floral shop in Clever for a flower arrangement. Jody planned to visit the grave of a nurse who lost her life in a medevac operation in Vietnam.

When they arrived at the Missouri Veterans cemetery in Springfield, she received instructions to where her friend was laid to rest. When Eddie and Jody were returning to the car, he saw a large monument made of white marble dedicated to the Korean War Veterans. They paused for a few moments to read the inscription. Not a word was shared between them, but they knew their hearts were impacted. It brought back some vivid memories. They later joined Walter in the car and drove from the cemetery.

When they arrived in the community of Ozark, they stopped off at the feed store first before they went about taking the necessary administrative steps to have someone check in on her father. It took nearly three hours before Jody was satisfied. They had done what was needed.

On the way out of Ozark, they stopped by a floral shop and bought a spray to take to her mother's grave. When they arrived at the cemetery, all three walked to where Eva Rauch was buried.

Eddie looked down at the double headstone and realized Walter had a point. At the base of the headstone beneath her name, a brief comment, 'Taken from this land but not my heart'. The other side of the stone had Walter's name engraved, but no other information. The area around the grave had been meticulously cared for with loving hands. The other plots in the cemetery were cared for, but not with a loving touch. Eva's grave showed he had been graveside a few days before.

Jody rested the arrangement on her mother's grave, as her father reached into his pocket producing a wad of leader fishing line, pulled out his pocketknife and began securing the flowers to the headstone. With authority he said, "Around here, the wind picks up a bit and if you don't take care of the flowers, they may be in the next county come morning."

That evening, Walter sat in his rocker, closed his eyes and slowly rocked back and forth. He would occasionally lift his hand to wipe at a sniffle or to brush away the tears from his face. He was not falling asleep, just swallowed up with grief and in deep thought. They waited until he was ready to speak. His hand reached out without opening his eyes and lifted a Bible from the end table. He cradled it in his weather-beaten hands, brought it to the bib of his overalls and pressed it against his chest. He opened his eyes, looked at Eddie for a moment, and then turned his attention to his daughter before he broke into tears. "I know, I don't have long to go. I don't want to be a burden on anyone. I love you and I want you to know that if I pass on, I'll meet you at heaven's doors with your mother at my side."

Jody reached over and placed her hand on her father's knee and said, "Daddy, I love you and I know Eddie does as well. You're my camping escort. Remember when I was young, you would come along with a bunch of us kids to camp out on the James River. We went way down by Hooten Town, just to fish. We would wade in the water instead of doing a lot of fishing. In the evening we would have a campfire for hot dogs and marshmallows on a stick. We were hungry because we never caught anything to eat, remember that?"

Eddie listened and at that moment, wished he had been a part of her life at an early age. She sure had a way of reaching into the past and putting a bit of humor on some of the things she had done. Most of her mishaps were in front of her father years ago, where he would ultimately pull her from several calamities she had created.

There were light chuckles, as the reminiscing began to bring out a cheerful tone to the visit after supper. The lighthearted conversation allowed Jody to talk to her father about his health and the importance of taking his medicine. He agreed with her and promised to take the medicine as prescribed by his doctor.

~ ~ ~ ~

The return trip to the homestead was finally behind them. When morning came, Jody would call the university and see how they were progressing in finding a prospect for her position. She was informed that there was a screening process taking place and was asked if she would agree to work until the screening board named a replacement. They assured her that it would be done within the upcoming month. She agreed and the date of her retirement was set to begin in less than two months.

At the event honoring Jody Day and her accomplishments at Montana State University at Bozeman, the bulk of the community, along with faculty and staff, turned out for the formal function. They heard dozens of speakers talk of her major contributions to the university, the State, the local tourist industry and to the church the Days attended. They were proud of her and Eddie was extra proud of what she had managed to do over the years. It was her night to shine.

Eddie and Jody had just stepped into the cabin, not even having time to put the formal clothing back into the closet, when the phone rang. "Jody, can you get the phone? I'll unload the car."

When Eddie returned from the car with all the plaques and memorabilia given to Jody at the banquet, he heard a lot of laughing coming from the kitchen. When he joined his wife, he knew that she was having a chat with their son Hanh from California.

Jody cupped the speaker of the phone and whispered to Eddie that Hanh was coming home with his girlfriend and they plan to get married. She said, "Yes, sure, we'd love to, yes, he's here right now, do you want to speak to him?" Then Jody handed the phone to Eddie.

When Eddie got on the telephone, he was informed of Hanh's and Linh's plans. They would be visiting Montana between semester breaks and would be getting married while they were home. "We'll be looking forward to seeing the both of you when you get here." Eddie hung up the telephone and looked at Jody. There was happiness written all over her face.

They both had a glass of milk and a piece of cake left over from earlier in the day and chose to sit at the table and make plans for the upcoming visit.

~ ~ ~ ~

When Hanh and Linh pulled their car to a stop in front of the cabin, Jody rushed from the cabin door. Eddie was making his way back to the house from the stables. Several paces behind were Lien and her Shoshone boyfriend, Buck. They planned to meet Hanh and his girlfriend, too.

Jody had wrapped her arms around Hanh, giving him a big hug and a kiss on the cheek. Then she stood back to see a very well-dressed young lady. She was not only physically beautiful, but radiated beauty and excitement from her dark eyes as she glided up alongside their son.

Hanh said, "Mom, this is Linh."

There was a rush of arms from Jody and a response from Linh as they embraced. Jody said, "I have heard so much about you, come inside where you can get comfortable."

They had no more entered the cabin, when Eddie made it to the front door and paused for a couple of moments looking back down the path at his daughter and Buck holding hands. As they made their way to the cabin, he held the door open for the younger set.

Inside the cabin, Hanh introduced Linh to Lien, Buck and Eddie. Lien and Buck greeted her verbally, but Eddie crossed the room and gave her a welcoming hug. He said, "I'm pleased to see that my son has brought additional beauty to the homestead."

A hasty attempt was made to put refreshments together and everyone sat down and began to visit. Jody liked Linh the instant they met and could relate to her partially because of the medical background. She hoped that Linh and Hanh would make a good match for each other because of their backgrounds and the medical field both of them enjoyed.

Eddie was overwhelmed by how Linh and Hanh seemed to fit, as if hand in glove. Unlike when he met Jody, he was enlisted and she was an officer. He was the patient and she was the nurse. He could only hope for his son that the bonds of matrimony would treat him as well as the marriage he had with Jody. The more he listened to Linh, the more he was convinced that his son was making a good choice.

Lien liked her because she was her Asian sister. Linh, like herself, was a child during the war. She had likewise lost her family, although never adopted. She was raised by a church organization in southern California shortly after the fall of Saigon. When she grew up, she entered college and was out on her own without any close family ties.

Buck liked Hanh and admired him for pursuing a degree in medicine. If he got sick, maybe he could trust him enough to go to him for treatment. All he knew was horses and was good at working with rough stock that was temperamental. Lien loved horses and she was

239

teaching him all there was to know about the administrative and management part of the operation.

Hanh liked Buck just a little because he was serious on courting his sister. After all, his sister had been his responsibility for a long time. After the death of their parents, he still harbored that responsibility. For the moment, all he could see was a tall willow shape of a man in jeans, a western shirt and a hat that he seldom took off his head. Although he had it off in the cabin, it showed the raven black hair that had a hat band crease around his head. The sweatband on the hat supported a large feather. Trusting in his sister's judgment, he began to realize he was enjoying this Shoshone man, who seemed to hold inner strength and wisdom. One thing for sure, Lien loved horses and if Buck loved horses, he could see where his sister might like him.

When Eddie and Jody excused themselves, they went to the kitchen and left the younger set visiting. As they departed, they could hear the razzing Lien was giving Hanh about getting married and the laughter it caused with Linh. Hanh was asking for moral support from Buck, who didn't know if giving it would not set well with Lien. There was laughter that resonated throughout the cabin.

When Eddie and Jody reached the kitchen, he said, "I like her very much and I believe Hanh will be happy."

Jody replied, "It sure looks as if they are a match made in Medical School," then she laughed. "I see two others out there that are on the verge of getting serious."

"Buck is a good man and he has been on the homestead for a long time. The horses and management duties Lien is involved with certainly have brought them together." Eddie said, "I hope they love each other as much as they love the horses. If they do, they will probably work well together. They certainly have a lot in common, just like Hanh and Linh."

Jody said, "We have a quick wedding to arrange in the next few days. I think we can draw on some of our experience to pull it off."

"We did," Eddie said laughingly. "We can and we will."

"Good," Jody quipped, "help me set the table. I'll get supper out of the oven and then you can call them in to eat. We'll get the wedding ball rolling in the morning."

~ ~ ~ ~

240

The hasty wedding was held at the Methodist church in Bozeman the day before Hanh and Linh had to return to Los Angeles for classes at UCLA. Despite the limited time, there was a good-sized crowd at the wedding to witness the happy event. This was not a typical ceremony, as Hanh had asked Buck to be the Best Man and Lien was asked to be the Maid of Honor.

Linh had asked Eddie and Jody to escort her down the aisle. When the minister asked, "Who brings this bride into this marriage?"

Eddie and Jody said in unison, "We do." And at that moment Hanh extended his hand to join Linh's and the four hands were held together as one, making a cross, while Eddie and Jody continued in unison, "And we wish you much love and happiness." Eddie and Jody took a seat and witnessed the remaining portion of the wedding ceremony.

When Hanh and Linh were introduced to those gathered as Mr. and Mrs. Hanh Day, everyone came forward and wished the happy couple much happiness and joy.

The following day, they were on their way back to California to begin another semester of classes and their marriage.

CHAPTER 16

Family Faith - Weddings And Grandchildren - 1988

When Hanh and Linh returned to UCLA, they graduated the following semester. Both were fortunate to find a position in the same facility to complete their internship. Eddie and Jody had attended the graduation ceremony and were later shuttled to the Santa Monica Pier for dinner. For a fun-filled day, they were whisked off to visited Disneyland and Knott's Berry Farm. One evening a couple of days later, Hanh had managed to acquire four tickets and they were off to the Forum for a Laker's basketball game.

While Eddie and Jody were visiting, the latest news was mentioned, when Linh said, "We are going to have a baby."

Jody was excited over the comment and asked, "When is the baby due?"

With a smiling face, Linh replied, "I believe it will arrive near the end of February, if I figured right, or at the latest, early March."

Eddie insisted, "You keep us posted. We're happy for the both of you. This is sure going to make us proud grandparents again and I like that."

When duty called them to report for their orientation and work, Eddie and Jody made preparations to return to Montana and await the new arrival.

~ ~ ~ ~

When they returned to the homestead, they both became more actively involved with the Little Britches Riding For Jesus group. They met the first and third weekend of each month. Eddie was kept busy tending to the many needs of the equestrian unit. He was deeply involved with the horse operation most of the day. Sometimes in the evening, he would invite some of the buyers down from the lodge to see what the kids were doing. When there were guests present, there was always time to show off their drills and their ability to ride. Buyers came from near and far: from Calgary, Canada area to southern California and back east as far as Tennessee and Kentucky. Jody made a special point to see that there were always refreshments and fresh pastries available while the guests were on the homestead. Lien and Buck would see that the horses were available for the Drill team to begin the weekend, but the group was responsible for the horses until they left the homestead. Mari would bring Chet and Chad to visit on the first weekend, Kari would bring Max and Tyler on the third weekend. Halfway through the summer, the boys got together and they staggered so that Chet and Max visited the same weekend, because of their ages and Chad and Tyler would visit the next time. Eddie and Jody were kept busy.

The Little Britches group adopted the colors of blue and gold for their extended saddle blankets. The blue blanket was bordered with a thin gold cord and at the flank of the blanket, the initial of the group was embroidered in gold. In the color guard, they had the American flag and the Montana State flag. Behind those riders came eight other riders with six-foot banners flying from their staffs with alternating colors of blue and gold. They were followed by riders two abreast to include all of the riders in the youth group. They enjoyed riding casually across the homestead, but excelled in the drills and precision movements that Eddie had choreographed for them. When they became polished, it was their intent to ride in local parades and perform at some of the local rodeos. The time spent on the homestead was put to good use as a ministry from the Bozeman Methodist church. This allowed the group to hold together with an interest and a good moral purpose. Their goal was to perform at the Big Timber rodeo, the one held at Red Lodge and the ultimate, to perform at the Midland Empire Fair in Billings.

~ ~ ~ ~

1989

Nearly three months had passed, when the phone rang around two o'clock in the morning. When Eddie answered the phone, he heard the excited voice of his son Hanh. "It's a girl, Dad, it's a girl and she is beautiful."

Eddie asked, "What are the particulars?"

Puzzled by the remark, Hanh answered, "She's beautiful and has a head of black hair."

There was a pause on the phone, before Eddie asked, "Hanh, how much does she weigh, how long is she and what name have you chosen for her?" While he was asking, he was stretched across the bed shaking his wife, as he held his hand over the phone, "Honey, it's Hanh, the baby is here."

Hanh replied, "I don't know all the small details. As for a name, Linh has it narrowed down to two, but I forget what she is favoring."

Feeling groggy, Jody rose from the pillow and pressed her head against Eddie's, so that they both could hear. "Hanh, how is Linh?" she managed to ask.

"She isn't back in her room yet," was the reply. "They sent me down to the nursery and said Linh would be in her room in a few minutes. I took one quick look at the baby and I had to call. She's beautiful!"

Hanh had agreed to call later in the day when they could also talk to Linh. They planned to come to Montana about midsummer and have the baby baptized. Jody's last words into the telephone were, "Keep in touch and tell Linh that we love her."

~ ~ ~ ~

It was late in the afternoon, while riding back across the field toward the stables, that Buck reined up his horse and dismounted. Lien did the same, wondering what Buck had on his mind. He reached over, grasped her hand and said, "Lien, you have told me to control my tongue, as it was a virtue in your culture. But I can no longer endure the situation. Will you marry me?"

Lien leaped into his arms and they kissed for a moment and when their lips parted, she answered, "Yes, Buck, I will marry you. First you must get my father's permission. That is a custom in the old country as well as ours."

Buck leaned over and began placing several loose rocks into a stack about two feet high only to hear her ask, "What on earth are you doing?"

He looked into her eyes and replied, "I ask for your love at this place and when we say our vows, I would like it to be at the same spot on Mother Earth, where I asked for and received your answer."

She smiled and said, "If that is your wish, it is mine also. I am glad that you have marked the land in such a manner. From where the stones now stand, we mark and make a new beginning. I like that."

He smiled, gave her another kiss and said, "Saddle up, we're going to see your father."

When they arrived at the stables, they were a bit behind Eddie, as he had already headed for the cabin. They took care of the horses and walked the narrow path to the cabin door. Buck looked at Lien and smiled just before they went inside.

It was moments before supper when Lien and Buck entered the cabin. Once inside, they joined Eddie and Jody in the kitchen and all four began enjoying a cup of coffee. Jody had just finished informing them of Hanh and Linh's baby's birth and the exchange of phone calls that had taken place. "They plan to visit and have the baby baptized in July or August," Jody added.

Buck suddenly cleared his throat and said, "Mr. Day, I have come here today, hat in hand, to ask for the hand of your Lien in marriage. I love her and I truly hope you and Mrs. Day will grant me the privilege."

It was so quiet in the cabin; one might imagine they could have heard a rockslide as far away as Sacajawea Peak. It hadn't happened, but the inside of the cabin had fallen still. Eddie swished his coffee in a clockwise manner inside his cup. He looked first at the man who asked the question. Then he cast his loving eyes on the daughter they had adopted and raised. He glanced over at Jody and saw a woman ready to bust loose and say something. But she was going to allow him to answer first. She was smiling. Eddie returned the look back to Buck and said, "Jody and I are most honored that you came here today, hat in hand and the answer is yes. You both have our blessings. I hope you both find the happiness between you that Jody and I have in our marriage."

Buck's shoulders seemed to drop a bit, as if the weight of asking the question seemed to slip away. "We have discussed it at length and agree that the time has come."

Jody busted loose, "When is the happy occasion going to take place?

Lien said, "I believe we have settled on the month of August, but haven't set the date. Hey, that would be a good time for Hanh and Linh to bring the baby home. I went to their wedding when they were here, now they can go to ours, isn't that right Buck?"

Buck was agreeable to anything. He had asked the hardest question and got his answer, "That would be nice if they would," he replied.

Jody spoke up, "Won't the two of you stay for supper? It's about ready to be put on the table?"

Lien helped in the kitchen and the men took refuge in the center of the cabin, joking and talking of horses.

~ ~ ~ ~

It was early June when Lien and Buck's wedding was planned for August sixth. The ceremony would be held outdoors, under the Montana skies, in the open field just north of the homestead's housing area. A small stack of rocks marked the place where Buck proposed and Lien accepted. This was where they would say their vows. The Sacajawea Peak was directly to the north and the cabins of the homestead were to the south. Buck and Lien would visit the site every day to be alone and to discuss their love for one another. It was their time to be together and the togetherness bonded them as one.

~ ~ ~ ~

It was early August when Jody caught sight of the car coming down the lane and she stood ready at the door. When Hanh drove the car into the yard and pulled to a stop, Jody was out the door in a flash and making her way to the passenger side of the car. She had only seen Anh in photographs and wanted to see her up close and to hold her. When Linh handed Anh over to Jody, she took the baby and cradled her in her left arm and pulled the blanket from her face long enough to see the latest grandchild staring back at her with dark button eyes. "You're beautiful," Jody cooed, as if the infant could understand and possibly answer back.

There was a brisk breeze prompting Jody to place the blanket back over the baby's face. She held her close and walked back into the cabin with Linh. Hanh was close behind struggling with the luggage.

Hanh asked, "Is Dad around?"

Jody replied, "He's up at the lodge with Lien and Buck. They moved the office up there where they could be close to the buyers when they visited the homestead." She was interested in her granddaughter being unwrapped so she could get a good look at her.

"I'll wait to talk to him when he gets back," Hanh uttered.

Linh took the blankets that were unwrapped from around her

247

daughter and folded them before she asked, "Is everything set for the baptism this weekend?"

"We have made the arrangements with the minister and he said they will have it just prior to the benediction." Jody added, "He did say that he would like to talk to the both of you prior to Sunday's services." As Jody looked into the eyes of Anh, she was compelled to say, "My, my young lady, you are simply the most precious looking little bundle Grandma has seen in a long time." Then she cradled the child in her arms and rocked her gently.

Hanh said, "I'll call the church office and see what the pastor wants to talk to us about."

"Get all the particulars together before you call," Jody advised. "Sometimes they want to include the information on the baptism certificate. Have you two considered who the Godparents might be?"

Hanh said, "We were thinking of having Lien and Buck."

Linh came up behind Hanh's chair and rubbed the top of his head just enough to mess up his hair and said, "Maybe we better ask them first, before you go and call the pastor."

No sooner had Linh spoken when the front door to the cabin opened and in walked Lien, Buck and Eddie. There was a squeal from Lien when she saw the baby. She rushed to get her first real look at Anh. Hanh got up from his chair to meet the men near the center of the cabin. He shook hands with Buck, then shook hands with his father and gave him an extended hug.

Lien held out her hands in a gesture to have the baby passed into her waiting arms. When the exchange took place, Lien whispered, "If my Asian-born parents could only see you, they would be so proud. Oh, you're so beautiful." She held the child and took her finger and touched Anh on the forehead followed by the nose and then the chin, causing the infant to smile.

Bits of chatter filled the air before Linh said, "Lien, Hanh and I would like to have you and Buck as Anh's Godparents. Would you?"

Lien looked up and said, "I would and I'm sure Buck would also. Buck!"

Hearing his name called out, he turned to Lien and gave her his undivided attention to hear his future wife say, "We'll be Godparents to Anh, won't we?"

Buck looked on and said, "That we will, and we need to have Hanh as Best Man and Linh you're going to have to fill in as Matron of Honor." The trade-off caused much laughter and when the time came, Hanh and Linh stood side by side when he called the church office to talk with the pastor. Eddie held little Anh in his arms for the first time and pranced around the cabin, working off nervous energy.

While Hanh was on the telephone, Jody quietly asked Linh, "How did you come to name her Anh?"

Linh said, "She lit up our lives and made us so happy, so we called her Anh. In Vietnamese, it stands for Intellectual and Brightness."

"That is so fitting," Jody replied. "She sure brings out a lot of talk of her beauty and she sure has most certainly brightened up our world."

When Hanh got off the telephone, he asked, "Sis, tell us about the wedding, where and when and all that stuff."

Lien smiled and replied, "Well, for starters we're going to have an outside wedding."

"You're kidding," Hanh managed to say. "How did this all come about?"

"We were riding back from checking on some of the horses, when Buck reined up and right out in the middle of the field, he proposed. He thought it would be nice to have the wedding at the same spot where he proposed and I agreed."

~ ~ ~ ~

Buck Willow had contacted all the Shoshone he knew and told them of his upcoming marriage to Lien. The ceremony would be shared with a pastor from the Methodist church out of Bozeman. Buck met with several of the elders to include the spiritual leader and sought their advice. The ceremony was to take place in the open air, a short distance from the cabins on the Weismann homestead, on August tenth at two in the afternoon. There was much coordinating to do and Buck was informed by his elders of his responsibility in helping out.

Lien had visited the Methodist church office and talked with Pastor Keith Bishop who was excited to be part of the wedding ceremony. She explained how the decision was made to have the wedding outdoors. Casual western attire, jeans and western wear, was encouraged. She said, "We're not going to have an elaborate wedding that requires a lot of money. We have decided on a small simple, get-it-done kind of wedding.

249

It is to be held before family and friends in a casual setting, at the exact point where he asked and I accepted. We would like to have you officiate and we plan to have the spiritual leader from the Shoshone take part in the ceremony."

Following the exchange of vows, there will be the cutting of the cake with nuts and mints available along with a punch that best not be spiked. We'll recognize the gifts at that time. That way if some of the guests need to leave and go home, they will have seen most of what will be happening. There will be an outdoor barbeque available with all the trimmings and request that nonalcoholic beverages be consumed, starting from about 5:30, but no later than 6:30 in the evening. There will be entertainment from the Little Britches Riding For Jesus group that will precede the singing and dance, along with some entertainment from the Shoshone. Nothing special is planned. It's just a casual way to top off the day.

Pastor Bishop commented, "You and your husband-to-be are encouraged to come into the office for premarital counseling and we will talk of what your plans are. It will also give me time to talk with the spiritual leader of the Shoshone who is going to be a part of the ceremony."

Their visit was lengthy with Lien leaving the church happy, knowing that her part of the wedding ceremony planning was beginning to take shape. She knew the congregation would be happy for her. She knew they would understand why the ceremony was going to be conducted as they wished. There was planning, but she didn't want to make it a lot of work for either of them. That evening, she planned to finalize her guest list and was in hopes Buck had his completed. Then they could start addressing the invitations.

~ ~ ~ ~

On the morning of August sixth, the spiritual leader met with Pastor Bishop and they went over their last few notes. They sat on the Weisman porch in comfortable chairs. Gun sat in his wheelchair, taking in what the two religious men were talking about. Susie had brought out some iced tea for the three of them to enjoy while they waited for the crowd to arrive.

250

~ ~ ~ ~

In the cabin Jody, and Linh fussed over Lien and helped her into her white silk wedding gown that had a Vietnamese flare at the chest and neckline. Jody teased, "Your hair is piled atop your head in such a way that it gives you the appearance of being taller than you are."

Linh handed Jody the veil that was attached to the head piece. The netting was shorter in front and the back draped down past Lien's shoulder blades. The netting held a baby's breath pattern that brought out the beauty of something sheer and delicate. Jody took the head piece and placed it in Lien's hair to make sure they had her hair in place to hold it properly. She removed it and set it aside until they were ready to leave the cabin.

It was a time to be nervous and Lien found herself pacing in her hose barefoot, not wanting to put on the shimmering patent leather white flats until she was ready to leave the room. She planned to have a coin from Vietnam in one shoe and in the other a quarter, both with their heads up. She felt it would be nice to have a coin from her past and one from the present with her during the ceremony. They would later turn into a keepsake. Buck had agreed and would respond likewise.

Calm as after the storm, Linh wasn't nervous. She had weathered the jitters and was aware of what Lien was going through. She laughed and teased a bit saying, "You're going to look back on your feelings of today, laugh and ask yourself, 'Why?' I guess every bride has to go through it at least once."

The preparation was going smoothly and things seemed to fall into place in its own time. Linh was called downstairs to check on Anh moments before she had to get ready herself. Jody tended to the rest of what Lien had to have done. Edward and Kathy were sitting back and enjoying the gathering. Kari and David kept a watchful eye on Chet and Chad, Mari and Gordon kept a tight rein on Max and Tyler's behavior. It was a gathering of family and all seemed to be having a good time.

Buck had been smuggled to the arena area by some well-intended friends, keeping him from seeing the bride too early. Members of his tribe were giving him a bad time because he was required to leave his hat and boots behind. He had his hair trimmed, although it showed some length by touching his collar. He wore a white shirt under a cream-colored wedding buckskin vest. It had been traditionally smoked, cured and

251

handed down from his father. His father had given him a hand-crafted silver piece to gather in the extended purple and white twisted neckerchief that rested under his collar. He wore black dress slacks and would walk in moccasins that bore the Shoshone design. In one moccasin was an old Shoshone marker chip and in the other a folded dollar bill with George Washington looking up. A marker chip from his past and the dollar bill marked the current currency. He would later remove them and give them to Linh to be placed with the other coins for keepsakes.

~ ~ ~ ~

It was nearly 12:30 when the road to the homestead looked as if there had been a major detour sign put up on the interstate. Numerous cars, pickup trucks of different models, some new, others old and showing marks of rough treatment, were coming down the road, bumper to bumper. There were trucks hauling trailers, some modern others homemade and others that looked as if they had been rolled down a hillside before being repaired. The trailers were loaded with horses and they lined the drive leading down to the stable area near the Day family cabin and Mr. Weisman's house. The cars and pickup trucks were directed to park in one of the open fields. The adjoining sloping hillside was matted with a variety of wild yellow and white flowers. The trucks with stock were directed toward the stable area where they could park and unload their horses. There they could take them into the arena area for feed and water while the riders made preparations for their part in the day's event.

As the guests parked their vehicles, they made their way to the front of Mr. Weisman's house and gathered on his front lawn to momentarily talk with friends. They could see some of the Montana bitter root flowers gathered in clusters randomly between the pasture fence lines and the path leading to his house.

The fields that joined the nerve center of the homestead were a lush green for this time of year. The grass had grown higher than the last cutting of hay stubbles in the field. Random floral clusters of Indian paintbrush, lupine, yarrow, columbines, arrowhead and balsamroot dotted the fence line like the border of a large elaborate handmade quilt. In the distance, the flowers blurred and became indistinguishable only leaving faded color to mark their presence. It was peaceful here and

Mother Nature intended to show off her tapestry to the guests that visited this part of Gallatin County.

When the guests arrived, they gathered near the Weisman house and would walk to the wedding site as a group. Those with wedding gifts took them to a special table near the arena before joining the others. At 1:30, several young Shoshone braves in tribal dress rode their ponies two abreast and created an avenue for the wedding party and guests to enter the field. Gun and Susie led the guests to the wedding site. Pastor Bishop put on his robe and stole and placed a Bible in his hand. The Shoshone Spiritual Leader held eagle feathers, a beaded cloth across one arm and a handful of cedar. They were joined by the Robe Bearer, who carried a buffalo robe. The guests would lead the way for the wedding party to the designated site.

By foot, the journey began with the guests entering the avenue. It was less cumbersome for those who wore boots and challenging for those who chose to wear high heels. The field held a layer of short grass and the walking was relatively easy but barely manageable for a wheel-chair. When the guests had arrived, they stood and waited for the ceremony to begin. The guests had divided and made an aisle for the wedding party to walk through at the site. They turned to look back at the house and cabin where they could see Pastor Bishop, the Shoshone Spiritual Leader and Robe Bearer followed closely by the groom, best man and matron of honor.

The Robe Bearer walked forward and stood to the north of the pillar of rocks holding the buffalo robe. Reverend Bishop and the Spiritual Leader stood on the south side of the pillar of rocks and waited for the wedding party to arrive.

When Buck, Hanh and Linh arrived, they walked up the makeshift aisle and stood some distance from the pillar of rocks in their proper positions and waited.

The bride was escorted by her mother and father. They began the walk from Mr. Weisman's front yard. They headed into the field to a designated point before the wedding would take place. Jody and Eddie would escort their daughter up the aisle when the time was right.

The Spiritual Leader was in Shoshone attire with a traditional Shoshone choker around his neck, a beaded cloth draped across one arm and he held an eagle feather in his left hand the other gripped a small amount of cedar. Pastor Bishop wore a black shirt with the clerical collar

253

and black slacks beneath his robe and a stole that reflected the Methodist emblem embroidered near each end.

When the last of the wedding party passed, each Shoshone brave would ride off to complete a circle of braves around those gathered.

When the air was filled with the music of several Shoshone songs played on the flute, the ceremony was about to begin. At the end of the flute playing, the Spiritual Leader stepped toward the helper and placed the cloth of beaded design atop of the buffalo robe. He lit the cedar he held in one hand on fire. The fire quickly snuffed out and the smoke billowed from the green cedar. The spiritual leader moved the cedar smoke over the rock pillar and on the ground in front of the stone marker, where the wedding party would stand. In the purification process, he waved the smoke toward the ground and then skyward, with the eagle feathers. He returned to his Robe Bearer's side and they unfolded the robe and placed it atop the pillar of stone and positioned the strip of Shoshone bead work on top. With his work completed, the Spiritual Leader spoke in his native tongue. With his arms outstretched and facing the heavens, he chanted a prayer. With his prayer completed, he stepped to the side.

Pastor Bishop stepped forward and placed the open Bible atop the beadwork, centering it on the robe above the stone pillar. When he turned, he invited the groom, best man and matron of honor to step forward onto the sacred ground.

When Lien and her parents began entering the aisle, two Shoshones pressed their flutes to their lips and began playing the "Wedding March"; the tone and high-pitched fluttering accentuated the melody. Lien held a large bouquet of flowers tied off with several streamers of ribbon resting in her arms. When they arrived before the minister, he asked, "Who gives this woman into this marriage?"

Eddie and Jody spoke in unison and said, "We do."

Stepping aside, Eddie and Jody left their daughter standing near the man she would soon marry. They had joined the others to witness the exchange of vows. Not only was their daughter getting married, but the joining of two cultures. Lien is Vietnamese and Buck is a Shoshone Indian, their union marked a ceremony that bonded east and west in a special way.

When he turned to face the crowd, Pastor Bishop said, "Dear honored guests, we are gathered here today to witness and bind in Holy matrimony Buck Willow and Lien Day. Please bow your head in prayer,"

Keith Bishop prayed aloud for the couple that was about to enter into their vows and asked for the blessings upon their union, then he closed with an "Amen."

The guests were quiet in an attempt to hear all that was said during the exchange of vows. Pastor Bishop spoke louder than usual and encouraged the bride and groom to do likewise. Before long the vows had been completed and the rings exchanged, before the Minister said, "You may now kiss the bride."

The Shoshone Spiritual Leader came forward and blessed the bride and groom in their union before he stepped aside.

The Methodist Minister asked them to turn and face those gathered, before he said, "I now introduce you to Buck and Lien Willow."

No sooner had his actions been completed, when there was a screeching from the heavens. With everyone looking upward, they could see two eagles circling overhead screeching, as if giving their blessings. The crowd was awed by the display of the eagles at this particular moment. The Spiritual Leader said, "It is a blessing like no other."

When the stirring moment with the eagles had passed, there was applause from the group for the newly-married couple. Tradition took over when Lien turned her back to the group and a flurry of single ladies rushed to get behind the bride, as she slowly bent at the waist and with enthusiastic energy, tossed the bouquet back over her head. The young lady that caught the bouquet of flowers squealed with excitement, hoping that tradition was corrected and she would be the next to marry.

When the wedding was complete, the Shoshone braves rode off and provided an avenue for the guests and wedding party to follow on their way back to the homestead.

When Lien turned around, she placed her hand on Buck's arm. They followed the Minister and the Spiritual Leader down the aisle. Eddie, Jody, Gun in his wheelchair and Susie along with Buck's parents, Storm and Snow Bird Willow, and the immediate families fell in behind and walked from the field, followed by the guests.

The Shoshone braves rode their ponies off to the side near the arena and secured them before changing clothing.

In the yard, several tables had been set up where the wedding gifts had been placed. One of the tables held the paper plates, napkins and utensils and a tray of nuts, mints and three large punch bowls. On another table was the wedding cake. Buck and Lien were on one side and the guests on the other, some snapping photos of the event. Buck picked up the knife and Lien rested her hand on his and the wedding cake was about to be cut.

Several of the guests began singing the Shoshone Love Song. They sang it once in the Shoshone native tongue and again in English. When they had finished Lien was overwhelmed and said "My heart has been touched by such a song, thank you." Buck only nodded in agreement. Beaming with excitement, they looked at each other, picked up the knife and cut the cake. When the guests had passed by the tables and gathered in their refreshments and a piece of wedding cake, the bride and groom went to the table with the gifts. They opened each one and recognized the giver graciously. Buck spoke up and said, "Before long, the barbeque will be ready and we invite you to stay and take part in it. Following the barbeque, we have impromptu entertainment, so please stick around and see what will happen next."

Lien excused herself and rushed to the cabin where she exchanged her wedding dress for white blouse and dark slacks and a pair of boots before returning to the crowd.

Pastor Bishop was invited to go into Gun's house to change his clothing. He accepted and only removed his robe and stole. He returned to the gathering with his black shirt, clerical collar and black trousers.

Before the barbeque took place, the Little Britches Riding For Jesus group rode and displayed the intricate maneuvers and drills they had been practicing. The young Shoshones showed off their riding skills and introduced the guests to a game they played on horseback with a ball and hoop sticks. As the barbeque came to an end, the sun was beginning to set in the western skies and a brilliant display across the heavens blessed those gathered at the homestead.

After the sunset the bon fire provided a glow as the Shoshone danced around the fire and sang Shoshone songs. Later, the crowd was asked to add their voices to several Methodist spirituals.

There were several stock buyers that witnessed the wedding and other activities, before venturing back to the lodge. They enjoyed their relationship with those on the homestead.

The entertainment went well into the night, before they discovered, the newlyweds had slipped away on a honeymoon. It was late in the night when the festivities came to an end.

~ ~ ~ ~

The day after the wedding, Eddie took his grandsons fishing at their favorite fishing hole. When Chet and Max ventured upriver looking for a good spot to fish, they discovered an eagle's nest high up in a sycamore tree on an island in the middle of the Gallatin River. "The nest was about seven feet across and about ten feet deep," Chet boasted.

Max bragged, "I saw it first."

Chad and Tyler had talked their grandpa into getting them started at fly fishing. They were spread out on the gravel bar a short distance down river from where the nest was discovered. Chad had a dusty miller and Tyler relied on the Royal Coachman. Chad had insisted he would fish from the gravel bar and Tyler thought upriver was a bit was more to his liking.

When Chet and Max came back to tell Eddie about the nest, the other two decided that fishing was more fun than going to look at a bunch of twigs up in a tree. Eddie trusted the two younger lads because they were avid fly fishermen at this point. He decided to go with the older boys to look at the nest.

Chet led the way and Max was right behind him. They hurriedly made their way up through some willows and across a couple of fallen logs. They finally got to the point where they could look directly across the river toward the island. The tall sycamore tree was huge and reached to the heavens. When the boys stopped, they were both pointing across the water to the island. "See there," Chet managed to say, half out of breath from the return trip.

"Sure, as thunder," Eddie remarked. "That's an eagle's nest alright. Have either of you seen an eagle near the nest?"

Chet bragged, "I bet that is the nest that belongs to those two eagles that flew over the wedding yesterday."

Max looked at Eddie and said, "He likes to bet on things he isn't really too sure about."

With a comforting hand, Eddie placed a hand on each of his grandson's shoulders and said, "Nature is funny at times. Sometimes you look for something and when you find it, it's practically in your own back yard. I have seen one flying way back two or three months ago. I thought they would be making their nest in the higher country. Just goes to show you grandpas can miscalculate sometimes."

257

Max said, "I take it as a lucky spot right here to flip my line. Chet you can either go upstream or down, but I'm fishing right here."

"I'm going upstream a short way and catch them before they get down to your line." Chet added, "I bet I'll catch more than you, cousin."

Max looked at Eddie and said, "See, there he goes again."

Out of curiosity, Eddie decided to stay with the older boys for a while longer in hopes of seeing one of the eagles return to its nest. As time went by, he gave up his waiting and returned downstream to check on the younger set.

When Eddie was making his way off a mud bank at the end of a willow patch, he looked up and saw both boys dancing on the rocks and handling their fly rods with enthusiasm. Each lad had a trout on and they were feverishly feeding line or reeling it in. They were doing what it took to keep control of the rod. Tyler was the first to land his and before he had his hand into the net, Chad was leaning down with his net in hand making an attempt to haul his in. Eddie stood still looking at the two cousins who loved fly fishing and being able to land some pretty good-sized trout. He was proud of them and remembered the days when they tried to become experts overnight.

Eddie approached each lad to see the trout they had landed and said to each one, "Not too shabby, that one is a pretty good size."

He stayed with Chad and Tyler for a short time and his curiosity grew even stronger. Seeing that they were back casting and teasing the water with their flies, he excused himself and ventured up stream.

Eddie stayed occupied keeping tabs on four fishermen on the same day, while having the urge to check out Mother Nature. Chet and Max had both caught two trout and were sitting on the bank chatting with each other when Eddie arrived. They were tired of fishing and were ready to go back to the cabin.

When they stepped out of the willows and down off the mud bank, a length of line with a fly attached whizzed in front of their faces. It caused all three to duck, as if the hook was an angry bee. It came by once more, before Tyler had let his line sail out through the loops and eye of his fly rod. The fly rested atop the swift moving current of the Gallatin. Tyler had moved upstream on the gravel bar and was nervously trying to catch up on the fish count, as Chad was one up.

Eddie said, "Careful boys, Tyler is getting serious."

They moved away from the area allowing Tyler to cast. His line sailed through the air with a magical flow and landed upstream a short distance allowing it to float downstream. Without warning, the slack in the line became taut and the tip of the rod was lifted to the heavens, as it bowed. Tyler fed the line out and lowered the rod. He was a young master at work and he enjoyed having a fighter on the end of the line. Moments later he grabbed his net and with the greatest of ease ran the net beneath the trout and lifted it from the cold flowing river water.

Tyler called out to Chad, "We're even."

Eddie told the boys, "Reel in your line. We need to do some cleaning before we take the fish up to the cabin."

As they squatted at the edge of the river cleaning the trout, they looked up at the shadow of a bird flying overhead and saw an eagle swoop down and pull a trout from the water and disappear over the tops of the cottonwood and sycamore trees that were bordered with willows. When they got back to the cabin, each would have a story to tell.

~ ~ ~ ~

Weeks after the many guests and family members had gone home from the wedding and christening, Eddie and Jody were sitting and relaxing in the double rocker following supper with Buck and Lien. They all were getting ready to witness another one of the splendid sunsets at the end of the day in big sky country. Buck and Lien were sitting in the two older rockers. They relaxed after eating a roast with all the trimmings, including fresh bread and for dessert, a freshly baked wonderberry pie.

Eddie asked, "Are you two settled down enough from your abbreviated honeymoon to take on some responsibility around here?"

Buck took the comment as a joke about their married life and said, "The honeymoon was short, but it was sweet. We're back to do what is necessary around the homestead."

Jody raised an eyebrow at Eddie's comment and smiled over at Lien, who took her father's comment in stride.

"We enjoyed the first few days," Buck reminisced, "but when Lien started talking of the problems with some of the horses and keeping tabs on the account ledger, I knew her love was back here at the homestead. She has taught me a lot about her style of management and I try to keep up with her, without making too many mistakes. We share the love of horses and I guess we can't get that out of our blood, so we gladly returned."

Lien spoke up, "Daddy, I think we're happier here than being out and about trying to enjoy ourselves. Especially when we know there's work that needs to be done."

"That sounds more like dedication to me," Jody replied. "Some people have it, while others don't."

As the sun began to fall behind a bank of clouds that was etching the western landscape, the colors began to change, moment by moment. The searing glow of the sun began to fade and the reflective rays began to touch the scattered clouds with a soft touch of color, from pink to lavender to a light blue. A thin orange glow spread out over the top of the layer of dark clouds to the west, like butter on hot toast. The heavenly display marked the end of the day as the homestead lights in the yard began to flicker and glow.

Eddie said, "I'm asking the both of you to consider what Jody and I have discussed in depth. We are at an age where we would like to settle back and enjoy what few years we have left. What I'm saying is we'd like to hand over the management and overall operation of my share of the homestead to the two of you."

Lien panicked, "Is there something you're not telling us? Are you sick or what?"

"No, no," Jody tried to calm her daughter, from going into hysterics. "We have talked about this for a while and thought there would come a day when we would hand over our responsibilities here on the homestead. It should go to someone more energetic that understands the whole operation, that's all."

"Does Hanh know what you two have planned?"

Jody replied, "Your brother and Linh have their chosen field in medicine. They have their positions in a hospital in southern California, which is where their love is. The two of you share the same love for the horse operation as your father and I do. This is why we are asking the two of you."

Buck said, "I'm honored that you would consider me. I'm still learning some of the management skills that Lien possesses."

Eddie said, "Buck, your part of the family now and by choosing the two of you, we figure two heads are better than one." He laughed and tried to put a light spin on his having to ask. "You understand and have a feel for horses like no other that I have ever run into. You're a good man and an excellent judge of horse flesh."

The rest of the evening was spent with laughter and lighthearted comments, aside from the business at the homestead. There would be a time for transition before they took over complete control of the managing and functions within the horse operation. They knew it would take time to have all this done.

Before the evening grew any longer, Jody got up from the double rocker and went to the kitchen and brought back a pan of cinnamon rolls, she had baked earlier. Lien had followed and was pouring a cap on everyone's coffee. She took the pot back into the kitchen and returned with a skip in her step.

It was late in the evening when they called it a day. Buck and Lien stayed downstairs that night, instead of venturing to their home.

CHAPTER 17

Rose Parade – Hometown On Veteran's Day – 1995

The past month had been filled with the transition of several managerial responsibilities on the homestead. Eddie and Jody had made their choice to step aside and enjoy their senior years and watch from a distance as the horse business continued. Buck and Lien had taken over and had planned a horse show extravaganza. All the horse associations within the state would come together one last time. They would recognize Eddie Day for his accomplishments before he retired. The show had a dual purpose, Lien and Buck planned to use the show to make a statement, 'this is where the heart of the horse business was located.'

When Friday came the road to the homestead was filled with pickup trucks and trailers loaded with a variety of horses. Some of the overflow had to be parked in the adjoining open field. The arena grounds were filled to near capacity with some of the stockmen hitching their horses near their stock trailers. Businesspeople and horse buyers from as far away as Calgary, Canada, southern California, Kentucky and Tennessee had already booked reservations at the lodge for the weekend.

Early Saturday morning, there was a two-hour veterinary clinic, held at the arena grounds with the stands filled to capacity. Following the clinic, the Little Britches Riding For Jesus group put on a demonstration of drills and horsemanship for the crowd. They introduced the Christian Horse-lovers Club from Wisconsin that had a motto; 'Saddle up for a great adventure with God.' A youthful team from the Eastern Team Penning Association gave an exhibition of their skills. They were rowdy, but seemed to have the most fun while riding hard and penning their calves. The American Quarter Horse Association, United Professional

Horsemen's Association was represented along with the Purebred Morab Horse Association that came in from Indiana and Kentucky. The American Saddlebred Horse Association came in from Calgary, Canada. They had made the trip without bringing down their stock across the border. The Canadian government had issued health concerns for those crossing into the United States with livestock. From Tennessee, six riders from the Bluegrass State Appaloosa Horse Club showed off their horses and their riding abilities. The National Cutting Horse Association was the last to perform in the morning. The crowd enjoyed seeing the ability of the horse to do the cutting and the rider seemingly sitting relaxed in the saddle. There were five riders who picked out a different calf on each round. Some of the calves were far from cooperating, but the skills of the horse and rider won out in the end.

During the noon hour, the barbeque fixings had been prepared at the lodge by the Shoshone and catered to the arena area. The lunch hour was cut short in order to fit in all the other programs and the crowd returned to the stands for more excitement.

Several riders from the American Painted Horse Association put on a demonstration of the walker and trotters' class and were joined by eight riders from the Arkansas Gaited Horse Show Association, who gave their demonstration with the Missouri Fox Trotters and Tennessee Walker Class. This was a show within itself, as the two groups put on a magnificent display.

The Sierra Empire Arabian Horse Association and the Comstock Arabian Association from California and Nevada had a limited number of Arabians with them. But the elegance and the Arabian formal dress of the riders was stunning. It was a show display that many of the guests marveled over. Most of the crowd that had their roots in and around Montana hadn't seen such a display in person.

The E Z Run Pro Barrel Racing Association brought out their horses and showed them off to the crowd before the competition began. They emphasized the skills needed in a horse to qualify as a pro barrel racer. When the competition began, there were a total of nine female riders. This was a timed event with each contestant riding fast to round the barrels without knocking them down and beating the others' time. The group made it clear that they were there to buy, if there was a horse that looked promising.

The next two events were meant for entertainment. The first was a father and son, under ten years of age, team roping and untying the ribbon off a calf's tail, a timed event. When the calf was released, the father would rope the calf. He had two tries before being disqualified. When he had the calf roped, his son on foot was to chase down the calf and remove a ribbon from its tail. When he raised the ribbon in the air, his time was marked. The crowd cheered after the calf was caught, encouraging the youth as they tried to chase the calf down and untie the ribbon. The laughter filled the stands, as each team tried to beat the others' time. It wasn't long before they had a winner.

The arena was nearly filled with calves. All of the riding youth and those in the crowd under fifteen were invited to participate in a calf scramble. When the youth were gathered at one end of the arena, they were told by a voice over the PA system, "There are five ribbons tied to the tails of the calves. Each white ribbon was worth $25.00 and the red ribbon was worth $50.00. When we begin, you will need to race down to the calves and find the calf with a ribbon and untie it from the tail. When all five of the ribbons are accounted for, the fun is over. Get ready get set, go!"

Laughter erupted from the crowd, as the storm of young children running toward the calves caused the calves to go wild and run as best they could. As exciting as it was, three children fell. From the stands, it looked as if they may have been hurt, but when it was over, not one was injured.

Buyers and folks interested in the line of horses raised on the homestead were invited for a hayride tour covering the many pastures and a slide presentation that would be available for viewing at the lodge later in the day.

When the entertainment ended, the crowd returned to the lodge and prepared for the banquet dinner and dance in the large ballroom. A conference room was made available for the younger set with entertainment.

When the banquet and dance was nearing an end, there was the recognition from many of the horse associations for Eddie's contribution to their organizations and the standard of excellence in which he held his horse operation. Every plaque and certificate were important to Eddie and before the night was over, there was one request from the Sierra Empire Arabian Horse Association. "Mr. and Mrs. Eddie Day, it is the request of our organization that you ride with our group in the Tournament of Roses Parade in Pasadena, California on New Year's Day. This is an all-expense paid round trip from Bozeman. It is our way of saying thanks for your dedication in raising the finest of horses." The remainder of the

265

evening was enjoyed on the dance floor, listening to some of the finest local country music.

~ ~ ~ ~

At year's end, Eddie and Jody made their trip to Los Angeles and landed at LAX on Friday in the afternoon. When they were walking down the ramp from the plane into one of the satellite pods located around the airfield, they were met by their hosts Mr. and Mrs. Ellis Campbell. They were from Santa Clarita, a community northeast of Los Angeles on Highway 5.

The Campbell family held a small sign with one simple word, 'DAY' written in large letters. Eddie and Jody saw the sign moments before the Campbell family saw them.

Ellis greeted Jody and introduced his wife, "This is Elsa and honey this is Jody and Eddie Day." The meeting was brief and before long they headed down the escalator to walk on the moving walkway. It ran under the runways and came out at the airline's ticket office near the turn-style luggage carousel. The luggage area was inside a large glassed-front window that faced Century Boulevard. When they claimed their luggage, they walked across one of the loops of Century Boulevard into a parking lot, where Mr. Campbell had parked his ranch's station wagon.

They headed east on Century Boulevard until they turned on the ramp for the San Diego Freeway, Highway 405 and headed north. Above the San Fernando Valley, they turned on Highway 5 and some eight miles later, they were in Santa Clarita and making their way outside the town to their ranch.

From the highway, it looked like a small ranch tucked into the foothills of the Angeles National Forest. Ellis asked Eddie to accompany him to the stables for a quick tour of the stable and ranch. Elsa, on the other hand, invited Jody into the ranch house.

When Eddie followed Ellis to the stables, he saw an efficient facility with several stable hands tending to the horses. Eddie said, "I'm impressed with the operation you have here."

Ellis replied, "The horses that I have here today will be those taking part in the parade. The pavement will take a toll on the horses if their shoes aren't properly cared for beforehand. We get them curried and otherwise prepared, along with all the parade regalia that will decorate each horse."

"Seeing what you have here on the ranch is impressive," Eddie remarked, "I can see why you and your buyers were so particular when you came to buy."

"The rest of the horses are out to pasture," Ellis added. "They run up close to the Angeles National Forest that borders the property."

They walked out of the stable area and looked over the back side of the ranch. There the Arabians were enjoying their freedom in the open pasture. Eddie's first impression of the ranch when they had arrived was that it was relatively small. However, the ranch was larger than he first thought. Eddie was impressed.

~ ~ ~ ~

When Jody followed Elsa into the spacious ranch house of Spanish Stucco, the inlaid tile and the heavy wooden doors gave off a masculine appearance. Inside, the high ceilings were marked with heavy beams. The walls were decorated with southwestern rugs and tapestries. As Jody walked past one of the rooms, she could see it was the trophy room for the ranch. They went to the center of the house where the ceiling was the highest and the room was decorated with the finest of leather furniture. The walls displayed large pictures of the Arabian horses they had on the ranch.

Elsa ordered tea for two from the maid, while saying to Jody, "Please make yourself comfortable. We'll sit in here and wait for the men to join us. It will give us time to get to know each other." They had tea and visited. Jody summarized her role in life and her experiences before meeting Eddie. Elsa talked of her growing up in Chattanooga, Tennessee and coming to California as a student at UCLA. She had a scholarship and became a registered nurse. She explained, "I worked for a number of years at County General, a hospital in Los Angeles, before I met Ellis."

Jody asked, "Is that where you met him?"

"Goodness, no," Elsa answered. "A friend of mine asked me to accompany her and her fiancé to an equestrian horse show at Rancho Palos Verdes. I met Ellis there and fell in love with him and that beautiful horse he was showing. My life took a big right turn the day I met him. Life as I knew it, from that point on, has never been the same."

Jody said, "My life hasn't been the same since Eddie entered into it, either, and I wouldn't change it for a moment."

"It is odd," Elsa replied. "Here we are both with a history in nursing and married to men that are so involved with horses."

They enjoyed their talk and with the similarities in their lives, they found comfort in talking with the other. Elsa would talk of Tennessee and California and Jody would talk of Missouri and Montana.

~ ~ ~ ~

In the evening hours, the two couples sat in the living room near a large fireplace and talked of one subject and then another. Before the night came to an end, Ellis asked, "We have an equestrian unit in the parade and we also have a carriage. The parade is some two hours long and covers five and a half miles. I'll leave it up to the two of you, if you would rather ride in the saddle that distance, or in the carriage."

Elsa said, "You'll get a matching shirt, Eddie. Jody, we'll get you a blouse with the rose design on it, as our gift to the both of you for being our guests."

Turning to Elsa, Jody said, "Thank you very much. I see that I'll be leaving California with a very special memento."

Eddie looked at Jody and said, "I'm up to the ride if you would rather do that, or would you prefer the carriage?"

"I believe we'd enjoy riding horseback, if it isn't any trouble," Jody said, while displaying a smile on her face. There was laughter and they visited deep into the night, the same way as folks in Montana do.

~ ~ ~ ~

Two days later, on January 1, 1996, Eddie and Jody found themselves in a church parking lot, not far from Ellis Street and Orange Grove Boulevard in Pasadena. The horses were still in the trailers for the moment, as the parade floats and various marching bands were assembling and passing by.

Eddie and Jody stood in awe at the size of the floats. The floats made their way to their positions and began making their way to the parade route. The horses were unloaded and the equestrian group lined up in the order they would ride in the parade. The Days were both impressed with their mounts and honored that they were able to ride with the Sierra group in such a nationally-known parade.

268

It wasn't long before one of the parade volunteers, a white-suiter, notified them their position was coming up and had them enter the parade as scheduled. When they turned onto Colorado Boulevard, it was a short distance before they were approaching the Grandstand area. Along the parade route, nine TV networks broadcasted the Rose Parade live. Eddie and Jody waved to the crowd, but when it came time to be in front of the cameras, they waved into the cameras, in hopes that people back in Montana would get a glimpse of them. The folks back home knew they were riding with the Sierra Empire Arabian Horse Association entry.

After they passed the Grandstands, it was a matter of riding and waving to the crowd along Colorado Boulevard, which ran through the community of Pasadena, California. Before them were many floats and several marching bands. As they looked down the boulevard, they could see the tops of the floats several blocks away and they could hear the different bands from a distance. It was a warm day with the green grass and palm trees lining the street. The sky was obscured because of the smog that blanketed the Los Angeles basin. But it was a great day to be in a parade. As honored guests, they were thankful their hosts allowed them to ride with their group.

The parade turned north on Sierra Madre Boulevard and came to an end at Villa Street. The Sierra group rode their horses to the trucks and horse trailers that were parked a short distance away from the floats. As they rode by several entries, Eddie and Jody had one last chance to view the floats up close.

When the horses were cared for, Ellis had his car at the parking area and they rode back to the ranch. Later in the day, they settled down to watch the televised Rose Bowl football game from the comfort of Ellis' home. When they sat down to enjoy the game, Ellis handed Jody a tape of the parade and said, "I hope you enjoy it. Maybe you'll see something you missed at the parade."

Jody smiled and said, "How thoughtful, we appreciate it and when we view it, we'll think of the two of you."

~ ~ ~ ~

The day after the parade, Eddie and Jody left the ranch early. Ellis and Elsa had made arrangements for a surprise lunch at the Santa Monica Pier and a brief shopping trip before going to LAX. When they arrived at

269

one of the more exclusive restaurants, they were ushered to a table where Hanh, Linh and little Anh were seated. The lunch was abbreviated because Hanh and Linh had to get back to their hospital positions, after Anh was taken to the day care in the hospital. The visit was short but sweet and they enjoyed seeing Anh as well.

At the airport, they visited up until their plane was called to board. The departure of friends was made with mixed emotions. Eddie thanked them for their hospitality and for their equestrian group honoring him in this fashion. Jody had found a friend with whom she would keep in touch. They were leaving behind two friends, but it was nice to know they were heading back to Bozeman.

~ ~ ~ ~

When they returned to the Bozeman area, there were many phone calls. Many were from well-wishers who called to say they had seen them in the parade. A pleasant surprise one afternoon was the visit of Pastor Ronald Waters and his wife Edith. When they showed up at the door, there was a hug for Jody and a handshake for Eddie. Jody insisted, "You are staying for supper and I won't take no for an answer." They agreed.

After supper, they stayed around for a short visit and got to witness a sunset from the comforts of the cabin. Pastor Waters said, "I have retired from the ministry and will be going back to your hometown, Eddie. While we were there, Edith and I fell in love with the congregation and we have decided that is where we would like to settle down."

Eddie said, "I guess some of us have decided to hang up the spurs too. Jody and I have worked hard to get the horse business up and running and it has drained us at times. I guess we were both ready to retire and let the younger set take over."

"Time has a way of moving on," Edith said softly, "and we can do nothing to stop it."

Jody said, "Our daughter Lien will be disappointed to know that you have retired. She had mentioned in the past she wondered where you had gone and if you were available to baptize her baby, when the time comes."

Pastor Waters said, "When the time comes, you just let me know and we can get the baptismal situation taken care of."

The visit was short and sweet as Ronald and Edith wanted to head down the road and possibly make Billings before they called it a day.

They would be tired by then and to drive the added mileage on the other side of Billings would put them getting to their destination late at night. Their parting was one of mutual and sincere agreement, that they would keep in touch.

~ ~ ~ ~

One afternoon, Buck came running to the cabin, knocked and quickly opened the door in his excitement. "Hello, hello!" he called out. "I need your help, now! Lien is having pains and she's down at the stables. I think the baby is about to arrive."

Buck's plea didn't fall on deaf ears. Jody and Eddie practically raced past Buck and headed for the stables. When they arrived, they found Lien sitting on a bench outside one of the stalls, doubled over in pain.

Eddie hollered, "Lien, are you alright?"

Jody arrived at her daughter's side and was feeling her forehead and coaxing her to sit up straight. "Lien, sweetheart, take a deep breath and try to relax. How long has this been going on?"

Lien straightened up long enough to say, "The pain hit me all at once, then I was doubled over with another sharp pain."

Jody timed the contractions and it didn't take long before she said, "Buck, go to your house and bring what Lien has laid out. We'll meet you at the hospital, and for heaven's sake, be careful driving in." Turning her attention to Eddie, she said, "Get the car and bring it here to the stables. We're going straight to the hospital and we're going to be grandparents before supper, if I don't miss my guess."

Everyone on the homestead surely guessed what was going on when they witnessed the rooster tails of dust from two vehicles racing from the property and heading into town. No one in these parts of Gallatin County would drive that fast unless there was a good reason.

That evening, at 5:48, the first cries from Lewis Clark Willow filled the delivery room of the hospital. It was a happy moment. Buck was so nervous when a nurse told him and Eddie, "Please, go to the nursery. You both can see the baby there in a couple of minutes." Jody stayed with Lien and gave her comfort until she was assigned her room. Then Grandma would make a quick trip to the viewing window of the nursery.

When Jody arrived at the nursery, she asked, "Buck, how did you two agree upon the name?"

Buck smiled and explained, "If it was going to be a girl, Lien would have chosen a Vietnamese name to mark her past. But it was a boy, so I had the privilege of naming him. I chose Lewis Clark because Meriwether Lewis and William Clark chose Sacagawea, a Shoshone woman, to help them with their expedition. His name reflects Shoshone history."

Jody replied, "That is so fitting. I like the name and he appears to be quite a chunk with a head of black hair."

The fluorescent light above them illuminated Buck. He stood straight and tall, as if casted in bronze, his shoulders pulled back looking proud as any father could. Eddie and Jody embraced, sharing the moment. Lewis Clark Willow appeared to look up through the glass with dark button eyes, seeing them for the first time.

~ ~ ~ ~

In August, Ronald and Edith Waters made another visit to the homestead. Their mission was twofold: they wanted to see the baby and to deliver a letter from the mayor. Eddie was to be honored as the Grand Marshall in the Veterans Day Parade the Sunday before Veterans Day.

Pastor Waters was intrigued over the worn combat boots that rested on a box containing all the rocks that marked Eddie's life. "Goodness, Eddie," he commented, "Are these the pair of boots you wore in Korea?"

"That's them," Eddie replied, "And that box they're sitting on is a collection of rocks I have gathered over the years. When I was young and there was something important in my life, I would pick up a rock, mark it with a pen and enter it in a ledger to show why it was important. Sometimes old habits are hard to break. I kept it up and I have quite a collection.

"Would you feel offended," Ronald asked, "if I asked to see the ledger?"

Eddie smiled and said, "Not at all." He walked over to the box, lifted the boots from the top and retrieved the ledger. They sat in the rockers close to each other. Eddie opened the ledger and began flipping through it. Each rock was numerically marked. "On one of the pages," he said, "This one is marked on the day I was baptized." As they paged through the ledger, Eddie said, "This is from the creek where Mrs. Shomake had the accident with her car."

As they flipped through the pages in the ledger, the comments ranged from when the children were born to the day he was released from the Korean prison and one on his first day of freedom. There was an entry on the day he asked Jody to marry him. Pastor Waters listened in awe at the chronological ledger remarks logging Eddie Day's life."

"There is an importance in those boots, too," Jody interjected, adding another layer to the story. "You see, Eddie tried to save my first husband who was wounded on the battlefield, but they lost. Eddie was taken prisoner and my husband Donald was killed. Eddie took a dog tag and a note from my late husband and hid them in the leather of his boots. He had made a promise to deliver them to a nurse in San Francisco. He kept them there for nearly twelve years before he found out who they belonged to."

Pastor Waters said, "That was a long time and what a commitment to carry it through."

Jody said, "I recall crying the day Eddie handed them to me, realizing they were from my late husband. Now you can understand why I love this man."

Ronald turned to Eddie and asked, "Would you consider letting me take them back to the church to put on display for the congregation, along with any small memorabilia that reflects on your military life?"

Eddie said, "Tell the Mayor I'll accept the invitation to be the Grand Marshall and sure I'll let you take the items, as long as they have some safeguards; I'd like to leave them for my grandchildren."

The retired minister said, "They will remain at the church for as long as you allow."

Lien and Buck came over to the house and the Waters family got to see Lewis Clark Willow up close. They both explained how they came to choose the name, it's history and meaning.

Lien asked, "Mr. Waters, is it still possible for you to baptize our Lewis?"

He said, "Lien and Buck, I would be happy to baptize Lewis Clark. When would you like for it to be done? If you're both going to be at the parade in November, that would be a good time, or any time you feel it is appropriate."

Lien looked at Buck to hear him say, "When we visit on the weekend of the Veterans Day Parade will be ok. That way it wouldn't be imposing on you, making the trip this far, or us making another trip back east."

The visit was abbreviated, leaving Eddie and Buck to help load the box of rocks and other items into the back of the Waters' station wagon. The couple left before the sun set that evening.

~ ~ ~ ~

The family reunion was scheduled for early November 1996, before the parade. Hanh and Linh could only get seven days off from the hospital and were scheduled for work in the AM on the 13th. They would fly and rent a car in Billings. Anh would accompany them, as she was a toddler and into more mischief than her parents could tolerate. When they arrived at the homestead, they found the cabin was filled with immediate family. Mari and Gordon Shum had their two children Chet and Tyler, Kari and David Hostetler had brought their two children Max and Chad. Buck and Lien had stopped over with little Lewis Clark to visit and they found Eddie and Jody about as happy as anyone in the valley. The two-day visit allowed Eddie and Jody to shower love on the immediate family before visiting extended family at Edward and Kathy's farm on Friday.

Two days later, the group caravanned down the highway and arrived at the Edward Day farm on Friday afternoon. The dusty rooster tails from the lane gradually settled over the nearby acreage, pushed on by a light breeze.

The three-day visit with the extended family included a parade scheduled for Saturday and church on Sunday. Some planned to return home late Monday, while others at the reunion indicated they would leave on Tuesday. Time didn't permit having a lengthy reunion at Edward and Kathy's farm. Hanh explained, "We might be the first to leave the reunion, because we have a flight to catch in Billings."

The Days were pleased that everyone made the reunion, including Eric and Sarah. Edward and Kathy had a chance to hug and love the entire group. When the reunion would come to its eventual end, there would be photos to look at and memorable moments to talk about for a long time.

~ ~ ~ ~

November 9, 1996

Eddie and Edward Day slowly stepped into the house after doing the early morning chores. Each held a growing appetite. Kathy had no sooner placed a stack of hotcakes on their plates, when the telephone rang. Seeing that Kathy had turned a deaf ear to the telephone and was on her way to the kitchen tending to another set of hotcakes, Edward answered the phone. "Hello."

"Mayor Johnson here, are the lot of you going to make it into town, in time for the parade?"

"We wouldn't miss it for the world, despite the fact my bones are telling me there's a change in the weather coming. I'm fixing to eat first."

The mayor laughed, "You do remember that that boy of yours and his wife are Grand Marshalls, with you and Kathy being the Parade Honorees this year."

"I sure do," Edward replied, "don't you let them start without us."

"Remember, we're starting at ten this year and not eleven as we had in the past," the mayor added, "I'll see you up by the school."

Edward wiped at his unshaven face and answered, "Thanks for the call." He turned around after hanging up the phone and hadn't taken one step toward the table, when the phone rang again. Figuring it was the mayor again, ready to remind him of something else, he answered, "Yeah, what did you forget?"

There was a short pause on the other end of the telephone before the voice came through, "Edward, this is Spike down at the Legion Post. Did I catch you at a bad time?"

"Almost, I'm cutting things mighty thin on this end. Eddie and I haven't had our breakfast yet. Kathy and Jody are almost ready and my son and I are rushed. We have to make the parade and we're pinched for time."

Spike the newly elected Post Commander for the American Legion Post asked, "I have a few things to discuss with you before tomorrow, can I catch you right after the parade?"

Edward said, "I'll meet you up by the ball field where they will be handing out the awards for the participants."

"Great," Spike's happy voice chimed in the receiver, "I'll let you get back to doing whatever was so important."

When he hung up the telephone and turned around, he saw his wife Kathy removing the cold hotcakes from his plate and replacing them with a fresh batch. She was smiling and chuckled before adding, "Best eat then clean up, we've got a parade to go to."

They were on their way to their cars, when two cars raced down the lane and came to a screeching halt, causing the dust to boil into the air.

When the dust settled, the driver's door on the lead car opened and out stepped Neil Day, "We got here as fast as we could, are we too late?"

Edward answered, "Glad to see you, son, I see you have the family with you. I'm looking forward to seeing you right after the parade."

The window rolled down in the other car and Connie Summerfield called out, "Daddy, we had a flat a way back, or we would have been here sooner We'll follow you."

Kathy cried out, "We'll see you right after the parade. I have to see to it that grandma gets to smother you with lots of loving later today."

~ ~ ~ ~

At the high school, the parade coordinator, Bessie Margrave, was feverishly trying to get each unit lined up. When Edward drove his station wagon into the parking lot, he was followed by Eddie and Jody in their Malibu. Bessie called out, "Kathy and Jody, get those men of yours over here, we're about to begin the parade."

Kathy waved at her and said, "Edward we need to get to the parade car." Jody smiled at Eddie and walked proudly beside him.

"Well, they haven't started without us, have they," Edward replied. They made their way across the high school lawn to the waiting Mustang convertibles with their top down. A blanket was up and over the back seat and extended on the trunk, with protection on the seat. They stepped into the back seat and sat on the back part of the car. The door was closed and a last check of the tape supporting the paper banner marked 'Parade Honorees' was done.

Eddie and Jody were assigned the Mustang convertible in front of his parents. They stepped into the back seat and made themselves comfortable, sitting elevated on the back of the seat and part of the trunk. On the door a taped paper banner read 'Parade Grand Marshals'.

The flag girls from the high school led the parade, with a couple of girls out front carrying a large banner nearly eight-foot-long with the title 'Veterans Day'.

The mayor's car was followed by those belonging to the city council and then the local Boy Scouts color guard before the Grand Marshal's car. Behind them were Eddie's parents and five high school bands. A consolidated military color guard and one from the American Legion Post were next in the parade order. There was a group of Shriners from

Billings and a group of veterans wearing uniforms that dated back to various conflicts. They were followed by several Cub Scout packs, Girl Scouts and Brownies. Then there were the floats, decorated vehicles, three equestrian units and a collection of families who saddled up, honored to ride in the parade. Just for fun, the fire department led eleven older relics resembling cars, trucks of the past and four old steam-powered tractors.

As the parade made its way from the high school to one end of town, there were few spectators. But when they turned down Main Street, the crowd seemed unending and the many American flags lightly moving in the breeze punctuated the event. The crowd was cheering. As the color guards passed, there was a show of respect for flag and country that grew from the crowd. As the Grand Marshal's car began to make its way down the street, the crowd cheered. As the Parade Honoree car began to pass, several women would yell out "Hey, Kathy," and wave. Some of the older men who were veterans would rise to their feet and render a salute to them, as they had done for Eddie and Jody.

Jody turned to Eddie and said, "It is so nice that your hometown has seen fit to honor you in this fashion. The crowd is smaller than that of the Rose Parade, but the people here have your best interest at heart and it shows from the turn out." They waved to the crowd and when a veteran gave a salute, Eddie and Jody would both return it in a snappy fashion.

Kathy turned to Edward and said, "Would you look at that, are they saluting us?"

As they continued waving to the crowd, Edward replied, "It sure looks that way."

"I think it's nice," she replied, as she waved a recognition gesture with Edward doing the same.

The remainder of the parade followed them to the beat of the drummers. They set the cadence and the bands filled the air with patriotic marching music. It was near the end of the parade when Jody said, "I think this is one of the nicest experiences I've had. It only goes to show you what small town America does for their veterans."

In the car behind them, Kathy turned to her husband and said, "I don't know about you, but my arms are about waved out."

"Mine, too," Edward responded, "but what an experience."

Kathy replied, "Yes and on such a beautiful day, even if there's a light chill in the air."

"It's an indicator Old Man Winter is about upon us," Edward answered. "We could have had a mess of snow to deal with if the temperature had changed much."

When they arrived at the high school, Eddie and Jody joined Edward and Kathy as they strolled hand in hand, over to the football field. Some of the floats had returned and were being dismantled. Edward wasn't in the mood for walking too fast and was pleased to see his Kathy didn't plan to outrun him. Some of the parade organizers were busy with those who judged each unit and the process of arranging the awards was the responsibility of others. The Day family elected not to get too involved with those going about their task.

Several moments had passed, allowing Eddie and Jody to talk with his old school mates. Edward felt a light slap of a hand across one of his shoulders. He jumped a bit before he turned around, only to stare into the eyes of Sherman 'Spike' Workman, the American Legion Post Commander.

Spike said, "Didn't mean to scare you, Edward."

"I wasn't expecting you so soon. I guess my thoughts were else-where."

"The reason I called earlier this morning is I would like to call upon you and Kathy to say a word or so at the ceremony tomorrow."

Edward said, "We appreciate the offer, but we'd feel more comfortable sitting this one out. I hope you understand. Kathy and I would like to sit with Eddie and Jody and just enjoy the moment."

"I do understand," Spike said softly. "I'd like to see if Eddie's children would like to make a brief comment at the unveiling. Are they in town where I might talk to them?"

Edward said, "They're all in town for the weekend. They're around here someplace because they all made the trip to Bozeman yesterday, just to see this parade honoring Eddie."

"If you would, have them give me a call later today and I'll explain what I have in mind for the ceremony tomorrow."

With a smile on his face, Edward said, "No need to do that."

Spike had a surprised look on his face and asked, "What do you mean by that?"

Edward pointed to the side of the crowd and said, "Here they all come now. I'll introduce them to you and you can ask them, all at the same time."

When they arrived, Edward introduced them to Spike and allowed him to converse with them as to what he had in mind. They visited with him for a while, before Spike reached over and tapped Edward on the shoulder and said, "I've got to run. I'll see you tomorrow around noon, here at the high school, out front."

The Post Commander left as quickly as he appeared. Mari asked, "We're headed over to the café for a hamburger and fries, Would the four of you like to join us?"

Eddie spoke up and said, "We have plans to stick around here with Mom and Dad for a bit to see the awards being given out. You kids go do your thing and we'll see you back at the farm."

"Eat a burger for me," Edward chimed. "The mayor is going to call on your dad to say a word or so before the awards are presented and he'll be in their official photograph. We'll be along when that is done. Maybe I'll spring loose and buy lunch for two. I haven't had a milk shake to go with a burger in a long time. I think it sounds pretty good." Turning to Kathy he asked, "What do you think?"

"Well, Edward Day," Kathy chimed. "Are you trying to court me all over again, after all this time?"

"I might be at that," he replied, before he gave a laugh. "As for Eddie, he's on his own. I just hope he has enough jingle in his pocket to buy lunch for Jody."

"Sounds like the same old menu from way back when, doesn't it?" Kathy said, reminiscing, as she looked into his mischievous eyes.

The kids excused themselves and were seen heading to the parking lot. They were overheard when Kari remarked, "Grandpa's flirting with Grandma and I think it's so cute." They began laughing as they continued towards their cars.

When Connie and Neil arrived at the football field with their families, there was a lot of happiness turned loose. It had been a spell since the two families had visited with Kathy and Edward. The senior Days were looking forward to having a great time once they got back to the farm. Both families had made the long trip to visit with their parents and were in hopes of having some time to visit with Eddie and Jody at the farm following their recognition by the community.

~ ~ ~ ~

The Veterans Day church recognition Sunday services fell a day before the traditional holiday to be celebrated across America. Flag poles in front of every business were still flying Old Glory. The entire community was in a festive mood to celebrate. They planned to honor all of the men and women who had served in the military and those presently serving on active duty in the Armed Forces. This was a proud community. Most of the men, and a large number of women, had served from as far back as WWII. Today, an American hero, and the most recognized throughout Montana, was honored, not to mention that he was from this community. It caused them to pause and remember, if only momentarily, they knew and remembered Eddie Day. They were patriotic and turned out in full force to show their respect for a man they were proud of.

At the beginning of the services, Lien and Buck Willow brought their son Lewis Clark forward to be baptized. Hanh and Linh also stepped forward as Godparents, along with Eddie and Jody, Kathy and Edward as family witnesses. Each family had their part to respond to openly when asked. Then Pastor Waters turned to the congregation, they responded to their responsibilities as well. Moments later, the baptism was completed and the family returned to their pews.

The services at the Methodist church were nearing an end after honoring the many veterans with a musical tribute. Each veteran was asked to stand and be recognized on this Recognition Sunday. As each veteran stood to be recognized, they would give a brief comment about their service, their rank, where and when they served, along with a short comment or two. Jody and then Eddie were the last to stand and be recognized. In the foyer, the white drape that covered a glass cabinet had been removed as Pastor Waters spoke, "Today we are also remembering the service and sacrifice of Eddie Day, during a troubling time in our nation's history. Eddie and his lovely wife Jody are with us today. We are proud of the both of you, for your extended military service. For those of you who do not know, Eddie worshiped and was baptized here in this church. When he entered the Army, he was in our thoughts during that time and his faith saw him through some pretty rough times. The war was unkind to Eddie, but he felt blessed in so many other ways. Through tough times, he managed to keep his faith and when he returned, life began anew. He is a remarkable man and today it is fitting we celebrate his life. As we depart from our services today, to go out and witness to the world, we will pass by a cabinet in the foyer that holds a part of Eddie Day's life. It also holds a part of our lives in the case as well, hopes dreams and reflective memories. The church has borrowed the memorabilia from the Day family and it will remain in the foyer until we begin hanging the green. At that time Eddie has granted permission for it to be transferred to the high school and remain there until the end of the school term. Today we are invited, directly following services, to a tribute honoring Eddie Day at the high school, where he once attended. After the brief ceremony, the school will provide a light lunch. All the veterans will be at the head of the line in the cafeteria. The display in the foyer contains a homage to Eddie Day's life. The box contains rocks that mark the important events in his life. The boots are those he wore as a prisoner of war and he brought them home with a message for Jody. It was from her late husband who was killed on the battlefield in Korea. Eddie and Jody, would you please stand by the display? And to all our remaining veterans, I ask that you and your wives join Eddie and Jody now. Would you all please remain in the foyer, so that the congregation may thank all of you personally for your service?" With the last reminder spoken, Retired Pastor Ronald Waters began the benediction and ended with a resounding 'Amen.'"

As the congregation left the church, they paused momentarily in the foyer to view the contents on display in the glass case honoring Eddie Day's life. Then they would shake hands and say a brief comment to each veteran and their wives, before stepping into the chilly mid-November air on their way to the high school. In the glass case were items relating to Eddie's survival while a prisoner of war in Korea. There were pieces of significant memorabilia, photos and newspaper clippings that marked his life. Each item was placed in such a way that the light in the display case illuminated them. Some of the veterans stood briefly at attention in front of the display and rendered a salute to Eddie and Jody, before stepping aside to remain in the foyer. Before leaving, a few of the women raised their hands to their lips as if kissing their fingertips, before placing them on the frame of the glass case. They would pause for a moment before shaking hands with Jody, Eddie and the other veterans. The contents within the case brought back a variety of memories for so many of the parishioners.

Most of the families remained outside the church talking softly about the impact of what they had just witnessed. It seemed that the entire congregation had gathered on the sidewalk or on the lawn to show a moment of respect for each veteran and the entire Day family. Eddie and Jody were the last to leave the church. The congregation seemed to engulf them as they reached out to touch them once more, in friendship, as they passed by, a handshake here or a tap on the shoulder there. It was a caring and loving touch from the community of worshipers, extended to each veteran, to honor them on this day. Moments later, they were on their way to the high school.

The Sunday paper highlighted the Veterans Day Parade with a lengthy story. Across the front page in large letters the headlines read, 'A Box Of Rocks - A Pair Of Boots'. Several articles and editorials were wedged between the many photographs. This town was proud of Eddie Day and the paper accommodated the community with a host of photos that marked the special event.

~ ~ ~ ~

May in 1997

When the foliage was at its freshest green, moments before the Montana skies began to put on a heavenly display near sunset, Eddie and Jody sat in the double rocker within their cabin. They waited for the sky to begin its change in color. They began reminiscing back over the years of when they first met at the Presidio.

Jody said, "You were a physical and emotional wreck." She laughed and added, "I couldn't help but feel sorry for you. The years of captivity had scared you emotionally and physically. You were no Charles Atlas, but you hugged onto those boots pretty well."

Eddie adjusted his position in the rocker and said, "I didn't understand until you turned the photograph around that was on your desk and handed it to me. Then I realized why the tears were in your eyes."

"You kept a promise, Eddie. I don't think any other man in this world would have done what you did."

"I still remember some of the bad things that I witnessed in Korea and I also recall the time you remembered some of the bad things you experienced in Vietnam."

Jody sighed, "We have both had some things we had to work through together, haven't we?"

"That we have," Eddie softly replied. "I remember how my girls reacted after I returned. It was a trying time for both of them for a while, but they adjusted well. Looking back over the years, we have had a host of wonderful things happen to us after we were married. The children and grandchildren sure have put us through some of the most interesting situations at times, haven't they? And I'm glad we have hung up our spurs."

Jody smiled and said, "I was so proud of you when you agreed with me on adopting Hanh and Lien. Now look where they are and how they have grown." It's nice to remember the good times and have good friends like Gun and Susie and I agree with you on your last statement."

This sunset seemed like no other. The colors were beginning to show their brightness before they faded and blended into another color, painting the heavens above the rugged landscape. Each sunset is different in color or intensity, from simplicity to a display of gigantic proportion. How it is seen and how it touches the heart is what causes meaning in a person's life at the end of the day. Eddie turned to Jody as they sat in the double rocker and said, "We're not in our prime of life, just two tired old souls. Let us pause and give thanks."

Jody smiled and reverently bowed her head.

"Dear Lord," Eddie began, "Jody and I are most grateful and we are blessed. And thank you for the many sunsets we have been able to witness from our cabin, so lovingly built. We are also grateful for so many things in life. Thank you for all the challenges we have had the opportunity to endure. We thank you for our children and grandchildren and the joy of seeing them grow. We thank you for coming into our lives and guiding our behavior over the years. Thank you, Lord, we are truly grateful, Amen."

Jody looked up and when she looked into Eddie's eyes she said, "We are grateful. I know you spoke from the heart and they were the thoughts I harbor as well." The smiles they shared seemed to light up the interior of the cabin. They were in love and cherished each other's closeness and spirituality.

As the sunset began to fade beyond the western panes of glass in the cabin, an eagle was seen flying across the sunset. The Gallatin River had a reflective shimmer beyond the grassy fields full of energetic newborn colts pastured for the first time and there was peace within the valley.

283

ABOUT THE AUTHOR

Shirley Earnestine and Larry Antone Ludwig

This book was a labor of love for the both of us.

Larry was born and raised in Montana, enlisted in the US Navy for a period of four years in 1956. He was assigned to the USS Cimarron AO-22 a fleet oiler that operated in the pacific theatre. After leaving the Navy, he enlisted in the US Army and remained there for sixteen years. His assignments ranged from state-side duty as a military policeman, those duties were in the lower forty-eight and Alaska. As a recruiter and career counselor he had assignments in California and in Korea near the demilitarized zone. Ludwig retired after serving twenty years of active military service and moved to Springfield, Missouri.

He continued his education at Southwest Missouri State later renamed Missouri State. He holds a BS in communications and BAs in English and Writing. He lived in Marionville, Missouri with his wife Shirley Earnestine until her death from cancer Oct 13, 2015. She encouraged his writing and helped tremendously with her editing expertise. He has three children from a previous marriage and enjoys nine grandchildren and three great grandchildren.

Larry's additional writings are *'The Waiting', 'Remembering The Cimarron', 'Cille' and 'Duke 8F15'*.

TRIBUTE

In memory of the millions of men and women who served during the Korean Conflict. Many of them suffered terrible debilitating physical and emotional wounds upon the battlefield. A large number suffered the emotional scars inflicted upon them while being held as a prisoner of war, sadly many died while being held in captivity.

Not forgotten are the countless families who remained behind. They endured enormous pain, suffering and hardships, while supporting those they loved while they served.

They all have answered '**THE CALL**' and have paid a tremendous price to protect our way of life. May God bless each and every one of them, for what they did to preserve the precious rights and freedom we enjoy in this great land we call America.

AUTHOR'S COMMENT

It is my fondest hope that this book although a piece of fiction, may reflect favorably upon the men and women who served in Korea. Not to be forgotten are the families that remained behind holding down the home front, while a part of their hearts served in a conflict during a turbulent time.

THIS MEMORIAL IS DEDICATED TO THE BRAVE MEN AND WOMEN WHO FOUGHT COMMUNISM DURING THE KOREAN WAR 1950-1953

PRESERVED SOVEREIGNTY FOR SOUTH KOREA AND STOOD FIRMLY FOR DEMOCRACY AND IDEALS OF THE UNITED STATES OF AMERICA FOR THOSE WHO SERVED WE SALUTE OUR FALLEN COMRADES IN THIS BRUTAL WAR

"GOD BLESS YOU"

KWVA CHAPTER OF SPRINGFIELD, MO

DEDICATED JULY 27 2002

OUR HEROS
KOREAN VETERANS

Korean War Statistics

- The Korean Conflict began on June 25, 1950 and ended with the Armistice being signed on July 27, 1953.
- Historical facts: Actual hostilities occurred from June 27, 1950 to July 27, 1953.
- There were 6.8 million American men and women who served during the Korean War period.
- There were 54,000 deaths to Americans in service during the period of hostilities; of these 33,700 were actual battle deaths.
- There were 7,140 POW's during the Korean War. Of these 4,418

returned to the United States, 2,701 died and 21 refused repatriation.

- There have been 131 recipients of the Congressional Medal of Honor among Korean War Veterans.
- It was once called 'The Forgotten War', but in the hearts of many it is not.

Made in the USA
Middletown, DE
10 September 2022

72742559R00170